About the Authors

Jennie Lucas's parents owned a bookstore and she grew up surrounded by books, dreaming about faraway lands. At twenty-two she met her future husband and after their marriage, she graduated from university with a degree in English. She started writing books a year later. Jennie won the Romance Writers of America's Golden Heart contest in 2005 and hasn't looked back since. Visit Jennie's website at: jennielucas.com

Lynn Raye Harris is a Southern girl, military wife, wannabe cat lady, and horse lover. She's also the *New York Times* and *USA Today* bestselling author of the HOSTILE OPERATIONS TEAM® SERIES of military romances, and twenty books about sexy billionaires for Mills & Boon.

USA Today bestselling, RITA®-nominated, and critically-acclaimed author **Caitlin Crews** has written more than one hundred books and counting. She has a Masters and Ph.D. in English Literature, thinks everyone should read more category romance, and is always available to discuss her beloved alpha heroes. Just ask. She lives in the Pacific Northwest with her comic book artist husband, is always planning her next trip, and will never, ever, read all the books in her to-be-read pile. Thank goodness.

Italian Summers

June 2022
Scandalous Demands

July 2022
The Ultimate Revenge

August 2022
Secrets and Lies

September 2022
For Business or Pleasure

October 2022
The Billionaire's Bargain

November 2022
Seduced by the Sea

Italian Summers For Business or Pleasure

JENNIE LUCAS

LYNN RAYE HARRIS

CAITLIN CREWS

MILLS & BOON

First Published in Great Britain 2022
By Mills & Boon, an imprint of HarperCollins*Publishers*
1 London Bridge Street, London, SE1 9GF

www.harpercollins.co.uk

HarperCollins*Publishers*
1st Floor, Watermarque Building,
Ringsend Road, Dublin 4, Ireland

ITALIAN SUMMERS: FOR BUSINESS OR PLEASURE
© 2022 Harlequin Enterprises ULC

The Consequences of That Night © 2013 Jennie Lucas
Unnoticed and Untouched © 2012 Lynn Raye Harris
At the Count's Bidding © 2015 Caitlin Crews

ISBN 978-0-263-30582-1

THE
CONSEQUENCES
OF THAT NIGHT

JENNIE LUCAS

CHAPTER ONE

A BABY.

Emma Hayes put a hand over her slightly curved belly, swaying as the double-decker bus traveled deeper into central London in the gray afternoon rain.

A baby.

For ten weeks, she'd tried not to hope. Tried not to think about it. Even when she'd gone to her doctor's office that morning, she'd been bracing herself for some problem, to be told that she must be brave.

Instead she'd seen a rapid steady beat on the sonogram as her doctor pointed to the flash on the screen. "See the heartbeat? 'Hi, Mum.'"

"I'm really pregnant?" she'd said through dry lips.

The man's eyes twinkled through his spectacles. "As pregnant as can be."

"And the baby's—all right?"

"It's all going perfectly. Textbook, I'd say." The doctor had given her a big smile. "I think it's safe to tell your husband now, Mrs. Hayes."

Her husband. The words echoed through Emma's mind as she closed her eyes, leaning back into her seat on the top deck of the Number 9 bus. Her husband. How she wished there was such a person, waiting for her in a homey little cottage—a man who'd kiss her with a cry of joy at the news of his coming child. But in direct opposition to what she'd told her physician, there was no husband.

Just a boss. A boss who'd made love to her nearly three months ago in a single night of reckless passion, then disappeared in the cold dawn, leaving her to wake up alone in his huge bed. The same bed that she'd made for him over the past seven years, complete with ironed sheets.

I know the maid could do it, but I prefer that you handle it personally. No one can do it like you, Miss Hayes.

Oh, boy. She'd really handled it personally this time, hadn't she?

Blinking, Emma stared out the window as the red double-decker bus made its way down Kensington Road. Royal Albert Hall went by in a blur of red brick behind the rain-streaked glass. She wiped her eyes hard. Stupid tears. She shouldn't be crying. She was happy about this baby. Thrilled, in fact. She'd honestly thought she could never get pregnant. It was a miracle.

A lump rose in her throat.

Except...

Cesare would never be a real father to their baby. He would never be her husband, a man who would kiss her when he came home from work and tuck their baby in at night. No matter how she might wish otherwise.

Because Cesare Falconeri, self-made billionaire, sexy Italian playboy, had two passions in life. The first was expanding his far-flung hotel empire across the globe, working relentlessly to expand his net worth and power. The second, a mere hobby when he had an hour or two to spare, was to seduce beautiful women, which he did for sport, as other men might play football or golf.

Her sexy Italian boss annihilated the thin hearts of supermodels and heiresses alike with the same careless, seductive, selfish charm. He cared nothing for any of them.

Emma knew that. As his housekeeper, she was the one responsible for arranging morning-after gifts for his one-night stands. Usually Cartier watches. Bought in bulk.

As the bus traveled through Mayfair, the lights of the Ritz Hotel slid by. Looking down from the top deck of the bus, Emma saw pedestrians dressed in Londoners' typical festive autumn attire—that is to say, entirely in black—struggling with umbrellas in the rain and wind.

It was the first of November. Just yesterday, the warmth of Indian summer had caressed the city like a lover, with promises of forever. Today, drizzle and rain had descended. The city, so recently bright and warm, had become melancholy, haunted and filled with despair.

Or maybe it was just her.

For the past seven years—since she'd first started as a maid at Cesare's hotel in New York, at the age of twenty-one—she'd been absolutely in love with him, and absolutely careful not to show it. Careful not to show any feelings at all.

You never bore me with personal stories, Miss Hayes. I hardly know anything about you. He'd smiled. *Thank you.*

Then three months ago, she'd come back from her stepmother's funeral in Texas and he'd found her alone in his darkened kitchen, clutching an unopened bottle of tequila, with tears streaming down her cheeks. For a moment, Cesare had just stared at her.

Then he'd pulled her roughly into his arms.

Perhaps he'd only meant to offer comfort, but by the end of the night, he'd taken the virginity she'd saved for him, just for him, even when she knew she had no hope. He'd taken her to his bed, and made Emma's gray, lonely world explode with color and fire.

And today, a new magic, every bit as shocking and unexpected. She was pregnant with his baby.

Emma traced her fingertip into the shape of a heart against a fogged-up corner of the bus window. If only his playboy nature could change. If only she could believe he'd actually wish to be a father someday, and even fall in love with Emma, as she'd fallen for him…

The double-decker bus jolted to a stop, and with an intake of breath she abruptly wiped the heart off the glass. Cesare, *love?* That was a laugh. He couldn't even stick around for breakfast, much less commit to raising a family!

Ever since she'd woken up alone in his bed that cold morning after, Emma had faithfully kept his mansion in Kensington sparkling clean in perpetual hope for his arrival. But she'd found out from one of the secretaries that he'd actually returned to London two days ago. Instead of coming home, he was staying at his suite at the flagship London Falconeri near Trafalgar Square.

His unspoken words were clear. He wanted to make sure Emma knew she meant nothing to him, any more than the stream of models and starlets who routinely paraded through his bed.

But there was one big difference. None of his other lovers had gotten pregnant.

Because unlike the rest, he'd slept with her without protection. He'd believed her when she'd whispered to him in the dark that pregnancy was impossible. Cesare, who trusted no one, had taken Emma at her word.

Her hands tightened on the handrail of the seat in front of her. Here she'd been fantasizing about homey cottages and Cesare miraculously turning into a devoted father. The truth was that when he learned their one-night stand had caused a pregnancy, he'd think she'd lied. That she'd deliberately gotten pregnant to trap him.

He'd *hate* her.

So don't tell him, a cowardly voice whispered. *Run away. Take that job in Paris. He never has to know.*

But she couldn't keep her pregnancy a secret. Even if the odds were a million to one that he'd want to be part of their baby's life, didn't even Cesare deserve that chance?

A loud burst of laughter, and the stomp of people climbing to the top deck, made Emma glance out the window. She leaped to her feet. "Wait, please!" she cried to the bus driver, who obligingly waited as she ran down the bus stairs, nearly tripping over her own feet. Out on the sidewalk, buffeted by passersby, she looked up at the elegant, imposing gray-stone Falconeri Hotel. Putting her handbag over her head to dodge the rain, Emma ran into the grand lobby. Nodding at the security guard, she shook the rain off her camel-colored mackintosh and took the elevator to the tenth floor.

Trembling, she walked down the hall to the suite of rooms Cesare occasionally used as an office and a pied-à-terre after a late evening out in Covent Garden. Cesare liked to be in the thick of things. The floor wasn't private, but shared by those guests who could afford rooms at a thousand pounds a night. Trembling, she knocked on the door.

She heard a noise on the other side, and then the door was abruptly wrenched open.

Emma looked up with an intake of breath. "Cesare…"

But it wasn't her boss. Instead a gorgeous young woman, barely covered in lingerie, stood in his doorway.

"Yes?" the woman said in a bored tone, leaning against the door as if she owned it.

A blade of ice went through Emma's heart as she recognized the woman. Olga Lukin. The famous model who had dated Cesare last year. Her body shook as she tried to say normally, "Is Mr. Falconeri here?"

"Who are you?"

"His—his housekeeper."

"Oh." The supermodel's shoulders relaxed. "He's in the shower."

"The shower," Emma repeated numbly.

"Yesss," Olga Lukin said with exaggerated slowness. "Do you want me to give him a message?"

"Um…"

"There's no point in you waiting." The blonde glanced back at the mussed bed, plainly visible in the hotel suite, and gave a catlike smile. "As soon as he's done, we're going out." Leaning forward, she confided in a stage whisper, "Right after we have another go."

Emma looked at Olga's bony shape, her cheekbones that could cut glass. She was absolutely gorgeous, a woman who'd look perfect on any billionaire's arm. *In his bed.*

While Emma—she suddenly felt like nothing. Nobody. Short, round and drab, not particularly pretty, with the big hips of someone who loved extra cookies at teatime, wearing a beige raincoat, knit dress and sensible shoes. Her long black hair, when it wasn't pulled back in a plaited chignon, hadn't seen the inside of a hairdresser's in years.

Humiliation made her ears burn. How could she have dreamed, even for an instant, that Cesare might want to marry someone like her and raise a baby in a snug little cottage?

He must have slept with her that night out of *pity*—nothing more!

"Well?"

"No." Emma shook her head, hiding her tears. "No message."

"Ta, then," she said rudely. But as she started to close the door, there was a loud bang as Cesare came out of the bathroom.

Emma's heart stopped in her chest as she saw him for the first time since he'd left her in his bed.

Cesare was nearly naked, wearing only a low-slung white towel around his hips, gripping another towel wrapped carelessly over his broad shoulders. His tanned, muscular chest was bare, his black hair still damp from the shower. He stopped, scowling at Olga.

"What are you—"

Then he saw Emma in the doorway, and his spine snapped straight. His darkly handsome face turned blank. "Miss Hayes."

Miss Hayes? He was back to calling her that—when for the past five years they'd been on a first-name basis? *Miss Hayes?*

After so long of hiding her every emotion from him, purely out of self-preservation, something cracked in her heart. She looked from him, to Olga, to the mussed bed.

"Is this your way of showing me my place?" She shook her head tearfully. "What is *wrong* with you, Cesare?"

His dark eyes widened in shock.

Staggering back, horrified at what she'd said, and brokenhearted at what she'd not been able to say, she turned and fled.

"Miss Hayes," she heard him call behind her, and then, "Emma!"

She kept going. Her throat throbbed with pain. She ran with all her heart, desperate to reach the safety of the elevator, where she could burst into tears in privacy. And start planning an immediate departure for Paris, where she'd never have to face him again—or remember her own foolish dreams.

A father for her baby. A snug home. A happy family. A man who'd love her back, who would protect her, who'd be faithful. A tear fell for each crushed dream. She wiped her eyes furiously. How could she have ever let herself get in this position—with Cesare, of all people? Why hadn't she been more careful? *Why?*

Emma heard his low, rough curse behind her, and the hard thud of his bare feet. Before she reached the elevator, he grabbed her arm, whirling her around in the hall.

"What do you want, Miss Hayes?" he demanded.

"Miss Hayes?" she bit out, struggling to get free. "Are you kidding me with that? We've seen each other naked!"

He released her, clearly surprised by her sharp tone.

"That doesn't explain what you're doing here," he said stiffly. "You've never sought me out like this before."

No, and she never would again! "Sorry I interrupted your date."

"It's not a— I have no idea what Olga is doing in my room. She must have gotten a key and snuck in."

Hot tears burned behind her eyes. "Right."

"We broke up months ago."

"Looks like you're back together."

"Not so far as I'm concerned."

"Now, that I believe," she choked out. "Because once you have sex, any relationship is pretty much over where you're concerned, isn't it?"

"We didn't just have sex." He set his jaw. "Have you ever known me to lie?"

That stopped her.

"No," she whispered. Cesare never lied. He always made his position brutally clear. No commitment, no promises, no future.

Yet, somehow many women still managed to convince themselves otherwise. To believe they were special. Until they woke alone the morning after, to find Emma serving them breakfast with their going-away present, and ended up weeping in her arms.

"I really don't care." Emma ran an unsteady hand over her forehead. "It's none of my business."

"No. It's not."

She took a deep breath. "I just came to…to tell you something."

The dim lighting of the elegant hotel hallway left hard shadows against Cesare's cheekbones, the dark scruff of his jaw, and his muscular, tanned chest. His black eyes turned grim. "Don't."

Her lips parted on an intake of breath. "What?"

"Just don't."

"You don't even know what I'm going to say."

"I can guess. You're going to tell me all about your feelings. You've always shared so little. I convinced myself you didn't have any. That I was just a job to you."

Emma almost laughed hysterically in his face. Oh, if only he knew. For years, she'd worked for him until her brain was numb and her fingers were about to fall off. Her first thought each morning when she woke—was him. Her last thought before she finally collapsed in bed each night—was him. What he needed. What he wanted. What he would need and want tomorrow. He'd always been more than a job to her.

"It kept things simple," he said. "It's why we got along so well. I liked you. Respected you. I'd started to think of us as—friends."

Friends. Against her will, Emma's gaze fell to the hard planes of his muscular, tanned chest laced with dark hair. Wearing only the low-slung white towel wrapped snugly around his hips, he was six feet three inches of powerful, hard-muscled masculinity, and he stood in the hallway of his hotel without the slightest self-consciousness, as arrogant as if he were wearing a tailored suit. A few people passed them in the hallway, openly staring. Emma swallowed. It would be hard for any woman to resist staring at Cesare. Even now she… God help her, even now…

"Now you're going to ruin it." His eyes became flinty. "You're going to tell me that you *care*. You've rushed down here to explain you still can't forget our night together. Even though we both swore it wouldn't change anything, you're going to tell me you're desperately in love with me." He scowled. "I thought you were special, but you're going to prove you're just like the rest."

The reverberations of his cruel words echoed in the empty hallway, like a bullet ricocheting against the walls before it landed square and deep in her heart.

For a moment, Emma couldn't breathe. Then she forced herself to meet his eyes.

"I would have to be stupid to love you," she said in a low voice. "I know you too well. You'll never love anyone, ever again."

He blinked. "So you're not—in love with me?"

He sounded so hopeful. She stared up at him, her heart pounding, tears burning behind her eyes. "I'd have to be the biggest idiot who ever lived."

His dark gaze softened. "I don't want to lose you, Emma. You're irreplaceable."

"I am?"

He gave a single nod. "You are the only one who knows how to properly make my bed. Who can maintain my home in perfect order. I need you."

The bullet went a little deeper into her heart.

"Oh," she whispered, and it was the sound someone makes when they've been punched in the belly. He wanted to keep her *as his employee*. She was irreplaceable in his life—*as his employee*.

Three months ago, when he'd taken her in his arms and kissed her passionately, her whole world had changed forever. But for Cesare, nothing had changed. He still expected her to be his invisible, replaceable servant who had no feelings and existed solely to serve his needs.

Tell me this won't change anything between us, he'd said in the darkness that night.

I promise, she'd breathed.

But it was a promise she couldn't keep. Not when she was pregnant with his baby. After so many years of keeping her feelings buried deep inside, she couldn't do it anymore. Maybe it was the pregnancy hormones, or maybe the anguish of hope. But emotions were suddenly bleeding out of her that she couldn't control. Grief and heartbreak and something new.

Anger.

"So that was why you ran away from me three months ago?" she said. "Because you were terrified that if I actually woke up in your arms, I'd fall desperately in love with you?"

Cesare looked irritated. "I didn't exactly run away—"

"I woke up alone," she said unsteadily. She ran her trembling hand back through the dark braids of her chignon. "You regretted sleeping with me."

He set his jaw. "If I'd known you were a virgin…" He exhaled, looking down the gilded hallway with a flare of nostril before he turned back to her. "It never should have happened. But you knew the score. I stayed away these past months to give us both some space to get past it."

"You mean, pretend it never happened."

"There's no reason to let a single reckless night ruin a solid arrangement." He folded his arms over his bare chest, over the warm skin that she'd once stroked and felt sliding against her own naked body in the dark hush of night. "You are the best housekeeper I've ever had. I want to keep it that way. That night meant nothing to either of us. You were sad, and I was trying to comfort you. That's all."

It was the final straw.

"I see," she bit out. "So I should just go back to folding your socks and keeping your home tidy, and if I remember the night you took my virginity at all, I should be grateful you were such a kind employer—comforting me in my hour of need. You are truly too good to me, Mr. Falconeri."

He frowned, sensing sarcasm. "Um…"

"Thank you for taking pity on me that night. It must have felt like quite a sacrifice, seducing me to make the crying stop. Thank you for your compassion."

Cesare glared at her, looking equal parts shocked and furious. "You've never spoken like this before. What the hell's gotten into you, Emma?"

Your baby, she wanted to say. *But you don't even care you took my virginity. You just want me back to cook and clean for you.* Anger flashed through her. "For God's sake, don't you think I have any feelings at all?"

He clenched his hands at his sides, then exhaled.

"No," he said quietly. "I hoped you didn't."

The lump in her throat felt like a razorblade now.

"Well. Sorry. I'm not a robot. No matter how inconvenient that is for you." She fought the rush of tears. "Everything has changed for me now."

"Nothing changed for me."

Emma lifted her gaze to his. "It could, if you'd just give it a chance." She hated the pleading sound of her voice. "If you'd only just listen…"

Cesare's eyes were already hardening, his sensual lips parting to argue, when they heard a gasp. Emma turned to see an elderly couple staring at them in the hotel hallway. The white-haired man looked scandalized at the sight of

Cesare wearing only a white towel, while his wife peered at him through her owlish glasses with interest.

Cesare glared at them. "Do you mind?" he said coldly. "We are trying to have a private conversation."

The man looked nonplussed. "I beg your pardon." He fled toward the elevator, pulling his wife with him, though she shot Cesare's backside one last look of appreciative regret.

He turned back to Emma with a scowl. "Nothing can change for me. Don't you understand?"

It already had. He just didn't know it. Emma swallowed. She'd never thought she'd be forced to blurt out news of her pregnancy in the middle of a public hotel hallway. She licked her lips. "Look, can't we go somewhere? Talk about this in private?"

"Why? So you can confess your undying love?" His voice was full of scorn. "So you can tell me how you'll be the woman to make me love again? How you've imagined me proposing to you? How you've dreamed of standing next to me in a white dress?"

"It's not like that," she tried, but he'd seen her flinch. It was exactly like that.

"Damn you, Emma," he said softly. "You are the one woman who should have known better. I will not change, not for you or anyone. All you've succeeded in doing with this stunt is destroying our friendship. I don't see how we can continue to maintain a working relationship after this…."

"Do you think I'll even *want* to be your housekeeper after this?"

His eyes widened, then narrowed.

"So much for promises," he bit out.

She flinched again, wondering what he would say when she told him about the far worse promise she'd unknowingly broken—the one about it being impossible for her to get pregnant.

But how could she tell him? How could she blurt out the precious news of their child, standing in a public hallway with him staring at her as if he despised her? If only they could just go back to his room—but no. His suite was already filled, with a hard-eyed blonde in skimpy lingerie.

Everything suddenly became clear.

There was no room for a baby in Cesare's life. And Emma's only place there, as far as he was concerned, was scrubbing his floor and folding his sheets.

Cesare's expression was irritated. "If things can't be like they were…"

"What? You'll fire me for caring? That's your big threat?" Looking at the darkly handsome, arrogant face that she'd loved for so long, fury overwhelmed her. Fury at her own stupidity that she'd wasted so much of her life loving a man who couldn't see a miracle when it was right in front of him. Who wouldn't want the miracle, even if he did see.

How could she have loved him? How could she have ever thought—just as he'd accused her—that she could change his playboy nature?

He exhaled, and moderated his tone in a visible effort. "What if I offered to double your salary?"

Her lips parted in shock. "You want to *pay* me for our night together?"

"No," he said coldly. "I want to pay you to forget."

Her eyes stung. Of course he would offer *money*. It was just paper to him, like confetti. One of his weapons, along with his power and masculine beauty, that he used to get his way. And Cesare Falconeri always got his way.

Emma shook her head.

"So how can we get past this? What the hell do you want from me?"

She looked up at him, her heart full of grief. What did she want? A man who loved her, who would love their child, who would be protective and loyal and show up for breakfast every morning. She whispered, "I want more than you will ever be able to give."

He knew immediately she wasn't speaking of money. That was clear by the way his handsome face turned grim, almost haunted in the dim light of the hallway. He took a step toward her. "Emma…"

"Forget it." She stepped back. Her whole body was shaking. If he touched her now, if he said anything more to remind her what a fool she'd been, she was afraid she'd collapse into sobs on the carpet and never get up again.

Her baby needed her to be strong. Starting now.

Down the hall, she heard the elevator ding. Glancing back, she saw the elderly couple hesitate in front of the elevator, obviously still watching them. She realized they'd been listening to every word. Turning back to Cesare, she choked out, "I'm done being your slave."

"You tell him, honey," the white-haired woman called approvingly.

Cesare's expression turned to cold fury, but Emma didn't wait. She just ran for the elevator. She got her arm between the doors in time to step inside, next to the elderly couple. Trembling, she turned back to face the man she'd loved for seven years. The boss whose baby she now carried, though he did not know it.

Cesare was stalking toward her, his almost-naked body muscular and magnificent in the hallway of his own billion-dollar hotel.

"Come back," he ground out, his dark eyes flashing. "I'm not done talking to you."

Now, that was funny. In a tragic, heart-wrenching, want-to-burst-into-sobs kind of way. "I tried to talk to you. You wouldn't let me. You were too terrified I'd say those three fatal words." She gave a bitter laugh. "So here are two words for you instead." Emma lifted glittering eyes to his. "I quit."

And the elevator doors closed between them.

CHAPTER TWO

I'M DONE BEING your slave.

Cesare's body was taut with fury as the elevator doors closed in front of Emma's defiant, beautiful face. He could still hear the echo of her scornful words.

I want more than you will ever be able to give.

And then she'd quit.

Cesare couldn't believe it.

It was true that in the past few months, he'd thought once or twice about firing Emma rather than face her again. But he'd promised himself he wouldn't fire her. As long as she didn't get silly or ask for a *relationship*. After all they'd been through together, he didn't want to lose her.

He'd never expected this. He was the one who left women. They didn't leave *him*. Not since...

He cut off the thought.

Turning, he stalked back down the hall, passing a wealthy hotel guest, a heavily bejeweled white-haired lady dressed in vintage Chanel, holding a small Pomeranian in her arms. An entourage of three servants trailed behind her. She glared at him.

Ah. Cesare's lip curled in a mixture of admiration and scorn. The wealthy. He hated them all sometimes. Even though he himself had somehow become one of them.

Returning to his suite, he realized he had no key. And

he was still wearing only a towel. At any moment someone would snap an embarrassing photograph, to add to the rest of his indiscretions already permanently emblazoned all over the internet. Irritated, he pounded on his own door with the flat of his hand.

Olga opened the door, still in her lingerie, holding a lit cigarette.

"There's no smoking in this hotel," he snapped, walking past her. "Put that out."

She took a long puff, then snuffed it out in the bottom of a water glass. "Problems with your housekeeping staff?" she asked sweetly.

"How did you get in here?"

"You sound as if you're not glad to see me." Pouting, Olga slinked forward, swaying her hips in a way that was no doubt supposed to be enticing. He almost wished it were. If he'd still been attracted to her, maybe he wouldn't have made such a mess of things with Emma. Because he couldn't go back to thinking of Emma Hayes just as an employee, no matter how he wished he could. Not when every time he closed his eyes, he remembered the way she'd felt beneath him in the hot breathless hush of night.

Don't worry. I can't get pregnant, she'd whispered, putting her hand over his as he'd reached for a condom in his bedside stand. *It's impossible. I promise you...*

And he'd believed her. Emma Hayes was the first, and only, woman he'd ever slept with without a condom. In his whole life.

The way it had felt—the way *she* had felt...

Cesare ground his teeth. His plan of dealing with the aftermath had not gone well. After three months apart, he'd convinced himself that surely, cool, sensible, emotionless Emma had forgotten their night together.

But she hadn't. And neither had he.

Damn it.

"You haven't been photographed with any other women for ages," Olga purred. "I knew that could only mean one thing. You've missed me, as I've missed you."

Looking up, Cesare blinked. He'd forgotten she was there.

She gave him a sultry smile. "We were good together, weren't we?"

"No." Cesare stared at her. "We weren't." Picking up the designer clothes and expensive leather boots she'd left in a neat stack by the bed, he held them out to her. "Please get out." In his current frame of mind, he was impressed with himself for managing the *please*.

Olga frowned, licking her red, bee-stung lips. "Are you kidding?"

"No."

"But—you can't send me away. I'm still in love with you!"

Cesare rolled his eyes. "Let me guess. You're having some sort of crisis because your bookings are down. You're ready to give up the difficulties of the modeling business and settle down, marry rich, have a child or two before you devote the rest of your life to shopping for jewels and furs."

Her cheeks turned red, and he knew he was right. It would have been funny, but this had happened too often for him to find it amusing anymore.

Her long lashes fluttered. "No one understands you like I do, Cesare. No one will ever love you like I do!"

Crossing the suite, he opened the door, and tossed her clothes and boots into the hallway.

"Cara," he drawled, "you're breaking my heart."

Olga's eyes changed from pleading to anger in a moment, leaving him to feel reasonably assured that her so-called love was worth exactly what the sentiment usually was: nothing, a breath of wind, once spoken, instantly lost.

"You'll be sorry!" She stomped past him, then stopped outside the doorway, wiggling her nearly-bare bottom at him. "You'll never have all *this* ever again!"

"Tragic," he said coldly, and closed the door.

His suite went quiet. Cesare stood for a moment, unmoving. He felt weary as the emotion of the past hour came crashing around him.

Emma. He'd lost her. She'd acted like all the other women, so he'd treated her like one.

The trouble was that she was different.

Maybe it's for the best, he thought. Things had gone too far between them. It had become...dangerous. Scowling, he dropped his towel and pulled a black shirt and pants from his wardrobe. The pants were slightly wrinkled, and the shirt had been oddly ironed. They didn't even have the right smell, because Emma hadn't been the one to wash, dry and fold them.

But it wasn't her laundry skills he missed most. He looked out the window. The lights of London's theater district were already twinkling in the dusk.

Cesare had always liked the environment of hotels, the way the faces of the people changed, the sameness of the rooms, the way a man could easily move out of one hotel and change to the next without anyone questioning his constancy, or thinking there was a flaw in his soul.

He'd known Emma Hayes's value since she'd first joined the housekeeping staff of his hotel on Park Avenue in New York. She'd been in charge of the penthouse floor, where he stayed while in the city, and he'd been so impressed by her work ethic and meticulous skills that she'd become assistant head housekeeper within the first year, and then head housekeeper when he'd opened the Falconeri in London. Now, she supervised the staff of his Kensington mansion. Taking care of him exclusively.

But she didn't just keep Cesare in clean socks. She kept him in line. Unlike other employees, unlike even his friends, Emma wasn't overly impressed by him. She'd become his sounding board. Almost like…family.

How could he have let himself seduce her? He needed her. He could always count on Emma. She always put his needs first. She never even asked for time off. Not until three months ago, when she'd abruptly left for a long weekend.

The Kensington house had felt strangely empty without her. He'd avoided coming home. On the third night, he'd returned from an unsatisfactory date at two in the morning, expecting to find a silent, dark house. Instead, he'd heard a noise from the kitchen and felt a flash of pleasure when he realized Emma must have returned early.

He'd found her sitting alone in the dark kitchen, holding a tequila bottle. Her black dress was wrinkled. Her eyes had dark smudges beneath them, as if she'd been crying, and her long black hair was unkempt, cascading thickly down her shoulders.

"Emma?" he'd said, hardly believing his eyes. "Are you all right?"

"I just came back from Texas," she whispered, not looking at him. "From a funeral."

He'd never seen her drink before, he realized—not so much as a glass of champagne. "I'm sorry," he said uncomfortably, edging closer. He didn't know anything about her family. "Was it someone you loved?"

She shook her head. "My stepmother." Her fingers clutched compulsively around the bottle. He saw it was still unopened. "For years, I sent money to pay her bills. But it never changed her opinion. Marion always said I was selfish, a ruiner of lives. That I'd never amount to anything." She drew in a shaking breath. "And she was right."

"What are you talking about?" he said, taking an instant dislike to this Marion person, dead though she might be.

Emma flung an unsteady arm around to indicate the immaculate, modern kitchen. "Just look."

Cesare looked around, then turned back. "It's perfect," he said quietly. "Because you're the best at what you do."

"Cleaning up other people's lives," she'd said bitterly. "Being the perfect servant. Invisible like a ghost."

He'd never heard her voice like that, angry and full of self-recrimination. "Emma…"

"I thought she'd forgive me in the end." Her voice was muffled as she sagged in the kitchen stool, covering her face with a trembling hand. "But she left me no message in her will. Not her blessing. Not her forgiveness. Nothing."

"Forgiveness—for what?"

She looked at him for a long moment, then she turned her face toward the shadows without answering. She took a deep breath. "Now I'm truly alone."

Something had twisted in Cesare's chest. An answering pain in his own scarred heart, long buried but never completely healed. Going to her, he'd taken the bottle from her hand. He'd set it on the kitchen counter. Reaching out, he'd cupped her cheek.

"You're not alone." His eyes had fallen to her trembling pink lips as he breathed, "Emma…"

And then…

He'd only meant to offer solace, but somehow, he still wasn't sure how, things had spiraled out of control. He remembered the taste of her lips when he'd first kissed her. The look in her deep, warm green eyes as he covered her naked body with his own. The shock and reverence that had gone through him when he realized he was her very first lover.

She was totally different from any woman he'd taken to his bed before. It wasn't just the alluring warmth of her makeup-free face, or her total lack of artifice, or the long, dark hair pulled back in an old-fashioned chignon. It wasn't just her body's soft plump curves, so different from the starvation regime demanded by starlets and models these days.

It was the fact that he actually respected her.

He actually—liked her.

Everything about Emma, and the way she served him without criticism or demand, was comfort. Magic. *Home.*

But if he'd known she was a virgin, he never would have—

Yes, you would, he snarled at himself, remembering the tremble of her soft, tender lips beneath his, the salt of tears on her skin that night. The way she'd felt to him that night…the way she'd made him feel…

Cesare shook his head savagely. Whatever the pleasure, the cost was too high. Waking up the next morning, he'd realized the scope of his mistake. Because there was only one way his love affairs ended. With an awkward kiss-off, a bouquet of roses and an expensive gold watch, handed over by his one indispensable person—Emma herself.

He clawed back his short dark hair, still damp from his shower. His jaw was tight as he remembered the stricken expression on her pale, lovely face when she'd seen Olga in lingerie, standing in front of a bed which had been mussed, not with lovemaking, but from his hopeless attempt at sleep after a night on the phone with the Asia office. Of course Emma wouldn't know that, but why should he be obligated to explain?

What is wrong with you, Cesare?

Nothing was wrong with him, he thought grimly. It was the rest of the world that was screwed up, with stupid promises and rose-colored illusions. With people who pretended words like *love* and *forever* were more than sentiments on a Valentine's Day card.

He'd told himself Emma had no feelings for him, that their night together had been just an escape from grief. It meant nothing. He'd told himself that again and again. Told himself that if Emma tried to call it love, he'd break in a new housekeeper—even if that meant replacing her with someone who'd have the audacity to expect tea breaks and four weeks off every August.

But he'd never expected that Emma herself would just walk away.

Cesare looked out into the deepening autumn night. She'd done him a favor, really. She couldn't be his friend *and* his lover *and* know all his household secrets. It was too much. It left him too—vulnerable.

You are truly too good to me, Mr. Falconeri.

Cesare rubbed the back of his neck. He didn't deserve that. He *had* been a good employer to Emma. Hadn't he done everything a boss could do—paying her well, respecting her opinion, giving her independence to run his home? For the past few years, as they'd grown closer, he'd resisted an inconvenient desire for her. He wasn't used to ignoring temptation, but he'd done it, at least until three months ago. And as for what had happened that night... virgin or no—the way she'd licked her full pink lips and looked up at him with those heartbreaking eyes, how could he resist that? *Christo santo,* he was only a man.

But for that momentary weakness, she was now punishing him. Abandoning him without so much as a by-your-leave.

Fine. He growled under his breath. Let her quit. He didn't give a damn. His hands tightened. He *didn't*.

Except…

He did.

Cursing himself, he started for the door.

Emma wearily climbed out of the Tube station at Kensington High Street. Making her way through crowds of early evening commuters, she wiped rain from her cheek. It had to be rain. She couldn't be crying over Cesare.

So he'd never given her a chance to tell him he was going to be a father. So she'd found him in a hotel room with his ex-girlfriend, the lingerie model. So Emma was now all alone, with a baby to raise and nothing to help her but the memory of broken dreams.

She was going to be fine.

She exhaled, shifting her aching shoulders. She'd phone Alain Bouchard and accept that job in Paris. He'd give her decent hours, along with a good paycheck. She needed to be more sensible, now that she'd soon be a single mother.

Passing a shop selling Cornish pasties, she breathed in the smell of beef and vegetables in a flaky crust, vividly reminding her of her father's barbecues in Texas when she was a child. Going to the counter, she impulsively bought one. Taking the beef pasty out of the bag, she ate it as commuters rushed past her. Tears fell down her cheeks as she closed her eyes, savoring every bite. She could almost hear her father's voice.

Let me tell you what I know, kiddo. You're going to make it. You're stronger than you think. You're going to be fine.

It did make her feel a little better. Tossing the bag into the trash, she looked out at Kensington High Street. The lights of the shops glimmered as car lights streaked by in the rain.

She barely remembered her mother, who'd died when she was four, but her dad had always been there. Teaching her to fish, telling her stories, helping with homework. When Emma had gotten ill as a teenager, he'd been by her side every day, even as he pulled extra overnight shifts at the factory to fight the drowning tide of medical bills.

Her throat ached. That was the kind of father her unborn baby deserved. Not a man like Cesare, who'd loved once, and lost, in a terrible tragedy, and was now unable to love anyone but himself.

Maybe it was for the best he would never know he was a father. She could just imagine how Cesare's careless lack of commitment would affect a child.

Why didn't Daddy come for my birthday, Mommy? Why doesn't he ever come see me? Doesn't he love me?

Emma's eyes narrowed. No more romantic illusions. No more false hopes. She'd never give Cesare the chance to break their child's heart, as he'd already broken hers.

Pulling her raincoat tighter around her body, she gripped her handbag against her shoulder and went out into the drizzly night, walking down the street and past the town hall. Her footsteps echoed loudly past the expensive townhouses on Hornton Street, in counterpoint to the splatters of rain, until she finally reached Cesare's grand three-story mansion.

It was a palace of white brick, which had cost, including renovations, twenty million pounds. For years, she'd buried herself in work here, waiting for her real life to begin. Trying to decide if she even deserved a real life.

You selfish girl. Her stepmother's hoarse voice came back to her. *It should have been you who died.*

The memory still caused a spike of pain. She pushed the thought away. Marion was the one who'd ruined her father's life. She'd made a bad choice. It wasn't Emma's fault.

Though it sometimes felt that way. She swallowed. If only her father were still alive. He always had known the right thing to do....

She walked past the gate. Her lips pursed as she remembered meeting Alain Bouchard for the first time six months ago, here in the front garden. He'd shown up drunk and wanting to start a fight with Cesare, his former brother-in-law, blaming him for his sister's death. Fortunately Cesare was away, on a business trip to Berlin; Emma knew he'd never gotten over Angélique's tragic accidental death ten years before.

Emma could have called the police. That was what the rest of the staff had wanted her to do. But looking at Alain's grief-stricken face, she'd invited him into the house for tea instead, and let him talk himself out.

The next day, Alain Bouchard had sent her flowers and a handsome note of apology for his drunken ravings. That was the proper way of showing someone appreciation, Emma thought. Not by throwing expensive jewelry at them, bought in bulk, via a paid employee.

She stalked up the shadowy steps to the mansion, punched in the security code and entered. The foyer was dark, the house empty, gloomy as a tomb. None of the other staff lived in. When Cesare was gone, which was often, she was alone. She'd spent too long in this lonely tomb.

Well, no more. Throwing down her handbag, Emma ripped off her coat and ran up the stairs, taking them two at a time. She was going to pack and leave for France immediately. Before she'd even reached her bedroom at the end of the hall, she was pulling off her knit dress, the pretty dress that hit her curves just right, that she'd bought that very day in a foolish attempt to impress Cesare. Yanking it over her head, she tossed it to the hall floor. She'd wear comfortable clothes on the train, black trousers and a plain shirt. She'd be in Paris within three hours—

A small lamp turned on by her bed. Startled, she turned.

Cesare was sitting in her antique chair with blue cushions by the marble fireplace.

She gasped, instinctively covering her lace bra and panties. "What the hell are you doing here?"

"I live here."

She straightened, and her expression hardened. "Oh, so you just remembered that, did you?"

His eyes were black in the dim light. "You left the hotel before we could discuss something important."

"How did you—" she breathed, then cut herself off. He couldn't possibly know about the baby. And she didn't intend to let him know now.

Cesare rose to his feet, uncoiling his tall, powerful body from the chair. He looked down at her.

"I've decided not to accept your resignation," he said in a low voice. "I want you here. With me."

For a moment, they stared at each other in the shadows of her bedroom. She heard a low roll of thunder outside, the deepening patter of rain. Water dripped noisily from her hair onto the glossy hardwood floor.

Her arms dropped. She was no longer trying to cover her body. Why should she? He'd already seen everything. And she meant nothing to him. Never had. Never would.

"I don't belong here," she said. "I won't stay."

"Just because we slept together?" His eyes narrowed dangerously. "Do you really have to be such a cliché?"

"You're the cliché, not me."

"One stupid night—"

"No," she cut him off. She looked at him, and said deliberately, "I'm in love with you, Cesare."

Oh, that did it. She saw him flinch. He'd taken the words like a hit. Which was fine, because she'd meant it that way.

His black eyes glinted with fury as he grabbed her shoulders. "You don't love me. It's just because I was your first experience in bed. You haven't learned the difference between sex and love."

"But you have?"

Cesare didn't answer. He didn't have to. The whole world knew his tragic story: how he'd married young, and had been desperately in love with his wife, a beautiful French heiress, before she'd died just three years later. His heart had been buried with her.

She'd known this. And she'd still let herself hope…

Pulling away from him angrily, Emma went to her closet and reached up to the top shelf for the beat-up old suitcase that had once belonged to her father. Tossing it open on the floor, she turned back to her wardrobe to reach for her clothes.

He put his hand over hers, stilling her.

"Emma. Please."

Just that one word. The word he'd never said to her before. *Please.* She swallowed, then looked at him.

"Let me go. It's better for you this way. Better for all of us."

"I can't," he said in a low voice. "There are so few people in my life I trust. So few who actually know me. But you do. That's why I know—I *know*—you can't really love me."

His words were strangely bleak. Her heart twisted. He was right about one thing. She, of all people, did know him. She knew he was not the emotionless man the world believed him to be.

Emma ached to reach up and stroke the roughness of his cheek, to whisper words of comfort. Her hand trembled.

Shadows from the closed window blinds left lines across his dark, handsome face. His eyes burned through her.

But even more: her secret burned inside her, with every beat of her heart. She was pregnant with his child. Her silence in this moment was the biggest lie any woman could tell any man.

"Why ever did you think you couldn't get pregnant, Mrs. Hayes?" her physician had asked, looking shocked. "Childhood cancer, especially ovarian cancer, can occasionally cause difficulties, yes. But in your case it worked out just fine. I see it's a surprise, but this baby is wanted, yes?"

"Of course this baby is wanted," she'd answered. Oh, yes. Emma had believed for so long that she'd never be a mother. That it wasn't even a possibility. Fighting the same deadly, silent disease years before, her mother had never been able to have another child. Caroline Hayes had ultimately died when Emma was only four, at the age of twenty-nine. Barely older than Emma was now.

"Cara." Cesare's handsome face was almost pleading as he gave an awkward laugh. "How many times did we joke about it? That I wasn't worthy of any good woman's love?"

She blinked hard. "Many times."

"So you must see. What you think you feel—it's not love. Just sex."

Hot tears burned at the backs of her eyes and she feared at any moment tears would spill over her lashes. "For *you.*"

"For both of us. You just aren't experienced enough to realize it yet," he said gently. "But someday soon, you will…"

Emma stiffened. Was he already picturing her moving on, finding sex or love with another man? Cesare could imagine this, without it ripping out his heart?

Not Emma. It had nearly killed her to find him with

Olga. And even if he hadn't slept with her—that time—she knew there had been other women. Many, many others. And there would always be.

She ripped her hand away. She didn't have to live like this. Not anymore. She'd never have to spend another lonely night staring at her ceiling, listening to the noise down the hall while he had yet another vigorous one-night stand with yet another woman he'd soon forget. She was done.

It was like a burst of sunlight and fresh air after years of imprisonment.

"I don't want to love you anymore," she whispered.

He tried to smile. "See—"

"Do you realize that I've never taken a single vacation in seven years? No personal days, no time off, except for my stepmother's funeral?"

"I just thought you were devoted to your work, like I am."

"I wasn't devoted to my work. I was devoted to *you*." She shook her head. "I've lived in London for years and still only seen Trafalgar Square from the bus. I've never been inside the museums—or even had a picture of myself taken in front of Big Ben."

He stared at her incredulously. "I'll call my driver, take you down to Trafalgar Square and take your picture myself, if that's what it takes. I'll lower your schedule to thirty hours a week and give you two months off every year." He tried to give his old charming smile. "Forget our night together, and I'll forgive your infatuation. So long as it ends now."

She shook her head. "I'm done working for you."

"And there's nothing I can do to change your mind?"

The deep, sexy timbre of his voice caused a shudder to

pass through her body, all the way to her fingertips. She forced herself to ignore it.

"I can't change your nature," she choked out. "And you can't change mine. There is nothing either of us can do." She looked away. "Please ask Arthur to cut my last paycheck. I'll pick it up on the way to St. Pancras."

"St. Pancras?"

"I'm taking the train to Paris." She licked her lips. "For a new job."

He stared at her.

"You're not even giving me two weeks' notice?"

"Sorry," she mumbled.

Silence fell between them. In the distance, she heard the sounds of a police siren, with its European sound, so different from New York's.

"It seems I've been an awful boss to you these past years." Something in Cesare's tone made her look up. From where he stood on the other side of the bed, his handsome face was half-hidden in shadow. "Let me save you the trouble of a trip to the office. I'll pay you now."

"It's not necessary."

"But it is," he said coldly. In his long-sleeved black shirt and trousers, he looked sophisticated, like the international tycoon he was. But the power of his muscled shoulders and cold fury in his black eyes were anything but civilized. "Here."

Pulling a handful of fifty-pound bills out of his wallet, he tossed them toward her. Wide-eyed, Emma watched them float like feathers to the bed.

"Your paycheck," he said grimly. Reaching back into his wallet, he threw out American money next. "The vacation time you refused to take." He tossed out Euro notes. "Your Christmas bonus." Then Japanese yen. "Overtime."

Dirhams and Russian rubles flew next. "The raise I should have given you."

Shocked, Emma watched the blizzard of money fall like snowflakes onto the bed, a flurry of money from all over the world, pesos and reals and kroner, dollars from Canada and Australia.

Frowning, Cesare suddenly looked into his wallet. Empty. It seemed even billionaires had a limit to ready cash. Pulling the platinum watch off his tanned wrist, he dumped it on the bed, on top of the Matterhorn of money.

"There," he said coldly. "Will that compensate you for all the anguish you suffered working for me? Are we done?"

She swallowed. Even now, in his generosity, he was being cruel—using his wealth as a weapon against her. Making her feel small.

"Yes," she choked out. "We're done."

"So you're no longer my employee. As of this moment."

Head held high, Emma walked toward the money on the bed. *Just take it,* she told herself. She had earned that money—all of it and more! The money he'd tossed at her so carelessly was nothing to him, barely more than he might spend impulsively on an amusing night out, buying thousand-pound bottles of scotch for all his rich friends.

But still. There was something truly awful about reaching for a pile of money left on her bed. Something sordid.

She tried to force herself forward, then stiffened. She exhaled, pulling back her hand.

"What's wrong now?"

"I can't take it," she said. "Not like this."

He slowly walked around the bed toward her. "It's yours. You earned it."

"Earned it how?" she whispered.

"For God's sake, Emma!"

She whirled back to him. "I can't take it off the *bed*. As if I were your..."

She couldn't say the word, but he did.

"My whore?" Cesare came toward her, his dark eyes like fire. "You are driving me insane," he ground out. "If you do not want the money, then leave it. If you are so determined to go, then go. I don't give a damn what you do."

"You've made that painfully clear," she said hoarsely.

"And you," he snarled, "have made it clear that there is no way I can win. You think I'm a selfish bastard, you hate me, you hate yourself for your so-called *love* for me. You're sick of the sight of me and you're using our night together as an excuse to quit."

She sucked in her breath.

"An *excuse*?" It was humiliating how her voice squeaked on the word.

"Yes." Cesare was close to her now, very close. She was suddenly very aware that she was wearing almost nothing and they were alone in her dark bedroom. Her nipples were hard beneath her white lace bra. Her own breathing seemed loud in her ears. His powerful body towered over hers, and she could feel the warmth emanating off his skin. The heat in his gaze scared her—almost as much as the answering heat in her own body. He said in a low voice, "You're running away from me like a coward."

She gasped, "Are you kidding? *I'm* running like a coward?"

Cesare's hand reached out to touch her cheek, and as she felt his fingertips against her skin, it was all she could do not to turn her face into the warmth of his caress, even now. "You mean nothing to me, Emma," he growled. His dark eyes burned through her. "You never have. You never will."

"Good," she choked out. "Because I can hardly wait

to leave you. I'm so happy that after tonight I'll never see you again...."

His hand trailed down her cheek, to her neck, to her bare shoulder. She barely heard his harsh intake of breath over the pounding of her own heart. She trembled, knowing she was on the knife's edge.

Cesare roughly seized her in his arms, and crushed her lips with his own.

CHAPTER THREE

CESARE'S KISS WAS angry and searing. His lips plundered hers, and all her anger and grief and pain seemed to explode beneath the fire of his touch, into an inferno.

He wrapped a strong arm around her waist, holding her tight against him, and his other hand ran along her bare arm, up her shoulder, down her naked back. She felt his body, hard against hers, and against her will a soft moan came from the back of her throat. Her skin felt scorched everywhere he touched. She was desperate to have him closer.

Now.

Her hand cupped the rough edge of his jawline, then moved back to tangle in his dark hair, pulling his mouth harder and deeper into hers.

She heard his hoarse intake of breath as he cupped her full, aching breasts over the lace of her bra. She was overflowing the cups now, and her belly was starting to get fuller as well. Would he notice? Would he guess? Would Cesare be able to see how he'd permanently branded her body as his, always and forever, without her saying a single word?

"All this time, I've been hating myself for a lack of self-control," he said in a low voice. "Now I can hardly believe I had such restraint." He lifted his gaze to hers, even as one of his hands slowly stroked her nearly naked body, over her white lace, causing her to tremble with need. "I can't believe I waited so long." His sensual lips curved as he cupped her face, tilting back her head. "No other woman has even interested me since that night…."

Her lips parted. No. Surely he couldn't mean what she thought he meant….

With their bodies so close, standing together beside her bed, she felt his warmth and strength. She breathed in the bare hint of masculine cologne. She felt the electricity of his words, of his touch—the overwhelming sensual force of his complete attention. And Emma's only defense, anger, crumbled.

He kissed her softly, briefly, butterfly kisses to each of her cheeks, tantalizingly close to the corners of her mouth. But hope, like a fragile spring bud unfolding in the snow, began to build inside her. She could hardly believe his shocking confession.

He'd been faithful….

"There's really been no other woman for you since our night?" she breathed.

He shook his head, his eyes dark. "Has there been someone for you?"

The question made her choke out a laugh. "How could there be?"

"Does that mean no?"

"Of course not!"

"Good."

His sudden masculine smugness irritated her. "You admit something, too," she said sharply.

"What?"

"You didn't seduce me three months ago just because I was crying. You weren't just trying to comfort me."

He stared at her, then said quietly, "No."

Her soul thrilled at the concession. She gloried in it. "You wanted me, too."

He spoke a single grudging word, as if it were pulled from deep inside him. "Yes."

"For how long?"

"Years," he bit out.

"Why didn't you tell me?" she whispered.

"I was afraid you'd do exactly what you did today." His hands undid the plaits of her braids, causing her long dark hair to fall down her back. She trembled as his hands stroked her long, tumbling waves of hair. "You'd get some crazy delusion of loving me, and then I'd have to fire you."

"I am in love with you."

He snorted. "If you really loved me, wouldn't you be begging me to stay?"

"Because begging works so well with you."

Slowly he lowered his head until his mouth was inches from hers.

"It's just lust, *cara,*" he whispered, his lips almost brushing hers. "Not love…."

And holding her against his hard body in the shadowy bedroom, he kissed her, clutching her as if he were a drowning man and only she could save him. His lips plundered hers, teasing, gentling, searing.

As they stood together, he slowly kissed down her throat, his fingertips roaming softly over her naked skin. She felt the warmth of his hands cupping her breasts, stroking tight, aching nipples that peeked through white lace.

Leaning back in his arms, she gasped with pleasure and need. Until she lost her balance, and fell back against the bed, his arms still around her, their bodies entangled in their embrace.

The bed felt made of feathers beneath her. Still in her bra and panties, Emma slid against the duvet cover, and felt something sharp and cold beneath her thigh. She pulled it out and looked at the shining platinum face with confusion. "Your watch."

"Forget it." Taking it from her hand, he tossed the expensive watch across the room, causing it to scatter noisily across the hardwood floor before it hit the wall with a soft thunk.

She realized what the "feathers" she'd felt beneath her body actually had to be. Twisting, she tried to look beneath her. She was lying almost naked beneath him *on a bed of money.* "Everything's still on the bed—"

"I don't care," he said roughly, and kissed her, until she forgot about the money, and wouldn't have cared if she did.

Pulling away, he pulled off his shirt in an abrupt movement. Emma's throat constricted as she reached out to touch the intoxicating vision of his naked chest, muscular and hard, with tanned skin that felt like silk over steel. She stroked down to the flat six-pack of his belly, laced with a scattering of dark hair. He was flesh and blood, this man she'd wanted so hopelessly, and loved for so long.

Covering her body with his own, Cesare kissed her. She felt his weight crushing her breasts, felt the slide of his warm bare skin against her own. He released the clasp of her bra and pulled off the slip of white lace, tossing it aside. He pulled her panties slowly past her hips, over her thighs, down her legs.

She was naked beneath him. Lying on a pile of money. She shouldn't be doing this, she thought. Then he pulled off his pants and silk boxers, and rational thought left her entirely.

She gasped as she saw how large he was, how huge and hard. Slowly, he kissed down her body, licking and suckling her breasts. He caressed down the curve of her belly, then kissed her lips in a long, deep embrace that seemed to last forever, until she forgot where she ended and he began. Their bodies fused together in heat, skin to skin, slick and salty and sweet. Moving down her body, he pushed her legs apart with his knee, spreading them wide with his hands. Lowering his head, he nuzzled between her thighs. She felt his hot breath.

She gasped as, holding her hips firmly against the bed, he spread her wide and tasted her.

She twisted, rocking beneath him. The pleasure was too sharp, too explosive. Beneath the ruthless insistence of his tongue, she trembled and shook, gasping on the bed. Every time she moved, money went flying into the air. Durhams and dollars, pounds and pesos flew violently, then fell back softly like snow, sliding down the naked bodies clutched together on the bed.

The money felt whisper-soft, brushing against Emma's face or shoulder or breast while she felt the hard, bristly roughness of his masculine body between her legs.

"Lust," Cesare said in a low voice.

Their eyes locked over the curves of her naked body. She shook her head.

"Love…"

With a low growl, he lowered his head back between her legs. She felt the heat of his breath on her tender skin, and his tongue took another wide taste of her, then another. Slowly he caressed her, licking her in delicate swirls until her breathing came in gasps and her hands were gripping the bedsheets beneath her, along with fistfuls of yen and euros.

"Lust," he whispered against her skin.

"No," she choked out.

He thrust his tongue an inch inside her. She gave a shocked gasp in a voice she hardly recognized as her own. His hands roamed possessively over her, cupping her breasts, her waist, her hips. Reaching beneath her, he pressed her bottom upward, lifting her more firmly against his mouth, and impaled her more deeply with his tongue. His lips and soft wet tongue suckled the aching center of her need as he moved two thick fingertips inside her, where his tongue had been. She cried out, overwhelmed by the intensity of pleasure.

Her back arched from the feel of his fingers inside her and his tongue swirling over her and she gripped his shoulders as waves of ecstasy started to pull reality beneath her feet, crashing over her. She exploded, and as if from a distance, she heard herself scream—

Rolling beside her, he pulled her into the warm haven of his arms. Emma looked up at him with tears in her eyes.

It wasn't just lust between them. It *wasn't*.

If he'd only just give her a chance. If only he'd say something that would make her think she could tell him about the baby...

Leaning up, Emma put her hand on his cheek and kissed him in a deep, lingering embrace that left her chin and cheeks tingling from the rough bristles of his jaw. She could still feel his body straining against her. As he kissed her back, holding her tight, breathless hope ripped through her. She could show him he had nothing to fear. That their relationship could be so much more than lust. She knew the man he really was, yes. But she also knew the man he could be....

"Love," she whispered silently against his lips.

Emma abruptly rolled him beneath her on the bed. He looked up at her, surprised. She smiled, her soul welling up with sudden certain joy. If he wouldn't let her speak words of love...

She would show him.

* * *

Cesare stared up at the woman who'd just rolled him beneath her on the bed. He felt Emma's hands stroke down his chest, as her legs straddled his hips.

She was so impossibly beautiful, he thought, dazzled by the pink flush of her creamy skin, the emerald gleam of her eyes. She looked down at him fiercely, like an ancient warrior queen who commanded an army of thousands eager to die in her name. Power emanated from her proud, curvaceous body like light. Power he'd never seen in her before.

"Emma," he breathed. "What's gotten into you?"

"Haven't you figured it out?" Her full red lips curved into a smile as she lowered her head. She whispered against his mouth, "You have."

She kissed him, and he felt that something had changed in her. Something he didn't understand. She seemed— different. New. Beneath her touch, sparks flew up and down his body, a fire that burned him to blood and bone.

He'd wanted her for months. Years. But never like this. His body shook with need. She'd never, ever made the first move before.

He could hardly believe he'd once thought of Emma as having no feelings. This was who she really was: a seductive sex goddess, innocent and wanton, powerful and glorious...

As her lips caressed his, her long dark hair tumbled over his body, sliding over his overheated skin. Her full breasts brushed against his chest. With a moan, he cupped them with his hands. Breaking off their kiss, he wrenched his head to suckle a taut, pink nipple, licking it, pulling it into his mouth. His hand tangled in her hair, stroking down her naked back. He heard her moan. Felt her thighs tighten around his hips. He felt the soft, wet core of her brush the tip of his hardest edge as she swayed in innocently tantalizing torture.

Twisting away with a choked gasp, he started to reach for the wallet in his jacket hanging on a nearby chair, intending to retrieve a condom, but she stopped him.

"It's not necessary." She hesitated, then said slowly, "This time because I'm actually—"

"You're still on the Pill?" He exhaled. "Thank God." She stiffened, and he wondered if he'd said something rude, though he couldn't imagine what. Women could be sensitive, and even though Emma was the most rational woman he knew, she was still undeniably a woman. Oh, yes. Running his hand down the curve of her bare breast— even fuller than he remembered—he looked up at her with heavy-lidded eyes. "I love that you are always prepared, Miss Hayes."

She leaned forward, allowing her long dark hair to trail sensuously across his bare chest as she said pointedly, "Emma."

"Emma," he groaned as her fingertips trailed down his body. "Oh, God—Emma—"

Reaching up, he kissed her, and as she leaned down to kiss him back, he could wait no longer. Pulling her down on him with his hands, he simultaneously thrust up with his hips, pushing inside her, and heard her gasp as he filled her soft, wet body.

God. He'd never felt anything like this. He rammed inside her, filling her hard and deep. She slid over his hips, riding him, and his whole body started to tighten. No. No, it was too soon. The intensity of pleasure was too much. But being inside her without a condom…skin to skin…

He gripped her shoulders. "I'm not sure how long I can last," he said hoarsely. "Give me… Give me a minute to…"

But it seemed Emma's days of obedience were over. She

continued to slide against him. He looked up, intending to protest. He stopped when he saw how her eyes were closed, her beautiful face rapt and shining in ecstasy.

No! He squeezed his eyes shut. He couldn't see her like that! Not when at any moment he could… He could… But even with his eyes closed, he could still see her shining face, see her full breasts swaying above him as she moved. He felt tighter—tighter—about to explode…

"You feel so good," she whispered. "So—good…"

"Oh, my God," he said in a strangled voice. "Stop!"

Gripping his shoulders, she leaned forward, so close he could feel the brush of her lips against his earlobe, and whispered, "Love."

It was the one thing that made him cold.

"Lust," he growled back, and flung his body over hers, lying her beneath him on the bed. He ran his hands down her body, licking and sucking every inch of her skin. Sitting back against the pillows, he pulled her into his lap, wrapping his arms around her.

Tangling his hands in her hair, he tilted back her head and kissed her deeply. Lifting up her body, he lowered her hips heavily against him, thrusting slowly inside her. He rocked against her, controlling the rhythm and speed, slowing down when he came too close to exploding. Face-to-face, breath to breath, their eyes locked, their arms wrapped around each other, as close as two lovers could possibly be. He made love to her for what felt like hours until finally she gasped against him one more time, closing her eyes with a cry.

Cesare could hold back no longer. Kissing her shoulder, he sucked hard against her skin, and let himself go. He thrust inside her four times, so deep and hard that he exploded, so close to heaven that he saw only stars.

He saw only *her.*

Exhaling, he collapsed, still holding her tight.

It took long moments for Cesare to fall back to earth. He slowly became aware of the ticking of the old antique clock on the mantel. Blinking in the darkness, he saw he was in Emma's bed, in her suite of rooms on the second floor of his Kensington house. Moonlight was creeping in through the edges of the window shades as he still cradled her in his arms. He felt her cheek against his chest. Against his heart.

He shifted, cuddling her in the crook of his arm, her naked body against his own. He saw a small mark on her shoulder, where he'd sucked a little too hard in a love bite. That would leave a bruise, he thought. He'd marked her as his own. And for some reason he didn't want to examine, he was glad.

Emma blinked, smiling up at him sleepily before she glanced down at the bed. "What a mess we've made."

He looked down. The duvet and sheets were twisted at their feet and there were banknotes *everywhere.*

Cesare prided himself on discipline. He'd tried to do the sensible thing with Emma, to make them both forget their intoxicating night and return to their employer-employee relationship.

He'd failed. Massively.

And he was glad.

Now they could both have what they actually wanted. Yes, his home might fall apart without her in charge. At the moment he didn't give a damn. Who cared about milk in the fridge or having his bed made perfectly? Who cared about it being made at all, so long as he had her in it?

Emma yawned, her eyes closing as she settled deeper into his arms. Leaning forward, he kissed her softly on the temple. His own eyelids were heavy.

As she drowsed in his arms, he still shuddered with aftershocks of pleasure from their lovemaking. Making love without a condom, to a woman he liked and trusted, was a wholly new experience.

He'd certainly never had it with his wife.

Cesare looked down at Emma's face, half-hidden in shadow as she slept in his arms. She looked like a slumbering angel, her black eyelashes stark against her pale skin, and masses of her long, glossy dark hair tumbling over the pillow.

He felt exhausted, utterly spent. But as he closed his eyes, he smiled. He'd proved his point, and he was suddenly glad Emma had quit her job with him. That meant she'd be available for full-time pleasure. Their relationship might last for weeks, even months, now she understood there was no love involved. There would be no arguments, no goals of marriage or children to fight over. They could just enjoy each other's company for as long as the pleasure lasted.... He fell asleep, smiling and warm.

When he woke, the shadows of the room had changed to the soft gray light of dawn. Emma was stirring in his arms. He saw she was looking up at him with big, limpid eyes.

"Good morning," she said shyly.

Cesare stroked her cheek with amusement. "Good morning."

She bit her lip. "Um. If you want to go sleep in your own room, I'll understand...."

He placed a finger to her lips, gently stopping her. "I don't."

Her expression suddenly glowed. "You don't?"

He didn't blame her for being surprised. He was somewhat surprised himself. Usually he couldn't wait to get out of a woman's bed the morning after. He usually left long before morning, in fact.

But he felt oddly comfortable with Emma. He didn't

need to pretend with her, or play games, or be polite. It was strange, but he felt like he could just be himself, without trying to hide his flaws. How could he hide them? She knew them all.

"I'm hungry," Emma confessed, sitting up. "I can't stop thinking about fried eggs and bacon and oranges…"

Cesare kissed her bare shoulder. He was not thinking about food. "We could go down to the kitchen." He let his fingertips trail over her breast. "Or we could have a little breakfast in bed first…."

"Yes," she whispered, lifting her lips toward his. He stroked back her wildly tousled black hair.

"I'm so glad you came to your senses," he murmured as he kissed her.

She drew back with a frown. "My senses?"

He smiled, twisting a long black tendril of her hair around his finger. "You are going to be a very enjoyable bit of carry-on baggage."

"Oh, so now I'm baggage, am I?"

"I've decided you were right."

Her green eyes suddenly shone. "You did?"

"I'm glad you quit," he said lazily, running the pad of his thumb over her nipple, for the masculine pleasure of watching it instantly pebble beneath his touch. "I need to be in Asia tomorrow, Berlin on Friday."

Lifting a dark eyebrow, she said lightly, "And I need to take that job in Paris."

"You're thinking about your job?" He snorted. "I want you to come with me."

"Give up my career to do what—just hang out in your bed?"

"Can you think of a better idea?"

"I like my career." Her voice had a new edge to it. "I'm good at it."

"Of course you are. The best," he said soothingly. He hadn't meant to insult her. "But I'll cover your expenses while you're with me. We can just both enjoy ourselves. For however long this lasts."

"Are you joking?" She sounded almost angry.

Cesare was still waiting for her burst of excited joy and arms to be thrown around him at the brilliance of his plan. Her joy didn't seem to be forthcoming. "Don't you understand what I'm offering you, Emma?"

"I must not," she said. "Because it sounds like you expect me to drop everything for you, when all you want is sex."

"Sex with *you*," he pointed out. He would have thought that would be obvious. "And friendship," he added as an afterthought. "It'll be…fun."

"Fun?" she said in a strangled voice.

"What's wrong with that?"

"Nothing. Wow. It's the answer to all my childhood dreams. *Fun*."

He was starting to grow irritated "You can throw away your mop and broom. No more twenty-four-hour days with a jerk for a boss." He tried to laugh, but she didn't join him at the joke. He continued weakly, "You'll travel with me—see the world…"

Pulling away from him entirely, she looked at him in the gray dawn.

"For how long?" she said quietly.

"How should I know?" Sitting up straighter against the headboard, he folded his arms grumpily. "For as long as we're enjoying ourselves."

"And you'll kindly pay me for my time."

He ground his jaw. "You're twisting this all around, making it sound like I'm trying to insult you. Why aren't you happy? You should be happy—I've never offered any woman so much!"

She rebelliously lifted her eyes. "We both know that's not true."

A cold chill went down his spine. "You're talking about my wife."

She didn't answer. She didn't have to.

"Christo." Cesare clawed back his hair. This couldn't be happening. "We've been together only two nights, I've barely asked you to be my mistress, and you're already pressuring me to marry you?"

"I didn't say that!"

"You don't have to." He could see it in her face: that terrible repressed hope. The same expression he'd seen in so many women's faces. The desire to pin him down, to hold him against his will, in a place he didn't want to be. To make iron chains of duty and honor replace delight or even pleasure.

"You did get married once. You must have had a reason."

Anger rushed through him. The memory of Alain Bouchard's hateful voice. *You married my sister for her money and then made her life a living hell. Is it any wonder she took the pills? You might as well have poured them down her throat.*

Cesare's lips parted to lash out. Then he forced himself to focus on Emma's lovely, wistful face. It wasn't her fault. He choked back furious, hateful words.

"I married for love once," he said flatly. "I'll never do it again."

"Because you still love her," she whispered. "Your wife."

Cesare could see what Emma believed. That he'd loved Angélique so much that even a decade hadn't been enough to get over the grief of losing her. He let it pass, as he always did. The beautiful, simple lie was so much better than the truth.

He set his jaw, facing her across the bed, not touching. Just moments before, they'd been so close. Now an ocean divided them.

"I thought I made myself clear. But it wasn't enough. So hear this." He looked at her. "I will never love you, Emma. I will never marry you. I will never want to have a child with you. Ever."

In the rising pink dawn, every ounce of color drained from Emma's beautiful, plump-cheeked face, causing the powerful light of joy to disappear, as if it had never existed.

It was hard to watch. Cesare took a steadying breath. He had to be cruel to be kind. If they were to be together, even for just a few weeks, she had to accept these things from the beginning.

"My feelings in this matter will never change," he said quietly. "I thought you understood. I thought you felt the same." He reached for her hand, trembling where it rested on the bed. "Lust."

In a flash of anguish, her luminous eyes lifted to his. She shook her head. His eyes narrowed.

"You must accept this," he said, "for us to have any future."

A low, bitter laugh bubbled to her lips—the most bitter thing he'd ever heard from her. She ripped her hand away. "Future? No love, no marriage, no child. What kind of future is that?"

His jaw tightened. "The kind that is real. No promises to be broken. No pretense. No fakery. We just take it day by day, enjoying each other's company, taking pleasure for as long as it lasts."

"And then what?"

"We part as friends." He looked at her. "I don't want to lose your friendship."

"My friendship?" Her lip curled. "Or my services?"

"Emma!"

"You want to stop paying me as your housekeeper, and hire me straight out as your whore. No, I get it." Holding up her hand, she said coldly, "I'm sorry, this is awkward for you, isn't it? Usually I'm the one who handles this, who puts out your trash the morning after." She looked past the tangled mess of bedcovers at the foot of the bed, still surrounded by an explosion of money, to his platinum watch lying on the floor. "You even gave me a watch. Just like all the rest."

His own personal watch was even more expensive than the Cartier ones, but he sensed telling her that wouldn't impress her. "Emma, you're being idiotic...."

"I really am just like the rest." She threw the sheets aside and stood up from the bed. "I'll just collect my things and buy myself some roses on the high street, shall I?"

But as she started to walk away from the bed, Cesare grabbed her wrist.

"Don't do this," he said in a low voice.

"Do what?"

"This." He looked up at her, his eyes glittering. "I want you in my bed. For now. For as long as it's fun for both of us. Can't that be enough? Why do you need false promises of more? Why can't you just accept what I freely offer you?"

Their eyes locked. He could see the pain in her gaze.

"I want more. I want it all," she whispered. "Love. Marriage." She swallowed, looking up at him. "I want a baby. Our baby."

The air around him suddenly felt thin. He shrank back from her words. Literally. "Emma..."

"I don't need a wedding proposal. Or for you to say you're ready to be a father." Her eyes met his. "I just need to know you might want those things someday." She blinked fast. "That you might be open to the possibility… if something ever…"

"No," Cesare choked out. Still naked, he scrambled back on the bed, putting his hand to his neck, feeling as if he had something tight around his throat. He took a deep breath, forcing his hands down, trying to calm down, to breathe. "Either this is a fun diversion, a friendship with benefits, or it's nothing. You decide."

She stared at him for a long moment, her face as pale as marble. Then, violently, she grabbed her white bra and panties off the floor and yanked them on her body. Walking to her closet, she pulled out big armfuls of clothes. "What was I thinking—" she kicked open her old suitcase "—to believe—" she tossed the clothes inside "—in miracles!"

Cesare rose to his feet. Still naked, he padded across the hardwood floor. Without her warmth next to him, the bedroom felt chilly in the autumn morning. He heard traffic noise from the street outside. Soon, the house's day staff would arrive. He desperately wanted this settled before they were interrupted. He felt Emma was slipping away from him. He didn't understand why. With a deep breath, he tried once more.

"Why are you throwing everything away for the sake of some distant future? Think about today." Wrapping his arms around her waist from behind, he nuzzled the side of her neck and said in a low voice, "Let tomorrow take care of itself…."

Her skin was cold to the touch. She pulled away. Her beautiful face looked more than forlorn now—she looked frozen.

He sucked in his breath. He searched her face. "You're still going to leave, aren't you," he breathed. "You're still going to throw everything away for dreams of love, marriage and children. For a *delusion.* I can't believe you'd be such a…"

Emma's eyes were stony. She looked as if her soul had been shattered.

"…fool?" she finished.

He gave a single stiff nod.

She shook her head, wiping her eyes. "You're right. I have been a fool. A stupid romantic fool who believed a man like you could ever change."

Kneeling down, she gathered all the piles of money off the floor and dumped it into her suitcase. Picking up the platinum watch, she tossed it inside, then closed the suitcase with a bang. She looked down.

"Thank you for your offer," she said in a low voice. "I'm sure some other woman will take you up on it." She looked up, her eyes luminous with tears. "But I'm going to have a baby, and a home. And a man who loves us both."

Her words, spoken with such finality, hit him like a blow. He'd just offered Emma more than he'd offered any woman in ten years. And this was his reward for letting himself be vulnerable. Though he stood in front of Emma right now in flesh and blood, she was still rejecting him for some ridiculous fantasy of love and a child.

Something Cesare hadn't felt in a long, long time— something he'd thought he would never feel again—sliced through his heart.

Hurt.

His arms dropped. He stepped back.

"Bene," he said stiffly. "Go."

She pulled on jeans and a T-shirt. She picked up a few errant fifty-dollar banknotes off the floor and tucked them securely in her pocket, then lifted her chin. "Don't worry. I won't bother you again. I'll leave you alone to live the life you want. I give you my word." She held out her hand as if they were strangers. "Goodbye, Cesare."

His lips tightened, but he shook her hand.

"*Arrivederci,* Signorina Hayes. I hope you find what you're looking for."

Her green eyes shimmered, and she turned away without a word. Gathering her suitcase, her coat and her bag, Emma left the tidy bedroom. Cesare listened to her suitcase *thump, thump, thump* down his stairs. He listened to the front door open—and then latch closed.

She'd really gone. He couldn't believe it.

Going to the window, he looked down and watched her walk away, down the sidewalk toward Kensington High Street, in the drizzling rain of London's gray morning. He watched her small, forlorn figure with an old suitcase and a beige mackintosh, and felt a strange twist in his chest.

It's better this way, he told himself fiercely. Better for her to go, before the small hole in his heart had a chance to grow any larger. He watched her get smaller and smaller.

"Go," Cesare said aloud in the empty room. "You mean nothing to me."

But still, his hands tightened at his sides. *She'll be back,* he thought suddenly. No woman he wanted had ever been able to resist for long. And the sex had been too good between them. Emma wouldn't be able to stay away.

She'd soon be back, begging to negotiate the terms of her surrender. He exhaled, his shoulders relaxing. He allowed himself a smile. She'd be back. He knew it.

Within the week, if not the day.

CHAPTER FOUR

Ten months later

CESARE LOOKED OUT the window as his driver pulled the Rolls-Royce smoothly through the traffic of the Quai Branly, past the Pont de l'Alma. The September sun was sparkling like diamonds on the Seine.

Paris was not Cesare's favorite city. Yes, the city was justly famous for its beauty, but it was also aloof and proud. Like a coquette. Like a cold, distant star. Like his late wife, Angélique, who was born here—and took her lover here, a scant year after their marriage.

Sì. He had reason to dislike Paris. Since his wife's death over a decade before, he'd avoided the city. But now he was building a Falconeri Hotel here, upon the demand of his shareholders.

But Paris had changed since his last visit, he realized. The city felt…different.

Cesare looked up at the elegant classical architecture of cream-colored buildings. Through the vivid yellows and reds of the trees, the golden sun was bright in the blue sky. The city had a new warmth and charm he'd never felt before.

Because we finished the business deal, he told himself. After months of mind-numbing negotiations, his team had finally completed the purchase of an old, family-run hotel on the Avenue Montaigne, which—after it was exhaustively remodeled—would become the first Falconeri Hotel in France. *I'm just pleased about the deal.*

But he shifted in his leather seat. Even he didn't buy that.

Closing his eyes, he felt the sun on his skin. Against his will, he thought of her, and his body flashed with heat that had nothing to do with sunlight.

Emma lived in Paris.

You don't know that, he told himself fiercely. It had been almost a year since she'd left him in London that dreary November morning. For all he knew, she'd moved on to another job, another city. For all he knew, she'd changed her mind and never taken a job in Paris at all. For all he knew, she'd found another lover, a man who would love and marry her and be willing to have a child with her, just as she'd wanted.

For all he knew, she was already his wife. Pregnant with his child.

Cesare's hands tightened involuntarily.

For ten months, he'd made a point of not knowing where Emma was or whom she was with. He'd told himself he didn't care. At first, he'd been sure she'd soon return. It had taken him months to finally accept she wasn't coming back. Cesare knew she'd wanted him, as he wanted her. He'd been surprised to discover she'd wanted her dreams even more.

He'd been furious, hurt; and yet he'd respected her the more for it. She was the one who'd gotten away. The one he couldn't have. But she'd made the right choice. They wanted different things in life. Emma wanted a love, a home, a husband and a family of her own.

Cesare wanted—

What was it he wanted?

He tapped his fingers on the leather armrest as he stared out at the sparkling river. More, he supposed. More money. More hotels. More success for his company. More, more, more of the same, same, same.

His PR firm would soon announce how absolutely ecstatic the Falconeri Group was to finally have a hotel in this spectacular French city. His lips twisted. Well, Cesare would be ecstatic to leave it. This magical city seemed to have a strange power to steal any woman he actually tried to keep for longer than a night.

He wondered suddenly if Emma's dreams had been haunted, as his had been. Or if all she felt for him now was indifference. If she'd forgotten him entirely. If he alone was cursed with the inability to forget.

His driver stopped at a red light. Resentfully Cesare watched smiling tourists cross the street, walking from the popular *bateaux* of the Seine to the nearby Eiffel Tower. He still saw Emma in his dreams at night. Still felt her breath against his skin. Still heard her voice. Even by the light of day—hell, even now—his feverish imagination…

Cesare's eyes widened as he saw a woman crossing the street. She passed by quickly, before he could see her face. But he saw the black, glossy hair tumbling down her shoulders, saw the way her hips swayed and the luscious curve of her petite frame as she walked away from him. No. It couldn't be her. This woman was pushing a baby stroller. No, he was imagining things. Paris was a city of over two million people. There was no way that…

Cesare gripped the headrest of the seat in front of him.

"Stop the car," he said softly.

The chauffeur frowned, looking at Cesare in the rear-view mirror. "Monsieur?" he said, sounding puzzled.

When the light turned green, he drove the Rolls-Royce forward with traffic.

Cesare watched the woman continue walking away. It couldn't be Emma for a million reasons, the most obvious being the stroller.

Unless she'd really meant what she said about finding a man who would give her a child, and she'd done it in a hurry.

I'm going to have a baby. And a home. And a man who loves us both.

Watching her disappear down the street, he remembered the cold, gray morning last November, when he'd watched Emma walk down Hornton Street. He'd been so sure she'd come back. She never had. Not a message. Not a word.

He watched this woman go, with one last sway of her hips, one last shimmering beam of sunlight on her long, glossy black hair, before she turned toward the Champ de Mars. Disappearing…again…

Cesare twisted his head savagely toward the driver. "Damn you!" he exploded. "I said stop!"

Looking a little frightened, the driver immediately plunged through traffic to the side of the road. The Rolls-Royce hadn't even completely stopped before Cesare opened the door and flung himself on the sidewalk, causing several pedestrians to scatter. People stared at Cesare like he was crazy.

He felt crazy. He turned his head right and left as he started to run, getting honked at angrily by a tour bus as he crossed the street.

Where was the dark-haired woman? Had he lost her? Had it been Emma? He clawed his dark hair back, looking around frantically.

"Attention—monsieur!"

He moved just in time to avoid getting run over by a

baby carriage pushed by a gray-haired woman dressed in Gucci. *"Excusez-moi, madame,"* he murmured. She shook her head in irritation, huffing. Even Parisian grandmothers, even the *nannies,* wore designer clothes in this arrondissement.

He ran down the Avenue de la Bourdonnais, where he'd last seen her, and followed the crowds into the nearby park, the Champ de Mars, looking right and left, turning himself in circles. He walked beneath the shadow of the Eiffel Tower, past long queues of people. He walked down the paths of the park, past cheery couples and families having picnic lunches on this beautiful autumn day. Wearing his suit and tie, Cesare felt unbearably hot, running all over Paris in pursuit of a phantom from his past.

Cesare stopped.

He heard the soft whir of the wind through the trees, and looked up at the blue sky, through leaves that were a million different shades of green, yellow, orange. He heard the crunch of gravel beneath his feet. He heard children's laughter and music. In the distance, he saw a small outdoor snack stand, and beyond that, a playground with a merry-go-round.

What the hell was he doing?

Cesare clawed back his hair. *Basta.* Enough. Scowling, he walked to the snack stand and bought himself a coffee, then did something no true Parisian would ever do in a million years—he drank it as he walked. The black, scalding-hot coffee burned his tongue. He drank it all down, then tossed the empty cup in the trash. Grimly he reached into his pocket for his cell phone, to call his driver and get back on schedule, back to sanity, and return to the private airport on the east of the city where his jet waited. Walking, he lifted the cell phone to his ear. "Olivier, you can come get me at..."

He heard a woman gasp.

"Cesare?"

He froze.

Emma's voice. Her sweet voice.

"Sir?" his driver said at the other end of the line.

But Cesare's arm had already gone limp, the phone dropping to his side. Even now, he was telling himself that it wasn't her, it couldn't possibly be.

He turned.

"Emma," he whispered.

She was standing in front of a park bench, the stroller beside her. Her green eyes were wide and it seemed to Cesare in this moment like every bit of sunlight had fled the sky to caress her pink blouse, her brown slacks, her long black hair with a halo of brilliant golden light. The rest of the park faded from sight. There was only *her,* shining like a star, ripping through his cold soul like fire.

"It is you," she breathed. She blinked, looking back uneasily at the stroller before she turned back, biting her lip. "What are you…doing here?"

"I'm here…" His voice was rough. He cleared his throat. "On business."

"But you hate this city. I've heard you say so."

"I bought an old hotel on the Avenue Montaigne. Just this morning."

He'd somehow walked all the way to her without realizing it. His eyes drank her in hungrily. Her cheeks were fuller, her pale skin pink as roses. Her dark hair fell in tumbling soft waves over her shoulders. She'd put on a little weight, he saw, and it suited her well. The womanly softness made her even more beautiful, something he wouldn't have thought possible.

"It's—a surprise to see you," she faltered.

"Yes." His eyes fell on a dark-haired, fat-cheeked baby

sleeping in the stroller. Who was this baby? Perhaps the child of her employer? Or could it possibly be…hers? His gaze quickly fell to her left hand. No wedding ring.

So the baby couldn't be hers, then. She'd been very specific about what she'd said she wanted. *A husband, a home, a baby.* She surely wouldn't have settled for less—not after she'd left him for the sake of those dreams.

The pink in Emma's cheeks deepened. "You didn't come searching for me?"

His pride wanted him to say it was pure coincidence he'd stumbled upon her in the park. But he couldn't.

"I came to Paris for the deal," he said quietly. "But on my way out of town, I thought I saw you cross the street. And I couldn't leave without knowing if it was you."

They stood facing each other in the sunlit park, just inches away, not touching. He dimly heard birds sing in the trees above, the distant traffic of tour buses at the Eiffel Tower, the laughter of children at the merry-go-round.

"I was so sure you would return to me," he heard himself say in a low voice. "But you never did."

Her green eyes scorched through his heart. Then, in a voice almost too quiet to hear, she said, "I…couldn't."

"I know." Before he even realized what he was doing, he'd reached out a hand to her cheek.

Her skin was even softer than he remembered. He felt her shiver beneath his touch, and his body ignited. He wanted to take her in his arms, against his body, to kiss her hard and never let go.

Just moments before, he'd felt admiration about how she'd sacrificed the pleasure they might have had together, in order to pursue her true dreams. But in this instant, all those rational considerations were swept aside. He searched her gaze. "Did you ever wonder what we could have had?"

A shadow crossed her face.

"Of course I did."

He barely heard the noises around them, the soft coo of the baby, the chatter around them in a multitude of languages as tourists strolled by.

He'd missed her.

Not just her housekeeping skills. Nor even her sensual body.

Emma Hayes was the only woman he'd ever trusted. The only one he'd ever let himself care about, since the nightmare of his marriage so long ago.

Standing with Emma in this park in the center of Paris, Cesare would have given a million euros to see her smile at him the way she used to. To hear her voice gently mocking him, teasing him, putting him politely but firmly in his place. They'd had their own private language, he saw that now, and he suddenly realized how unusual that was. How special and rare.

No one called him on his arrogance anymore. No one else could challenge him with a single dimpled smile. No one kept him on his toes. Kept him breathless with longing.

He'd found a different housekeeper to keep his kitchen stocked and do his laundry. Perhaps, someday, he'd find a woman equally alluring to fill his bed. But who could fill the void that Emma had left in his life?

She'd been more than his housekeeper. More than his lover. She'd been his friend.

His hand moved down her neck to her shoulder. He felt her warmth through the soft pink fabric of her blouse.

"Come back to London with me," he said suddenly.

She blinked, then, glancing at her baby, she licked her lips. Her voice seemed hoarse as she asked, "Why?"

Cesare hesitated. If there was one thing he'd learned in life, it was that a man should never show weakness. Not even with a woman. *Especially* not with a woman. "The housekeeper I hired to replace you has been unsatisfactory."

"Oh." With a sigh, she looked down. "Sorry. I am working for someone else now. He's been good to me. I have no desire to leave him."

I have no desire to leave him. Cesare didn't like the sound of those words. He had a sudden surge of irrational jealousy for this unknown employer. He glanced back at the stroller. And who was this baby?

He said only, "I'll pay double what you're paid now."

Emma's eyes hardened. "We've already had this conversation, haven't we? I won't work for you at any price. It's not a question of money. We want different things. And we always will. You made that painfully clear to me in London."

The dark-haired baby gave an unhappy whimper from the stroller. Going down on one knee, she grabbed a pacifier from a big canvas bag and gave it to the baby, who instantly cheered up. She looked at the plump-cheeked, dark-eyed baby, then slowly rose to her feet, facing Cesare.

"Don't come looking for me again. Because nothing is going to change. And all you will bring us—all of us—is unhappiness."

Who was this baby? The question pounded in his heart. Her employer's? Emma's? But he couldn't ask. To ask the question would imply that he cared.

She stared at him for a moment, then turned away.

"I don't want you as my housekeeper," he said in a low voice. "The truth is…I miss you."

She looked back at him with an intake of breath, her lovely face stricken. She glanced at the baby in the stroller, who was simultaneously sucking like crazy on the pacifier, and trying to reach for his own feet. "I have other responsibilities now."

Cesare followed her gaze. The baby looked familiar somehow....

"I need a man I can trust. One I can count on to be permanent in my life. An equal partner. A father...for my baby."

For a moment, Cesare stared at her. Then as the meaning of her words sunk in, he literally staggered back. "*Your* baby?"

Emma nodded. Her eyes looked troubled, her expression filled with worry.

He could understand why.

"So much for all your big dreams," he ground out. "You left me for the wedding ring and the white picket fence." He couldn't control the bitterness in his voice as he flung his arm toward her bare left hand. "Where is your ring?"

"My baby's father didn't want to marry me," she said quietly.

"So you gave yourself away to some playboy? Someone who couldn't even give what I offered?" Jealousy raced through him. Once again, the woman he'd wanted, the one he'd chosen—had thrown herself away on another man. His hands curled into fists and he took a deep breath, regaining control. "I thought better of you." He lifted his chin. "So who is the father? Let me guess. Your new boss?"

"No," she said in a low voice. Slowly she lifted her eyes to his. "My old one."

He snorted. "Your old—"

Cesare gave an intake of breath as he looked down at the chubby black-haired baby.

I don't need a wedding proposal. He heard the echo of her trembling voice from long ago. *Or for you to say you're ready to be a father. I just need to know you might want those things someday. That you might be open to the possibility...if something ever...*

And he'd told her no. Flat-out. *Either this is a fun diversion, a friendship with benefits, or it's nothing.*

I'm going to have a baby, she'd said then. He'd thought she was trying to pin down his future. He hadn't realized she'd been talking about the present.

Cesare stared down at the baby's familiar black eyes—the same eyes he looked at every day in the mirror—and his knees nearly gave way beneath him.

"It's me," he breathed. "I'm the father."

CHAPTER FIVE

EMMA'S HEART POUNDED as she waited for Cesare's reaction.

She couldn't believe this was happening. For the past ten months, she'd dreamed of this. She'd thought of him constantly as their baby grew inside her. The day Sam was born. And every day since.

But now, she was afraid.

Alain Bouchard had been a wonderful boss to Emma, looking out for her almost like a brother through the months of her pregnancy and the sleepless nights beyond. But Alain hated Cesare, his former brother-in-law, blaming him for his sister Angélique's death. For ten months, Emma had waited for this day to come, for Cesare to find out about the baby—and the identity of her employer.

Over the past year, as she walked through the streets of Paris doing Alain's errands, shopping for fresh fruit and meats in the outdoor market on the Rue Cler, whenever she'd seen a tall, broad-shouldered, dark-haired man, she held her breath. But it was never Cesare. He hated Paris. It was partly why she'd chosen this job.

So today, when she'd seen a tall, dark-haired man pacing across the park, looking around with a strange desperation, she'd forced herself to ignore her instincts, because they were always wrong. She'd simply sat on the bench as her baby dozed in his stroller, and felt the warmth of the

September sun on her skin. It had been almost a year since she'd last seen Cesare's face, since she'd last felt his touch. So much had happened. Their baby was no longer a tiny newborn. Sam had grown into a roly-poly four-month-old who could sleep seven hours at a stretch and loved to smile and laugh. Already, she could see his Italian heritage in his black eyes, the Falconeri blood.

But still, as Emma sat in the park, she hadn't been able to look away from the dark-haired man in a tailored suit, who seemed out of place as he stomped down the path, gulping down a coffee. She'd told herself her imagination was working overtime. It absolutely *was not* Cesare.

Then he'd walked past her, barking into his cell phone. She saw his face, heard his voice. And time stood still.

Then, without thought, she'd reacted, leaping to her feet, calling his name.

Now, as she looked up at him, the world seemed to spin, the tourists and trees and dark outline of the Eiffel Tower a blur against the sky. There was Cesare. Only Cesare.

For so long, she'd craved him, heart and soul. Cried for him at night, for the awful choice she'd had to make. He'd told her outright he didn't want a child, but she'd still struggled with whether she'd made an unforgivable mistake, not telling him. Twice she'd even picked up the phone.

Now he was just inches away from her, close enough to touch. All throughout their conversation, she'd glanced at their baby out of the corner of her eye. How could he not instantly see the resemblance? How could he not see little Sam in the stroller, and *know?*

Well, Cesare knew now.

"I'm the father," he breathed, looking from Sam to her.

"Yes." Emma felt a thrill in her heart even as a chill of fear went down her spine. "He's yours."

Cesare's dark eyes were shocked, his voice hoarse. "Why didn't you tell me?"

"I…"

"How could you not tell me?" Pacing back two steps, he clawed back his dark hair. Whirling back to face her, he accused, "You knew you were pregnant when you left London."

She nodded. His dark eyes were filled with fury.

"You lied to me."

"I didn't exactly lie. I said I was going to have a baby…."

He sucked in his breath, then glared at her. "I thought you meant *someday*. And you let me believe that. So *you lied*."

She licked her lips. "I wanted to tell you…"

"You were never on the Pill."

"I never said I was!"

His eyes narrowed. "You said—"

"I said I couldn't get pregnant," she cut him off. "I didn't think I could. When I was a teenager, I was—very sick—and my doctor said future pregnancy might be difficult, if not impossible. I never thought I could…" She lifted her gaze to his and whispered, "It's a miracle. Can't you see that? Our baby is a miracle."

"A miracle." Cesare glowered at her. "And you never thought you should share the miracle with me?"

"I wanted to. More than you can imagine." Emma set her jaw. "But you made it absolutely clear you didn't want a family."

"Did you get pregnant on purpose?" he demanded. "To force me to marry you?"

Emma couldn't help herself. She laughed in his face.

"Why are you laughing?" he said dangerously.

"Oh, I'm sorry. I thought you were making a joke."

"This isn't a joke!"

"No. It isn't. But *you* are!" she snapped, losing patience.

He blinked as his mouth fell open.

She took a deep calming breath, blowing a tendril of hair off her hot forehead. "I've gone out of my way not to trap you. I'm raising this baby completely on my own. I wouldn't marry you even if you asked me!"

"Really?"

She stiffened, remembering that she had indeed once yearned to marry him—even hinted at it aloud! Her cheeks burned with humiliation. She lifted her chin. "Maybe once I was stupid enough to want that, but I've long since realized you'd make a horrible husband. No sane woman would want to marry a man like you."

"A man like me," he repeated. He looked irritated. "So you'd rather be a housekeeper, slaving for wages, instead of a billionaire's wife?" He snorted. "Do you really expect me to believe that?"

She glared back at him. "And do *you* really believe I'd want to sell myself to some man who doesn't love me, when I can support myself and my child through honest work?"

"He's not just your child."

"You don't want him. You said so in London. Right to my face."

"That was different. You made it sound like a choice. You didn't tell me the decision was already made." He folded his arms, six feet three inches of broad-shouldered masculine stubbornness. "I want him tested. To have DNA evidence he's my child."

She ground her teeth. "You don't believe me?"

"The woman who swore she couldn't get pregnant? No."

Ooh. She stamped her foot. "I'm not having Sam pricked with a needle for some dumb DNA test. If you don't believe me, if you think I might have been sleeping around and now I'm lying just for kicks, then forget about us. Just leave. We'll do fine without you."

He clenched his hands at his sides. "You should have told me!"

"I tried to, but when I started hinting at the idea of a child, you nearly fainted with fear!"

"I absolutely did *not* faint—" he began furiously.

"You did! From the moment I found out I was pregnant, I wanted to tell you. Of course I wanted to tell you. What do you take me for? My parents were married straight out of high school and loved each other until my mom died. That's what people do in my hometown. Get married and stay married. Buy a home and raise a family. Do you honestly think—" Emma's voice grew louder, causing nearby people in the park to look at them "—that I wanted to be a single mother? That this is something I *chose?*"

Cesare looked astonished, his sensual lips slightly parted, his own tirade forgotten. Then he scowled.

"Don't even try to—"

"Even now," she interrupted, feeling the tears well up, "when I've just told you you're a father, what are you doing? You're yelling at me, when any other man on earth would be interested in—I don't know—meeting his new *son!*"

He stopped again, staring at her, his mouth still open. Then he snapped it shut. He glared at her. "Fine."

"Fine!"

Cesare turned to the baby. He knelt by the stroller. He looked into Sam's chubby face. As Emma watched, his eyes slowly traced over the baby's dark eyes; exactly like his own. At the same dark hair, already starting to curl.

"Um," he said, awkwardly holding out a hand toward the baby. "Hi."

The baby continued to suck the pacifier, but flung an

unsteady hand toward his father. One little pudgy hand caught his finger. Cesare's eyes widened and his expression changed. He moved closer to Sam, then gently stroked his hair, his plump cheek. His voice was different as he said more softly, "Hi."

Seeing the two of them together, Emma's heart twisted.

"You named him Sam?" he asked a moment later.

"After my dad."

"He looks just like me," Cesare muttered. Pulling away from the baby, he rose to his feet. "Just tell me one thing. If I hadn't come to Paris, if I hadn't seen you today—would you ever have told me?"

She swallowed.

"You really are unbelievable," he ground out.

"You don't want a family." Her voice trembled. "All you could have given him was money."

"And a *name*," he flung out.

"He already has both." She looked at him steadily. "I've given him a name—Samuel Hayes. And I earn enough money. Not for mansions and private jets, but enough for a comfortable home. We don't need you. We don't want you."

Cesare ground his teeth. "You're depriving him of his birthright."

She snorted. "Birthright? You mean you'd have insisted on sending him to a fancy school and buying him something extravagant and useless at Christmas, like a pony, before you ignored him the rest of the year?" She shook her head. "And that's the best-case scenario! Because let's not pretend you actually want to be in the picture!"

"I might..." he protested.

"Oh, please." Her eyes narrowed. "All you could have offered was money and heartbreak. Better no father at all than a father like you. My child will never feel like an ignored, unwanted burden." She straightened her shoulders, lifting her chin. "And neither will I."

Cesare stared at her. Then his mouth snapped shut.

"So that's what you think of me," he muttered. "That I'm a selfish bastard with nothing but money to offer."

She stared at him for a long moment, then relented with a sigh. "You are who you are. I realized last year that I could not change you. So I'm not going to try."

His handsome face looked suddenly haggard. In spite of everything, her traitorous heart went out to him. Living with him for seven years, learning his every habit, she'd seen glimpses of the vulnerability that drove Cesare to a relentless pursuit of money and women he neither needed nor truly wanted. When he came home late at night, when he paced the hallways in sleepless hours, she'd seen flashes of emptiness beneath his mask, and the despair beneath his careless charm. There could never be enough money or cheap affairs to fill the emptiness in his heart, but he kept trying. And Emma knew why.

He'd lost the woman he'd loved, and he'd never be able to love anyone again.

Even through her anger, she felt almost sorry for him. Because without love, what could there be—but emptiness?

"It's not your fault," she said slowly. "I understand why you can't let anyone into your heart again. You loved her so much—and then you lost her…" At his expression, she reached her hand to his rough cheek. Her voice trembled as she whispered, "Your heart was buried with your wife."

Cesare seemed to shudder beneath her touch. "Emma…"

"It's all right." Dropping her hand, she stepped back and tried to smile. "We're fine. Truly. Your son is happy and well. I have a good job. My boss is a very kindhearted man. He looks out for us."

Something in her voice made him look up sharply.

"Who is he? This new boss?"

She licked her lips. "You don't know?"

He shook his head. "After you left, I tried my best to forget you ever existed."

It shouldn't have hurt her, but it did. Emma put her hands on the handlebar of the stroller. "That is what you should do now, Cesare. Forget us...."

But he grabbed the handlebar, his hand over hers. "No. This time, I'm not letting you go. Not with my son."

She swallowed, looking up at his fierce gaze.

"You only want us because you think you can't have us. *No* is a novelty, it's distracting and shiny. But I know, if I ever let myself...count on you, you'd leave. I won't let anyone hurt Sam. Not even you."

She tried to pull away. He tightened his grip.

"He's my son."

"Let us go," she whispered. "Please. Somewhere, there's a man who will love us with all his heart. A man who can actually be a loving father to Sam." She shook her head. "We both know you're not that man."

The anger in Cesare's face slid away, replaced by an expression that seemed hurt, even bewildered.

"Emma," he breathed. "You think so little of me—"

"You heard her," a man growled behind them. "Let her go, damn you."

Alain Bouchard stood behind them with two bodyguards.

Cesare's eyes widened in shock. "Bouchard...?"

Alain was a powerful man, handsome in his way. In his mid-forties, he was a decade older than Cesare. His salt-and-pepper hair was closely clipped, his clothing well-tailored. His perfect posture bespoke the pride of a man who was CEO of a luxury goods firm that had been run by the Bouchard family for generations. But the red hatred in the Frenchman's eyes was for Cesare alone.

"Let her go," Alain repeated, and Emma saw his two burly bodyguards, Gustave and Marcel, take a step forward in clear but unspoken threat.

For an instant, Cesare's grasp tightened on her hand. His eyes narrowed and she was suddenly afraid of what he might do—that a brutal, juvenile fistfight between two wealthy tycoons might break out in the Champ de Mars.

Desperate to calm the situation down, she said, "Let me go, Cesare. Please."

He turned to her, his black eyes flints of betrayed fury. "What is he doing here?"

"He's my boss," she admitted.

"You work for Angélique's brother?"

She flinched. Strictly speaking, that might seem vengeful on her part. "He offered me a job when I needed one. That's all."

"You're raising my son in the house of a man who hates me?"

"I never let him speak a word against you. Not in front of Sam."

"That's big of you," he said coldly.

She saw Gustave and Marcel draw closer across the green grass. "Please," she whispered, "you have to let me go…."

Cesare abruptly withdrew his hand. There was a lump in Emma's throat as she turned away, quickly pushing the baby stroller toward Alain.

"Are you all right, Emma?" Alain said. "He didn't hurt you?"

Out of the corner of her eye, she saw Cesare stiffen.

"Of course I'm all right. We were just talking." She glanced behind her. "But now we're done."

"This isn't over," Cesare said.

His handsome face looked dark as a shadow crossed the sun. She took a deep breath. "I know," she said miserably.

"Allons-y," Alain said, putting a hand on the stroller handle, just where Cesare's had been a moment before. They walked together down the path and out of the park, and at every step, she felt Cesare's gaze on the back of her neck. She didn't properly breathe until they were out of the Champ de Mars and back on the sidewalk by the street.

"Are you really all right?" Alain asked again.

"Fine," she said. But she wasn't. A war was coming. A custody war with her precious baby at the center. She could feel it like the dark clouds of a rising storm. Trying to push aside her fear, she asked, "What were you doing at the park? How did you know we were there?"

"Gustave called me."

Her brow furrowed. "How did Gustave know?"

Alain's cheeks colored slightly. "I sometimes have my bodyguards watch you, at a distance. Paris can be a dangerous city…"

His voice trailed off as they were passed by two elegant women dripping diamonds and head-to-toe Hermès.

"This neighborhood?" Emma said in disbelief.

He gave a graceful Gallic shrug. *"On ne sait jamais."* His expression darkened. "And it seems I was right to have you followed, with that bastard Falconeri showing up. He's Sam's father, isn't he?"

She was sure he meant to be protective, but her privacy felt invaded. "Yes," she admitted. "But I don't blame him for being upset. I never told him I was pregnant."

"You obviously had reason. Is he going to try to take the baby?"

"I don't know," she said in a small voice.

"I won't let him." He stopped, looking down at her with

his thin face and soulful eyes. "I'd do anything to protect you, Emma. You must know that."

She looked at her boss uneasily. "I know." In spite of all his kindness, she'd found herself wondering lately if he might be more interested in her than was strictly proper for an employer. She'd told herself she was imagining things. But still… She shook her head. "We'll be fine. I can take care of us."

Ahead, she saw Alain's black limited-edition Range Rover parked illegally on the Avenue de la Bourdonnais, with his chauffeur running the engine.

"After what he did to my sister, I won't let any woman be hurt by Cesare Falconeri, ever again," Alain vowed. Emma stiffened.

"Cesare didn't do anything to her. It was a tragic accident. He loved her."

"Ah, but you think the best of everyone." His expression changed from rage to gentleness as he looked down at her. His jaw tightened. "Even him. But that bastard doesn't deserve you. He'll get what he deserves. Someday."

Looking at him, Emma's heart trembled at what she might have unthinkingly done by accepting a job with Alain. He was convinced that his sister's death had been something more than a tragic accidental overdose. But Cesare was innocent. He'd never been charged with any crime. And Emma, of all people, knew how he'd loved his wife. She took a deep breath and changed the subject.

"Sam and I will be fine," she said brightly. "Cesare doesn't want a family to tie him down. He'll soon return to London and forget all about us."

But as dark clouds crossed the bright sun, Emma thought of the tender expression on Cesare's face when he'd first caressed his baby son's cheek. And she was afraid.

* * *

"To the airport, sir?"

Cesare leaned back heavily in the backseat of the Rolls-Royce. For a moment he didn't answer the driver. He pressed his hands against his forehead, still trembling with shock and fury from what he'd learned.

He had a child.

A son.

A baby born in secret, to the woman who'd left him last November without a word. And gone to work for his enemy.

Closing his eyes, he pressed his fingertips against the lids. He didn't believe Emma had gotten pregnant on purpose. No. She'd been right to laugh at his knee-jerk reaction earlier. She was clearly no gold digger. But leaving him in London, without a word, taking his child away, taking his *decision* away...

He took a deep breath. She'd done it all as if Cesare didn't even matter. As if he didn't even *exist.*

"Sir?"

"Yes," he bit out. "The airport."

The limousine pulled smoothly back into the Paris traffic. Cesare's throat was tight. He struggled to be fair, to be calm, when what he wanted to do was punch the seat in front of him and scream.

His baby was being raised in the house of Alain Bouchard, a man who unfairly blamed him for his sister's death. Bouchard didn't know the truth, and knowing how the man had loved his sister, Cesare had kept it that way.

But now, he pictured Bouchard's angry face, the way he'd stepped protectively in front of Emma.

Was it possible that over the past year, while Cesare had been celibate as a monk hungering for her, Emma had become Bouchard's lover?

No, his heart said. Impossible. But his brain disagreed. After all, the two of them were living in the same house. Perhaps she'd been lonely and heartsick. Perhaps he'd found her crying in the kitchen, as Cesare once had, and she'd fallen into the other man's bed, as she'd once fallen into his.

He hopelessly put his hands over his ears, as if that could keep his own imagination away. Anger built inside Cesare, rising like bile in his soul.

As the car turned west, heading toward the private airport outside the city, he looked out the window. He could see the top of the Eiffel Tower above the charming buildings, over two young lovers kissing at a sidewalk café.

He ground his teeth. He'd be glad to leave this damn city. He hated Paris and everything it stood for. The romance. The *love.*

Whether Emma was Bouchard's mistress or not, she had no love for Cesare anymore. She'd made her low opinion of him, as a potential father or even as a human being, very clear. She didn't want a thing from him. Not even his money. The thought made him feel low.

It would be simple to take the easy out she offered. Leave Paris. Go back to London. Forget the child they'd unintentionally created.

His child.

He could still see the baby's face. His soft black hair. Those dark eyes, exactly like his own.

He had a son.

A child.

He closed his eyes. Over the memory of the baby's sweet babble, he heard Emma's voice: *We don't need you. We don't want you.*

Cesare's fist hit the window with a bang.

"Sir?" His driver quivered, looking at him in the rear-view mirror.

Cesare's eyes slowly opened. Perhaps he wasn't ready to be a father. But that no longer mattered.

Because he was one.

"Go back."

"Back?"

"To my hotel." Cesare rubbed at the base of his skull. "I'm not leaving Paris. Take me back now."

Pulling his phone from his pocket, he dialed a number in New York City. Mortimer Ainsley had been his uncle's attorney, twenty years ago, and presided over his will when he'd died and Cesare gained possession of his aging, heavily mortgaged hotel. Later, Mortimer Ainsley had looked over the prenuptial agreement given to Cesare by Angélique Bouchard, the wealthy older French heiress who had proposed after just six weeks.

Morty, who'd appeared old to Cesare's eyes even then, had harrumphed over the terms of Angélique's prenup. "If you leave this Bouchard woman, you get nothing," he'd said. "If she dies, you get everything. Not much of a deal for you. She's only ten years older so it may be some time before she dies!"

Cesare had been horrified. "I don't want her to die. I love her."

"Love, huh?" Morty had snorted. "Good luck with that."

Remembering how young and naive he'd been, Cesare waited for Morty to answer the phone. He knew the old man would answer, no matter what time it was in New York right now. Morty would know the right attorney in Paris to handle a custody case.

Better no father at all than a father like you.

Cesare's jaw tightened. Emma would realize the penalty for what she'd done. She'd see that Cesare Falconeri would not be ignored, or denied access—or even knowledge!—of his own child.

"Ainsley." Morty's greeting was gruff, as if he'd just woken from sleep.

"Morty. I have a problem…." Without preamble, Cesare grimly outlined the facts.

"So you have a son," Morty said. "Congratulations."

"I told you. I don't have a son," Cesare said tightly. "*She* has him."

"Of course you can go to war over this. You might even win." Morty cleared his throat. "But you know the expression, *Pyrrhic victory?* Unless the woman's an unfit mother…"

Cesare remembered Emma's loving care of the baby as she pushed him in the stroller through the park. "No," he said grudgingly.

"Then you have to decide who you're willing to hurt, and how badly. 'Cause in a custody war, it's never just the other parent who takes it in the neck. Nine times out of ten, it's the kid who suffers most." Morty paused. "I can give you the number of a barracuda lawyer who will cause the sky to rain fire on this woman. But is that what you really want?"

As his Rolls-Royce crossed the Seine and traveled up the Avenue George V, Cesare's grip on his phone slowly loosened. By the time he ended the call a few minutes later, as the car pulled in front of the expensive five-star hotel where he'd stayed through the business negotiations, Cesare's expression had changed entirely.

The valet opened his door. "Welcome back, monsieur."

Looking up, Cesare didn't see the imposing architecture of the hotel as he got out. Instead he saw Emma's troubled expression when they'd parted in the Champ de Mars.

She was expecting him to start a war over this. *Christo*

santo, she knew him well. Now that he knew about Sam, she expected him to fight for custody, to destroy their peace and rip their comfortable life into shreds. And then after that, after he'd made a mess of their lives for the sake of his pride, she expected Cesare to grow bored and quickly abandon them both.

That was why she hadn't told him about the baby. That was why she thought Sam was better off with no father at all. She truly believed Cesare was that selfish. That he'd put his own ego over the well-being of his child.

His lips pressed into a thin line. He might have done it, too, if Morty hadn't made him think twice.

You have to decide who you're willing to hurt, and how badly. 'Cause in a custody war, it's never just the other parent who takes it in the neck. Nine times out of ten, it's the kid who suffers most.

Before his own parents died, Cesare'd had a happy, almost bohemian childhood in a threadbare villa on Lake Como, filled with art and light and surrounded by beautiful gardens. His parents, both artists, had loved each other, and they'd adored their only child. The three of them had been inseparable. Until, when he was twelve, his mother had gotten sick, and her illness had poisoned their lives, drop by drop.

His father's death had been quicker. After his wife's funeral, he'd gone boating on the lake in the middle of the night, after he'd drunk three bottles of wine. Calling his death by drowning an *accident,* Cesare thought, had been generous of the coroner.

Now his hands tightened. If he didn't go to war for custody, how else could he fulfill his obligation to his son? He couldn't leave Sam to be raised by another man—especially not Alain Bouchard. Sam would grow up believing Cesare was a monster who'd callously abandoned him.

Cesare exhaled.

How could he bend Emma to his will? What was the fulcrum he could use to gain possession of his child? What was her weakness?

Then—*he knew.*

And if some part of him shivered at the thought, he stomped on it as an irrational fear. This was no time to be afraid. This time, he wouldn't be selling his soul. There would be no delusional *love* involved. He would do this strictly for his child's sake. *In name only.*

He had a sudden image of Emma in his bed, luscious and warm, naked in his arms....

No! He would keep her in his home, but at a distance. *In name only,* he repeated to himself. He would never open his heart to her again. Not even a tiny corner of it.

From this moment forward, his heart was only for his son.

Grabbing the car door as it started to pull away, he wrenched it open and flung himself back into the Rolls-Royce.

"Monsieur?"

"I changed my mind."

"Of course, sir," replied the driver, who was well accustomed in dealing with the inexplicable whims of the rich. "Where may I take you?"

Emma expected a battle. He would give her one. But not in the way she expected. He would take her completely off guard—and sweep her completely into his power, in a revenge far sweeter, and more explosive, than any mere *rain of fire.*

"Around the corner," Cesare replied coldly. "To a little jewelry shop on the Avenue Montaigne."

CHAPTER SIX

EMMA JUMPED WHEN her phone rang.

All afternoon, since she'd left Cesare in the park, she'd been pacing the halls of Alain's seventeenth-century *hôtel particulier* in the seventh arrondissement. She'd been on edge, looking out the windows, past the courtyard gate onto the Avenue Rapp. Waiting for Cesare to strike. Waiting for a lawyer to call. Or the police. Or… She didn't know what, but she'd been torturing herself trying to imagine.

When her cell phone finally rang, she saw his private number and braced herself.

"I won't let you bully me," she whispered aloud to the empty air. Then she answered the phone with, "What do you want?"

"I want to see you." It shocked her how calm Cesare's voice was. How pleasant. "I'd like to discuss our baby."

"I'm busy." Standing in the mansion's lavish salon with its fifteen-foot-high ceilings, she looked from the broom she hadn't touched in twenty minutes to Sam, lying nearby on a cushioned blanket on the floor, happily batting at soft toys dangling above him in a baby play gym. She set her jaw. "I'm working."

"As mother of my heir, you don't need to work, you

know." He sounded almost amused. "You won't worry about money ever again."

He was trying to lull her into letting down her guard, she thought.

"I don't worry about money *now*," she retorted. As a single mother, she'd been even more careful, tucking nearly all her paycheck into the bank against a rainy day. "I have a good salary, we live rent-free in Alain's house and I have a nice nest egg thanks to you. I sold your watch to a collector, by the way. I couldn't believe how much I got for it. What kind of idiot would spend so much on a— Oh. Sorry. But seriously. How could you spend so much on a watch?"

But Cesare didn't sound insulted. "How much did you get for it?"

"A hundred thousand euros," she said, still a little horrified. But also pleased.

He snorted. "The collector got a good deal."

"That's what Alain said. He was irritated I didn't offer the watch to him first. He said he would have paid me three times that…." She stopped uneasily.

"Bouchard takes good care of you."

Cesare's good humor had fled. She gritted her teeth. What was the deal between those two? She wished they'd leave her out of it. "Of course Alain takes care of me. He's an excellent employer."

"You can't raise Sam in his house, Emma. I won't allow it."

"You won't allow it?" She exhaled with a flare of nostril. "Look, I told you that Sam's your child because it was the right thing to do…"

"You mean because I gave you no choice."

"…but you can't give orders anymore. In case you haven't noticed, you're no longer my boss."

His voice took on an edge. "I'm Sam's father."

"Oh, you're suddenly sure about that now, are you?"

"Emma—"

"I can't believe you asked me for a paternity test! When you know perfectly well you're the only man I've ever slept with in my whole life!"

"Even now?"

His voice was a little tense. Cesare was worried she'd slept with other men over the past year? She was astonished. "You think I was madly dating while I was pregnant as a whale? Or maybe—" she gave a low laugh "—right after Sam was born, I rushed to invite men to my bed, hoping they'd ignore the dark hollows under my eyes and baby spit-up on my shoulder." She snorted. "I'm touched, really, that you think I'm so irresistible. But if I have a spare evening I collapse into bed. For sleeping, not orgies, in case that was your next question."

For a moment, there was silence. When next he spoke, his tone was definitely warmer. "Leave Sam at home with a babysitter. Come out with me tonight."

"Why?" She scowled. "What do you have planned—the guillotine? Pistols at dawn? Or let me guess. Some lawyer is going to serve me a subpoena?"

"I just want to talk."

"Talk," she said doubtfully.

"Perhaps I was a little rough with you in the park...."

"You think?"

He gave a low laugh. "I don't blame you for believing the worst of me. But I'm sure you'll forgive my bad manners, when you think of what a shock it was for me to learn I have a son, and that you'd hidden that fact from me for quite some time."

He sounded reasonable. Damn him.

"What's your angle?" she asked suspiciously.

"I just want us to share dinner," he said, "and discuss

our child's future. Surely there is nothing so strange in that."

Uh-oh. When Cesare sounded innocent, she *knew* he was up to something. "I'm not giving up custody. So if that's what you want to discuss, we should let our lawyers handle it." She tried to sound confident, like she even *had* a lawyer.

"Oh, *lawyers.*" He gave a mournful sigh. "They make things so messy. Let's just meet, you and me. Like civilized people."

She gripped the phone tighter, pacing across the gleaming hardwood floors. "If you're thinking of luring me out of the house so your bodyguards can try to kidnap Sam, Alain's house is like a fortress...."

"If you're going to jump to the worst possible conclusion of everything I say, this conversation is going to take a long time. And I wouldn't mind a glass of wine," he said pointedly.

She watched her baby gurgle with triumph when he caught the end of his sock. Falconeri men were such determined creatures. "You're not going to try to pull anything?"

"Like what?" When she didn't answer, he gave an exaggerated sigh. "I'll even take you someplace crowded, with plenty of strangers to chaperone us. How about the restaurant at the top of the Eiffel Tower?"

She pictured the long circling queues of tourists. Surely even Cesare couldn't be up to much, amid such a crowd. "Well..."

"You left London without a word. You kept your pregnancy secret and went to work for Bouchard behind my back. I don't think a single dinner to work out Sam's custody is too much to ask."

Emma was about to agree when her whole body went on alert at the word *custody.* "What do you mean, custody?"

"I'm willing to accept your pregnancy was an accident. You didn't intentionally lie. You're not a gold digger."

"Gee, thanks."

"But now I know I have a son, I can't just walk away. We're going to have to come to an arrangement."

"What arrangement?"

"If you want to know, you'll have to join me tonight."

"Or else—what?"

"Or else," Cesare said quietly. "Let's just leave it at that."

"You don't want to be a father," she said desperately. "You couldn't be a decent one, even if you tried—not that you would try for long!"

For a moment, the phone fell silent.

"You think you know me," he said in a low voice.

"Am I wrong?"

"I'll pick you up at nine." There was a dangerous sensuality in his voice that caused a shiver down Emma's body. She suddenly remembered that Cesare had ways of making her agree to almost anything.

"Make it seven," she said nervously. "I don't want to be out too late."

"Have a curfew, do you?" he drawled. "He keeps tight hold on you."

"Alain doesn't have anything to do with—"

"And Emma? Wear something nice."

The line went dead.

The sun was setting over Paris, washing soft pink and orange light over the white classical facades of the buildings as Emma stood alone on the sidewalk of the Avenue Rapp.

It was three minutes before seven. She'd dressed carefully, as requested, in a pink knit dress and a black coat.

She'd considered showing up in a T-shirt and jeans, just to spite him. Instead she spent more time this afternoon primping than she'd spent in a year. For reasons she didn't like to think about. For feelings she was trying to convince herself she didn't feel.

Emma had stopped wearing the severe chignon when she'd come to Paris. Now her black hair had been brushed until it shone, and fell tumbling down her shoulders. Her lipstick was the same raspberry shade as her dress. She was even wearing mascara to make her green eyes pop. She hoped.

No. She ground her teeth. She *didn't* hope. She absolutely didn't care what Cesare thought she looked like. She *didn't*.

It was only for Sam's sake she was meeting Cesare tonight. Where her own romantic dreams were concerned, she'd given up on him that cold, heartbreaking morning in London when he'd informed her he would never ever: 1. love her, 2. marry her or 3. have a child with her. He'd said it outright. What could you do with a man like that?

What indeed…

Emma shivered in her thin black wool coat, tucking her pink scarf more firmly around her neck. Pulling her phone out of her pocket, she glanced at the time: six fifty-eight.

She sighed, wondering why she'd bothered to be on time. Cesare would likely be half an hour late, as usual, and in the meantime she was standing out here looking like a fool as taxi drivers gawked at her standing on the sidewalk. She would have gone back to wait inside, except the bad blood between Alain and Cesare made her reluctant to allow the two men to meet.

She'd already tucked her baby son into bed, leaving him

with Irene Taylor, the extremely capable young woman who until recently had been an au pair for the Bulgarian ambassador. Irene was bright, idealistic and very young. Emma had never been that young.

Her eye was caught by a flash of light. Looking up over the buildings, she could see the tip of the Eiffel Tower suddenly illuminated with brilliant sparkling lights. That meant it was seven o'clock. Her lips turned down. And just as she'd thought, Cesare was late. He'd never change....

"Buona sera, bella."

With an intake of breath, Emma turned to see Cesare on the sidewalk, looking devastatingly handsome in a long black coat.

"You're on time," she stammered.

"Of course."

"You're never on time."

"I am always on time when it matters to me."

Her cheeks turned hot. Feeling awkward, she looked right and left. "Where's your car?"

Cesare came closer. "It's a beautiful night. I gave my driver the night off." He tilted his head. "Why are you waiting on the sidewalk? I would have come to get you."

"I didn't want to start World War III."

He snorted. "I don't hold any grudge against Bouchard."

She looked at him steadily. "He holds one against you. The things he has said..."

His eyes narrowed. "On second thought, perhaps you are right to separate us. I am starting to resent the way he's taken possession of something that should belong only to me."

Emma trembled at the anger in his dark eyes. He meant Sam. He had to mean Sam.

"You look beautiful tonight," he said huskily.

"Oh. Thanks," she said, suddenly shy. Cesare looked

even more handsome than she remembered, and cripes, was that a tuxedo beneath his black coat? "So do you." Her cheeks flamed. "Er, handsome, I mean. Not that it matters," she added hastily, "because we're just going out to talk about our son...."

She stopped talking as he took her hand in his own. She felt the warmth of his palm against hers. He glanced at her high-heeled shoes. "Do you mind walking a few blocks?"

In this moment, it was hard for Emma to remember what pain felt like. Wordlessly she shook her head.

He smiled, an impossibly devastating smile, and her heart twisted in her chest. "Too bad. I would have offered to carry you."

Carry her? Against his chest? Her mouth went dry. She tried to think of a snappy comeback but her brain suddenly wasn't working quite right. His smile increased.

Still holding her hand, he led her across the street and up the narrow, charming rue de Monttessuy. The Eiffel Tower loomed large, directly ahead of them. But it wasn't that world-famous sight that consumed her.

She glanced down at Cesare's hand as they walked up the quiet street, past the brasseries and shops. He held her hand as if she were precious and he never wanted to let her go.

"Is something wrong, *cara?*"

Emma realized she'd stopped on the sidewalk right in front of the boulangerie. "Um..."

He pulled her closer, looking down at her with dark intense eyes as his lips curved. "Perhaps you want me to carry you, after all?"

She swallowed.

Yes.

No.

She took a deep breath of air, scented with warm, buttery croissants and crusty baguettes, and reminded herself she wasn't in London anymore. She didn't love Cesare. She'd left that love behind her. He had no power over her here. None.

"Absolutely none," she whispered aloud.

Moving closer, he stroked her cheek. "None?"

She pulled away from him, trembling. "Why are you acting like this?"

"Like what?"

"Like you care."

"I do."

She shook her head, fighting tears. "I don't know what you're planning, but you—"

"Just dinner, Emma," he said quietly. "And a discussion."

"Nothing more?"

He gave her a lopsided grin that tugged at her heart. "Would I lie?"

"No," she sighed.

He pulled her across the Avenue de la Bourdonnais, which was still busy with early-evening traffic. They walked down the charming tree-lined street into the Champ de Mars, to the base of the Eiffel Tower. She exhaled when she saw the long lines of tourists. In spite of all his promises, she still almost feared Cesare might try something. Not seduce her, surely?

No, why would he?

Unless it was a cold-blooded calculation on his part. Unless he thought he could overwhelm her with sensuality until she was so crazy she agreed to give up custody of Sam. Her hands tightened at her sides. He wouldn't even get a single kiss out of her if he tried. And the next time he contacted her, she really would have a lawyer....

"Elevator or stairs?" he asked, smiling.

Tilting her head back to look up the length of the tower, Emma had a sudden image of tripping on the stairs in her high heels, and Cesare sweeping her up into his arms. She could almost imagine how it would feel to cling to him, her arms around his body, her cheek against his chest.

"Elevator," she said quickly.

They went to a private elevator at the south pillar of the Eiffel Tower. There was no queue here. *Strange,* she thought. She'd heard this restaurant was really popular.

She was even more shocked when the elevator opened with a ding on the second platform of the Eiffel Tower, and they walked into a beautiful restaurant...

And found it empty.

Emma stopped cold. With an intake of breath, she looked at Cesare accusingly. "Where is everyone?"

He shrugged, managing to look guilty and innocent at the same time. "What do you mean?"

She looked over all the empty tables and chairs of the modern restaurant, with its spectacular views of Paris from all sides. "No one is here!"

Coming behind her, he put his hands on her shoulders. "*We* are here."

Slowly he pulled off her coat, then handed it to a host who discreetly appeared. Cesare's eyes never left hers as he removed his own coat, revealing his well-cut tuxedo. Emma shivered beneath his gaze for reasons that had nothing to do with being cold. As he led her to a table by the window, the one with the best view, she felt suddenly hot, as if she'd been lying beneath the sun. No, worse. As if she'd been *standing* on it.

They sat down, and a waiter brought them a bottle of wine. Emma glanced at the tables behind them and saw they were all covered with vases of long-stemmed roses.

"Roses?" she said. Her lips curled humorlessly. "To go

along with the watch you gave me? The finishing touch on the parting-gift extravaganza for one-night stands?"

"I should think it's obvious," he drawled, pouring wine into her glass, "you're not a one-night stand."

"A two-night stand, then."

He looked at her without speaking. Her cheeks burned.

"I won't let you talk me into signing custody away," she said hoarsely. "Or seduce me into it, either."

He gave a low laugh. "Ah, you really do think I'm a coldhearted bastard." He held out her glass, filled with wine a deeper red than roses. "That's not what I want."

"Then, what?"

He just looked at her with his dark eyes. Emma's heart started pounding.

Her hand shook as she reached out for the glass. She realized she was in trouble. Really, really big trouble.

He held up his own wine. "A toast."

"To what?"

"To you, *cara,*" he murmured.

He clinked her glass and then drank deeply. She looked down at the glass and muttered, "Should I wonder if this is poisoned?"

He gave a low laugh. "No poison, I promise."

"Then, what?" she whispered.

Cesare's dark eyebrow quirked. "How many times must I say it? I want to have *dinner.* And *talk.*" He picked up the menu. "What looks good?"

"I'm not hungry."

"Not hungry? With a menu like this? There's steak— lobster…"

"Will you just stop torturing me with all this romantic nonsense and tell me why you've brought me here?"

He tilted his head, looking at her across the table, before he gave a low laugh. "It's the roses, isn't it? Too much?"

"I'm not one of your foolish little starlets getting tossed out after breakfast, sobbing to stay." She narrowed her eyes. "You never try this hard. You never have to. So it must be leading up to something. Tell me what it is."

Cesare leaned forward across the candlelit table, his dark eyes intense. Her whole body was taut as she leaned toward him, straining to hear. He parted his sensual lips.

"Later," he whispered, then relaxed back in his chair as if he had not a care in the world. He took another sip of wine and looked out the huge wall of windows overlooking the lights of Paris, twinkling in the twilight.

Emma glared in helpless fury. He clearly was determined to take his own sweet time, to make her squirm. Fine. Grabbing her glass, she took a big gulp of the wine. Since she'd moved to Paris, she'd grown to appreciate wine more. This was a red, full-bodied Merlot that was equal parts delicious and expensive. Setting down her glass, she looked around them.

"This restaurant is kind of famous. It's hard to even get reservations here. How on earth did you manage to get the whole place?"

He gave a low laugh. "I pulled some strings."

"Strings?"

"It wasn't easy."

"For you," she said darkly, "everything is easy."

"Not everything." He looked at her across the table. His eyes seemed black as a midnight sea. Then he looked past her. Turning around, she saw the waiter approaching their table.

"Monsieur?" the man asked respectfully. "May I take your order?"

"Yes. To start, I'd like…" Cesare rattled off a list that included endives, foie gras, black truffle sauce, venison and some kind of strange rose-flavored gelatin. It all sounded very fancy to Emma, and not terribly appetizing.

"And for madame?"

Both men looked at her expectantly.

Emma sighed. "I'm afraid I don't much care for French food."

The waiter did a double take. So did Cesare. The scandalized looks on both male faces was almost funny. Emma stifled a laugh.

"Of course you like French food," Cesare said. "Everyone does. Even people who hate Paris love the food."

"I love Paris," she said. "Just not the food."

"I can give madame some suggestions from the menu…" the waiter tried.

She shook her head. "Sorry. I've lived here for almost a year. Trust me, I've tried everything." She looked at him. "What I would really like is a cheeseburger. With French fries. *Frites,*" she amended quickly, as if that would make her order sound more gourmet, which of course it didn't.

The waiter continued to stare at her with a mix of consternation and bewilderment. In for a penny, in for a pound….

"And ketchup." She handed him the menu with a sweet smile. "Lots and lots of ketchup. *Merci.*"

The waiter left, shaking his head and muttering to himself.

But Cesare gave a low laugh. "Nice."

"Shouldn't I order what I want?" she said defensively.

"Of course you should. Of course a nice American girl, on a romantic night out at the Eiffel Tower, would order a cheeseburger with ketchup."

"Romantic night?" she said with a surge of panic. He gave her an inscrutable smile. To hide her confusion, she looked out the window. "I can still enjoy the view."

"Me, too," he said quietly, and he wasn't looking at the window. A tingle of awareness went up and down Emma's body.

"This is my first time inside the Eiffel Tower," she said, trying to fill the space between them. She gave an awkward laugh. "I could never be bothered to wait in the lines."

"Doesn't Bouchard ever give you time off?"

She glanced at him with a snicker. "You're one to talk."

He had the grace to look discomfited. "I was a difficult boss."

"That," she said succinctly, "is an understatement."

"I must have been an awful employer."

"A monster," she agreed.

"You never even got to see inside the British Museum." He had a hangdog look, like a puppy expecting to be kicked. "Or take a picture of Big Ben."

She squelched an involuntary laugh, covering it with a cough. Then sighed.

"Perhaps you weren't entirely to blame," she admitted.

He brightened. "I wasn't?"

"I blamed you for not having time to tour London. I swore Paris would be different. But even though Alain has bent over backward to be the most amazing employer I could possibly imagine…"

Cesare's expression darkened.

"…I still haven't seen much of the city. At first, I was overwhelmed by a new job in a new city. Then I had the baby, and, well…if I have extra time, I don't tour a museum any more than I go on a date. I collapse in a stupor on the couch." She sighed, spreading her arms. "So it seems I'm full of excuses. I could have climbed the Eiffel Tower before now, and brought Sam with me, if I'd made it a priority. Instead I haven't been willing to wait in line or pay the money."

"What if I promised you'd never have to do either, seeing the sights of London?"

She tried to laugh it off. "What, there's no line to see the Crown Jewels anymore?" she said lightly. "It's a free ride for all on the London Eye?"

He took another sip of his wine, then put it back down on the table. His dark eyes met hers. "I want you both to come back to London with me."

She set her jaw. She'd been afraid he'd say that. "There's no way I'm leaving my job to move back to London with you. Your interest in Sam will never last."

"You have to know I can't abandon him, now I know. Especially not in Bouchard's house."

"I thought you said you didn't bear Alain any grudge."

"I don't. But that doesn't mean I'll let him raise my son." The votive candle on the table left flickering shadows on the hard lines of his handsome face. He said quietly, "Bouchard wants you for himself, Emma."

"Don't be ridiculous," she said uncomfortably, then recalled her own recent concerns on that front. "And anyway, I don't see him that way."

"He wants you. And he already knows that taking care of Sam is the way to your heart." His voice was low. Behind him, she could see the sparkling lights of Paris in the night. "As you yourself said—Sam deserves a father."

"Yes, he does," she said over the lump in her throat. "An actual father who'll love him and kiss his bruises and tuck him in at night. A father he can count on." Looking up at him, she whispered, "We both know you're not that man."

"How do you know?"

The raw emotion in Cesare's voice made her eyes widen. She shook her head.

"You said yourself you don't want a child. You have no idea what it means to be a parent…."

"You're wrong. I do know. Even though I'm new at being a father, I was once a son." He looked away. "We had no money, just an old house falling down around us. But we were happy. My parents loved each other. And they loved me."

She swallowed. "I've never heard you talk about them before."

"There's not much to tell." His lips twisted down at the edge. "When I was twelve, my mother got sick. My father had to watch her slowly die. He couldn't face life without her, so after her funeral, he went drinking alone on the lake at night. The empty boat floated to shore. His body was found the next day."

"I'm sorry," she choked out, her heart in her throat. "How could he do that—leave you?"

"I got over it." He shrugged, his only sign of emotion the slight tightening of his jaw. "I was sent to a great-uncle in New York. He was strict, but tried his best to raise me. I learned English. Learned about the hotel business. Learned I liked hard numbers, profit and loss. Numbers made sense. They could be added, subtracted, controlled. Unlike love, which disappears like mist as soon as you think it's in your arms."

His wife. He was still brokenhearted over his loss of her. Emma fought back tears as she said, "Love makes life worth living."

His lips twisted sardonically. "You say that, even after you wasted so many years trying to get love from your stepmother, like blood from a stone? All those years trying and failing, with nothing but grief to show for it."

Pain caught at her heart.

"I'm sorry," Cesare said, looking at her. "I shouldn't have said that."

"No. You're right." Blinking back tears, she shook her

head. "But others have loved me. My parents. My mother died when I was four, even younger than you were. Ovarian cancer. Just like…" She stopped herself. *Just like I almost did,* she'd almost said.

"I'm sorry," he said.

"It's all right. It was a long time ago. And my father was an amazing man. After my mom died, it was just the two of us. He gave me my work ethic, my sense of honor, everything." She pressed her lips together. "Then he fell in love with a coworker at his factory…."

"Cruel stepmother, huh?"

"She was never cruel." She sobered. "At least not at first. I was glad to see my father happy, but I started to feel like I was in their way. An outsider interrupting their honeymoon." She glanced up at the waiter, who'd just brought their meals. He set the cheeseburger and fries before her with the same flourish he used on Cesare's venison and risotto with black truffle sauce. It must have been hard for him, she thought, so she gave him a grateful smile. *"Merci."*

"So you left home?" Cesare prompted after the waiter left.

"Well." She dipped a fry into a ramekin of ketchup, then chewed it thoughtfully. It was hot and salty and delicious. She licked her lips, then her fingers. "At sixteen, I fell head over heels for a boy."

Cesare seemed uninterested in his own food as he listened with his complete attention. "A boy."

"The captain of the high school football team." She gave a smile. "Which in Texas can be a big deal. I was flattered by his attention. I fell hard. A few kisses, and I was convinced it was love. He talked me into going all the way."

"But you didn't." Taking a bite of his food, he grinned at her. "I know you didn't."

"No." She swirled another fry through the ketchup. "But I went to the doctor to get birth control pills." With a deep breath, she looked him in the eye. "That's how I found out I had cancer."

His jaw dropped. "Cancer?"

"Ovarian, the same as my mom had had." She kept stirring the fry in the ketchup, waiting for him to freak out, for him to look at her as if she still had one foot in the grave. "I was on chemotherapy for a long time. By the time I was in remission, Mark had long since dumped me for a cheerleader."

Cesare muttered something in Italian that sounded very unkind. She gave a grateful smile.

"He did me a huge favor. I'd had no symptoms. If I hadn't gone to the doctor then, I never would have known I was sick until it was too late. So in a funny way—that broken heart was the price that saved my life." She ate a bite of French fry, then made a face when she realized the bite was almost entirely ketchup. She set it down on her plate. "Though for a long time I wished I *had* died."

"Why?"

"My illness took everything. My childhood. My dreams of having a family someday. The medical bills even took our house." Her throat ached, but she forced herself to tell the worst. "And it killed my father."

Reaching across the table, he grabbed her hand. "Emma…"

She took a deep breath. "It was my fault. My father wasn't the kind of man who could declare bankruptcy and walk away from debt. So to pay all the bills, he took a night job. Between his jobs and taking care of me, he started to neglect my stepmother. They started fighting all the time. But the day my doctor announced I was in remission, I convinced my father to take me home early. It was Valentine's Day. I talked him into stopping at the florist to buy flowers. As a surprise." She paused. "Marion was surprised, all right. We found her at home, in bed, with the foreman from their factory."

Cesare sucked in his breath. "And?"

"My father had a heart attack," she whispered. She ran her hand over her eyes. "He was already so run-down from taking care of me. From working two jobs. Marion blamed me for everything." Her voice caught as she covered her face with her hands. "She was right."

His voice was gentle as he pulled back her hands. "It wasn't your fault."

"You're wrong." Emma looked at him across the table, and tears ran unchecked down her face. "If I hadn't fought so hard to live, I'd never have been such a burden. My father wouldn't have had to work two jobs, my stepmother wouldn't have felt lonely and neglected, and they'd still be together. It's my fault. I ruined their lives."

"Your stepmother said that?"

She nodded miserably. "After the funeral, she kicked me out of the house. I was eighteen. She had no legal obligation to take care of me. A friend let me stay until I graduated high school, then I left Texas for New York. I wanted to make something of myself, to prove Marion wrong." She blinked fast. "But nothing I ever did, not all the money I sent her, ever made her forgive what I did."

Rising to his feet, Cesare came around the table. Gently pulling Emma from the chair, he wrapped her in his arms. "So that's why you looked so stricken," he murmured. "The night we first… The night you came back from her funeral."

"Yes. Plus…" She swallowed. It was time to tell him the worst. To tell him everything. She thought of all her lonely years, loving him, devoting herself only to him. She looked up, barely seeing his face through her tears. "When

I told you I loved you last year, you tried to convince me it was just lust. But there's a reason I knew all along that it wasn't." She took a deep breath and said, "I've loved you for years, Cesare."

His hands, which had been caressing her back, abruptly stopped. He looked down at her. "Years?"

"You never knew?"

Wide-eyed, he shook his head.

"I loved you from almost the first day we met," she said quietly. She gave a choked laugh. "I think it was the moment you said you were glad to have me, because I looked smart, and the previous housekeeper on the penthouse floor had just been fired for being idiot enough to fall for you."

He looked bewildered. "That made you love me?"

She gave a low laugh. "I guess you were wrong when you said I looked smart."

"I thought you had no feelings. I never knew…"

"I hid it even better than I thought." Her lips quirked. "I knew you would fire me if you ever guessed."

"But why? Why would you love me in silence for years? I ran roughshod over you. Bossed you around. Expected you to be at my beck and call."

"But I saw the rest, too," she said over the lump in her throat. "The vulnerability that drove you to succeed, as if the devil himself were chasing you. The way you were kind to children when you thought no one was looking. Giving money to charity, helping struggling families stay in their homes—anonymously. So no one would know."

He abruptly released her, pacing back a step in his tuxedo. His handsome face looked pale.

"But now." He took a deep breath, then licked his cruel, sensual lips. "But now, surely you don't…love me."

She saw the fear in his eyes.

"Don't worry," she said softly. "I got over loving you the day I left London. I knew we'd never have a future. I had to leave my broken heart behind me, to start a new life with my child."

For a moment he didn't reply. Then he pressed his lips together. "*Our* child."

"Yes." She sighed. She looked straight into his eyes, her heart aching as she said, "But not for long."

"What do you mean?"

"You won't last."

He stepped toward her. "You really think I would abandon him? After everything I've said?"

She matched him toe to toe. "I won't be a burden, or let Sam feel like one, either, wondering what's wrong with him that his own father can't be bothered to spend time with him." She lifted her chin, but as their eyes locked, she faltered. "You're not a bad person, Cesare. But trying to raise him separately, together, it's just not going to work."

"So you can find some other man to raise my son."

Her eyes shone with tears as she whispered, "You can't promise forever. You know you can't. So if you have any mercy in your heart—if you truly do care for Sam—please, let us go."

His expression changed. He took a long, dragging breath.

"Everything you're saying," he said slowly, "is bull."

Her lips parted in a gasp.

Cesare glared at her. "You didn't keep the baby a secret because you were trying to protect me from this choice. You didn't do it to protect Sam, either. You did it for one person and one person only. Yourself."

"How can you say that?" she demanded.

"Are you honestly telling me that it's better for Sam to believe his own father abandoned him? Yes, I'm selfish. Yes, I work too much. Yes, it's possible I might buy him a pony. Maybe I wouldn't be a perfect father. But you wouldn't—won't—even give me a chance. It isn't Sam that you fear will be a burden." He looked at her. "*It's you.* You're afraid I will take charge of him, and you'll be left behind. You're afraid for yourself. *Only yourself.*"

Emma stared at him, her lips parted in shock. The accusation was like a knife in her heart.

Was he right? Could he be?

She shook her head fiercely.

"*No.* You're wrong!"

"You don't want to lose him," he growled. "Neither do I. From this moment, his needs must come first." He paused. "I did think of suing you for full custody…"

Those words were an ice pick in Emma's heart. She made a little whimpering sound. "No…"

"But a custody battle would only hurt my son. I'm not going to leave him in Bouchard's care, either. Or abandon him, whatever you say. I'm not going to shuttle a small child between continents, between two different lives. That leaves only one clear path. At least it's clear to me." Pulling a small jewelry box from his tuxedo pocket, he opened the box, revealing an enormous diamond ring.

"Emma Hayes," he said grimly, "will you marry me?"

CHAPTER SEVEN

CESARE STOOD BEFORE her, waiting for her answer. He hadn't even thought of bending down on one knee. His legs were shaking too badly. He was relieved his voice hadn't trembled at the question. The words felt like marbles in his mouth.

Hearing a soft gasp, he glanced behind him. Five members of the restaurant's staff were peeking from the kitchen door, smiling at this moment, waiting for Emma's answer, in that universal interest in the drama of a wedding proposal.

Will you marry me?

Four simple words. A promise that was easy to say, though not so easy to fulfill.

Cesare had the sudden memory of his father's bleak face after his beloved wife had died in his arms. The same look of stark despair on Angélique's face when Cesare had come home and found her dead, an empty bottle of sleeping pills on the floor beside her.

No. He wouldn't let himself remember. This was different. *Different.*

Cesare held the black jewelry box up a little higher, to disguise how his hand was shaking.

"Marry you?" Emma's eyes were shocked. Even horrified. She gave an awkward laugh. "Is this a joke?"

"You think I would joke about this?"

Biting her lip, she looked at the ring. "But you don't want to get married. Everyone on earth knows that, and from the day I've known you, every woman has tried to marry you anyway. We used to laugh about it."

"I'm not laughing now," he said quietly. "I'm standing in front of you with a twenty-carat ring. I don't know how much more serious I can be."

Her beautiful face looked stricken. "But you don't love me."

"It's not a question of love—at least not between us. It's a question of providing the best life for our son."

Her gaze shuttered, her green eyes filling with shadows in the flickering candlelight of the restaurant. She backed up one step—physically backed away—wrapping her arms across her body, as if for protection.

Nothing prepared him for what came next.

"I'm sorry, Cesare," she said quietly. "My answer is no."

He was so shocked, his hand tightened on the jewelry box, closing it with a snap. He'd assumed she would say yes. Instantly and gratefully.

He heard gasps behind him and whirled to face the restaurant staff hanging about the kitchen doorway.

"Leave us," he growled, and they ran back into the kitchen. He turned to face Emma, his jaw taut. "Might I ask—why?"

She swallowed. He saw her face was pale. This was hard on her, too, he realized. "I told you. I won't be a burden."

"Burden. You keep using that word. What does it mean?"

His dangerous tone would have frightened most. But standing her ground, she lifted her chin.

"You know what it means."

"No, I don't. I know you've lied to me for months, that you stole my son away without a word. But instead of trying to take him away from you, instead of seeking revenge, I'm trying to do the right thing—a new experience for me, I might add—while you keep whining words like *love* and *burden.*"

Her shoulders drooped as, biting her lip, she looked down. For a long moment, she didn't answer, and he looked at her in the darkness of the restaurant. She looked so beautiful in the flickering candlelight, with all of the lights of Paris at her feet.

Cesare's throat tightened.

He thought of the night he'd found her in the dark kitchen, after her stepmother's funeral. He'd taken one look at her tearstained face, at the anguish in eyes which had never shown emotion before, and his own long-buried grief had risen in his own soul, exploding through his defenses. He'd thought he was offering her solace, but the truth was that he'd been seeking it himself. Against his will, in that moment, Emma had made him *feel* again....

Now he heard her take a deep breath.

"Whatever you think now, this desire to commit won't last. You don't want the burden of a wife and child. We both know it. You don't know what marriage means."

"We both know I do," he said quietly.

Her eyes were anguished as tears sparkled—unheeded, unfought—down her cheeks like diamonds. "But you don't love me," she whispered again.

"And you don't love me," he said evenly. "Do you?"

Wordlessly she shook her head. He exhaled. "This marriage has nothing to do with romance."

She gave a half-hysterical laugh, swooping her arm to indicate the roses, the view of Paris, the twenty-carat diamond ring. "What do you call that?"

He gave her a crooked half grin. "I call it...strategic negotiation."

Emma gave another laugh, then her smile fell. "A marriage without love?"

"Without complications," he pointed out. "We will both love our son. But between us—the marriage will be in name only."

"In name only?" He'd shocked her with this. He saw it in her face. "So you wouldn't expect us to…"

He shook his head. "Sex complicates things." Not to mention made it hard to keep the walls around his heart intact. At least where she was concerned. He hesitated. "Better that we keep this relationship…"

"Professional?"

"Cordial, I was going to say."

She took a deep breath.

"Why would I agree to give up any chance at love?"

"For something you want more than love," he said quietly. "For a family. For Sam."

"Sam…"

"I will love him. I'll be there with him every step of the way. Every single day. Isn't that better than trying to shuttle him between two separate lives, where he never knows where he belongs?"

Raw yearning filled her soft green eyes. Blinking fast, she turned away, to the dark, sparkling view of Paris. "I've worried about what would happen to Sam, if anything ever happened to me…" Looking up at him, she swallowed. "I've been in remission a long time, but there are no guarantees. If the cancer ever came back…" She looked up at him. "I've been selfish," she whispered. "Maybe you're right. Maybe even a flawed father is better than none."

"I will be the best father I can be."

"Would you?" she said in a small voice. Her beautiful face was tortured, her pink lips trembling, long dark lashes sweeping against pale cheeks. "Or, if I were crazy enough to accept, would you panic within a month and run off with some lingerie model?"

Coming toward her, he took both her hands in his own. "I swear to you, on my life," he said softly. "Everything your father was for you—I will be for him."

He felt her hands tremble in his.

"I won't let you break his heart," she whispered.

"I don't lie, and I don't make promises. You know that."

Her voice was barely audible. "Yes."

"I don't make promises because I consider myself bound by them." Gently he placed the black jewelry box with the silver Harry Winston logo into her palm. "I'm making you a promise now."

Her anguished eyes lifted to his. "Please…"

"You are the mother of my child. Be my wife." Brushing back long tendrils of black hair from her shoulder, he lowered his head to her ear. He took a deep breath, inhaling the scent of her. She smelled like vanilla and sunlight, like wildflowers and clean linen and everything good he'd once had but had lost so long ago. He felt a shudder of desire, but pushed it aside. He wouldn't let sex complicate this relationship. He couldn't. Pulling back, he said softly, "Be my wife, Emma."

Were her hands still trembling? Or were his?

"Cesare…." He saw how close she was to falling off the precipice. She tried, "We don't have to marry. We can live apart, but still raise Sam together…."

"In separate houses? In separate cities? Sending a small child with a little suitcase back and forth between two lives? You already said that wouldn't work. And I agree." Slowly, so slowly it almost killed him, he pulled her into the circle of his embrace, encircling her like a skittish thoroughbred into an enclosure. His gaze searched hers. "Marry me now. Take my name, and let my son be a Falconeri. I swear to you. On my life. That I will be the father you dreamed he could have."

She swallowed. "You swore you'd never get married again," she breathed. "We both know—" their eyes met "—you're still in love with your lost wife, and always will be."

He didn't deny this. It was easier not to.

"But we won't be lovers," he said. "We'll be equal partners." His fingers stroked her black hair, tumbling in glossy waves down her back. "And together—we'll raise our son."

She exhaled, visibly trying to steady herself. "For how long?"

"For always," he said in a low voice. "I will be married to you…until death do us part."

Her skin felt almost cold to the touch. He could almost feel her heart pounding through her ribs. "It would be a disaster."

"The only disaster would be to let any selfish dreams—yours or mine—destroy our son's chance for a home." Stroking down her cheek, he cupped her face. "Say you'll be my wife, Emma," he said huskily. "Say it."

Tears suddenly fell off her black lashes, trailing haphazardly down her pale cheeks.

"I can't fight you," she choked out. "Not when you're using my own heart against me. My baby deserves a father. It's all I've wanted since the day I found out I was pregnant." Her beautiful eyes were luminous with emotion, her body tense, as she stood in his arms in the rose-strewn restaurant of the Eiffel Tower, all the lights of Paris beneath them. "You win," she said. "I'll marry you, Cesare."

"Do you want me to come up with you?"

For answer, Emma shook her head, though she didn't

let go of Cesare's hand. She hadn't let it go for the whole walk home from the Eiffel Tower. Her knees still felt weak. Now, as they stood outside Alain's gated courtyard, she was trembling. Possibly from the weight of the enormous diamond on her left hand.

Either that, or from the knowledge that she'd just thrown all her own dreams away, her precious dreams of being loved, for someone she loved more than herself: her son.

"Are you sure? Bouchard might not be pleased at the news."

"It will be fine." She still couldn't believe she'd agreed to Cesare's marriage proposal. He'd loved only one woman—his long-dead wife—and would never love another. Knowing that, how could she have said yes?

But how could she not? He'd offered her everything she'd ever wanted for Sam. A home. A family. A real father, like she'd had. How could she not have made the sacrifice of something so small and inconsequential as her own heart?

At least she didn't need to worry about falling in love with Cesare again. She'd burned that from her soul. She *had*...

"You won't change your mind the instant I let you out of my sight?" he said lightly.

She shook her head.

"I think I'd better stay close, just to be safe." Cesare's voice was husky as he carefully tucked her jaunty pink scarf around her black coat. "Bouchard might try to talk you out of marrying me."

Even though she didn't love him anymore—*at all*—having Cesare so close did strange things to her insides. Emma took a deep breath. But she couldn't let herself feel anything. Not love. Not even lust. Not this time.

She was going to be his wife. In name only. She'd have to keep her distance, while living in the same house.

"Seriously, don't come," she said. She looked past the gate at Alain Bouchard's mansion. "I'd better give Alain this happy news on my own."

Cesare gave her a lopsided grin that made her heart go thump, thump in her chest. "I'll get the car, then. Meet you back here in ten minutes?"

"Ten?" she said incredulously.

"Twenty?"

"Better make it an hour. It's amazing how long it takes to pack up a baby."

"Really? He seems small."

"*He* is, but he has a lot of stuff." At his bemused expression, she snorted. "You'll learn."

"Can't wait." Pulling her close, Cesare looked down into her eyes. Cupping her face, he looked down at her one last time as they stood on the street with the lights of Paris twinkling around them. "Thank you for saying yes. You won't regret it."

"I regret it already," she mumbled, then gave a small laugh to show she was joking, holding up her left hand. "This diamond ring weighs, like, a thousand pounds. See you in an hour."

Turning, she went through the gate, past the security guard into Alain's courtyard. One of his personal bodyguards was waiting by the mansion door.

"Monsieur Bouchard is not happy with you, mademoiselle," Gustave said flatly.

She stopped. "Were you—following me?"

The man jutted his chin upward, toward the house. "He's waiting for you."

Emma had meant to tell Alain her news in the most gentle way possible. Instead it seemed he already had a good guess what was coming. Well, fine. She narrowed her eyes. He shouldn't have had her followed.

Going upstairs, she walked right past Alain's office, but not before she saw him scowling at his desk. First, she went to check on her baby, and found him sleeping in his crib. For a moment, she listened to his soft breath in the darkness. Tenderness and joy caught at her heart. Smiling to herself, she whispered aloud, "You're going to have a family, Sam. You're going to have a real dad."

Creeping out, she closed the door, and went to the next-door sitting room, where she found Irene Taylor reading tranquilly in an armchair.

"How was everything?" Emma asked.

"Oh, he was perfect. An angel." Smiling, Irene tucked her book, a romantic novel by Susan Mallery, carefully into her handbag. "Did you have a nice evening?"

Wordlessly Emma held out her left hand. Irene gasped, snatching up her hand and staring at the ring.

"Are you *kidding?*" She made a big show of rubbing her eyes. "Ah! It's blinding me!" She looked up at Emma with a big grin. "You sly girl, I didn't even know you were dating someone."

"Well—I wasn't. But Sam's father came for a visit, and one thing led to another…"

"Oh, how wonderful," Irene sighed. "True love prevails."

"Um. Right." Emma's cheeks went hot. She couldn't tell Irene that love had nothing to do with it, that she'd kept her pregnancy a secret and now they were only getting married for Sam's sake. "Well. I'm leaving for London with him right now. Would you mind helping me pack Sam's things?"

"I'd love to. All his cute, tiny baby things. And now you're off to London, swept away to be wed like a princess in a story." Irene looked wistful. "I hope I find a love like that someday, too."

Her friend's idealistic notion of love, the same dreams she'd once had for herself, cast a pall over Emma's heart. How could she tell Irene that she had nothing to be envious about—that Emma was settling for a loveless marriage so her baby would have a father?

Sam deserves it, she told herself again. She tried to remember the calmness she'd had about her decision just a moment before, when she'd stood in her baby's room, listening to him sleep. She turned away. "I'll be back."

Squaring her shoulders, Emma went down the hall to Alain's office. She took a deep breath and went in.

Her employer was sitting at his desk. He didn't look up. When he spoke, his voice was sour. "Have a good time at the *Tour Eiffel?*"

She was glad he was taking that tone with her. It made this so much easier. "Yes, I had a wonderful evening," she said sweetly. "Thank you."

Alain glared at her. "I don't appreciate you staying out so late. I was worried."

"I don't appreciate you having me followed."

"I wanted to keep you safe."

"Safe," she said.

"I don't trust Falconeri. You shouldn't, either."

"Right. Well. I'm sorry to tell you, but I have to turn in my notice."

Alain's eyes widened. He slowly rose to his feet. "What?"

"And by *notice,* I mean I'm leaving right now." Her cheeks flamed. "I am actually sorry to do it to you, Alain. It's not very professional. In fact it's completely rude. But Cesare and I are going back to London with the baby...."

"He's stringing you along, Emma, toying with you! I

can't believe you would fall for his lines. He'll leave you high and dry when…"

"We're getting married," she said flatly.

Alain's mouth literally fell open.

"What?"

Emma held up her engagement ring, then let her hand drop back to her side. "You've been good to me, Alain. I know you deserve better than me leaving you like this." She swallowed. "But I have to take this chance, for Sam's sake. I'm sorry. I'll never forget your kindness and generosity over the past year…."

"I'm sorry, too," Alain said shortly. "Because you're making a mistake. He ruined Angélique's life."

"Your sister's death was a terrible tragedy, but the coroner ruled the overdose an accident…."

"Accident," he said bitterly. "Falconeri drove my sister to her death. Just as surely as if he'd poured the sleeping pills down her throat."

"You're wrong." Steadying herself, she faced him in his office, clenching her hands at her sides. "He loved her. I know that all too well. He loves her still," she said quietly.

"She gave him everything," Alain continued as if he hadn't heard. "He lured her into marrying him. She loved him. Trusted him." His eyes were wild. "But from the moment they were wed, he neglected her. So much so that she told me she meant to divorce him—then she mysteriously died before she could."

Emma blinked at his implication. "You can't think—"

"If she'd divorced him, he would have gotten nothing. A few hundred thousand dollars. Instead he got her entire fortune. He used that money to turn his shabby little hotel in New York into a multibillion-dollar international hotel conglomerate. You know he's ruthless."

"But not ruthless like that," she whispered. She reminded herself that Alain's words were spoken in anger, that he was a grief-stricken brother. Going toward him, she put her hand gently on his shoulder. "I'm sorry about Angélique. I truly, truly am. But you have to stop blaming Cesare. Her death wasn't his fault. He loved her. He never would have hurt her."

Alain slowly put his hand over her own. "Someday you'll see the man he really is. And you'll come back to me. I'll give you your old job back...or better yet..." His eyes met hers. "I'll give you exactly what Falconeri is offering you now."

Marriage. He meant marriage. Emma swallowed, then pulled her hand away. "I'm sorry, Alain. I care about you deeply, but not in that way." She stepped back from him and said with her heart in her throat, "I wish you all the best. Please take care of yourself." She turned away. "Goodbye."

"Wait."

She turned back at the door. Alain's jaw was tight as he looked at her.

"My sister shone like a star," he said. "She was so beautiful, the life of every party. But even Angélique couldn't keep his attention for long. Don't think you will, either." He faced her across the shadows. "Loving him destroyed her, Emma. Don't let it destroy you."

CHAPTER EIGHT

WHAT A RIDICULOUS warning. Emma still couldn't believe it. It was laughable.

Yes, laughable. Emma felt pleased at the word. She hardly knew which was more ridiculous: the idea that Cesare would have caused his wife, the only woman he'd ever loved, to kill herself with sleeping pills, or that Emma would still be stupid enough to love him, knowing he'd never love her back.

Because she wouldn't.

Love him.

At all.

Ever again.

Even though Cesare had been so wonderful since they'd arrived in London two weeks ago. He'd taken days off from work just to spend time with them, walking across the city, seeing the sights, pushing Sam together in his baby buggy, strolling like all the other happy families along the Thames. But what did Emma care about that?

She certainly wouldn't fall in love with him just because they'd shared champagne while riding the huge Ferris wheel of the London Eye. Or because he'd agreed to a lunch of fish and chips at the Sherlock Holmes pub, when he'd wanted sushi, purely because she'd begged. She didn't care that they'd gone to Trafalgar Square to show Sam the stone lions, and Cesare had taken about a thousand pictures, and let her take some of him making funny faces as he pretended to fall from the stone pedestal. Those memories didn't matter. Her heart was made of stone.

Stone.

They'd visited the National Gallery. The British Museum. They'd gotten a tour of the new Globe Theatre, then bought fresh bread and cheese at the outdoor Borough Market. But her heart was completely safe. Cesare wasn't doing this for her. He was just following through on his promise to be an amazing father to Sam. That was all.

But he was keeping that promise beyond her wildest dreams.

Just yesterday, he'd insisted on going to Hamleys on Regent Street, where he'd bought so many toys that they'd needed to order an extra car to bring all the bags back to the Kensington house.

"When exactly are you expecting Sam to be interested in this?" Emma had asked with a laugh, looking from their sleeping five-month-old baby to the cricket bat and ball on the top of the toy pile.

"He is already fascinated with cricket. Can't you tell?" Cesare had leaned the foam cricket bat across Sam's lap, placing it in the baby's tiny hand as he slept on with a soft baby snore in the stroller. He stepped back. "Look. He's clearly a prodigy."

Holding a foam ball, Cesare elaborately wound his arm, then gently tossed the ball underhand. It bounced off the plastic edge of the stroller and rolled across the floor.

"Prodigy, huh?" she said.

He picked the ball up with a grin. "It might take a bit of practice."

"For him or you?"

"Mostly me. He already seems to have the knack."

"You're just a big kid yourself," she'd teased. "Admit it."

They'd looked at each other, smiling—then the air between them suddenly changed, sizzled with electricity.

Cesare had looked away, muttering something about going to the cashier to pay. And Emma's hands had gripped the stroller handle, as in her mind she repeated the words *In name only* about a thousand times.

Now she shivered as she went up the stairs of the Kensington house. He'd shown her every bit of attention he'd promised, and more. And as promised, he hadn't once tried to kiss her. Not even once.

But that was starting to be a problem. Because in her heart of hearts, she was starting to realize that she wanted him to…

She veered past his bedroom, and continued to her own bedroom, down the hall, where Sam was currently sleeping.

Emma told herself she was being stupid. They weren't even married yet, and she wanted to give him her body? Stupid, stupid. Because how much harder would it be not to give him her heart in the bargain?

We won't be lovers, he'd said in Paris. *We'll be equal partners.*

Her brain had accepted this as the best possible course when she'd agreed to his proposal. And yet…

She was supposed to be planning the wedding right now. But every time she started, something stopped her. Something that had nothing to do with choosing the cake or venue or church.

She was sacrificing her heart. For her son. She could accept that. There was one thing she was trying not to think about.

A marriage in name only would inevitably mean that Cesare would take lovers on the side.

What else could it mean—that Cesare would do as she planned to do, and go without sex for the rest of her life? No. For a red-blooded man like him, that would be impossible.

She was trying not to think about it. Trying and failing.

Emma leaned heavily back against her own bedroom door, closing it behind her. She didn't want to be jealous. She didn't want to be afraid.

But the day they'd returned to Kensington, Emma had fired the housekeeper. Miss Maddie Allen was an attractive young blonde, and Emma had instantly felt she hadn't wanted her within a million miles of Cesare. He'd said he was glad to see her go, that she was the worst housekeeper imaginable and had regularly left iron marks on his shirts. But Emma had given her a year's salary as severance, out of guilt for the real reason she'd fired the beautiful Miss Allen—out of pure, raw fear.

She didn't want to feel this way. With a sigh, Emma walked across her bedroom. A garment bag from a designer shop on Sloane Street was laid carefully upon her bed. Zipping open the bag, she looked down at the gown she would wear tonight at their official engagement party.

For a moment, she just stood there looking at it. Then she reached out and stroked the slinky silver fabric. Pulling off her clothes, she put on a black lace bra and panties and black garter she'd gotten from a French lingerie shop. She didn't dare look at herself in the full-length mirror as she put them on, for fear she'd lose her nerve.

Tonight, she would be introduced to Cesare's friends, and London society in general, not as his housekeeper, but as his future wife, and the mother of his child. She didn't want to embarrass him.

And if, by some miracle, he thought she looked pretty, maybe their marriage could become real. Maybe he'd take her in his bed, and she'd never have to feel insecure again....

Even Angélique couldn't keep his attention for long. Don't think you will, either.

She pushed away the memory of Alain's words. She had to stop this ugly insecurity! After all her jealousy, she'd found out Cesare hadn't slept with Maddie Allen anyway. Emma knew this because—her blush deepened—she'd blurted out that question immediately after the housekeeper had departed. His reply had been curt.

"No. I did not sleep with her." His jaw had been tight as he looked at the fire in the fireplace, leaving flickering red-and-gold light across the spines of the leatherbound books. He'd parted his lips, drawing in breath as if he meant to say something more, then stopped.

Nearly jumping out of her own skin, she'd said, "But did you ever..."

"No more questions. I won't have you torture us both by asking for a list of my lovers. You of all people know the list is long." Putting his hands on her shoulders, he'd looked down and said softly, "This home is yours now, Emma." He'd cupped her face. "I will never disrespect you here."

His words had thrilled her. *Then.* Later, she'd parsed his words. *This home is yours. I will never disrespect you here.* Meaning—he'd disrespect her elsewhere? At a hotel?

Now, reaching down for the silver dress, long and glamorous like the gown of a 1930s film star, she let the whisper of fabric caress her skin as she pulled it up her body. She didn't want to be jealous. She didn't want to worry.

She wanted him to want—*her.*

Emma's throat tightened. Sitting in the chair at the vanity desk, she began brushing her dark hair with long, hard strokes. She looked at herself in the antique gilt mirror. She was nothing special. Just a regular girl, with round cheeks and big, vulnerable green eyes, who looked scared out of her mind.

How could she marry him, even for Sam's sake, knowing that Cesare would never uphold the promise of their wedding vows? How could she allow Sam to grow up watching his father repeatedly cheat on his mother—and her explicitly allowing him to do it? What kind of sick ideas would that teach her precious boy about love, marriage, trust and family?

If only Cesare would want her. Her hand slowed with the brush. If only they could truly be lovers, in the same bed, maybe he'd stay true to their wedding vows, and they could be a real family....

"Not ready yet?"

She twisted in the chair to see Cesare in the doorway. He was wearing a tuxedo a little different than the one in Paris—less classic, more cutting edge. But with his dark hair and chiseled good looks, he melted her, whatever he might be wearing. Even wearing nothing.

Especially wearing nothing.

She gulped, turning away. She couldn't stop thinking about the two hot nights he'd made love to her. So long ago now. Almost a year since he'd touched her...

"You look beautiful," he said huskily, coming into her bedroom.

"Oh," she said. "Thank you." Their eyes met in the mirror. Her cheeks turned pink.

"You're just missing one final touch." Coming up behind her, he pulled a sparkling diamond necklace from his pocket and placed it around her neck. Emma's lips parted as she saw it in the mirror, huge diamonds dripping past her collarbone. Involuntarily she put her hand against the necklace, hardly able to believe it was real.

"Almost worthy of the woman wearing it," he murmured.

"You...you shouldn't have." Nervously she rose to her feet, facing him. Realizing her fingertips were still resting against the sparkling stones, she put her hand down.

"It's nothing. A mere trinket." His black eyes caressed her. Leaning forward, he brushed long tendrils of glossy black hair from her bare shoulders, back from the necklace, and whispered, "Nothing is too good for my future wife."

Emma felt the warmth of his breath against her bare skin. She shuddered with a sudden pang of need. Of desire.

She couldn't let herself want him like this. Couldn't. It left her too vulnerable. And the one thing she knew about Cesare was that he detested needy women. She wouldn't, couldn't, be one.

And yet...

Turning away, she went back to the mirror and put on her bright red lipstick with a shaking hand. She tried to ignore his gaze as she ran the red tube carefully over her lips. Sitting back on the bed, she reached for her high-heeled shoes, gorgeous Charlotte Olympia pumps with bamboo on the platform sole and pink cherry blossoms crisscrossing the straps. Emma had seen them in a shop on Sloane Street and in spite of her best efforts—since they were quite expensive—had fallen instantly in love with the 1930s Shanghai glamour.

"Mr. Falconeri said you're to have whatever you wish, madame," the salesgirl had insisted, and Emma, with baby Sam in his stroller next to Cesare's personal bodyguard, had quickly succumbed. It was so wrong to buy shoes that were so expensive. Wrong to want something so forbidden. So clearly out of reach. Emma looked at Cesare.

Or was it?

She rose to her feet, her long black hair tumbling over

the low cowl neck of her gown, which melted like liquid silver against her body. She felt transformed—like a glamorous, mysterious starlet from a black-and-white film. She'd never felt so beautiful, or less like the plain, sensible person she'd always been. She took a deep breath, and looked at Cesare.

"I'm ready," she said softly.

He stared at her. She saw his hands tighten at his sides as his gaze slowly went down the length of her dress. And when he spoke, was it her imagination or was his voice a little strained?

"You look…fine." Clearing his throat, he held out his arm. "Ready to meet the firing squad?"

"That's how you refer to your friends?"

He gave her a wicked grin, quirking his dark eyebrow. "You should hear how they refer to me."

"I already know." As she took his arm, Emma's smile fell. "You're the playboy who will never be caught by any woman."

He winked at her, a gesture so silly and unexpected that it caused her heart to twist in her chest. "They'll understand when they meet you."

Their eyes locked, and the squeeze on her heart suddenly became unbearable.

I love you. The words pushed through her soul, through her heart. *I love you, Cesare.*

It was a realization so horrible, Emma sucked in her breath in a gasp so rough and abrupt that it made her double over, coughing.

He rubbed her back, his voice filled with concern. "Are you all right?"

She held up her hand as she regained her breath. Downstairs, she could hear the rising noise of guests arriving at the Kensington mansion for the engagement party. All of his snooty rich friends, and their beautiful girlfriends—half of whom Cesare had probably slept with over the years. Half? Probably more.

"Cara?"

She finally straightened, her eyes watery. "I'm fine," she said, wiping her eyes. It was a lie.

She loved him.

Almost a year ago, she'd left him in despair, believing they had no chance for a future. But now, after just two weeks of wearing his engagement ring on her hand, an awful, desperate hope had pushed itself into her soul. Against her will.

She was in love with him. The truth was she'd never stopped loving him. She was utterly and completely in love with her former boss, the father of her baby.

A man who was going to marry her out of pure *obligation*. Who didn't even want to touch her. Who wanted their marriage to be *in name only*. For their son's sake. A shell. A sham…

"Emma?"

She couldn't let him see her face. Couldn't let him guess what she felt inside. Pretending not to see his outstretched arm, she walked swiftly ahead.

"Wait," he said sharply.

Emma stopped. She took a deep breath, and looked back at him in the hallway.

Smiling down at her in a way that caused his eyes to crinkle, he took her arm and wrapped it around his own. "It's an engagement party. We should enter the ballroom together."

Together. How she wished they could truly be together.

"Are you cold?" He frowned. "You're trembling."

"No… Yes… Um." She twisted her ankle deliberately. "It's the shoes."

He snorted, looking at the four-inch heels. "No wonder."

As they walked down the stairs, she clutched his arm as if her beautiful shoes were really the problem, trying to convince herself everything would be just fine. All right, so she was in love with Cesare and he'd never love her back. All right, so her whole body yearned for him to touch her, but he insisted on separate bedrooms and was likely planning to hook up with the next gorgeous actress who struck his fancy.

But they had a child together. Their marriage would be like a business partnership. That counted for something, didn't it?

Didn't it?

Her throat tightened.

As they approached the mansion's ballroom, she saw his friends—tycoons, actresses, diplomats and royalty. The women were thin and young and beautiful, in chic, tight clothes with no stretch marks from pregnancy. They all turned to look at her speculatively. She could see their sly assumption: that Emma had gotten pregnant on purpose. That was how a gold-digging housekeeper trapped an uncatchable playboy.

Their expressions changed as they looked from her to Cesare. And she realized that being in love with him just made Emma exactly the same as every other woman in the room. They all wanted him. They all broke their hearts over him.

She swallowed, glancing up at him through her lashes, suddenly desperate for reassurance, unable to fight this green demon eating her alive from the inside out.

Cesare abruptly stopped at the bottom of the stairs, in front of the open ballroom doors. "Time to face the music."

His voice was strangely flat. All the emotion had fled from his expression. Meeting her eyes, he gave her a forced smile, as if he already regretted his unbreakable, binding promise to marry her. "Let's get this over with, shall we?"

She suddenly wanted to ask him if those were the words he'd say to himself on their wedding day, too. She looked down at her diamond necklace. At her enormous engagement ring.

I can do this, she told herself. *For Sam.*

Cesare led her into the ballroom, and as she walked across the same marble floor she'd once scrubbed on her hands and knees, she pasted a bright smile on her face as she was formally introduced to London society: the housekeeper who'd been lucky and conniving enough to trap a billionaire playboy into marriage.

"So the great Cesare Falconeri is caught at last," Sheikh Sharif bin Nazih al Aktoum, the emir of Makhtar, said behind him. His voice was amused.

"Caught?" Cesare turned. "I haven't been caught."

The sheikh took a sip of champagne and waved his hand airily. "Ah, but it happens to all of us sooner or later."

Cesare scowled. The two men were not close; he'd invited the sheikh as a courtesy, as his company sought to get permission to build a new resort hotel on one of his Persian Gulf beaches. He'd never thought the man might actually come, but he'd showed up at the Kensington mansion in a black town car with diplomatic flags flying, in full white robes and trailing six bodyguards.

Six. Cesare had to stop himself from rolling his eyes. Bringing two bodyguards was sensible, six was just showing off. He bared a smile at his guest. "I'm the luckiest man on earth to be engaged to Emma. It took me a year to convince her to marry me." Which was true in its way.

The sheikh gave a faint smile. "Some men are just the marrying kind, I suppose."

Cesare raised his eyebrows. "You think *I'm* the marrying kind?"

He shrugged. "Clearly. You've experienced it once and choose willingly to return to it." The dark eyes looked at him curiously, as if Cesare were an exhibit in a zoo. "As for myself, I'm in no rush to be trapped with one woman, subject to her whims, forced to listen to her complain day and night—" He cut himself off with a cough, as if he'd just realized that saying such things at an engagement party might be poor form. "Well. Perhaps marriage is different from the cage I picture it to be."

A cage. Cesare felt the sudden irrational stirrings of buried panic. He could hear the harsh rasp of Angélique's exhausted voice, a decade before.

If you ever loved me, if you ever cared at all, let me go.

But Angélique, you are still my wife. We both gave a promise before God....

Then He will forgive, for He knows how I hate you.

We can go to marriage counseling. He'd reached for her, desperate. *We can get past this.*

Her lip had curled. *What will it take for you to let me go?* She narrowed her eyes maliciously. *Would you like to hear how long and hard Raoul loves me every time we meet, here and in Paris, all this past year, while you've been busy at your pathetic little hotel, trying to make something of yourself? Raoul loves me as you never will.*

Cesare had tried to cover his ears, but she'd told him, until he could bear it no longer and went back on everything he'd ever believed in. *Fine,* he told her grimly. *I'll give you your divorce.*

Twenty-four hours later, Angélique had returned from Buenos Aires and swallowed an entire bottle of pills. Cesare had been the one to find her. He'd found out later that Raoul Menendez was already long married. That he'd laughed in Angélique's face when she'd shown up on his doorstep.

So much for love.

So much for marriage.

Oh, my God. A cold sweat broke out on Cesare's forehead as he remembered that panicked sense of failure and helplessness. The sheikh was right. A cage was exactly what marriage was.

"Your bride is beautiful, of course," the man murmured. "She would tempt any man."

Cesare looked up to see Emma floating by on the dance floor in the arms of Leonidas, his old friend and former wingman at London's best nightclubs. The famous Greek playboy had a reputation even worse than Cesare's. Emma's beautiful face was laughing, lifted to the Greek's admiring eyes. Cesare felt a surge of jealousy.

Emma was his woman. *His.*

"Ah. So lovely. Her long dark hair. Her creamy skin. And that figure…" The sheikh's voice trailed off.

"Don't even think about it," Cesare said dangerously.

He held up his hands with a low laugh. "Of course. I sought merely to praise your taste in a wife. I would not think of attempting to sample her charms myself."

"Good," he growled. "Then I won't have to think of attempting to knock your head off your body."

The man eyed him, then shook his head with a rueful snort. "You have it badly, my friend."

"It?"

"You're in love with her."

"She's the mother of my son," Cesare replied sharply, as if that explained everything.

"Naturally," the other man said soothingly. But his black eyes danced, as if to say: *you poor fool, you don't even see how deeply your neck is in the noose.*

Reaching up his hand in an involuntary movement, Cesare loosened the tuxedo tie around his neck. Then he grabbed a glass from a passing waiter and gulped down an entire glass of Dom Perignon in one swallow before he said, "Excuse me."

"Of course."

Going to the other side of the dance floor, Cesare watched Emma dance. He saw the way her face glowed. *Sì.* Think of her. Beautiful. So strong and tender. It wouldn't be so awful, would it, having her in his house?

As long as they didn't get too close.

As long as he didn't try to seduce her.

That was the only way this convenient marriage would ever work. If they kept their distance, so she didn't get any crazy ideas back about loving him. And he didn't start thinking he needed her, or let his walls down.

Vulnerability was weakness.

Love was pain.

Cesare's face went hot as he remembered how he'd felt last year when she'd left him staring after her in the window like a fool. He'd been so sure she'd be back. That she wouldn't be able to resist him.

But she had. Very well.

While he hadn't even slept with another woman since their last night together, almost a year ago.

How the world would laugh if they knew *that* little truth about Cesare Falconeri, the famous playboy. They would laugh—*sì*—they would, because it was pathetic. Fortunately he had no intention of sharing it with anyone. Not even Emma.

He almost had, the first day they'd arrived here, when she'd been so strangely jealous of the silly blonde housekeeper. He'd almost told Emma the truth, but it had caught in his throat. He couldn't let her know that secret. He would never allow himself to be that vulnerable to anyone ever again.

You love her, the sheikh had accused. Cesare snorted. Love? Ridiculous. Love was a concept for idealistic young souls, the ones who thought *lust* was not a big enough word to describe their desire. He'd been that way once. He'd married his wife when he was young and stupid. He'd thought sex meant love. He'd learned his lesson well.

Now his eyes narrowed as he watched Emma smile up encouragingly at Leonidas.

Before he realized what he was doing, he was on the dance floor, breaking up their little duo. "I'd like to dance with my fiancée, if you don't mind."

Emma had been in the middle of laughing but she looked at Cesare in surprise, as if, he thought grimly, she'd already forgotten his existence. As if she already suspected her power over him, and knew his weakness.

Leonidas looked tempted to make some sarcastic remark, but at Cesare's scowl, thought better of it. "Alas, my dear," he sighed to Emma. "I must hand you over to this brute. You belong to him now."

She gave another low laugh, and it was all Cesare could do not to give the Greek shipping tycoon a good kick on the backside to help speed him off the dance floor. With narrowed eyes, he took Emma in his arms.

"Having fun?" he growled as he felt her soft body against his, in her slinky gown of silver.

"It's been dreadful." She peeked up at him. "I'm glad to see you. I know he's your friend, but I didn't think I could take much more. Thank you for saving me!"

"Are you sure?" he said through gritted teeth. "The two of you seemed so cozy."

She blinked. "I was being nice to your friend."

"Not much nicer, I hope," he ground out, "or I might

have found the two of you making use of a guest bedroom!"

"What's gotten into you? You're acting almost—"

"Don't say it," he warned.

She tossed her head. "Jealous!"

Cesare set his jaw. "Tell me, what exactly was Leonidas saying that you found so charming?"

Sparks were starting to illuminate her green eyes. "I'm
not going to tell you."

He glared at her. "So you admit that you were flirting."

"I admit nothing. You are the one who said we shouldn't
ask each other questions!"

"About the past, not the present!"

"That's fine for you, because as you well know, *you* are
my only past, while *your* past could fill every bedroom in
this mansion. And probably has!"

Her voice caught, and for the first time he heard the
ragged edge of repressed tears. He frowned down at her.
When he spoke again, his voice was low, barely audible
over the music. "What's wrong?"

"Other than you accusing *me* of flirting, while I torture
myself with questions every time I meet one of your beautiful guests—wondering which ones you've slept with in
the past? And suspecting—all of them!"

Her voice broke. Her green eyes were luminous with
unshed tears. He glanced around uneasily at the women
around them. Emma was right. He'd slept with more than
one of them. No wonder she was upset. He'd nearly exploded with irrational jealousy, just seeing Leonidas talking to her.

Pulling her tighter in his arms, he swayed them to the
music, continuing to dance as he spoke to her in a low
voice.

"They were one-night stands, Emma. Meaningless."

"You called our first night together *meaningless,* too. The night we conceived our baby."

He flinched. Then emotion surged through him. He glared at her.

"This is why I wanted our marriage to be in name only. To avoid these arguments and stupid jealousies."

"You mean the way you practically hit your good friend in the face for the crime of dancing with me and making me laugh?"

For a moment, he scowled at her. Then, getting hold of himself, he took a deep breath.

"Sorry," he muttered. "I never meant…to make you cry."

Emma looked away, blinking fast. "That's not why I was crying."

"What is it, then?"

"It's stupid."

"Tell me."

She swallowed.

"They all think I'm a sly gold digger. All your friends." She wiped her eyes. "A few women actually *congratulated* me on tricking you into marriage. Some of them could hardly believe a woman as—well, fat—as me could do it. Others just wanted tips for how to trick billionaire husbands of their own. They wanted to know if I poked holes in the condom wrapper with a needle or what."

Cesare's hands tightened on her back. He stared down at her, vibrating with rage as they swayed to the music. "I will take a horsewhip to all of them."

She gave a small laugh, even as tears spilled down her cheeks. "It doesn't matter," she said softly, but he could feel how much that wasn't true. To her, the simple question of honor and a good name did matter. Her pride had been hurt.

He fiercely wiped a tear off her cheek with her thumb. "You and I, we know the truth."

"Yes. We do. But I still wish," she whispered, "we were a million miles from here."

"From London?"

"As long as we're in London, I'll always be your gold-digging housekeeper. And you'll be the playboy who's slept with every woman in the city." She looked up at him with tearful eyes. "I wish we could just go. Move away. Somewhere I'll never have to wonder, every time I see another woman, if she's ever been in your bed." She shuddered. "I hate what my imagination is doing to me—"

"Since the first night we slept together, I haven't touched another woman."

Her lips parted. "What?"

Cesare was almost as surprised as she was that he'd said it. But damn it—how could he not tell her? He couldn't see her pain and do nothing. "It's true."

"But—why?"

He stopped on the dance floor.

"I haven't wanted to," he said quietly.

"I don't understand." Emma shook her head. "If that's the case, why would you say you wanted a marriage in name only?"

Reaching out, he brushed back some dark hair from the soft skin of her bare shoulder above her gown. "Because all my love affairs have ended badly."

She swallowed. "Mine, too."

"Our marriage is too important. I cannot let it end in fights and tears and recriminations. The only way to make sure our relationship never ends…is never to start it in the first place."

"It won't work. Listen to us! We're still fighting any-way."

"Not like we would if—" He cut himself off, then shook his head. "You know lovers are a dime a dozen to me. But you… You are special." Reaching up, he stroked her cheek. "I need you as a partner. As my friend." He set his jaw. "Sex would ruin everything. It always does."

Swallowing, she exhaled, looking away.

"All right," she said finally. "Friends." There was a shadow of worry behind her eyes as they lifted to his. "You really haven't slept with any other women?" she said in wonder. "Since the night we conceived Sam?"

He gave her an unsteady grin. "Don't tell anyone. It would ruin my reputation."

"Your secret is safe with me." She smiled up at him, even as her eyes still shone with tears. "And you might as well know—your friend Leonidas is a very clumsy dancer. That's why I was laughing at his dumb jokes. To try to disguise yelps of pain every time he stomped on my foot."

A hard pressure in Cesare's chest suddenly released. For a moment, they just looked at each other, and though they were in the middle of a dance floor surrounded by a hundred guests, it was as if it were just the two of them in the world.

He never should have brought her back to London, Cesare thought suddenly. Of course not. How could he have expected Emma to return as a wife to the house where she'd once been his employee, and sleep in the same lonely bedroom down the hall from the bed where he'd seduced other women, again and again? The house where he'd once expected her, as a matter of course, to make breakfast for his one-night-stands and escort them out with gifts and a shoulder to cry on?

"We don't have to stay here," he said slowly. "There's someplace else we can go. A place where we can be married and start fresh, just the three of us. As a family."

"Where?"

His heart twisted to remember it. But he forced himself to meet her gaze. To smile.

"Home," he said simply.

CHAPTER NINE

THE TWO-HUNDRED-year-old villa on the shores of Lake Como stood like an ancient castle, caught in the shadows between the gray water and lowering clouds of dusk.

Emma took a deep breath, savoring the cool air against her cheeks and crunch of gravel beneath her feet as she walked along the forest path around the lake toward home. From the cushioned front pack on her chest, Sam let out another low cry, waving his plump arms. She sighed, looking down at her baby, then rubbed his soft downy hair.

"I thought for sure that a walk would do it," she said mournfully. He was irritable because he hadn't gone down for a nap all day, not for lack of her trying. "Ah, well. Let's see what we can rustle up for dinner, shall we?"

Her own stomach was growling after their long walk. She had spent hours trying to coax him to sleep, but as tired as Sam was, as soon as he started to nod off, he kept jerking himself awake. Now, she was finally forced to admit failure. The darkening October sky was drawing her back home.

That, and knowing Cesare was waiting for them...

Emma smiled to herself as she walked the lake path back toward the villa, which had been in the Falconeri family for hundreds of years. They'd been living here a month now, and it was starting to feel like home, though their first day, when he'd shown her around, she'd been shocked. "You grew up in this palace?" she'd blurted out, thinking of her two-bedroom bungalow on the Texas prairie.

He'd snorted. "It didn't always look like this. When I was a child, we barely had indoor plumbing. Our family ran out of money long before I was born. And that was even before my parents decided to devote their lives to art." His lips quirked. "Five years ago, I decided I wouldn't let it fall apart." His voice turned grim. "Although I was tempted."

"I remember you talking about the remodel." Emma had walked through room after room, all of them with ceilings fifteen feet high, with gilded details on the walls and even a fresco in the foyer. "I never imagined I might someday live here as your wife."

She could see why the remodel of this house, which she remembered him grumbling about, had required so much money and time. Every detail of the past had been preserved, while made modern with brand-new fixtures, windows, heated floors and two separate kitchens.

She'd been amazed when she saw a beautiful oil painting of Cesare as a young boy of maybe three or four, with chubby cheeks and bright innocence in his eyes—along with a determined set to his jaw. His clothes were ragged and covered with mud. She'd pointed at it with a laugh. "That was you?"

"My mother painted me perfectly. I was always outside in the garden, growing something or other."

"You liked to garden?" It astonished Emma. She couldn't reconcile the image of the happy, grimy boy in the painting with the sophisticated tycoon who now stood before her.

He rolled his eyes. "We were that kind of family. If I wanted fruit, I had to grow it myself. My parents' idea of childcare was to give me a stick and send me outside to play in the dirt." He fell silent. "But for all that, we were happy. We loved each other."

"I'm sorry," she'd whispered, seeing the pain in his eyes. She'd put her arms around him. "But we're here now."

For a moment, Cesare had allowed her to hold him, to offer comfort. Then he'd pulled away. "It all worked out," he said gruffly. "If I hadn't had my little tragedy and been sent to New York, I might never have started Falconeri International." His lips curved. "Who knows. I might still have been living here in a ruin, growing oranges and flowers, digging in the garden."

Now, as Emma walked along the lake's edge with her baby in her front pack, she stared at that overgrown garden. Alone of everything on the estate, the villa's garden had not been touched. It had been left untended and wild, choked with weeds. It was as if, she thought, Cesare could neither bear to have it destroyed, nor have it returned to its former glory.

A white mist was settling across the lake, thick and wet. Emma shivered as she pushed open the tall, heavy oak door that led into the Villa Falconeri. The scrape of the door echoed against the checkered marble floor and high ceiling with its two-hundred-year-old fresco above, showing pastoral scenes of the countryside.

"Cesare?" she called.

There was no answer. Emma heard a soft snore from her front pack and looked down. After hours of trying, Sam had finally dropped to sleep. His dark eyelashes fluttered downward over his plump cheeks. Smiling to herself, she went upstairs to tuck him into his crib.

She was sharing her beautiful bedroom with her baby. There was plenty of room for his crib and changing table. The room was enormous, in powder-blue, with a canopy bed and a huge window with a balcony overlooking the lake. Gently lifting her sleeping baby out of the carrier, she tucked him into his bed.

Alone in the room, without her baby's warmth against her, she felt a shiver of cold air in the deepening twilight. Even here, in this beautiful place, she slept alone.

You are special. I need you as a partner. As my friend. Sex would ruin everything.

Emma took a deep breath.

Tomorrow, their three-day wedding celebration would begin, first with a church ceremony, followed by a civil service the next day. Private celebrations with just a few friends: a white dress. A cake. Vows that could not be unspoken.

How she wished it all could be real. She longed to be his real wife. She looked at her empty bed. She wanted to sleep in his arms, to feel his lips on hers, to feel his hard, naked body cover hers at night. A flash of heat went through her and she touched her lips with her fingers. She could remember him there...

She shivered, closing her eyes.

As much as her brain told her that marriage was the rational solution, as much as her heart longed to be permanently bound to the man she loved, her body was tense and fighting the wedding every step of the way.

Marry a man who would never touch her?

A man who was still in love with his long-dead wife?

A man who would satisfy his sexual needs elsewhere, discreetly, leaving Emma to grow old and gray and die in a lonely, solitary bed?

Emma had been shocked when Cesare had told her in London that he hadn't slept with another woman since their first night together. But as amazing as that was, she knew it wouldn't last. It couldn't. Cesare wasn't the kind of man to tolerate an empty bed for the rest of his life. There were too many women in the world who would eagerly join him, married or no.

Cesare didn't equate sex with love the way she did, either. To Cesare, satisfying a sexual need was no different than satiating a hunger for food or sleep. It was just physical. Not emotional.

Lovers are a dime a dozen to me.

Emma swallowed, crossing her arms over her body.

She could ask him outright if he planned to be unfaithful to her. But she was afraid, because if she asked, he would tell her the truth. And she didn't think her heart could take it.

No, it was easier to live in denial, in the pretty lie of marriage vows, and to try not to think about the ugly truth beneath....

"There you are, *cara*."

Whirling around to see Cesare in the doorway, she put a finger to her lips. "Shh. Sam is finally asleep," she whispered, barely loud enough to hear. "I just got him down."

His handsome face looked relieved. *"Grazie a dio."* He silently backed away, and she followed him out of the room. She closed the door behind them, and they both exhaled.

"What made him sleep? Was it your walk?"

"No," she said softly. "I think it was coming home."

For a long moment, they looked at each other.

"I'm glad you are thinking of it as home, *cara*." He smiled. "And starting tomorrow, we will be husband and wife."

A lump rose in her throat. She tried to stay silent, but her fear came out in blurted words. "Are you still sure it's what you want?"

The smile slid from his face. "Why wouldn't I be?"

"A lifetime without love—without…" She gulped, then forced herself to meet his gaze. "Without sex…"

"The decision has already been made." His voice had turned cold. "I've made you dinner. Come."

She was very hungry after her walk, but she hesitated, glancing behind her. "I can't just leave Sam up here. Not until the baby monitor arrives. This house is so big and the old walls are thick. Downstairs in the dining room, we'd never hear him if he cried…."

"I thought you might feel that way." Cesare tilted his head, looking suddenly pleased with himself. "We're not going far."

Placing his hand in the small of her back, he pushed her gently down the hall. A sizzle of electricity went up her body at even that courteous, commanding touch. Biting her lip, she allowed him to lead her…

…a mere ten steps, to his own bedroom next door.

"We're having dinner in your room?" she said, a little sheepish that he'd guessed her feelings about the baby so well.

He nodded. "A private dinner for two on my balcony."

"Lovely," she said. "Um…any particular reason?"

"I just thought before our guests arrive in the morning, it would be nice to have a quiet dinner. To talk."

"Oh." That sounded ominous. The last time they'd had a private dinner and a talk she'd walked out engaged, with her whole life changed forever. She was afraid what might come out of it this time. The questions she might ask. The answers he might give. All words that could never be unheard or forgotten.

She licked her lips and tried to smile as she repeated, "Lovely."

Cesare led her into his enormous en suite bedroom, with a fireplace and a huge bed that she tried not to look at as they walked past it. He led her out to the balcony, where she found a charming table for two, lit by candle-light, and two silver plates covered by lids. Beyond the table, the dark sweep of Lake Como trailed moonlight in a pattern of gold.

Emma looked at Cesare, noticing for the first time how he had carefully dressed in a crisp black shirt and pants. With his dark hair, black eyes and chiseled jawline, he looked devastatingly handsome. He was the man every woman wanted. While she… Well.

Emma touched her hair, which was tumbling over her shoulders, messy from Sam tugging on it, and from the wind of their walk. She looked down at her simple pink blouse and slim-fit jeans. "I'm not dressed for this." For all she knew, she might have baby spit-up on her shoul-der. She tried to look, but she couldn't see. "Um. I should go change…"

"Go back to your bedroom and risk waking up our son? Don't you dare. Besides." He looked over her body with a heavily lidded gaze. "You are perfect just as you are." He held out her chair with a sensual smile. *"Signorina, per favore."*

Nervously Emma sat down. He sat down across from her, poured them each a glass of wine, then lifted off the silver lids of the plates. She took a deep breath of fettuccine primavera, with breaded chicken, salad and fresh bread. Placing the linen napkin in her lap, she picked up her heavy fork, also made of solid silver. "This looks delicious."

"It is an old family recipe."

"You cooked it yourself?"

"Not the bread, but the pasta, yes. I had to do something to be useful while you were fighting the war to put Sam to sleep." He paused. "I had Maria pick up the vegetables from town, but I made the sauce as well."

"I had no idea you knew how to cook."

He gave a low laugh. "When I was a boy, I helped with everything. Milked our cow. Made cheese and grew vegetables in the garden."

"Your life is very different now." She sipped red wine. She wasn't going to ask him if he planned to be faithful after their marriage. She *wasn't*. Placing a trembling hand over her throat to keep the question from popping out, she asked in a strained tone, "So why have you let the garden grow so wild and unloved? I could cut back the weeds, and bring it back to its former glory...."

His hand tightened on his wineglass, even as he said politely, "It's not necessary."

"I wouldn't mind. After all, it's my home, too, now...."

The candlelight flickered in the soft, invisible breeze. "No."

His short, cold word echoed across the table. As their eyes locked, Emma's heart cried out. For all the things they both weren't saying.

Was this to be their marriage? Courtesy, without connection? Proximity without words?

Would this beautiful villa become, like the Kensington mansion had been, her empty, lonely tomb?

Taking another gulp of wine, she blinked fast, looking out at the dark, quiet night. Lights of distant villas sparkled like stars across the lake. She heard the cry of unseen night birds, and the soft sigh of wind rattling the trees.

"How did you first meet her?" she asked softly. "Your wife?"

"Why do you want to know?" He sounded guarded.

"I'm going to be your wife tomorrow. Is it so strange that I'd want to hear the story of the first Mrs. Falconeri? Unless—" she bit her lip and faltered "—you still can't bear to speak of her..."

For a moment, she thought he wasn't going to answer. Then he exhaled. "I was twenty-three." He paused. "I'd inherited my uncle's hotel. Not the hotel you worked at on Park Avenue, but an old, rickety fleabag on Mulberry Street. I struggled to keep it afloat, working each day until I dropped, doing everything from carrying luggage to bookkeeping to making breakfast." He paused. "Angélique stumbled into the lobby one evening, taking cover from a rainstorm."

He fell silent. He cut a piece of chicken, took a bite. Set his fork and knife down. Emma leaned forward over the table, on edge for what he would say next, barely aware of the cool night breeze against her overheated skin.

Cesare looked out at the dark, moonswept lake, haunted with October mist. "For me," he said softly, "it was love at first sight."

Emma's heart lurched in her chest.

"She was so glamorous, ten years older, sexually experienced and—well, French…"

Everything she was not. Emma felt the pain twist more deeply beneath her ribs.

"We were married just six weeks after we met."

"That's fast," Emma mumbled. He'd known her for almost eight *years.*

"I was dazzled by her. It seemed like a miracle that she wanted to marry me. After we wed, I was more determined than ever to make the hotel a success. No one would ever accuse me of living off my wife."

"No," she whispered over the lump in her throat. She took another gulp of wine, finishing off her glass.

"She was unique," Cesare said in a low voice. "My first."

He couldn't mean what she thought he meant. "Your—first?"

"Yes," he said quietly.

"But—you were *twenty-three*."

"Amusing, yes?" His lips curved. "The famous playboy, a virgin at twenty-three. My uncle was strict, and after he died, I was too focused on the hotel. I had no money, nothing to offer any potential wife."

It was a good thing she hadn't been drinking wine or she would have spit it out in shock. "You were trying to save yourself—for marriage?"

"I was idealistic," he said quietly. "I thought love was supposed to be part of it." He glanced behind him at the villa, then at the dark water, scattered with gold and silver moonlight like diamonds on citrine. "Then it all died."

Yes. She'd died. His one and only love.

"You still love her, don't you?" Emma choked out. "And you always will."

Cesare's dark eyes abruptly focused on her. He put his hands over hers and said softly, "It doesn't matter."

She felt the warmth of his hands over hers, beneath the dizzying stars in the wide black-and-violet sky. Her heart beat frantically in her chest. She wanted to throw herself at his feet. To beg him to be faithful. To beg him to forget his long-dead wife and love her, instead.

"Of course it matters," she said hoarsely. "My father used to say love is all that matters. It's the only thing we leave behind."

His expression hardened. "We both love Sam."

"But is that truly enough for you to be happy?"

"Marriage isn't about happiness," he said. "It's about keeping a promise. Until death do us part. And the truth is, you and I are already bound together. By our child."

Bound, Emma thought unhappily. Bound like a rope around his wrists. Like a shackle. Like a chain.

She rose unsteadily to her feet. "I can't do this."

"What?"

"Marry you." She shook her head tearfully. "I can't let this beautiful villa be turned into a tomb, like your house was for me in Kensington, with nothing but silence and shadows to fill my bed.... I can't spend the rest of my life alone. Trapped with a man who doesn't even want me."

"You think I don't want you?" His voice was dangerous.

"You say that I am special," she said bitterly. "Your partner. Your *friend.* But we both know, once we are wed, you'll take lovers. But I won't. Because—I..." *I love you,* she almost said, but her throat closed when she saw Cesare's face.

"Not *want* you. My God." There was fury in his black eyes as he stood in the moonlight. "I told you I haven't touched another woman in over a year, and you think I don't want you?"

Her mouth suddenly went dry. "You—"

"You have no idea how hard it's been not to touch you." Reaching out, he slowly stroked down her neck, then leaned forward and whispered, "I've yearned to have you in my bed. Every night. I've thought of nothing else— but you."

Sparks flew up and down her body everywhere he touched.

"But I was trying to do the right thing for once in my damned life," he ground out. "In sickness and in health. For richer or for poorer. I was trying to do the right thing for our son. But the truth is all I've been able to think about, every single night, is having you naked beneath me."

Emma couldn't breathe.

Cesare's gaze dropped to her lips. "And this is my reward for my sacrifice. You mean nothing more to me now than the housekeeper you were. You think—"

His voice ended with a growl as he ripped her into his

arms. Holding her against his chest in the moonlight, he lowered his head, then stopped, his mouth an inch from hers.

Emma trembled at the warmth of his breath. She could almost taste his lips. Electricity seared through her veins.

"Please," she whispered, hardly knowing what she was asking for. She licked her lips, felt her tongue almost brush against his skin. She shuddered with blinding need, from her body to her heart. *He doesn't love me. His heart is buried with his wife.* "Lust," she breathed aloud, staring at his lips. "It's just lust."

She heard his harsh intake of breath. In sudden movement, he pushed her against the wall, and lowered his mouth to hers in a savage, hungry kiss.

Sparks sizzled down her skin as she felt his body, hard against hers. His hand roamed down her neck, ruthlessly reaching beneath the neckline of her blouse, to cup her breast beneath her bra. She gasped as she felt his hand brush her aching nipple. As her lips parted in the gasp, he deepened the kiss, twining and flicking his tongue against hers. He took her mouth roughly, in a way that left no doubt who was master.

A soft moan came unbidden from deep inside her. Her arms rose of their own accord to wrap around his shoulders. His tall, muscular body pressed against hers, hip to hip, and she felt lost in his passionate embrace. She clutched his back, feeling the steel of his muscles beneath his shirt. His hips swayed, grinding against her.

Cesare kissed her, his tongue twisting hot and hard in her mouth, tangling, giving and taking. And Emma knew that whatever her brain told her she should want, that in her body and heart she'd wanted this, only this, for the past year. For years before that.

The truth was that she'd waited for it all her life.

But this wasn't just lust for her. No matter how she'd tried to convince him otherwise. The truth was trembling inside her. *I love you. I never stopped loving you.*

Her hands reached up, tangling in his short black hair. She pulled him closer, clutching his shoulders, lifting on her tiptoes to kiss him with all the anguished love in her heart. He gripped her hard against the rough stone wall.

They kissed on the balcony, with the moonswept lake at their feet, and if a cool October wind blew against Emma's overheated skin, she no longer felt it. Cesare's hands moved over her body, sliding down her thin blouse, up her arms. Her breasts were crushed against his hard chest, and every inch of her was on fire.

His kiss possessed her with an intensity and force she'd never felt before. It was as if she alone could save him from destruction, as if he were taking her very breath to live.

When he drew back, he looked down at her, his eyes wide. Tilting back her head, he gently ran his thumbs over her full, swollen lips.

"Tell me to stop," he said with a shuddering breath. "For God's sake. Tell me now…"

But she couldn't. She could no more tell him to stop than she could tell herself to stop breathing, or the stars to stop shining. She loved him, and for one more night, the pathetic truth was that she was willing to do anything, pay any price.

With a low groan, he lifted her up into his arms as if she weighed nothing at all and carried her through the balcony door into his bedroom. He set her down gently on the enormous bed.

Still dressed, he covered her body with his own, pressing her back against the softness of the white pillows and thick white comforter as he kissed her. She felt the roughness of his chin against her skin, felt the heat and strength of his body. His hands trailed down her throat, to the hollow of her collarbone, then along the sides of her body, over her blouse. Her breasts felt full and heavy, her nipples tight.

She felt him unbuttoning her blouse. Never breaking their kiss, he slowly pulled it off her body, in a whisper of fabric skimming against her skin. Her hands trembled as she did the same with his black shirt, overwhelmed with desire to feel his heat. Her fingertips ran down the muscles of his back, and she tossed his shirt to the floor.

Looking up at him in the moonlight, she saw the stark shadows beneath the lines of his hard chest, the trail of dark hair down his taut belly. Her fingers traced down his velvety-smooth skin, over the powerful muscles of his body.

With a low growl, he kissed and stroked down her skin, nibbling her chin, down her neck to the valley between her breasts. Undoing the front clasp of the bra with a well-practiced movement, he cupped her full breasts with his large hands. She shivered at the sensation, but he continued down her body, flicking his tongue in her belly button, grasping her hips. Unbuttoning her jeans, he slowly pulled them down her legs, along with her panties, before tossing them to the floor.

She felt his shoulders between her bare legs, the heat of his breath on the sensitive, tender skin between her thighs. She gripped his shoulders in agonizing anticipation, then felt his tongue slide between her legs to her deepest, most secret place. He brushed his tongue against her, pushing two fingertips inside her—slowly, so slowly—until her body was so tight that she gripped his shoulders, holding her breath.

"Wait…" she gasped.

He refused to obey. He ruthlessly pushed her to the limit, and beyond, until with a soft scream she exploded beneath the unrelenting pleasure of his tongue between her legs. The moment she cried out, gripping her fingernails into his flesh, he ripped off the rest of his clothes. He shoved himself roughly inside her, ramming to the hilt in a single deep thrust.

The sensation of him filling her, just seconds after her ecstasy, caused a shocking new wave of pleasure to build inside her. He thrust again, and she gasped with the sensation of a new wave of desire, taking off from the level it had been a moment before, climbing higher and higher, tighter and tighter. She began to rock back and forth, trembling with almost unbearable pleasure.

He rode her harder, faster, panting for breath, as their sweaty bodies clung together in the dark, hot night. A cool breeze whipped in from the Italian lake, banging back the balcony doors. But neither of them noticed as he was deep, pounding inside her, splitting her apart. She gasped, clutching his taut backside, feeling his muscles grow hard as stone beneath her hands. With a shuddering intake of breath, he slammed inside her one last time, and they both let go, flying, falling, collapsing into thin air.

Cesare landed on top of her, then, as if he feared he would hurt her with his weight, immediately rolled on one side of her. He pulled her against him on the bed, nuzzling her forehead, both of them so close, so close. Both of them the same.

Emma closed her eyes. She suddenly felt like weeping.

A moment before, all she'd wanted was this, only this. But now, she'd barely had what she wanted and already wanted more. Not just sex. She was greedy beyond all imagining. She wanted his love.

In this moment of glory, heartache filled her. She pulled away from him, moving into the shadows of the bed.

"What is it, *cara?*" he asked in a low voice, as his hand

gently stroked her bare back. She knew she shouldn't answer. She should just leave it.

But the words came out of her throat against her will.

"Will you be faithful to me?" she whispered. "Can you be?"

For a moment, he didn't answer. She couldn't see his face. And she knew she'd made a horrible mistake. She turned to face him on the bed.

"Is fidelity so important to you?" he said in a low voice.

The lump in her throat suddenly felt like a razorblade.

"No," she whispered. Really, what use was fidelity without love? What was it but cold pretense, the form of love without the heart of it?

"Tomorrow we wed." Sleepily he pulled her into his arms and kissed her forehead. "So many nights I dreamed of you, *cara,* did you know that? And now you are in my bed. Our wedding night before we are wed…"

"Yes." She ran her fingertips along the warmth of his bare chest. She would marry him tomorrow. She'd given her word. She would raise his child and sleep in his bed, and be at his command for the rest of her life. And Cesare, the onetime playboy who notoriously enjoyed such a variety of women, would do his best to accomplish his obligation of fidelity—at least for a month, or possibly a year…

Holding her in his arms, he closed his eyes. A few moments later, his breathing became even and deep.

But Emma didn't have the same peace.

She leaned against his naked body, so warm and powerful and protective around her own. She looked through the open balcony door, past the moonlight to the distant bright star, the first star of morning. In a few hours, the dark violet sky would change to red, then pink, then a glorious Italian blue as the sun would rise on her wedding day.

The first and only wedding day she'd ever know. She'd be married to the man she loved. The father of her baby.

Cesare would marry her. For Sam's sake.

But what happiness could they know, in a marriage where only one partner loved, and was faithful?

The truth was that, wedding or not, Emma was no better than any of the other women Cesare might take to his bed.

His real wife was, and always would be, Angélique.

Loving him destroyed her, Emma. Don't let it destroy you.

Emma shuddered this time as she remembered Alain's words. He knew how wildly his sister had loved Cesare. What he hadn't known was the fierce love Cesare had for her in return. Angélique hadn't been destroyed by loving him.

But Emma would be.

She looked at Cesare's handsome sleeping face in the shadowy bedroom. She listened to the sound of his breath. Could she really marry him? Knowing she'd be nothing more than the mother of his child, the keeper of his home, or at best—a warm body in the night?

Could Emma accept an eternity of knowing she was the other woman—that if given the choice, her husband would have traded her life in an instant for Angélique's?

You're stronger than you know, kiddo. She heard her father's words. *You'll get through this, and have a life more amazing than you can even imagine. Filled with sunshine and flowers and above all, love. All the things you deserve, Emma. I love you, sweetheart.*

Blinking fast, Emma stared out at the dark lake. The last streak of silvery moonlight stretched out before her like a path, like a single forlorn tear, leading to an unseen future.

* * *

Cesare held her hand tightly, unable to look away from her beautiful face.

Emma was wearing a beautiful wedding dress, holding a bouquet of pink roses. But somehow, as they left the chapel, her fingers slipped from his grasp. She ran ahead of him. He called her name, and she glanced back, laughing as she disappeared in the mist. He saw her plummet down the chapel steps, down, down, down, her bouquet exploding into a million pale pink petals falling thickly like snow.

His feet were heavy as concrete as he tried to reach her. It seemed an eternity before he found her, on a soft bed of grass. But something had changed. Emma's beautiful face had turned hollow-cheeked like his mother's, her eyes blank with despair like Angélique's. Emma was dying, and he knew it was his fault. Desperate, he jumped on a boat and took off across the lake to find a doctor. But halfway across, the boat's engine died, leaving him stranded and alone, surrounded by dark water, and he suddenly knew he was too late to save her. He looked down at water like black glass in the moonlight. There was only one thing to do now...only one way to end the pain...

With a shuddering gasp, Cesare sat up straight in bed.

Still panting for breath, he looked out the window. The sky was blue. The sun was shining. He heard birds singing. It was a dream, he told himself. All a dream. But his body was covered with cold sweat.

Today was his wedding day.

He looked down at the bed where he'd made love to her last night. Empty. He put out his hand. The sheets were long cold.

Cesare suddenly wondered if he might have woken her with his nightmare, tossing and turning or worse, crying out. He clawed back his hair, exhaling with a flare of nostril. The thought of being so vulnerable was horrifying.

But not as much as what he was about to do today.

Naked, he got up from the bed, and his legs seemed to shake beneath him. Downstairs, he could already hear guests arriving. Some twenty people, friends and acquaintances from London, Rome and around the world, would be staying at the villa for the next three days. Today, there would be a long prewedding lunch, followed by a ceremonial church wedding at twilight in the small, ancient chapel on his estate. Tomorrow they'd have the civil service in town.

The next three days would be nothing but one party after another, and the thought suddenly made him grit his teeth. He'd chosen this. Shouldn't he feel satisfaction, or failing that, at least some kind of resigned peace?

Instead his body shook with a single primal emotion—fear.

I can do it for Sam.

Closing his eyes, he pictured his sweet baby's face. Then the woman holding his son in her arms.

Emma. Her beauty. Her kindness. She was the perfect mother to Sam. The perfect homemaker. The perfect lover. He thought of the ecstasy he'd experienced last night in her arms. But reflecting on all the ways he valued Emma didn't calm the frantic beat of his heart. To the contrary. It just made him feel more panicked.

He'd sworn he'd never have a child. Then he'd found out about Sam.

He'd sworn he'd never marry again. Then he'd proposed to Emma.

He'd sworn their marriage would be in name only. Then he'd swept her straight into bed last night.

What was next? What fresh vow would he break?

There was only one left, and it was a line that he could not, would not cross. Because if he did, if he ever let himself love her, he'd be utterly annihilated. Just like before...

With an intake of breath, he paced across the bedroom, the same grand room which, decades before, had belonged to his parents. So in love, before everything came crashing down.

Whether by death, or divorce, love always ended. And ended in pain.

Cesare couldn't let himself love Emma. It would be the final bomb exploding his life into pieces. Any time he tried to love someone, to depend on them, they left—as far and fast as they possibly could. Through death.

He couldn't survive it again.

His heart pounded frantically. He looked out the window, past the overgrown garden, toward the lake. He should never have brought Emma here. Never should have let himself see the bright laughter in her eyes as she held their baby yesterday, carrying him through that garden. *This is a lemon tree, and this is verbena...*

Just as his own mother had once done. He could still remember his mother's warm embrace, back when he was very young and happy and thought the sunshine would last forever. He could hear his father's deep, tender voice. *Ti amo, tesoro mio.*

Cesare shuddered, blinking fast. He'd thought if he was careful not to love anyone, never to care, that he would be safe. Instead he'd accidentally created a child.

Or had it been an accident? Some part of him must have been willing to take that risk—since he'd never slept with any woman without protection before. Not even Angélique. But then, she'd been too selfish to want a child. All she'd wanted was a man to worship her, and when Cesare had gotten too busy with work, she'd found another man to offer her the worship she desperately craved.

Emma was nothing like Angélique. If the Frenchwoman had been cold and mysterious as moonlight, Emma was sunlight on a summer's day. Warmth. Life.

But he couldn't let himself love her. She could leave him. She could die. Her cancer could return, and leave Cesare, like his father, bereft at midnight on an endless black lake.

Looking out at Lake Como, he had the sudden impulse to throw on his clothes and run away from this house. From this wedding. Far, far away, where grief and pain and need could never find him again.

Stop it. Cesare took a deep breath, clenching his hands at his sides. *Get ahold of yourself.* He couldn't fall to pieces. He had to marry her. He'd promised. His child deserved a real home, like he'd once had. Before his parents had abruptly left, stripping his happiness away without warning…

Closing his eyes, he took a deep breath. He ruthlessly forced down his feelings. Shut down his heart.

Jaw tight, he opened his eyes. He would marry Emma today. Whatever he felt now, he'd given his word. He would marry her and never, ever love her.

And no irrational nightmare, no mere *terror,* would stop him from fulfilling his promise.

CHAPTER TEN

"OH, EMMA," IRENE whispered. Her eyes sparkled with tears. "You make such a beautiful bride."

Looking at herself in the gilded full-length mirror, Emma hardly recognized herself. The sensible housekeeper had been magically transformed into a princess bride from a nineteenth-century portrait. Her beautiful cream-colored silk dress had been handmade in Milan, with long sleeves and elaborate beadwork. Her black hair was pulled up in a chignon, tucked beneath a long veil that stretched all the way to the floor.

The green eyes looking back at her in the mirror were the only thing that seemed out of place. They weren't tranquil. They were tortured.

Just last night, passion had curled her toes and made her cry out with pleasure. That morning, she'd risen from the warmth of their bed early to feed Sam. She had drowsed off while rocking the baby back to sleep, and when she returned later, Cesare was gone.

But something had changed in him. All day, as they welcomed their newly arriving guests—who, with the exception of Irene, were all Cesare's friends, not hers—he'd barely looked at her. She'd told herself he was just busy, trying to be a good host. But the truth was that in the tiny corner of her heart, she feared it was more than that. No. She *knew* it was more than that.

This marriage was a mistake.

Emma looked at herself again in the mirror, at the beautiful wedding gown. She smoothed the creamy silk beneath her hands. *The decision is already made,* she told herself, but her hands were trembling.

Since she'd left his bed that morning, the day had flown by, in a succession of celebrations leading up to tonight's first wedding ceremony, at twilight in the chapel. Emma had been genuinely thrilled to see Irene, who'd been flown in from Paris courtesy of Cesare. But as she'd shown the younger woman around her new home, Irene's idealistic joy had soon become grating.

"It's all like a dream," she'd breathed, seeing her beautifully appointed guest room, with its Louis XV furniture and accents of deep rose and pale pink. She'd whirled to face Emma, her rosy face shining. "You deserve this. You worked so hard, you put your baby first, and now you've been rewarded with a wedding to a man who loves you with all his heart. It's just like a fairy tale."

Feeling like a fraud, Emma had muttered some reply, she couldn't even remember what. Later, as she was congratulated by his friends, even a sheikh of some sort with long white robes who, in perfect British English, wished her well, the feeling only worsened.

Out of everyone at the villa, only one person didn't speak to her. He didn't even look at her. Not since he'd made love to her last night.

How could he turn so fast from passion to coldness?

The answer was clear.

Cesare didn't want to marry her.

It was only his promise that was forcing him to do it. Emma's gaze fell on baby Sam, who was currently lying on her soft bed, proudly chewing the tip of his own sock, which was stretched out from his foot.

"Here's your bouquet," Irene said now, smiling as she wiped her own happy tears away. She handed her a small, simple bouquet of small red roses. "Perfect. This is all so romantic...."

Emma looked down at the flowers, feeling cold. How could she destroy Irene's dreams, and tell her that *romantic* was the last thing this wedding would be? She exhaled.

"I just wish my father were here," Emma whispered. With his steady hand and good advice, he'd know just what to do.

Irene's face instantly sobered. "It must be so hard not to have him here, to walk you down the aisle. But he's with you in spirit. I know he is. Looking down on you today and smiling."

Emma swallowed. That thought made it even worse. Because today, marrying Cesare, she was doing something her heart told her was wrong. Doing something that her heart told her could only ultimately end in disaster, no matter how good their intentions might be for their son.

It's too late to back out, she told herself. *There's nothing I can do now.*

Irene looked at the watch on her slender wrist.

"It's time," she said cheerfully. She picked up Sam, who was wearing a baby tuxedo in his strictly honorary capacity of ring bearer. "We'll be sitting in the front row. Cheering for you both. And probably crying buckets." She waved a linen handkerchief. "But I came prepared!" She tucked it in her chiffon sash. "See you in the chapel."

"Wait." Emma swallowed, feeling suddenly panicky. She held out her arms. "I need Sam with me."

Irene looked bemused. "You want to walk up the aisle holding a baby?"

"Yes. Because—" she grasped at straws "—we're a family."

"But your hands are full…."

Emma instantly dropped the bouquet on the floor in a splash of petals, and stretched out her hands desperately. She needed to feel her baby in her arms. She needed to remind herself what she was doing this for—marrying a man who was forever in love with his dead wife. His *real* wife. She needed to feel that she was sacrificing her life for a good reason. "Give him to me."

"Aw, your poor flowers," Irene sighed, looking at the bouquet on the floor. Then, looking up, she slowly nodded. "But maybe you're right. Maybe this is better. Here you go."

Emma took Sam in her arms. She felt the warmth of his small body and inhaled his sweet baby smell, and nearly cried.

Turning away, Irene paused at the door of Emma's bedroom. "The three of you are already a family," she said softly, "but today makes it official. Thanks for inviting me. Seeing what's possible…it makes me more happy than you'll ever know."

And her young friend left, leaving Emma holding her baby against her beaded silk dress, her throat aching as she fought back tears that had nothing to do with joy.

"All right, Sam. I guess we can't be late." She looked out the window, at the vast sky above the lake, already turning red in the twilight. "I only wish I had a sign," she murmured over the lump in her throat. "I wish I knew whether I'm making the right choice—or ruining all our lives."

Sam, of course, didn't answer, at least not in words she could understand. Holding her baby close, she walked out of her bedroom as an unmarried woman for the last time.

When next she returned, she would be the mistress of this villa. From now on, her place would be in Cesare's bed.

Until he grew tired of her. And started sleeping elsewhere. She pushed the thought aside.

Emma's white satin shoes trembled as she walked down the sweeping stairs. The villa was strangely silent. Everyone had gone to the chapel, even the household staff. She heard the echoing footsteps of her shoes against the marble floor before she pushed open the enormous oak door and went outside.

Holding her baby close, she walked down the path carved into the hillside, along the edge of the lake. "This marriage is for you, Sam," she whispered. "I can live without your father loving me. I can live without him being faithful to me. For you, I can live the rest of my life with a numb, lonely heart...."

Emma stopped in front of the medieval chapel, which was lit by torchlight on the edge of the lake. Such a romantic setting. And every drop of romance a lie.

Trembling, she walked toward it, nestling her baby against her hip as the veil trailed behind them.

The twelfth-century chapel had been carefully and lovingly restored to its Romanesque glory. The medieval walls were thick, with just a few tiny windows. The arched door was open.

Heart pounding, she stepped inside.

The dark chapel was illuminated by candlelight, its tall brass candlesticks placed along the aisle. She heard the soft music of a lute, accompanied by guitar. As she appeared in the doorway, there was an audible gasp as the people packed into the tiny chairs rose to their feet.

Emma's legs felt like jelly. She felt a tug on her translucent silk veil and saw Sam had grabbed it in his pudgy fist, and was now attempting to chew it. She smiled through her tears, then took a deep breath as the music changed to the traditional wedding march.

Looking at all the faces of the guests, she didn't recognize any of them as she slowly walked forward, feeling more dizzy with every step. She tried to focus on Cesare at the end of the aisle. She took another step, then another. She was six steps from the altar.

And then she saw his face.

Cesare looked green, sick with fear—as if only sheer will kept him from rushing straight past her in a panic. He tried to give her a smile.

Her footsteps stopped.

"Stop! Don't do it! Don't ruin your life!"

The man's voice was a low roar, as if from the deepest reaches of the earth, coming up through the stone floor. For an instant, Emma couldn't breathe. Her father's voice from beyond the grave…? Then she saw Cesare glare at someone behind her.

Whirling around, she saw Alain.

The slim salt-and-pepper-haired Frenchman took another step into the chapel. "Don't do this," he pleaded. "Falconeri has already caused the death of one woman I loved. I won't let him take another."

There was a gasp and growl across the crowd. Cesare gave a low hiss of fury. He was going to come down and smash Alain's face for doing this, she realized.

For stopping a wedding that Emma never should have agreed to in the first place.

"Don't marry him." Alain held out a trembling hand to her. "Come with me now."

She'd wanted a sign?

With tortured eyes, she turned back to Cesare.

"I can't do this," she choked out. "I'm sorry."

Cradling her baby, she picked up the hem of her cream-colored silk gown with one hand, and followed Alain out of the chapel. She ran from Cesare as if the happiness of her whole life—and not just hers, but Sam's and Cesare's—depended on it.

Which she finally knew—*it did.*

As a thirteen-year-old, coming home in a strange big city, Cesare had once been mugged for the five dollars in his pocket. He'd been kicked in the gut with steel-toed boots.

This felt worse.

As if in a dream, Cesare had watched Emma walk up the aisle of the chapel, a bride more beautiful than he'd ever imagined, with their child in her arms. Then, like a sudden deadly storm, Alain Bouchard had appeared like an avenging angel. Emma had looked between the two men.

Cesare had been confident in her loyalty. He'd known she would spurn Bouchard, and marry him as she'd promised.

Instead she'd turned on him.

She'd *abandoned* him.

For a moment, as the chapel door banged closed behind her, Cesare couldn't breathe. The pain was so intense he staggered from it.

The chapel was suddenly so quiet that he could hear the soft wind blow across the lake. The deepening shadows of the candlelit chapel seemed relentlessly dark as endless eyes focused on him, in varying degrees of shock, sympathy and worst of all—pity.

The priest, who'd met with them several times over the past weeks, spoke to him in Italian, in a low, shocked voice. He could barely hear.

Cesare's tuxedo tie was suddenly too tight around his throat. He couldn't let himself show his feelings. He couldn't even let himself *feel* them.

Emma had left him.

At the altar.

With Bouchard.

And taken their child with her.

He looked at the faces of his friends and business acquaintances, including the white-robed, hard-eyed sheikh of Makhtar in the back row, who alone had no expression of sympathy on his face. Cesare parted his lips to speak, but his throat was too tight. After all, what was there to say?

Emma had betrayed him.

Ripping off his black tie, he tossed it on the stone floor and strode grimly out of the chapel in pursuit of her.

So much for mercy. So much for the high road.

He never should have listened to old Morty Ainsley. Cesare's throat was burning, and so were his eyes. He should have sued Emma for full custody from the moment he learned of Sam's existence. He should have gotten his revenge. Gotten his war.

Instead he'd offered her everything. His throat hurt. His name. His fortune. His fidelity. Hadn't he made it clear that if she wished it, he would remain true to her? Hadn't he proven it with more than words—with his absolute faithfulness over the past year? How much more clear could he be?

And Emma had spurned all of it. In the most humiliating way possible. He'd never thought she could be so cruel. Making love to him last night—today, leaving him for another man.

He pushed through a grove of lemon trees. He would make her pay. He would make her regret. He would make her…

His heart was breaking.

He loved her.

The realization struck him like a blow, and he stopped. He loved her? He'd tried not to. Told himself he wouldn't. But all this time, he'd been lying to himself. To both of them. He'd been in love with her for a long time, possibly as long as she'd loved him.

He'd certainly been in love with her the night they'd conceived Sam. It wouldn't have made sense for him to have taken such a risk otherwise.

His body had already known what his brain and heart refused to see: he loved her. For reasons that had nothing to do with her housekeeping skills, or even now her skills as a mother, or her skills in bed. He didn't love her for any skills at all, but for the woman she was inside: loving, warm, with a heart of sunlight and fire.

And now, all that light and fire had abruptly been ripped out of his life, the moment he'd started to count on her. He wasn't even surprised. He'd known this would happen. Known the moment he let himself love again, she would disappear.

He had only himself to blame....

"Thank God you saw sense." Hearing the low rasp of Alain Bouchard's voice, Cesare ducked behind a thicket of orange trees. Peering through the branches, he saw two figures standing on the shore, frosted silver by moonlight. "Here." Bouchard's accented voice was exultant. "Get in my boat. You've made the right choice. I won't let him hurt you now."

Clenching his fists, Cesare took a step toward them. Then he saw Emma wasn't making a move to get in the boat. She had turned away, and was trying to calm the baby, who had started to whimper in her arms. Her long white veil trailed her like a ghost in moonlight.

"He didn't hurt your sister, Alain," she said in a low voice. "He would never hurt her. He loved her. In fact, he's still in love with her. That's why I...why I couldn't go through with it."

Cesare stopped, his eyes wide, and a branch broke loudly beneath his feet. Bouchard twisted his head blindly, then turned back to Emma. "Hurry. He might come at any moment."

"I'm not getting in the boat."

The Frenchman laughed. "Of course you are."

"No." Emma didn't move. "You have to accept it. Cesare is always brutally honest, even when it causes pain. Her death was a tragic accident. He's never gotten over it. Cesare is a good man. Honorable to his core."

Bouchard took a step closer to her on the moonlit shore.

"If you really believe that," he said, "what are you doing out here?"

Cesare strained to hear, not daring to breathe. He saw Emma tilt up her head.

"I love him. That's why I couldn't marry him."

Cesare stifled a gasp. She loved him?

Bouchard stared at her, then shook his head. "That doesn't make any sense, *chérie.*"

She gave a low laugh. "It actually does." She wiped her eyes. "He'll never love anyone but Angélique. Heaven help me, I might have married him anyway, except...except I saw his face in the chapel," she whispered. "And I couldn't do it."

Cesare took a deep breath and stepped out of the thicket of trees. Both figures looked back at him, startled.

"What did you see?" he asked quietly.

"Falconeri!" Bouchard stepped between them. "You might have fooled Emma, with her innocent heart. But we both know my sister's death was no accident."

"No."

"So you admit it!"

"It's time you knew the truth," Cesare said in a low voice. "I've kept it from you for too long."

"To hide your guilty conscience—"

"To protect you."

Bouchard snorted derisively. "*Protect* me."

"When she married me, she didn't want a partner. She wanted a lapdog." Cesare set his jaw. "When I threw myself into work, trying to be worthy of her, she hated the loss of attention. She hated it even more when I started to succeed. Once I no longer spent my days at her feet, worshipping her every moment, Angélique was restless. She cheated on me. Not just once, but many times. And I put up with it."

"What?" Emma gasped.

Bouchard shook his head with a snarl. "I don't believe you!"

"Her last lover was an Argentinean man she met while visiting Paris, who frequently traveled to New York on business. She decided Menendez was the answer to the emptiness in her heart."

Bouchard started. "Menendez? Raoul Menendez?"

"You know him?"

"I met him once, as he was having a late dinner in a hotel in Paris with my sister," he said uneasily. "She swore they were just old friends."

Cesare's lips curved. "Their affair lasted a year."

He frowned. "That's why she wanted a divorce?" For the first time, he sounded uncertain. "Not because you cheated on her?"

"I never could have done that," he said wearily. "I thought marriage meant forever. I thought we were in love." He turned to Emma and whispered, "Back then, I didn't know the difference between lust and love."

Emma caught her breath, her eyes luminous in the moonlight.

Bouchard stood between them, his thin face drawn. "She called me, the night before she died—sobbing that her only love had betrayed her, abandoning her like trash, that he'd been sleeping with someone else all the while. I thought she meant you. I never thought…"

Cesare shook his head. "She wore me down over that year, demanding a divorce so she could marry Menendez. She hated me, accusing me of being her jailor—of wanting our marriage to last longer just so I'd get more of her fortune. Do you know what it's like? To live with someone who despises you, who blames you for destroying her only happiness?"

"Yes," Emma whispered, and he remembered her stepmother. His heart twisted at the pain in her beautiful face. He wanted to take her in his arms and tell her she'd never feel that kind of grief again. Trembling, he took a step toward her.

"So you let her go," Bouchard said.

"I finally set her free so she could marry him," Cesare said. "She ran off to Argentina, only to discover Menendez already had a wife there. She came back to New York broken. I'm still not sure if she was trying to kill herself—or if she was just trying to make herself go to sleep to forget the heartbreak…."

Bouchard paced, then stopped, clawing back his hair. He looked at Cesare. "If this is true, why did you never tell me? Why did you let me go on believing you were at fault—that you were to blame?"

"Because you loved your sister," he said quietly. "I didn't want you to know the truth. That kind of blind love and faith is too rare in this world."

"I insulted you, practically accused you of…" He

stopped. "How could you not have thrown the truth in my face?"

Cesare shook his head. "I thought I loved her once. And I had my faults, too. Perhaps if I hadn't worked so much…"

"Are you kidding?" Emma demanded incredulously, juggling their baby against the hip of her wedding gown. He smiled.

"I'm telling you now because you both deserve to know the truth." He looked at Emma. "I didn't want anyone to know my weakness, or the real reason I never wanted to marry again. I thought love was just delusion, that led to pain." He paused. "Until I fell in love with you…"

Emma's lips parted in a soft gasp.

The Frenchman tilted his head, looking thoughtfully between them. "I think it's time for me to go." Stepping forward, he held out his hand. "*Merci,* Cesare. I have changed my mind about you. You are—not so bad. You must not be, for a woman like Emma to love you." Turning back, he kissed her softly on the cheek and gave her one final look. "*Adieu, ma chérie.* Be happy."

Climbing into his small boat, Alain Bouchard turned on the engine and drove back across the lake.

Cesare turned to face Emma. As he looked down at her beautiful stricken face, so haunted and young beneath the long white veil as she held his child, her eyes were green and shadowed as the forest around them. His heart was pounding.

"You left me at the altar," he said.

She swallowed. "Yes. I guess I did."

"You said you saw something in my face that drove you away," he said in a low voice. "What did you see?"

Moonlight caressed her beautiful face. She took a deep breath.

"Dread," she whispered. "I saw dread." Her voice caught.

"I couldn't marry a man with a face like that. No matter how much I was in love with you. I couldn't trap you into a loveless marriage for the rest of your life. And pretend not to notice as you—cheated on me, again and again."

"Cheated on you?" he demanded.

The baby started to whimper. Comforting him, she nodded miserably. "I assumed—"

"No." Going to her, he grabbed her shoulders and looked down at her. "Now you know the story, you have to know I would never betray you."

"I thought you still loved your wife," she whispered. "That I had no chance of holding your heart—"

"I was too proud to tell you the truth. I never wanted to appear vulnerable, or feel weak like that ever again. I did love her. I loved my parents, too. And all I learned was that when you love anyone—they leave."

"Oh, Cesare." Her eyes glimmered in the moonlight as she shook her head. "I'm so sorry…"

"I swore I'd never let anyone that close to me again." His lips lifted at the edges as he looked down at her. "Then I met you. And it was like coming home."

"You never said…"

"I told myself you meant nothing to me. That I'd only brought you from the hotel to be my housekeeper. But I think it was for you that I bought that house. Even then, some part of me wanted to settle down with you. With you, I lowered my guard as I never did with anyone else. And when I found you crying that night in the kitchen, it broke through me," he said hoarsely. "When I finally took you in my arms, I took everything I'd ever wanted and more…." He looked at Sam, then back at her fiercely. "Do you think it was an accident that I took such a risk? I've long since realized that my body and my heart must have known what my brain spent years trying to deny."

"What?" she whispered.

He looked down at her. "That you are for me. My true love. My only love."

She was crying openly now. "I never stopped loving you—"

He stopped her with a finger to her lips.

"I nearly died when I saw you leave with him," he said in a low voice. "It was like all my worst fears coming true."

"I'm sorry," she choked out. "When he broke into our wedding, I thought it was a sign, the only way to save us both from a life of misery—"

"Won't you shut up, even for a minute?" Since his finger wasn't working, he lowered his head and covered her mouth with his own. He felt her intake of breath, felt her surprise. He kissed her in the moonlight, embracing her with deep tenderness and adoration. Her lips were sweet and soft like heaven. When he finally pulled away, his voice was hoarse.

"All this time, I was afraid of loving anyone again. Because I didn't think I could handle the devastation of losing them. But I think I've always been in love with you, Emma." Reaching out, he cupped her face. "From the day we first met. And I told you that you looked smart. And that I was glad you came into my life."

A little squeak came out of her lips.

"Do you think I really came to Paris for some deal over a hotel? No." He searched her gaze. "I was looking for you. When I found out about the baby, I asked you to marry me. Then I slept with you. I did all the things I swore I'd never do. I kept breaking my own rules again and again. Over you."

"What are you saying?" she whispered.

He looked down at her in the moonlight, caressing her cheeks, running the pads of his thumbs over her pink full lips.

"Where you are concerned, from now on there is only one rule." He smiled, and her image seemed to shimmer as he said hoarsely, "I'm going to love you for the rest of my life."

"You—you really love me," she breathed.

He saw the incredulity in her eyes, the desperate hope. He thought of her years of devotion going far beyond that of any paid employee. Thought of how she'd always been by his side. How she'd always had the strength and dignity to stand up for what was right. Even today.

Especially today.

"You've shown me what love can be," he whispered. "Love isn't delusion, it isn't trying to avoid grief and pain, but holding your hand right through it, while you hold mine." He took her hand, cradling it in his own. "All this time," he said in a low voice, running his other hand along her pale translucent veil, "I was afraid of loving someone and losing them. I turned it into a self-fulfilling prophecy."

She swallowed, shifting Sam's weight against her shoulder. "It still could happen. I could get sick again. I could get hit by a bus."

"Or you could stop loving me. You could leave me for another man."

"Never," she cried, then suddenly blushed, looking down at her wedding gown. "Er, except for just now, I mean. And I didn't leave you for Alain, I never thought of him that way."

"I know."

"I couldn't marry a man who didn't love me. Because I've realized it's love that makes a family. Not promises."

Slowly Cesare lowered himself to one knee, as he should have done from the beginning. "Then let me love you for the rest of our lives. However long or short those lives might be." Taking her hands in his own, he fervently kissed each palm, then pressed them against his tuxedo jacket, over his chest. "Marry me, Emma. And whatever your answer might be, know that you hold my heart. For the rest of my life."

"As you hold mine," she said as tears ran down her face. Moving her hands, she cupped his face. And nodded.

"Yes?" he breathed, searching her gaze. "You'll marry me?"

"Yes," she said, smiling through her tears.

"Now," he demanded.

She snorted. "So bossy," she said with a laugh. "Some things never change." Her expression grew serious. "But some things do. I want to marry the man I love. The man who loves me." Her eyes grew suddenly shadowed as she shook her head. "And if anything ever happens to us…"

"We're all going to die someday." Cesare's eyes were suspiciously blurry as he looked down at her. Beneath her veil, several pins had fallen out of her chignon, causing her lustrous hair to tumble wildly down her shoulders. He pulled out the rest, tangling his fingers in her hair. "The only real question is if we're ever going to live. And from now on, my darling," he whispered as he lowered his lips to hers, "we are."

"Emma!"

"We're over here!" she called, but she knew Cesare wouldn't be able to see her in the villa's garden. It was August, and everything was in bloom, the fruit trees, the vegetables, even the corn. She tried to stand up, but being over eight months pregnant, it wasn't easy. She had to push herself up off the ground with her hands, and then bend around in a way that made Sam, now fifteen months old and digging in the dirt beside her with his little spade, giggle as he watched her flop around.

"Mama," he laughed, yanking a flower out of the ground.

"Fine, go ahead and laugh," she said affectionately, smiling down at him. "I did this for you, too, you know."

"Fow-a." With dark, serious eyes, he handed her the flower. Every day, he looked more like Cesare, she thought. But he'd also started to remind her of her own father, Sam's namesake. She saw that in the toddler's loving eyes, in his sweetly encouraging spirit.

"Emma!" Cesare called again, more desperately.

"Over here!" She waved her hands over the bushes, trying to make him see her. "By the orange grove!"

The garden had been transformed. Just like her life. The gold-digging supermodels of London would have been shocked and dismayed to learn that, as a billionaire's wife, Emma now spent most of her days right here, with a dirty child, growing fruits and vegetables for their kitchen and beautiful flowers to fill the vases of their home. Except, of course, when they had to fly down to the coast and go yachting along the Mediterranean, or take the private jet to see friends in London or New York. It was nice to do such things. But nicer still, she thought, to come back to their home.

The wedding had been even better than she'd imagined. After their breathless declaration and kiss by the lake, she and Cesare had gone back to the chapel arm in arm—only to discover their guests had already given up on them and started to mill back to the villa to gossip about them over some well-deserved limoncello. Even Irene looked as if she'd almost given up hope.

They'd called them all back to the chapel, and with some small, blushing explanation, the wedding had gone forward as planned. Right up to their first married kiss, which had been so passionate that it made all the guests burst into applause, and made Emma's toes curl as she'd thought she heard angels sing. The priest had been forced to clear his throat and gently remind them the honeymoon hadn't quite started yet.

She exhaled. They were a family now. They were happy. Cesare still had his international empire, but he'd cut back on travel a bit. Especially since they'd found out she was pregnant again.

"*Cara.*" Cesare came into the clearing of the garden and took her in his arms for a long, delicious kiss. Then he knelt by their son, who was still playing in the dirt, and tousled his dark hair. "And did you have a good day, *piccino?*"

Watching the two of them, father and son, tears rose in Emma's eyes. Slowly she looked over the beauty of the garden. The summer trees were thick and green, and she could see the roof of the Falconeri villa against the bright blue Italian sky. How happy her parents would be if they could see how her life had turned out. Cesare's parents, too. She could feel their love, every time she looked at Cesare. Every time she looked at their son.

And soon, their daughter would join them. Emma's hand ran over her huge belly. In just a few weeks, their precious daughter would be born. They had already picked her name: Elena Margaret, after her two grandmothers.

Emma felt the baby kick inside her, and smiled, putting both hands over her belly now. "You like that, do you?" she murmured, then turned her face back to the sun.

"What happened while I was gone today?" Cesare rose to his feet, a frown on his handsome face. "You are crying."

Smiling, she shook her head, even as she felt tears streak down her cheeks.

Reaching out, he rubbed them away. "What is it?" he said anxiously. "Not some problem with the baby? With you?"

"No." The pregnancy had been easy. She'd been healthy all the way through, in spite of Cesare's worry. All her checkups had put her in the clear. She was safely in remission, had been for over a decade, and all her life was ahead of her. "I can't explain. I'm just so—happy."

"I'm happy, too," he whispered, putting his arms around her. He gave a sudden wicked grin. "And I'll be even happier, after Sam is tucked in bed…"

She saw what he was thinking about, in the sly seduction of his smile, and smacked him playfully on the bottom. "I'm eight months pregnant!"

"You've never been more beautiful."

"Right," she said doubtfully.

"Cara." He cupped her face. "It's true."

He kissed her until she believed him, until she felt dazed, dazzled in this garden of flowers and joy. She knew they would live here for the rest of their lives. If they were lucky, they'd someday be surrounded by a half-dozen noisy children, all splashing in the lake, sliding up and down the marble hallways in their socks, screaming and laughing like banshees. She and Cesare would be the calm center of the storm. The heart of their home.

He pulled her against him, and they stood silently in the garden, watching their son play. She heard the wind through the leaves. She exhaled.

She'd gotten everything she'd ever wanted. A man who loved her, whom she loved in return. Marriage. A snug little villa. As she felt the warmth of the sun, and listened to the cheerful chatter of their son, she leaned into her husband's embrace and thought about all the love that had existed for the generations before them. Their parents. Their parents' parents. And the love that would now exist for generations to come.

We're all going to die someday, her husband had once said. Emma realized he was wrong.

As long as love continued, life continued. Love had made them what they were. It had created Emma, and created Cesare. It had created Sam, and soon, their daughter. Love was what lasted. Love triumphed over death.

And anyone who truly loved, and was loved in return, would always live on—in this endlessly beautiful world.

* * * * *

UNNOTICED AND
UNTOUCHED

LYNN RAYE HARRIS

To the men in my life—my husband, Mike, who has never met a sport he didn't like (and who patiently attempts to explain the rules to me every time), and to my dad and father-in-law, who both love motor sports. I still don't get that hockey thing, and I'll never understand what makes baseball on television so fascinating, or why anyone wants to watch cars go in circles for hours. But I do, finally, mostly understand American football. I think.

CHAPTER ONE

"MISS BLACK, you will accompany me this evening."

Faith's head snapped up. Her boss, Lorenzo D'Angeli, stood in the doorway to his office, looking every bit the arrogant Italian businessman in his custom suit and hand-made loafers. Her heart skipped a beat as she contemplated his gorgeous face—all hard angles and sharp planes, deeply bronzed skin, and eyes as sharp and clear blue as a Georgia spring sky. It wasn't the first time—and likely wouldn't be the last—but it irritated her that she reacted that way.

She knew all about men like him. Arrogant, entitled and selfish—she had only to look at the way he treated the women who paraded in and out of his life with ruthless regularity to know it was the truth, in spite of the fact he'd only ever been courteous to her.

"The dress is formal," he continued. "If you need clothing, take the afternoon off and charge your purchases to my account."

Faith's heart was skipping in earnest now. She'd often gone shopping for her boss in the six months she'd worked for him, purchasing silk ties or gold cuff links at his direction or picking up little gifts for whatever woman he was seeing at the time, but he'd never told her to shop for herself. It was, without question, unusual.

And perfectly impossible.

"I'm sorry, Mr. D'Angeli," she said as politely as she could, "but I don't believe I understand you."

His stance didn't soften an inch. "Miss Palmer is no longer going. I need a date."

Faith stiffened. Of course. But stepping in because he'd had a fight with yet another woman he was sleeping with was not part of her job description.

"Mr. D'Angeli," she began.

"Faith, I need you."

Four words. Four words that somehow managed to stop the breath in her chest and send a tremor over her. Oh, why did she let him get to her? Why did the mere thought of parading around town on his arm make her feel weak when he was the last person she would ever want to be with?

She forced herself to think logically. He wasn't saying he needed *her*. He needed the efficient PA at his side, ever ready to make calls or take notes or rearrange his schedule at a moment's notice.

He did not need the woman. Lorenzo D'Angeli needed no woman, she reminded herself.

"It's highly inappropriate, Mr. D'Angeli. I cannot go."

"Faith, you are the only woman I can count on," he said. "The only one who does not play games with me."

Her ears burned. For God's sake. Narcissus himself hadn't been that self-focused. "I don't play games because I'm your personal assistant, Mr. D'Angeli."

"Precisely why I need you with me tonight. I can trust you to behave."

Behave? She wanted to smack him. Instead, she gave him an even look, though her pulse was racing along like one of the superbikes that had made D'Angeli Motors famous. For as long as she lived, she'd never understand how she let this man get to her. He was darn pretty to look at, but he believed everything revolved around him.

Including her, it would seem.

"Shall I ring Miss Zachetti for you? Or Miss Price? I'm sure they're available. And if they are not, they certainly will be when they realize who's calling."

They'd fall all over themselves for another night in his company, Faith thought, frowning. She hadn't yet met a woman who wouldn't.

Renzo stalked toward her desk. Then he put his palms on it and leaned down until his eyes were nearly on a level with hers. She could smell his cologne, that expensive scent of man and spice and sleek machine that she always associated with him. No matter how beautifully groomed he was, how perfect, he still had an edge of wildness that made her think of the motorcycles he both built and raced.

He was famous the world over for his cool. Famous for staring down death at two hundred plus miles an hour on the track with nothing between him and the asphalt but a bit of leather, steel and carbon fiber. This was the man who'd won five world titles before a severe crash left him with pins in his leg and a cane that doctors said he would always need to walk.

But of course he hadn't accepted that fate. He'd worked hard to lose the cane, and even harder to get back on the racetrack. His determination had netted him four more world titles and the nickname of the Iron Prince. Iron because he was unbreakable and Prince because he ruled the track.

And now that iron-willed, determined, unbreakable man was staring at her with eyes so blue and piercing that she dropped her gaze nervously in spite of her determination not to. Faith reached for the telephone, her heart pounding in her throat.

"Which lucky lady will it be?" she asked, cursing herself for the falsetto note that betrayed her agitation.

Renzo's hand lashed out, lay against hers where it rested on the receiver. His skin was warm—shockingly so, she thought, as her flesh seemed to sizzle and burn beneath his. A surge of energy passed through her fingers, her wrist, up her forearm, down her torso and up her spine at the same time. Her body responded with a tightening that was very much unlike her.

"There is a bonus in it for you, Miss Black," Renzo said, his voice silky smooth as it caressed her name. "Whatever clothing you buy, you may keep. And I shall pay you one month's salary for complying with my simple request. This is good, *si?*"

Faith closed her eyes. Good? It was great. A month's extra pay would look very good in her bank account. It would put her that much closer to being able to buy a condo for herself instead of renting an apartment. When she had her own place, she'd finally feel like she'd accomplished something. Like she'd left the Georgia clay behind and made something of herself, in spite of her father's pronouncement that she never would amount to anything.

But she should still refuse. Wherever Lorenzo D'Angeli went, there were photographers and media and attention. She didn't want or need that, hadn't ever worried about it as a PA in an office. But as the woman on his arm, no matter that it was simply a job?

It wouldn't matter that it wasn't real. Her picture would be taken. She could end up on the front page of some tabloid....

And just as quickly the photo would disappear. It was one night, not a lifetime. What were the chances anyone would see a photo of Faith Black and connect her to Faith Louise Winston?

Poor, disgraced Faith Winston. She shivered inwardly. She would not live her life in fear of that single mistake returning to the fore. She was a grown woman now, not a naive teenager.

"Where is the event?" she asked, cursing herself even as she did so. It was a crack in her resolve, and he knew it.

The pressure of Renzo's hand eased, fell away. His eyes gleamed hotter than before—or perhaps she was hallucinating. Yes, of course. Hallucinating. Because there was no way he was looking at her with heat in his gaze.

"Manhattan," he said. "Fifth Avenue." He stood to his full height, and she tilted her head back to look up at him. A satisfied smile lifted the corners of his sensual mouth. "Please be ready by seven, Miss Black. My car will call for you then."

"I have not agreed to go," she said, her mouth as dry as a desert—but they both knew she was on the precipice of surrender. Yet some stubborn part of her refused to cave in so easily. Everything came so effortlessly to this man, and she had no desire to be yet another thing that fell into his lap simply because he wanted it to happen. The one time she'd allowed a man to talk her into something she'd been reluctant to do, the consequences had been disastrous.

But this man was her boss. He was not pretending an affection he did not feel simply to get her to comply with his request. And she was no longer an impressionable eighteen-year-old—how disastrous could the consequences really be?

"You have nothing to lose, Faith," Renzo said, his accent sliding over her name so sensuously that she shivered in spite of herself. "And much to gain."

"This is not part of my job description," she insisted, clinging to that one truth in the face of his beautiful persuasion.

"No, it is not."

They stared at each other without speaking—and then he bent to her level again, palms on the desk once more.

"You would be doing me a great favor," he said. "And you would be helping D'Angeli Motors in the process."

And then he smiled that killer smile of his, the one that made supermodels, nubile actresses and picture-perfect beauty queens swoon in delight. She was alarmed to realize she was not as unaffected as she'd always supposed she would be.

"You are of course free to refuse, but I would be most grateful to you, Faith, if you did not."

"This is not a date," she said firmly. "It's business."

He laughed, and she felt the heat of embarrassment slip through her. Why had she said that? Of course he wouldn't see her as a *real* date. She was too plain to ever be taken seriously as his date, but if he wanted to pay her to pretend, then fine. So long as they kept everything on a business foundation, she'd take the money and run.

"*Assolutamente, cara,*" Renzo said, gifting her once more with that smile, with the laser intensity of deep blue eyes boring into hers. "Now please, take the afternoon off. Go to Saks. My car will take you."

"I'm sure I can find something suitable in my closet," she insisted.

His look said he doubted it. "You happen to have the latest designer attire in your closet, Miss Black? Something appropriate for a gathering of New York's elite?"

Shame coiled within her. He paid her quite well, but she wasn't a fashionista. Not only that, but she had a condo to save for and no need to wear a formal gown. Until now. "Probably not," she admitted.

His smile was indulgent, patient. "Then go. This is part of the deal, Miss Black."

He disappeared behind his office door as if he had no doubts she would obey. Faith wanted to protest, but instead she sighed. And then she logged off her computer and gathered her purse. She'd launched herself into the deep end. She had no choice but to sink or swim.

Renzo's leg ached tonight. He set his laptop aside and rubbed his hand against the pain as the Escalade moved through Brooklyn traffic on the way to his PA's apartment. The discomfort was growing worse as the months went by, not better. He swore softly. His doctors had told him this might happen, but he'd worked too hard to let everything he'd gained slide away. He'd defeated the pain once; he would do so again.

He curled his hand into a fist and dug into the muscle. He wasn't finished yet. He refused to be.

Niccolo Gavretti of Gavretti Manufacturing was his biggest competitor, and Niccolo would love nothing more than to see Renzo lose not only the next world title but also D'Angeli's domination of the market. Renzo frowned as he thought of Niccolo. They'd been friends once, or at least Renzo had thought they had.

He knew better now.

And he would not lose. *He* would be the one to take the D'Angeli Viper onto the track and prove that he'd created the greatest superbike the racing world had ever seen—once the kinks in the design were worked out—and he would win another world title in the process.

His investors would be happy, the money would keep flowing and the next production version would be a huge hit with the public. Then Renzo would gladly retire from racing and leave it to the D'Angeli team to continue to dominate the motorcycle Grand Prix circuit.

Dio, per favore, one last title—one last victory—and he would stop.

Tonight was critical to his success, and he hoped he had not made a mistake in asking his plain but efficient secretary to accompany him. Desperate times, however, called for desperate measures.

He could appear at Robert Stein's party alone, of course. Perhaps everything would be fine if he did. But he had no desire to spend the evening avoiding Stein's daughter. Lissa was too young, too spoiled and too obvious in her attention.

And Robert Stein did not seem to appreciate his daughter's interest in Renzo one tiny bit. Though Renzo did not normally care what fathers thought, in this case he wanted it clear that he had no interest in Lissa Stein. For that, he'd needed a date, a woman who would stay close to his side and do his bidding when asked.

Everything had been perfect until this morning when he'd found himself saying the words to Katie Palmer that he usually said to a woman he'd grown tired of. He'd dated her for a month now, and she'd started to grow too clingy. The makeup bag tucked into one corner of his bathroom vanity wasn't too bad, nor was the toothbrush. Yet it was the shiny pink ladies' razor with several refills in his shower that, oddly enough, had been the last straw.

He had no problem with a woman spending the night when he invited her to do so. He was, however, quite irritated to find one starting to move herself in piece by piece after only a dozen nights together. Sex was an important and fulfilling aspect of his life, but he saw no need to confuse the issue with cohabitation. Renzo did not need to live with a woman to enjoy her, and he always made it clear in the beginning what his expectations were. Whenever someone crossed that line, they were summarily dismissed from his life.

Katie Palmer was a beautiful woman, an exciting woman, and yet she'd begun to leave him cold even before the pink razor and its endless refills had appeared. He wasn't quite sure why. She was exactly the sort of woman he usually dated—beautiful, slightly superficial and intellectually undemanding.

Renzo picked up his laptop again and stared at the report he'd been working on. He should have perhaps taken Faith's suggestion to invite a former girlfriend tonight instead of pressing her into service, but when the idea had first struck him as he'd sat at his desk and stared at a neatly typed memo with a helpful sticky note arrow pointing to the line for his signature, he'd had a sudden idea that taking his capable, mousy little PA with him would be far more productive than taking a woman who expected him to pay attention to her.

If he took Faith, it was business. She was a quiet, competent girl. She was not necessarily unattractive, he supposed, but he'd never really looked at her for signs of beauty. Why would he? She was his PA, and she was quite good at her job. His calendar had never been so orderly or his appointments so seamless.

Faith was perfect, even if she wasn't much to look at. She wore severe suits in dark colors that hid whatever figure she might have and scraped her golden hair back into ponytails and buns. She looked, truth be told, like a box. She also wore dark-rimmed spectacles.

But her eyes were green. He'd noticed that before, whenever she'd looked up at him through her glasses, her gaze sparking with intelligence. They were not dark like an emerald, but golden green like a spring leaf. And she smelled nice. Like an early-morning rain mingled with exotic flowers. There was no sharp perfume, no stale smell of smoke or alcohol or tanning solution.

But when she'd looked up at him this afternoon, her eyes flashing and a blush spreading over her cheeks, he'd had one wild, inconceivable moment when he'd imagined pulling her across the desk and fitting his mouth to hers.

Which made no sense. Faith Black was neat and efficient and smelled nice, but she wasn't the kind of woman he preferred. He liked her because she was professional and excellent at everything she did. He was not attracted to her.

It was, he supposed, an anomaly. A sign of the stress he'd been under for the past few months as his engineers worked to bring the Viper to top form. There were problems that had to be worked out or the bike would fail on the track.

And Renzo refused to accept failure. He'd poured a great deal of money and time into the development of this motorcycle, and he needed it to succeed. Success was everything. He'd known that since he was a teenager, since he'd realized that he actually *had* a father but that his father had not wanted to know him.

Because he wasn't a blue blood like the Conte de Lucano, or like the *conte*'s children with his wife. Renzo was the outcast, the unfortunate product of a somewhat hasty affair with a waitress. He hadn't been supposed to succeed—but he had, spectacularly, and he had every intention of continuing to do so.

Lorenzo D'Angeli never backed down from a challenge. He lived for them, thrived on them.

The limousine came to a halt in front of a plain concrete apartment building in a somewhat shabby neighborhood. Renzo winced as he moved his leg. It ached enough that he should allow his chauffeur to retrieve Faith, but he was just stubborn enough to refuse to permit even that small moment of vulnerability.

The car door opened and Renzo stepped onto the pavement, looking right and left, surveying the street and the people. The area didn't seem unsafe, yet it was worn. An unwanted memory tugged at his mind as he stood there. Another time, another place.

Another life, when he'd had nothing and had to struggle to feed his mother and younger sister. He'd been angry then, terribly angry. He'd always thought that if his mother had been more forceful, more demanding, she could have at least gotten the *conte* to make sure they had food and shelter. But she was weak, his mother, though he loved her completely. Too weak to fight back when she should have done so.

He ruthlessly squashed the feelings of helplessness the memory dredged up. Then he strode into the building and made his way to Faith's apartment on the second floor. There was no elevator. Renzo took the stairs quickly, in spite of the sharp throb in his leg. When he reached Faith's door, he took a moment to blank the pain from his mind before he rapped sharply.

She answered right away, the door whipping open to reveal a woman who might have made his jaw drop had he not had better control of himself. Faith Black was…different. A small spike of *something*—he did not know quite what—ricocheted through him as he studied her. She had not transformed into a voluptuous goddess, but she had transformed. Somehow.

The glasses were gone, and she was wearing makeup. He wasn't certain she ever wore makeup at the office, though perhaps she did. If she did, it wasn't quite like this, he was certain. Her lips were red, full and shiny from her lip gloss. Kissable.

Kissable?

"Mr. D'Angeli," she said, blinking in surprise.

"You were expecting someone else?" he asked mildly,

and yet the thought of her doing so caused a twinge of irritation to stab into him. Odd.

"I—well, yes. I had thought you were sending your car. I had thought I was meeting you at the event."

"As you see, this is not the case." He let his gaze drop slowly before meeting her pretty eyes again. She seemed surprised—and somewhat annoyed. She'd never been anything but professional in all their interactions, but what he saw in her eyes now made him wonder if it was possible that she did not like him.

Impossibile. Of course she did. He'd yet to meet a woman who didn't. He turned his best smile on her. "You look quite delightful, Miss Black."

And delectable, he was shocked to realize.

Her hair was piled on her head, but it wasn't quite as scraped back as usual; instead she'd pulled it into an elegant twist from which one disobedient tendril had escaped to lie against her cheek. Her pale lavender gown was demure, with a high neck, but it was also sleeveless and molded to her full breasts before falling away in ripples of fabric to the floor.

It was disconcerting, to say the least, to realize that she had a shape—and that shape was not a box. Quite the contrary, she was a study in curves, from the soft curve of her jaw to the curve of her bosom and down to the curve of her hips that he could just make out beneath the flowing fabric of her gown. He couldn't quite take his eyes from her, as if she might change back into the creature he knew if he looked away.

Color stained her cheeks as her green gaze fell from his. Satisfaction rippled through him. She was not immune after all. "Thank you. I—I was just searching for my earring backing. I dropped it and I'm not sure where it's gone."

He noticed then that she was only wearing one small

diamond earring. "Allow me to help," he said, pushing the door wider. She stepped back somewhat reluctantly, but she let him inside.

The apartment was small, but neat. The furnishings were worn, and there were a variety of magazines piled on a central table—including a couple of motorcycle magazines, it amused him to note. He was on the cover of the topmost one, in full leathers, looking grim as he stood beside a prototype of the Viper. And with good reason, considering the bike had fallen far short of what he'd been aiming for when he'd taken it out on the track. Not that the reporter had known, of course.

He dragged his gaze away from the magazine, continuing his study of Faith's home. A shelf stacked high with books ran along one short wall. The walls were industrial white, but she'd tried to punch it up with bright pictures and pillows on the furniture. It was a decidedly feminine space, though not in any overt way.

He thought of his mother decorating their tiny apartment in Positano with garlands of flowers and pretty fabric, and his jaw hardened as his thoughts turned dark. Did Faith also bring home an endless parade of men she hoped would fall in love with her? Did she cry at the end of the night—or series of nights—when she realized the current man was gone and never coming back?

"Over here," Faith said, leading the way to a tiny kitchen, which had barely enough room for two adults to stand together.

Her fragrance surrounded him as he joined her, that soft fresh scent he'd come to identify with her over the past few months. A sharp sensation rolled through him.

"I dropped it here," she said. "And it's rolled somewhere. It can't have gone far."

For a moment, he wasn't sure what they were talking

about. For a moment, for the barest of seconds, he wanted to press her soft body against the counter with his, wanted to drag the pins from her hair and see the golden mass tumble free. He shook the thought from his mind and focused on the task at hand.

"If you will allow me," he said, taking out his mobile phone and starting the application that turned the camera flash into a steady beam of light.

She couldn't leave the small space without brushing against him. A sliver of pleasure passed through him at the brief contact. *Stress*, he thought. *Simply stress*.

"And why were you putting on your earrings in the kitchen, Miss Black?" he asked as he stooped, ignoring the pain in his leg, and swept the light back and forth across the floor.

"I was in a hurry," she said. "I wanted to make it down to the street by the time your car arrived."

He tilted his head back to glance up at her. "You were planning to stand outside? Dressed like this?"

She shrugged. "I would have stood inside the building until I saw the car, but yes. I'm sorry you had to come up and get me."

The light flickered over something that glinted gold. Renzo swept the light into a corner again, found the small backing. He picked it up and pushed himself to his feet.

He gritted his teeth against the agony of spasming muscles and aching bone. "Miss Black, I am many things, not all of them pleasant, but I would hope that you realize I am not so callous as to make a lady wait in a dark and drafty hallway for my arrival."

"No, of course not," she said quietly, and he knew he must have looked severe. Yet he could not tell her why. Not without admitting what he would admit to no one— that he was weak, vulnerable, not made of iron after all.

Her gaze fell from his as she held her hand out to receive the tiny backing.

Renzo stared at the top of her golden head for a moment. He could have dropped it into her palm. That would have been easy. Prudent even. But he found he wanted to touch her again, wanted to see if he felt that same tiny jolt that he had this afternoon when he'd put his hand on hers before she could pick up the telephone. He'd dismissed the sensation as something akin to static electricity.

He put his fingers around her wrist and she gasped, her fingers curling inward on reflex before she forced them open again. He held her hand steady while he placed the backing in her palm. Her skin was soft, warm, and he wondered if the rest of her was equally as soft. Shockingly, a sliver of need began to tingle at the base of his spine. Renzo dropped her hand as if it had suddenly turned into a flaming brand.

Dio.

Her eyes were wide before she turned away. Her fingers shook as she fastened her earring in place, and he knew she must be affected, too. What was this sudden chemistry? Where had it come from? And why did he want to touch her again just so he could feel the jolt?

"There," she said unnecessarily when she completed the task. "I'm ready."

"Then we should be going," he said crisply. He helped her into her wrap and then waited while she locked the door. He had her precede him down the stairs, so that if he limped she would not know.

When they reached the street, his driver was standing at the ready with the door open. Renzo held his hand out to help Faith inside, but she did not take it, climbing into the custom Escalade on her own. He slid into the white leather seat beside her, and the door closed with a heavy thud.

They'd been gliding through the streets toward Manhattan for several minutes before she spoke. "Is there anything I should know about tonight, Mr. D'Angeli?"

Renzo glanced over at her. She was looking up at him with that focused look she usually got whenever he went over the morning reports with her.

Familiar ground, *grazie a Dio*. Perhaps now he could stop thinking about the way she smelled, about how delicate and feminine she seemed when he'd never quite noticed that about her before. Why had he noticed it now?

"We are attending a dinner at Robert Stein's residence," he said. "I am sure you realize why this is important."

She gave a firm nod. "Stein Engineering has patented a new form of racing tire. You wish them to build tires exclusively for the Viper instead of using stock tires. It would be an advantageous partnership."

"Ah, so you do pay attention in the meetings," he teased.

She looked surprised. And somewhat offended. "Of course I do. It's what you pay me for, Mr. D'Angeli."

Yes, it was what he paid her for. And tonight, he was paying her for something different. He, Lorenzo D'Angeli, was paying a woman to pretend to be his date. It was ludicrous, and yet he found he was rather looking forward to the evening in a way he would not have been had Katie Palmer been sitting beside him.

The Katie Palmers of the world were too obvious in their desire to own him, too certain of their sex appeal, and too jealous of his time and attention. He always found it amusing at first, but he quickly tired of it.

He knew it was his own fault, because that was the sort of woman he chose. But he'd watched his sweet, fragile mother pine for love for years, and he'd watched her be hurt again and again. She took things too seriously, thought every new man was her savior.

Because of that, Renzo had studiously avoided the kind of women in his own life who couldn't understand that sex was sex and love didn't enter the equation. He didn't believe in love, or at least not romantic love. If romantic love was real, then his mother should have found happiness years ago.

Faith wasn't like the women he usually dated. She wasn't superficial—and she wasn't fragile, either. In fact, she was looking at him now with what he thought might be thinly veiled disgust. A hot feeling blossomed inside him.

A challenge. He loved challenges.

Renzo couldn't quite stop himself from doing what he did next, if only to ruffle her cool. He reached for Faith's hand, took it in his while he traced small circles in her palm with his thumb. Her breath drew in sharply, and he could feel a tremor slide through her body. A current of satisfaction coiled within him. She was not impervious, no matter how hostile she looked, and that pleased him.

"Do you not think, *cara mia*," he purred, "that you should perhaps call me Renzo?"

CHAPTER TWO

FAITH's skin sizzled beneath his touch, as if someone had dropped cool water onto hot coals. Her breath froze in her chest, and her voice refused to work as he traced little whorls in her palm. His hand was warm and solid, his thumb perhaps the most sensual thing she'd ever experienced as it moved softly against her skin.

Faith blinked as if it were a mirage that would disappear as soon as she did so. It did not.

Surely, then, she was asleep in her bed, dreaming that Renzo D'Angeli was holding her hand and speaking in a sultry voice that entreated her to call him by his first name.

Because this could not be real. She'd worked for him for six months, and he'd never once shown the slightest bit of interest in her as a woman. Not that she'd ever wanted him to. He was precisely the sort of man she despised the most: handsome, arrogant and certain he was entitled to excessive adoration.

But he was not noticing her in that way. It was impossible. He was simply playing along with the expectation they would be less formal together when she was posing as his date.

Yes, that must be it. Of course.

"I will try, Mr. D—Renzo," she said quietly, her heart beating in her ears.

"Much better," he said, smiling his lady-killer smile. But the thumb didn't stop moving and a tendril of heat made its way up her arm and down through her core, pooling in the deepest, most secretive part of her. It figured. Of all the men to affect her, it would be this one. A man she couldn't have in a bazillion years, even if she'd wanted him.

Which she did not. He was gorgeous, but about as trustworthy as the viper he'd named his motorcycle after.

She wanted him to let her go. And she didn't. The languidness stealing over her at his touch was addictive. What would she feel if he pulled her into his arms and kissed her? Would she lose her mind the way his other women did?

The thought was not a pleasant one. She'd already lost her mind over a man—or at least everyone thought she had—and she had no desire to experience that ever again. One second of stupidity, and Jason Moore had shattered her trust in men—in people—forever.

She was just about to ask Renzo to let her go when his phone rang.

"*Perdono*," he said before he took the call.

Faith folded her hands over her evening bag and watched the news ticker on the muted television screen across from her. That had been close. She didn't like feeling even remotely attracted to this man. She pictured Katie Palmer sashaying out of his office just a few days ago, lipstick smudged, hair mussed, and felt her dislike of him swell.

Yes. That was precisely how it was supposed to be.

Faith shifted in her seat. She'd ridden in his limo before, accompanying him to meetings across town, but this was the first time she'd sat here in an evening gown. When she'd gone to Saks today, she'd been surprised to be met by a personal shopper whom Renzo had arranged for her.

Faith had viewed gown after gown, the personal shopper growing perplexed, to say the least, when she refused the more daring dresses that showed too much cleavage or leg. Obviously Renzo had a preferred style he liked his women to wear. And Faith had been determined to wear what she liked, regardless of who was paying for the gown.

When the woman had brought the lavender gown out, Faith had known it was the one. When she put this dress on, she felt elegant, pretty and demure enough to please even her upright father.

Renzo finished his phone call and turned to her. "I need you to stay by my side tonight," he said. "It is very important that you do so."

Faith swallowed. "Of course, Mr—Renzo."

She could see his frown in the light from the television. "I'm counting on you, Faith. You have never failed me yet."

But she *had* disappointed him when she'd nearly called him Mr. D'Angeli again, and it bothered her. Because this was part of the job and he expected her to be able to do what he asked. It shouldn't be difficult, yet she was letting her nerves get the best of her.

Faith turned her head to look out the window as she pressed her fingernails into her palm and dug in. She would do a good job. Because he'd asked her to, and she'd agreed. She owed him that much. Tonight was important to the success of the Viper.

She knew that the Viper meant everything to him. How many times had she left the office late while he was still there, only to come in the next morning and find he'd never left? He worked hard on the designs, worked with his team to implement the changes that were required to make the motorcycle a success, and he worked hard on the business of running D'Angeli Motors.

D'Angeli wasn't only known for its racing bikes, of course. They also made production motorcycles that were popular with enthusiasts everywhere. Sales were growing steadily in the States, though perhaps not as quickly as Renzo would like. She knew he counted on the Viper to usher in a new wave of prosperity and growth for his company. And what was good for D'Angeli Motors was also good for her. For all his employees.

His phone rang again. He looked at the display and swore in Italian before sending the call to voice mail.

A woman, no doubt. Probably Katie Palmer. Katie was an underwear model, Faith recalled. If Renzo couldn't be satisfied with a woman who looked that good naked, what on earth would it take to make him happy?

She shuddered to think it. No doubt he wanted a woman who fawned over his every move, who would feed him ice-cold grapes and fetch his slippers in her teeth were he to desire it. Arrogant, entitled man.

Eventually, the limo stopped in front of an ornate pre-war building on Fifth Avenue. A moment later, a uniformed doorman swung the door open and Renzo stepped out before turning and holding out his hand for her. Faith took a deep breath as she gathered her tiny, jeweled purse and tugged her wrap tighter. She thought about refusing his help like she had before, but it was darker now and this was unfamiliar ground. It would not do to land on her face in her finery.

She put her hand in his and let him assist her from the tall SUV. But as her foot hit the pavement, she wobbled in her high heels. She barely had time to lose her balance before Renzo steadied her, a broad hand coming to rest on her waist while the other held her hand firmly.

The hand on her waist seared her. It was like being struck by lightning. They looked at each other for some seconds before he spoke.

"You are full of surprises, Miss Black," Renzo said

softly, his fingers spanning her waist, scorching her through the silk georgette of her gown.

"Shouldn't you call me Faith?" she asked, her heart thrumming at both the feel of his hand on her body and the way he said she was full of surprises. As if he were *pleased*.

Oh for God's sake, stop. She could care less what he thought. Really.

His teeth flashed white in the night. "Of course. *Faith*. Are you ready to go up? We are expected."

Faith drew in a deep breath. "As ready as I'll ever be."

"You forgot something," he said, his voice sliding across her nerve endings like a shiver.

Faith blinked up at him, struck anew by the symmetrical beauty of his face. How could a man be so gorgeous?

"What did I forget?" she managed to say without turning into a stammering nitwit. She could feel her face flaming, and she wanted to turn and climb straight back into the Escalade. And then she wanted to berate herself for being a ninny.

"As ready as I'll ever be, *Renzo*," he said.

He watched her expectantly, and she realized they weren't moving until she got it right, no matter how difficult it was for her to think of him as Renzo instead of Mr. D'Angeli. No matter that it was far safer to think of him as Mr. D'Angeli. Far easier to maintain her professionalism that way.

But there was no getting around it. He wasn't moving, and she didn't want to stand on the sidewalk all night. She'd been lucky there'd been no paparazzi waiting for him and she didn't feel like tempting fate any further than she already had.

Not that she was important or her secrets all that earth-shattering—but she'd left her old life behind and she had no wish to revisit the pain and humiliation of it ever again.

She pulled in a breath. "As ready as I'll ever be, *Renzo*."

"*Fabuloso*," he said. "Already, you are perfect."

The Stein's penthouse apartment was magnificent. It took up two levels at the top of the building, and boasted a terrace planted just like a formal English garden. There were trees, arbors, a profusion of rosebushes and even a carpet of grass. Lights strung around the perimeter had the effect of softly illuminating the area and making one believe they were at a garden party. Central Park stretched out below, a dark inky spot in the night bordered by the bright lights of the Upper West Side across the way. If Faith stood near the edge of the terrace and looked left, she could see the Plaza gleaming white while the red taillights of taxis streamed by on Fifth Avenue.

She rarely came into Manhattan. The D'Angeli Motors factory was on Long Island, and she lived in Brooklyn. At the end of the day, she was too tired to venture into the city. And the weekends were her time to read, watch television and catch up on her laundry and housecleaning. She wasn't the sort of girl who had time to pop into the Plaza for afternoon tea.

But now, standing here, she almost wished she was. She could afford that much at least. But a place like the Stein's apartment was another story. This was how the supremely wealthy lived. It was at turns exhilarating and depressing.

She worked long hours to afford what she had and to save up for her own place someday, and other people had manicured grass growing on top of a building in Manhattan. Faith shook her head. Life was very strange sometimes.

She glanced over at Renzo. They'd only been here

twenty minutes, and already she felt that her coming had been a waste of time. He did not need her. He stood nearby, chatting with Robert Stein and a group of gentlemen. They were watching him raptly, laughing and agreeing with something he said, and then toasting him with their glasses held high. A moment later, Stein was turning away at an entreaty from his wife, and Renzo turned to look toward where Faith stood near the terrace wall, a glass of wine in her hand.

There was something electric in his gaze, something that shot straight to the deepest heart of her and twisted an emotion out of her. She took a sip of her wine. How very annoying to not be able to control her response to him. To be exactly like every other woman who couldn't control herself around him.

Except that she could control herself. And she would.

He said something to the men and then he was striding toward her, confident and sure. Until, for the briefest of moments, he seemed to favor his right leg. Faith frowned. A second later, he was moving as gracefully as ever. And yet she was positive he'd been in pain. That was the leg with the pins, the one that had been supposed to end his career several years ago.

"I'm sorry to have left you standing here alone," he said.

Faith shook her head, frowning at the thought his leg might be bothering him. "Not at all. You came here to talk to Mr. Stein. That should take precedence."

He tilted his head as he studied her. It disconcerted her until she wanted to drop her lashes and shield her eyes, but she would not shrink from him. It was not the first time tonight he'd looked at her that way. Each time, she felt as if he were dissecting her and viewing the parts individually. As if he weren't quite certain what to make of her.

Well, she wasn't certain what to make of herself. What

was she doing at a party full of rich people, pretending
to be the date of one of the most handsome and dynamic
men in the world? No one would believe it for a minute.

She didn't. She just wanted to be at home, wrapped in
her fuzzy robe and reading a book. That was believable.

"You are interesting, Faith," Renzo said.

She lifted her chin. She would not be flattered by his
smooth charm. "Not really. I'm just doing my job."

He arched an eyebrow. "Is that what you call it?"

"Yes," she said firmly. "I'm here because you asked me
to be, plus you offered to pay me. It's work."

He looked amused. "And what if I asked you to come
to Italy with me? Would you do it?"

Faith swallowed. Italy? She couldn't pretend that the
thought didn't excite her. She'd never been out of the country before, and she couldn't imagine a more wonderful
place to go. Pasta, pizza, cappuccino. Mmm. It made her
mouth water just to think it.

She'd always believed she would be shuffled to another
of the company's officers once Renzo returned to Europe.
She still believed it. He couldn't really be serious. He had
another factory in Italy, and another office that was no
doubt staffed with an efficient Italian PA.

"That depends," she said, her throat constricting around
the words.

"I need you, Faith. You keep my life together, and I don't
want to live without you."

Faith could only blink. And then she had to suppress
a laugh—because how many women would die to hear
Renzo say those words to them? Of course he meant them
a very different way, but it was still amusing.

"I wish I had a tape recorder," she said, and then bit her
lip when she realized she'd spoken aloud.

He looked perplexed. "Why is this?"

Faith shrugged, laughing. What was the use in denying it? "Because I could probably sell it many times over. I can think of a handful of women who would pay to hear those words from your lips. And I'm sure there are more trailing in your wake. I could retire early."

Renzo laughed. "Ah, *si*, it could be very profitable for you. And yet I hope you will consider my offer to accompany me to Italy."

"You haven't made the offer yet," she said, feeling bold and breathless at the same time.

His smile was turned up full force. "Have I not? Dear Faith, please accompany me to Italy. I will give you a twenty percent raise and cover all your expenses while we are abroad."

Twenty percent. Faith swallowed. "Well, as wonderful as that is, I think you've forgotten something." Because she had to be honest, no matter how much she might like to leap on the offer.

"And what is that?"

"I don't speak Italian. I don't speak anything but English, in fact."

His smile did not dim. "And yet the international language is English. How do you suppose people in Italy converse with people in Germany? No, this is not an issue. Besides, you will learn Italian while you live there."

"I—"

"Renzo, darling, there you are," a cultured female voice called out, interrupting them. "I've been looking everywhere."

Renzo stiffened as he turned toward the owner of the voice. The woman sauntering toward them was a stunning salon-blonde, dressed in a tight-fitting black sheath that showed a mile of tanned leg. Her hair hung long and straight down her back, and her makeup was absolutely perfect. She wore a fat diamond-drop necklace and matching earrings, and her shoes were gold.

"Lissa," Renzo said. "How nice to see you again."

Lissa's gaze fell to Faith and slid over her with no small measure of contempt. The look very clearly said *back away*. *Oh puh-leeze*. As if Faith were any competition. Still, she tilted her chin up and stood her ground.

Lissa turned her smile on Renzo. "Do I not get a kiss, darling? I had thought you Italians were all about the kiss when greeting friends."

"Of course." Renzo kissed her on both cheeks in the Italian manner and then turned and put an arm around Faith. Lissa's eyes narrowed to slits while Faith's entire body lit up like a firecracker as Renzo pulled her into the curve of his powerful frame.

This was not what she'd agreed to tonight, and yet in a way it had been. She was his date.

"Lissa, this is Faith."

Faith held her hand out, surprised it didn't shake when inside she was trembling so badly. Why, when she didn't even like him all that much?

Lissa took it after a moment's hesitation. "Very lovely to meet you," Faith said.

"Yes, lovely." Lissa's tone said it was anything but. "Renzo, I had hoped to speak with you. Alone," she added, her smile never wavering.

Renzo's fingers skimmed over Faith's bare arm, his touch setting off a chain of reactions inside her that ended with a sharp current of need settling between her thighs. She'd never felt anything quite like it. And she was furious it was happening now, here, with this man.

Her boss made Casanova look like an amateur, for pity's sake. She knew it, and yet she responded anyway.

"You may say whatever you wish to say in front of Faith," Renzo countered. "She is completely trustworthy."

Lissa pushed her hair over one shoulder with an indolent gesture. Her eyes sparked. "It can wait," she said tightly. And then she smiled. Faith had the impression of razor-sharp fangs lining the other woman's mouth. "Perhaps a bit later, then."

"Perhaps," Renzo said.

Someone called to her, and Lissa turned and waved. "If you will excuse me, I must mingle."

"Of course," Renzo replied. "Do not let us keep you."

Lissa insisted on kissing Renzo on both cheeks again and held her hand out to Faith, pressing it limply before gliding away in a cloud of malevolence that was quite possibly stronger than her perfume.

"Let me guess," Faith said coolly, moving out of his grasp when the other woman had joined a group of people a few feet away. "She is the reason you needed a date tonight."

"*Si*," Renzo said.

Faith turned to look up at him, exasperated, and just a little hurt. "Honestly, I don't know why you just don't do what you always do and be done with it."

His brows drew together. "What I always do?"

"Oh please, don't act as if you don't know. I've worked for you for six months, and I've yet to see a woman last more than a month with you. You wine them, dine them, give them presents and dump them."

It was bold of her, but she'd had just enough wine to loosen her tongue. To be on the safe side, she deposited the half-finished glass on the terrace wall. If she drank the whole thing, heaven knows what she might say to him.

Renzo grinned. Not at all the effect she'd been going for.

"You forgot one, Faith." She frowned, but he leaned toward her and spoke before she could say anything. "Bed them."

A flash of heat shot through her. Dammit! "Yes, of course. How could I forget that one? Silly me."

She realized she was standing before him with her arms crossed defensively when he put his hands on her shoulders and skimmed them down her arms. "I had no idea you were so outraged by my behavior," he teased.

Faith scoffed as she tried very hard not to react to his skin touching hers. Why didn't she just shove him away? "Outraged? I have no say in anything you choose to do. I am not outraged. It was merely an observation."

He put a finger under her jaw and tipped her chin up. His sharp eyes glittered with some hidden passion that hadn't been there only a moment ago. It shocked her. And intrigued her.

He was so close. Too close, the heat emanating from him enveloping her, making her long to press into him and see just how hot she could feel. Would she burn up in his embrace?

No. No, no, *no.* She would not think of her Italian playboy boss in that way. It wasn't safe. It was irresponsible. *Reckless.*

Faith did not do reckless. The one time she had, it had cost her far more than she could have ever dreamed. She was finished with reckless.

"But you disapprove," Renzo said.

"Not this time." And she almost meant it, except for the fact it would mean Renzo would actually sleep with that obnoxious woman. Though, on the other hand, the woman would pay for it in the end when Renzo dumped her. Faith might enjoy shopping for that parting gift. "Go for it."

He laughed. "And what makes you think I have not already? That she just doesn't understand I no longer want her?"

It was a valid point, but she knew better because she'd witnessed the fallout too many times. The tears, the desperate phone calls, the attempts to sneak past her and into his office in order to plead for another chance. Women could be, she'd decided, awfully pitiful sometimes. She wanted to tell them to get some dignity, to stop begging and go on with their lives. Men like Renzo were immune to histrionics.

"Because a woman who has been subjected to the D'Angeli treatment is usually angry with you. She wasn't. She wants you, and pretty badly I'd say."

The look in his eyes was sharp. He moved a step closer and she shuddered involuntarily. "What are you doing?" she asked.

"Nothing," he said, much too innocently. "I like the way you talk, Faith. It sounds like sweet syrup, all long and drawn out as if you had all day to speak. Not like the women in New York."

"That's because I'm from Georgia. It's hot there. We talk slow and walk slow and, well, do a lot of things slow." My God, she was babbling. To her urbane, gorgeous boss. Where was her dignity?

One of Renzo's dark eyebrows arched. "Really? I can imagine that some things are done best when done slowly. How wise you people from Georgia are."

Her heart was slamming into her ribs and a fine sheen of moisture was rising in the valley between her breasts. "I sound no different now than I have for the past six months. I can't imagine how you haven't noticed it before."

He took another step and she backed up, found herself against the wall of the terrace where it curved inward. He put a hand on the wall beside her, trapping her as his other hand came up and caressed her jaw.

It was electrifying.

"I have been wondering this myself," he said. "You have hidden yourself well, Faith."

Her body hummed with electricity that she feared would scorch her if it continued for much longer. "I've hidden nothing. I've come to work every day and sat at a desk not ten feet from your office door. I've brought you coffee, papers. I've fielded phone calls and given you reports. And I've gone shopping for those goodbye presents for your women—"

"Ah," he said softly, "you *are* offended."

"No," she replied. But then, because she couldn't help it, she added, "Though I think you should shop for your own presents."

Renzo laughed. "Perhaps you are correct, and yet you always choose the nicest things. How can I compete?"

"By employing a full-time personal shopper?"

His gaze dropped to her mouth for a moment and she sucked in a breath, trying to calm her racing heart. He hadn't backed away, hadn't taken his hand from her cheek in all this time they'd been talking. The sharp ache throbbing inside her was nearly unbearable.

And unfathomable.

"You have lovely eyes," he said. "Why do you hide them behind those hideous glasses all day long?"

She stiffened. "They're reading glasses. I need them to do my job." A different kind of heat scorched her now.

Someone laughed nearby, and then Lissa's voice drifted over the others. "So plain and unattractive. Honestly, I can't see what he sees in her. Must be an Italian thing."

Time seemed to stand still for a moment, hovering in the air above Faith's head, threatening her with old humiliations and hurts. And then it drifted down over her, covering her in feelings she would rather forget.

She told herself not to care, but she did anyway. It hurt, being the center of negative attention. Though nothing Lissa said could come close to what Faith had gone through in the past when Jason had betrayed her trust, she was surprised to realize that it still had the power to hurt her.

For a moment, she was back in high school. Hearing the taunts, the snickers, the innuendos. Feeling the anger, the urge to lash out, the urge to escape.

Renzo's jaw tightened. "I'm sorry, Faith."

"It's nothing," she said lightly, drawing on hard-won reserves of strength. "She's just jealous." But moisture swam in her eyes and her throat ached with the effort not to let any tears fall. She thought that she'd learned how to deal with this eight years ago, but she'd been wrong. You never got over people pointing their fingers and laughing at you.

"We will go now," Renzo said, his hands on her shoulders once more, this time imparting comfort rather than setting her on edge.

"No!" Faith swallowed the lump in her throat. She would not run. Not this time. "No, that's exactly what she wants. Besides, have you got what you came here for tonight?"

He'd spent a few minutes with Robert Stein, but it had been in the company of others. And she was fairly certain he'd not talked business upon first arriving. No doubt he'd been hoping to broach that subject a bit later.

He frowned. "That is unimportant."

Impulsively, she put a hand on his chest. The fabric of his tuxedo was smooth, cool, but beneath it his body was hard and hot. She knew he was in excellent shape considering that he was a top Grand Prix rider—not to mention she'd saved the heat-inducing magazine ad where he'd posed in his leathers with the zipper opened to his navel.

She'd been unable to deny how sexy he was in that ad, even if she did think him heartless when it came to women. The magazine had gone into her keeper pile, much to her dismay.

Still, after all that, she was unprepared for how his body felt beneath her hand.

Power and leashed strength waiting for the right instant to explode into action. At the moment, however, he seemed very still beneath her touch, nothing but the beat of his heart vibrating against her palm. It was almost as if he was purposely holding himself still.

Faith forced herself to focus. "Please, Renzo, the Viper is important to you. Talk with Mr. Stein. Don't worry about me. I can handle myself."

She'd learned how after a trial by fire she would never forget.

His fingers wrapped around hers where they rested on his tuxedo. He lifted her hand to his lips and pressed a kiss there that sent a shudder rocketing down her spine.

"You are quite remarkable, Faith," he said softly.

"Hardly," she replied. She needed to put distance between them, now more than ever. She didn't like this hot, achy feeling he called up inside her. It could come to no good for her. Even if he were interested in a plain girl like her, she had a lot more to lose than his usual women. Unlike the others, she'd find herself brokenhearted *and* jobless once he decided to dump her, were she foolish enough to give in to this silliness inside. "I'm thinking of my bottom line. If the Viper succeeds, then I can ask for an even bigger raise."

Renzo threw back his head and laughed. "Indeed. Then come with me, *cara*."

And, twining his fingers in hers, he led her into the center of the garden party.

CHAPTER THREE

RENZO was in a good mood. Aside from Lissa Stein's behavior—and the way his leg now throbbed after so much
time standing on it—it had been a good evening. Stein
had expressed interest in building custom tires for the
Viper, and an acute interest in an exclusive partnership
with D'Angeli Motors, should the Viper prove a success
during the time trials next month in Italy. The bike wasn't
quite ready yet, but Renzo had high hopes they'd be able
to begin training for the MotoGP season soon.

But, more interestingly, he was very much intrigued by
the woman sitting beside him in the limousine. He'd kept
her close for the rest of the evening, ushering her through
the gathering like a prized possession. Lissa Stein had
stayed far away, *grazie a Dio*.

While that had been his priority in bringing Faith tonight, he'd found that he rather enjoyed having her near.
She made no demands. She did not simper or whine or
pout. In fact, she seemed quite prickly, and she'd taken
him to task over the women in his life. Rather than finding it impertinent, he'd been amused.

She might bristle like a porcupine, but he couldn't help
noticing that she'd shivered and blushed when he'd touched
her. And that it seemed to infuriate her that she had.

When he'd backed her against the terrace wall and put

his hand on her cheek, he'd had every intention of kissing her even though he knew he should not. He'd never yet committed the sin of making love to a personal assistant, and he wasn't sure he wanted to cross that line now. But he *had* wanted to taste her. Just for an instant.

He still wasn't certain why. Faith Black was not a gorgeous model, but she had some indefinable quality about her that he couldn't quite pinpoint. She was strong, but also vulnerable. She'd experienced pain in her life, but that pain hadn't defeated her. He'd seen it in her eyes when Lissa had made those hurtful comments. He'd wanted to defend her, but she hadn't needed defending.

"I have not forgotten that you did not answer me about Italy," he said into the silence.

The interior of the car was dark, other than the lights from the street that shone inside as they drove back toward Brooklyn. One of Faith's earrings caught the light as she turned her head toward him.

"I've been thinking about it," she said.

"And what have you been thinking?"

"You didn't tell me how it would work once I got there. Where would I live? Would I need a car? I haven't driven in years, and I'm not sure I'd feel comfortable relearning that skill in a foreign country. It's not that I can't drive," she hurried on, "but since I've lived in New York, it's been unnecessary."

She sounded somewhat breathless, he noted, as if she were nervous and trying to hide it. Interesting.

"I have a very large house, *cara*. You would stay with me. And there is no need to drive, as you will travel with me wherever I go."

Wherever he went? Renzo surprised himself with the statement, but *si*, it made the most sense. How could she organize his appointments if she did not accompany him?

"I'm not sure I could do that," she said very quietly.

"Why not?" He sounded perplexed. Because he *was* perplexed.

"Because at least I have weekends off now. I have my own life, you know. It does not revolve around you twenty-four hours a day. And it sounds like it would in Italy."

A sudden thought occurred to him. Perhaps it should have occurred to him before, but the simple fact was that it hadn't. "Do you have a boyfriend, Faith? Someone you do not wish to leave behind?"

He knew what he wanted the answer to be, but he had no idea what she would say. If she would ruin his good mood by giving him a different answer than he desired.

"No, no boyfriend," she said.

A sliver of relief slid through him at her soft words. Not that he cared if she had a boyfriend, of course. But it would make it much easier if she did not.

"Any pets?"

"No. No pets. I had a cat, but he died last year."

"I'm sorry."

She shrugged, as if she were trying to say it was nothing. And yet he wasn't fooled. He could hear the sadness in her voice. "It's fine. He was old and it was his time. I wanted to get a kitten, but they need so much attention. Well, any cat does, really, and I work a lot so…"

Her voice trailed off and he found himself feeling somewhat guilty, as if he was at fault because she hadn't gotten another cat. He did work long hours, and sometimes she stayed behind, too, not leaving the office until after seven or eight in the evening.

No, a cat would not like that. Neither would a boyfriend.

She shrugged again. "I'm sorry. You didn't really want to know all that. I'm babbling."

"I've never heard you babble, Faith. I would hardly classify this as babbling." He knew babbling. Katie had been a babbler. He'd found it somewhat annoying that she couldn't ever stop talking, but he'd tried to keep her mouth too occupied to talk whenever they were together.

Renzo frowned. What had he ever seen in Katie? Besides the perfect body, of course? She'd been so shallow, so self-absorbed. Why had he surrounded himself with that?

"Well, I'm babbling now. My mom would say I—"

He heard her indrawn breath. "Would say what?" he prodded when she didn't continue.

"Nothing. It's nothing." She'd folded her hands on her lap again, and he found himself wanting to take one of her soft hands in his and rub circles in her palm the way he'd done before. Just to feel that tremor slide through her.

"You can tell me," he said.

"I'd rather not."

She sounded so prim, so controlled. It made him wonder. How had she worked for him for six months and he didn't know anything about her? She didn't seem to want to talk about her past. And though he wanted to command her to tell him what she'd been about to say, he could hardly do so. It wasn't like he enjoyed talking about his past—his family—either.

His mother was a good woman who'd worked hard all her life, but he was still somewhat embarrassed by his origins. He shouldn't be, but he was. Not because of her, but because of the Conte de Lucano. From the moment he'd learned who his father was when he was eight years old, the one time the man had come to see them and threatened his mother if she dared tell anyone who had fathered her child, he'd felt inferior. Damaged. Like garbage tossed on a scrap heap.

For all he knew, Faith felt the same. "You do not like talking about your family," he said.

She sighed. "No, I don't like talking about them. I left years ago and I'm never going back."

It was the closest thing to a vow he'd ever heard her utter. She said it with such conviction. Such bitterness.

Such passion.

Renzo felt a jolt of awareness curl through him. *Maledizione,* was he mad? She was his PA, and though he didn't quite understand where this sudden attraction to her sprang from, she was most definitely off-limits. She had to be. He needed to concentrate on the Viper, and he needed his efficient PA at his side, taking care of the business side of his life while he rode the hell out of the motorcycle and worked on the adjustments to the design. If he crossed the line with her, he could endanger everything—in so much as she might leave and he'd have to train a new PA when he did not have the time.

No, Renzo could not afford to endanger anything right now when time was critical. When Niccolo Gavretti was just waiting to find a weakness he could exploit in his quest to destroy Renzo and D'Angeli Motors. He should have crushed Niccolo when he'd had the chance, but he'd been sentimental. *Idiot.*

"I don't suppose you care to tell me why," he said, more than a little curious about what could make quiet, calm Faith Black run away from home.

Her head moved, the lights shining off her golden hair as she shook it. "Some families don't get along," she said. "Let's just leave it at that."

He could only stare. He'd thought her sweet, harmless, and here she was made of steel and wrapped in velvet. Faith did not speak to her family. It was a revelation, and he burned with curiosity as to why. He spoke to his mother and sister regularly, couldn't imagine not speaking to them. But here was this quiet girl telling him with such vehemence that she'd cut herself off from everyone in her life.

It stunned him. This was a woman with unsuspected depths. A woman who'd worked for him for six months, and he'd never once realized there was more to her than the face she presented him with every day.

The car pulled to a stop in front of her apartment building. He thought she might make a dash for it, but she waited for Stefan to come around and open the door. Renzo stepped out onto the pavement, his leg throbbing so badly now that he knew he would need a pain pill when he got home. At least, mercifully, the damn thing would make him sleep.

"You don't have to see me up," Faith said as he started toward the building door.

He turned toward her, saw the worry lines bracketing her mouth, and knew that she'd seen through him. For some reason, that made him angry.

"I do," he said shortly, his tone brooking no argument. A part of him was saying he was a fool, but the other part— the prideful, stubborn part—insisted he could still do any damn thing he wanted to do. It was simply an issue of mind over matter. If he couldn't conquer the little things, like stairs, how could he conquer the big things, like riding the Viper on the Grand Prix circuit?

Faith turned away in a huff and walked to the door. He followed her. She used her key to get inside the building, and then they were moving toward the stairs. She took her time, saying her high heels were bothering her, but he suspected she did it for him.

His leg cramped as he climbed the two flights, but then they were in the hall and standing before her door. Pain spiked into his leg then, radiating through his entire body so that he leaned against the wall, certain he wouldn't be moving for at least five minutes. *Per Dio.*

Faith unlocked her door and turned, a little gasp escaping her when she saw him standing there. "Renzo? Are you okay?"

"*Si,* of course," he said, but his voice sounded as if he were gritting his teeth. Which he was, he realized a moment later.

Faith didn't hesitate. She looped her arm in his. "Come in and sit down. Let me massage it for you."

Now why, in the midst of his pain, did that thought make his libido kick into gear?

"I'll be fine in a few moments. Just let me stand here." It wasn't an admission he'd wanted to make, but he wasn't so stubborn as to deny the truth when she could clearly see it.

She frowned up at him. "I had a roommate who was a massage therapist, and she taught me some things. I'm not a professional, but I can try to ease the cramp."

"It will go away in a moment."

Her expression said she didn't believe it for a minute. "I can massage it or you can stand here. Whichever you prefer. But know this. My feet hurt and I'm going inside and sitting down, with or without you."

He swore softly in Italian, but he let her help him into the cramped living space of her apartment. He didn't even bother trying to hide the limp this time. What was the point?

She eased him down on her sofa and then hastily moved magazines from her coffee table before bending to pick his foot up and prop it on the table. Renzo leaned his head back and closed his eyes as pain throbbed into his body.

"You shouldn't have stood on it so long tonight," Faith said.

"This rarely happens," he replied automatically, though

it was a lie. In truth it happened too often of late. And what if it happened on the track? He'd been asking himself that for months now. The consequences could be disastrous. He knew what it was like to wipe out at two hundred miles an hour. Knew how lucky he'd been to wake up from the accident with pins in his leg and his head intact.

"Yes, well, you should still think of it and take opportunities to rest the leg when you can." Faith sank down onto the couch beside him, her body pressing against his as she leaned over him and put her small hands on his thigh.

Renzo swallowed. Hard. He was in pain, yes, but he wasn't dead. His body wanted to respond to the feel of her hands pressing into him, but he refused to allow it. His senses were filled with her—with the sweet scent of her, the tactile pressure of her hands on his body, the sound of her breath and her voice. With his eyes closed, he didn't have to ask himself what it was about her. He could *feel* what it was, though he'd be damned if he could name it.

"The muscles are so tight," she said. "It would be much better if you took your pants off."

Renzo couldn't help but laugh, though the sound was nothing like his usual laugh. He wasn't quite sure if it was strained from the pain of his leg or the pain of fighting with himself not to reach for her. "*Cara*, you surprise me."

"That's not what I meant," she said, sounding all prickly and cool.

Renzo opened his eyes. She was looking at his leg, concentrating on massaging it, but a red flush had spread over her cheeks. Her face in profile was lovelier than he'd imagined. He couldn't stop himself from lifting his hand. From sliding his finger across her soft cheek.

"And yet I could almost wish you did," he said, and her head came up, her green eyes so wide and innocent. Innocent? He wasn't sure where he'd gotten that thought from.

"Are you flirting with me, Mr. D'Angeli?"

"Not if you prefer I didn't," he told her truthfully, disappointed that she'd retreated behind formality once more.

Her gaze dropped again. Her fingers kneaded his knotted muscles. It hurt, and yet he knew she was loosening them at the same time.

"That is exactly what I prefer," she said. "You *are* charming, but your charm is misdirected on me."

His brows drew together. She was bent over him, her head bowed, her cleavage frustratingly covered—and yet he would have sworn she felt the spark between them, too.

"Is it?" he asked, aggravated that she was so distant and formal.

"The last thing you need is another woman puffing up your already-outrageous ego," she stated firmly. "So, if you don't mind, while I am certain you could charm the panties off a nun, I'd prefer if you didn't attempt it on me."

Her heart thudded in her ears. Faith couldn't believe she'd actually said that to him. She was not unaffected by his male beauty, no matter how she protested otherwise. But he didn't need to know that, did he?

Except he wasn't a stupid man. When he'd touched her, she'd felt the blush bloom across her cheeks. Surely he'd seen it. Just as he'd no doubt heard the breathy note in her voice when she'd asked if he was flirting with her.

She'd denied she was affected, but it was a lie. What living, breathing woman wouldn't be attracted to this man?

Faith wanted to snort in disgust. Really, *she* should be the woman who wasn't because she'd watched him go through at least five girlfriends since she'd worked for him. Not only that, but she'd also seen the tabloid reports on his notorious love-them-and-leave-them lifestyle. How could she ever find a man like him attractive?

And yet she did.

"I don't believe I've ever charmed a nun," he said, his voice containing a hint of steel beneath the silk. "I only charm those who wish to be charmed."

"Then I'll consider myself safe." The tops of her ears burned.

"For now," he said.

Faith tried to concentrate on the ropes of muscle beneath her hands. It would be so much easier if she could touch his skin instead of his trousers, but this was definitely safer. Seeing his body, touching his skin—it made curls of heat sizzle into her just thinking of it. Even now, though there was fabric between her skin and his, it wasn't quite enough to block the sensuality of touching him.

Concentrate.

Faith pressed her thumbs into the muscle and worked at the knots. She wasn't a true massage therapist, but she'd thought she could help him by using a couple of the things that Elaine had taught her before moving back to Ohio.

What else could she do? She couldn't let him stand out there in the hall, and she couldn't let him go back downstairs when he was in such pain.

"Should I go down and tell Stefan what's happened?" she asked, suddenly remembering the uniformed man they'd left on the street.

"I'll call." Renzo took his phone out of his pocket.

"He can come up, if you like."

Renzo's eyes were flat. "No, that is not necessary."

Faith supposed Stefan was quite used to waiting outside women's apartments. The thought did not cheer her. Would the man think his boss was up here getting cozy with her? Did she care?

Renzo made the call, told Stefan to go home while Faith tried not to swallow her tongue, and then hung up and gave her an even look.

"Don't look so worried," he told her. "I'll take a taxi home."

She bit the inside of her cheek and told herself it didn't matter if Stefan thought Renzo was spending the night with her. It was getting late and Stefan would want to return home, so it was kind of Renzo not to make him wait.

"Is this helping at all?" she asked, still pressing her thumbs into his thigh muscle.

"*Si*, I think so."

"How long has this been going on, Mr. D'Angeli?"

His icy blue eyes glittered. "I refuse to discuss this with you unless you call me Renzo."

Faith's cheeks heated. "I had thought it best if we go back to the way things were before the party tonight."

Because she needed to put distance between them. She needed to remember that he was her boss, and not a man she could ever know more personally.

"And I disagree. If you wish to know about my leg, Faith, you will address me the way I have asked you to. It seems a bit ridiculous to call me Mr. D'Angeli considering where your hands are, yes?"

She barely resisted the urge to pinch him. "If this were a spa, I highly doubt you'd be asking the technician to call you Renzo."

He arched an eyebrow. "Depends on how attractive she was, I imagine."

"You're incorrigible," she said.

"And possessed of an outrageous ego, I understand."

Faith couldn't help but laugh. "Oh dear. I'm sorry I said that." It might be true, but she shouldn't have said it. One evening pretending to be his date didn't give her a license to insult him. He was still her boss when everything was said and done.

"You aren't sorry at all. And I don't mind." He shrugged. "Perhaps it is true."

"Will you tell me about your leg now?"

"Will you agree to call me Renzo?"

What else could she say? "Yes."

"*Bene*." He sighed. "It happens more lately than it used to. The doctors told me I would never walk without a limp, that I would always need a cane—but I proved them wrong. Except," he said with a hint of bitterness in his voice, "that it seems as if my victory was only temporary."

She stopped rubbing for half a second, her fingers going limp at the thought of this proud man needing a cane once more. "There is nothing that can be done?"

"Probably not. But I will not give in just yet." He leaned toward her then, took her chin in his fingers and forced her to look at him. "No one can know about this, Faith. It's very important that no one knows."

She could only blink at him. "I don't see how you can keep it a secret if something like this happens again."

He released her and sat back again. "I won't let it happen."

"That didn't work so well for you tonight, did it?" She was growing angry, and not because he was stubborn, but because he frightened her. She knew where this conviction sprang from, knew what he did not say. The Viper. The Grand Prix circuit. Though he had a racing team, he didn't feel anyone else could ride the bike to victory just yet. It was personal to him, though she did not quite know why.

The arrogant man intended to risk his neck on the track and to hell with everything else. It infuriated her.

She got to her feet, her entire body trembling with energy. She needed to move, needed to do something, or she might explode. *Why did she care?*

"Do you want something to drink?"

He was watching her carefully. "A brandy would be nice."

She wanted to laugh, but she did not. "I'm sorry, but this isn't the Ritz. I don't have a liquor cabinet. I may have some vodka, though."

Elaine had liked vodka and Faith was pretty sure she'd left half a bottle behind.

"And tonic water," she added. "I know I have that."

"Vodka and tonic would be fine," he said. Faith turned and fled to the kitchen. She found the vodka shoved in the back of a cabinet. Then she filled a glass with ice, added some vodka and poured tonic water on top. For good measure, she made another for herself. She wasn't much of a drinker, but she had the feeling she needed something to take the edge off.

This night had been strange, to say the least.

Renzo was sitting where she'd left him, his leg still propped up, his head leaning back against the sofa cushion. His eyes were closed, and she took a moment to admire the symmetrical beauty of his face. His nose was long and lean, his cheekbones high, his lips full and firm. He had a mouth made to kiss, she thought. His top lip dipped in the center, just slightly, and she found herself wanting to nibble on that sexy little dip.

It was a sensual mouth. A cruel mouth. A mouth she wanted on hers even though she knew better. Just for a moment. Just so she could see for herself what made all those women so willing to put up with this man.

His eyes snapped open, then went unerringly to her face. The heat she saw there was unmistakable. It nearly fixed her feet to the spot, but she forced herself to move

as if nothing was any different. As if they were still Miss
Black and Mr. D'Angeli, and this was simply a morning
at the office and she was taking him coffee.

She crossed the distance between them and held out the
drink. "*Grazie*," he said, taking it from her and sitting it
on the table beside him.

She set her own drink down and turned back to him,
prepared to ask if he wanted her to continue rubbing his
leg. But the look in his eyes scorched her.

Renzo reached up and took her hand in his. Her skin
sizzled as fire snaked through her.

"You feel it, too," he said. "I know you do."

Faith could not speak. She did feel it, whatever *it* was.
And she didn't like it. It made her achy and jumpy and worried. He was the wrong man, the man who could destroy
her present just as Jason Moore had destroyed her past.

With one tug, he pulled her down onto his lap, his arms
going around her to cradle her close. "Renzo," she started
to protest, but he bent and fitted his gorgeous mouth to
hers, silencing her.

CHAPTER FOUR

So MANY sensations crashed through Faith at once: confusion, fear, lust, passion, joy. She wanted to slide her arms around his neck, arch into him and beg him to show her what no man ever had before.

And she wanted to shove away from him, put as much distance between them as possible. She wanted him to go. And she wanted him to stay.

His mouth on hers was firm, sensual, demanding. His tongue slid across the seam of her lips, enticing her, entreating her. She was determined not to give in to the invitation, but he caressed her cheek and she gasped. His tongue slipped inside her mouth, stroked against hers.

It was, in its own way, heaven. Her heart hammered so hard in her ears that she could hear nothing else.

Faith made a sound, realized it was a moan. It was a needy sound from deep in her throat, the kind of sound that invited a man to continue, to take it further.

No! No, no, no. That was not at all what she wanted. She wanted it to stop—

And yet she made no move to stop it. In fact, she shivered in his embrace at the thought of more. The truth was that Renzo D'Angeli kissed like he'd been born to do so. His mouth moved over hers, fitted to hers, coaxed hers.

And she gave, gave as much as she was able, gave more than she thought she could.

She meant to push him away, but she wound her arms around his neck instead, let the hot sensations roll over her. She was electric, incandescent, her body sparking and tightening in ways she'd not thought possible. This was what drew the women, then. *This.*

A moment later she tilted, and then the world was shifting as he pressed her back onto the couch, his hard strong body pressing into hers. Panic shot through her. It suddenly reminded her of another time, another place, when she was young and innocent and thought she was in love. Jason had pressed her onto her parents' couch just like this, his body rubbing hers almost painfully, his hands grasping and groping beneath her dress.

Renzo did nothing of the sort, and yet Faith couldn't get the images out of her head. The fear, the panic. *A good girl wouldn't do such a thing, Faith. A good girl keeps her body sacred until she enters into the bonds of matrimony.*

It was her father talking, but she suddenly couldn't make the sainted Reverend Winston go away. And she couldn't allow that ugliness to ruin whatever beautiful feeling was crashing through her because of Renzo.

She put her hands on Renzo's shoulders and pushed. He lifted his head, a question in his blue eyes, and Faith took the opportunity to scramble out from under him. She fell onto the floor in a tangle of fabric, then shoved herself upright and retreated across the room.

Renzo stood, his features dark and alarmed. "Faith?"

Faith wrapped her arms around her body. "I'm sorry, but that was a mistake. I didn't mean for it to go that far, so please just forget it happened."

He looked stormy, and so sexy she wanted to weep. Had

that gorgeous, gorgeous man really been kissing her? Little
Faith Louise Winston of all damn people?

"Forget?" he asked dangerously. "I hardly think that is
possible, Faith."

"It was a mistake," she said. "I work for you, and tomorrow I'll be at the office like always, and you'll be there
doing what you always do, and it will be so awkward that
I'll want to scream. But I won't. And you'll find a new
girlfriend soon, and then you can forget about kissing me."

He shoved his hand through his hair, muttering in
Italian, and then picked up his vodka and tonic and drained
it. "Why would I want to forget it, Faith?"

"Because I'm nothing special," she said. Good Lord,
was the man dense?

"Don't talk like that," he commanded, his eyes flashing, and she laughed nervously.

"Don't worry. I don't think I'm awful or anything. I *am*
special, but in my world. Not in yours. You wouldn't even
be here if you hadn't dumped Katie Palmer today."

"Katie Palmer has nothing to do with this," he growled.

"But she does," Faith said, hoping she sounded as cool
and logical as she was trying so hard to be. She'd been
kissing Lorenzo D'Angeli, motorcycle magnate, Grand
Prix bad boy, right here in her humble little living room.
If he weren't still standing there in all his magnificently
male glory, she'd think she was making the whole thing up.
That the vodka and tonic she hadn't even taken a sip of had
gone to her head and made her hallucinate. "Katie Palmer
is the kind of woman you prefer. All your girlfriends have
looked like some version of her, you know."

His gaze narrowed, but she tumbled on recklessly. "Tall,
leggy, effortlessly beautiful, with long dark hair and perfect makeup and size zero bodies that could really probably
use a hamburger or two a bit more often..." She cleared

her throat, waved a hand down her body. "As you can see, I am none of those things. I'm short, curvy and not in the least bit effortlessly beautiful. And I like to eat. Pasta, hamburgers, the occasional French fry. No, you should really go find that Lissa woman and make her your next fling."

He looked utterly furious. "*Santo cielo,* I am not arguing with you over this." He took his phone from his pocket. "Perhaps you are correct. Lissa would certainly not argue with me when I wanted to kiss her."

"Not many women would," Faith said, stung in spite of everything she'd said to push him away.

"But you did." He made a call to a taxi company while she stood there feeling miserable, her heart squeezing tight as she wondered if she'd made a mistake.

Of course she hadn't. He was her boss!

"I need our relationship to be professional," she said when he finished his call, as much to convince herself as him. "I like my job and I don't want to feel uncomfortable there."

Renzo waved a hand as if it were nothing. Which, to him, it probably was. Women came and went with alarming regularity in his life. What was one more?

Indeed, his fury with her seemed forgotten as he moved toward the door with only the barest trace of a limp. "It never happened, Faith. Thank you for the massage, and for the drink. I will see you in the office tomorrow."

And then he walked out and left her standing there, her lips still tingling and her body aching with thwarted desire. Either she was the bravest woman in the world, or the biggest fool to send him away.

The problem was that she wasn't quite sure which.

Renzo got into the office early the next morning. Faith had not yet arrived when he walked past her desk and into his office with the tall windows and custom decor. Low-slung Italian leather couches faced each other in front of his desk, and he dropped onto one of them to read the reports that were sitting on the table there.

The Viper was nearly ready to take to Italy. The thought should fill him with triumph, and yet it only made him worry about what else might go wrong. He'd taken a pain pill last night, and this morning he felt perfectly fine—but when was the next time his leg would give out? And what would his rivals do if they learned he was not at his best? Niccolo Gavretti was looking for a chance to cream him. If his biggest rival knew about his weakness, he would exploit it whenever and however possible.

And then there was Faith. Renzo rubbed his temples for a moment and then dropped the reports. Where had his world-renowned cool gone last night when he'd needed it? He'd succumbed to the temptation to kiss her because she'd bent over him and her scent had driven him insane. He'd wanted just a taste. One brief taste, to see if he was losing his mind in lusting after his PA, or if there was something more beneath that buttoned-up surface.

He could still remember the utter shock he'd felt when his mouth touched hers. The lightning bolt of excitement that had rocketed through him with the same force as a fast ride on a fast track. There was nothing more exhilarating than opening up the throttle and giving the bike gas.

But kissing Faith had compared to that feeling. He'd wanted her. His body had gone from zero to two hundred plus in a matter of seconds. Even thinking of it now made him hard.

He knew when a woman wanted him, and she definitely had. And he'd had every intention of taking advantage of the chemistry between them at that moment. He'd been unable to stop himself from pressing her back on the couch when she'd kissed him with such fervor.

She was hot and sweet and more innocent than she seemed. She'd kissed him with all the finesse of a rank amateur, and yet it had done nothing but heat his blood. He usually liked his women polished and experienced, but Faith had managed to make him forget his preferences.

He'd wanted her and damn the consequences of sleeping with his PA. Hell, he still wanted her. He'd told her the kiss was forgotten, but he had forgotten nothing.

There was a knock on his door and he glanced at his watch. Eight o'clock on the dot, which meant it was probably Faith arriving. "Enter," he said, standing up and crossing to his desk.

The door slid open and Faith stood there in a boxy black suit, short heels, and with her hair scraped back on her head as always. "I wasn't sure if you were here," she said briskly. "Would you like coffee, Mr. D'Angeli?"

A trickle of annoyance filtered through him. "*Si,* that would be good, thank you."

She turned away.

"Faith," he called, and she stopped, pivoted to face him again.

"Yes sir?"

The formality grated on him, but he knew she did it to keep him at a distance. He wanted to tell her to take her hair down. To take off that ridiculous boxy jacket and unbutton her blouse to show some cleavage. To come over and wrap her arms around him so he could fit her body to his and kiss her thoroughly.

He would, of course, say none of those things. Another woman would smile and pout and do exactly what he wanted. But not Faith. If he said those things to her, she would slay him with a cold stare. And then she would walk out of his office and he'd be lucky if she ever came back.

"We're leaving for Italy in a week. Please make arrangements."

Her jaw dropped and for a moment he thought she would refuse. He waited for it, wondered how he would command her to go once she'd turned him down. Because he wanted her there with him. Because, *maledizione*, he *wanted* her. She intrigued him like no one else with her hidden beauty and prickly demeanor.

And her secrets. He wanted to know her secrets. What had made sweet Faith turn her back on her family?

Color bloomed on her cheeks, brought life and sparkle to her glorious eyes. She hesitated for a long minute. "Yes sir," she said. "I will."

Faith had never been outside of the United States before. She had her passport, because it had been required when she'd started working for D'Angeli Motors, but she'd never actually thought she would have reason to use it.

Now, as she stood in her apartment and looked around to make sure she'd forgotten nothing, she could hardly believe she was going. Renzo hadn't been able to tell her how long they would be gone, but he'd told her to continue to pay her rent here if it made her comfortable since she would be provided housing in Italy at no extra charge.

In his house. Faith gulped. She would be living in his house, a stone's throw away from him, for twenty-four hours a day. Why had she agreed to go? How could she live with him, as an employee, and watch him go about his life as if nothing had ever happened between the two of them? He had already forgotten it, as he'd assured her he would, while she could think of little else.

But that wasn't the worst of it. The worst was that she

imagined he would most certainly entertain women from time to time. In the same house she'd be living in. As an employee.

Faith made a noise that sounded suspiciously like a cry of distress. She'd meant to refuse to go. She'd meant to tell him that she couldn't go to Italy and could she please have a transfer to another office, but she'd stood there and looked at his handsome face, at the mouth she'd been kissing only hours earlier, and felt all her resolve crumble into nothing.

She'd said yes, just like some besotted female. She was furious with herself over it. For hours, she'd debated going back in there and telling him no, telling him she'd made a mistake and she wanted to stay right here, thank you very much.

But she hadn't. And now a car was waiting to take her to JFK for the flight to Italy. She took one last look around, and then locked the door behind her and headed down to the street. The driver had already taken her luggage down, so that when she emerged from the building, he popped out of the car and came around to open her door.

She slid into the plush interior of the black town car and belted herself in for the ride. It took nearly an hour in traffic to reach the airport, but once there she was ushered onto a huge Boeing business jet that belonged to D'Angeli Motors.

The interior was nothing like any plane she'd ever been on. She'd had no occasion to board the company's international jet before, but now she gaped at the sumptuous interior. Renzo was a wealthy man indeed if he could afford all this. Rich wood grains, buttery leather chairs and couches, a bar, televisions and custom carpeting that had the D'Angeli Motors logo woven into it. It was all so stunning, and it only served to remind her of how ridiculous it was to think he'd actually wanted her the night of the party. She was not the sort of sophisticated woman who matched this lifestyle.

In fact, she'd been thinking of other plane trips she'd taken in the past and she'd dressed for comfort with the typical economy class seating in mind. She wore stretchy jeans, a hooded sweatshirt and tennis shoes she could slip on and off without untying. In her carry-on backpack, she had a couple of books, an ereader, a music player and headphones, along with a few power bars and a bottle of water. She even had a travel pillow, which seemed silly since she was positive this jet was probably equipped with real pillows and blankets.

A sophisticated woman would have arrived wearing the latest fashions and carrying matching luggage—Louis Vuitton, no doubt—instead of dressed like a refugee and carrying snacks.

She was embarrassed suddenly, and it made her uncomfortable. She knew what it was like to feel like an outsider, like an idiot, and though wearing the wrong clothing and failing to be sophisticated didn't compare to what had happened before, the shame and anger were similar.

She felt stupid, useless, and she stood and clenched her fingers into fists, digging her nails into her palms. She'd left naive Faith Winston behind when she'd left home and changed her name, but that Faith sometimes crept up on her and made her feel as if she'd escaped nothing after all. As if she were still the preacher's daughter who'd been so stupid as to send a scandalous picture to a boy.

"Ah, Faith," Renzo said, and she looked up to see him standing just inside the entrance to the main cabin and smiling at her. She swallowed at the sight of him. His sharp blue eyes raked over her, appraising her—and no doubt found her lacking. He was dressed for comfort, too, she noted, but his jeans were designer labeled, and the soft cotton shirt he wore unbuttoned over a navy D'Angeli Motors T-shirt was probably hand woven by cloistered virgins or some such.

Because, if any man could afford such a thing, it would be Renzo.

He came forward and took her arm, leading her back toward the cabin he'd been in. "You look lovely," he said in her ear as he stopped just short of the entry.

Fire leaped along her nerve endings. "No, not really," she blurted, confusion and fear breaking through the surface of her calm.

His eyes dropped over her again. "And I say you do." He gave her arm a squeeze and then led her into the room he'd come from.

Two men sat at a table, papers spread out across the surface, but they stood as she entered the room with Renzo. She recognized them as two of the engineers on the project. "You have met Bill and Sergio before, have you not?" Renzo said, gesturing to the two men.

"I've met them, yes," she said, shaking hands with each man in turn. They were polite, but she was certain they were curious. Renzo had an entire staff at his Italian headquarters. Could he really not find a PA who kept his appointments straight?

Renzo put a hand on the small of her back. It was a possessive move, a familiar move, though it probably only looked gentlemanly to those observing. Faith could feel her color rising, and her gaze dropped away from the other men's.

"Let me show you where you will be most comfortable," Renzo said.

"Thank you," Faith murmured. What else could she say? That his fingers were burning into her where they lightly rested on her? That her nerve endings were tingling with awareness? That for the past week she had thought of little else than that kiss they'd shared?

Renzo steered her toward another area of the plane that had a long couch built along one wall and a flat-screen television that rose up from a cabinet at the touch of a button.

"You may watch until we take off," he said. "At that point, it will have to be turned off until we're in the air."

"Thank you," she said stiffly, standing with her hands folded together while she waited for him to return to his engineers. There was a wall between this room and the office he'd been in, and she could no longer see the two men.

Renzo laughed softly. "Relax. No one is going to bite you, *cara*. Unless, of course, you wish it?"

Her heart turned over. His blue gaze glittered hotly, and for one brief moment she thought he might actually pull her into his arms. Shockingly, a part of her wanted him to do so.

But only for a moment, only until she got her senses back and realized what a mistake that would be.

He did not touch her, however, and she began to believe she'd imagined that look that had said he would devour her if she let him. He was toying with her.

"I think I'll be fine without any biting," she said, unable to sound like anything but a prim preacher's daughter as she said it.

He laughed again. "You are a delight, Faith Black." And then he skimmed a finger down her cheek. "But I assure you that you would like it very much if I bit you. I know just where and how to nibble for the most impact."

Faith couldn't breathe. Molten heat rolled through her, pooling between her thighs, making her ache with longing. How did he do it? How did he make her want to forget every last bit of good sense she had and slip between the sheets with him? They were only words, and yet when he spoke them, they were dangerous. Seductive.

"You really shouldn't say things like that," she told him, proud that she managed to speak without choking.

He loomed over her, six feet two inches of gorgeous Italian male who smelled delicious and radiated a lethal sex appeal that had her wanting to wrap herself around him and to hell with the consequences.

Renzo's brow arched mockingly. "And you shouldn't refuse to consider the possibilities."

She had nothing to say to that. Renzo put his hands on her shoulders, then leaned down and brushed his lips across her forehead before turning and leaving without another word.

Her entire body hummed with electricity as she sank onto the couch in a daze. For a whole week, she'd convinced herself that he'd forgotten about their kiss in her apartment, that he'd put it from his mind as inconsequential, that the heat and excitement she'd felt had only been her imagination.

I know just where and how to nibble for the most impact.

Faith shuddered at the images that statement brought to mind. It was a long flight to Rome, and she wasn't going to sleep a wink.

CHAPTER FIVE

THEY arrived in Rome early the next morning. Though Faith had thought she wouldn't sleep at all, she in fact had, and woke feeling somewhat ready for the day. She'd dressed with care in a dark gray suit and heels, and put her hair into a tight knot. If Renzo was planning to work, she was ready.

Her heart had sped up at the sight of him. He'd been sitting in a plush leather chair by a window and sipping a cappuccino while reading something on his mobile tablet. Totally engrossed, he hadn't noticed her at first, and she'd let her eyes feast on him. His dark hair was full and lush, and it still looked slightly wild, as if he'd been racing on the track with the wind blowing through it. Artfully tousled, sexy, as if some woman had been running her fingers through it while he made love to her.

He was dressed in a navy pinstripe suit with a light blue shirt and a dark red tie. On his feet were custom-made Italian loafers. He looked every inch the billionaire and nothing like the daredevil Grand Prix racer at the moment.

She must have made a noise, because he'd lifted his head and spied her there. The frown on his face had not made her happy. No, it had made her feel about two inches tall, but she'd pushed through it and pretended she hadn't noticed while she took her seat in front of him and prepared to go over his appointments.

Now they were in a Mercedes limousine, moving toward the center of Rome, and Faith couldn't help but gape at the sights. She'd never seen anything so old and magnificent in her life. Everywhere you looked, there were crumbling ruins set beside ornate churches, and people moving around as if it were completely ordinary to be surrounded by such beauty.

The early-morning sun shone down on the city, picking out the bright whites of marble monuments and highlighting the red sandstone of ancient ruins. The traffic was heavy as they rounded the Colosseum, and tears pricked at the back of her eyes.

She'd always wanted to see it, and now it was here, huge, sandy-white and red, and imposing against the bright blue Roman sky. There was a cross set in the outer ring of stone that caught her eye.

Renzo looked up then and saw the question in her gaze. "It is actually a church now," he said. "The Pope holds a service in the Colosseum once a year."

Tourists ringed the grounds as they drove around the structure. Soon, they were passing the ruins of the Forum Romanum. People walked along the sidewalks between the Forum and the Colosseum, and vendors lined the way, selling food, scarves and other trinkets. The ride grew bumpy as they drove over the vast swath of cobblestones near the Vittorio Emanuele military monument. Cars converged in the giant circle and honked, scooters blaring past, before traffic straightened out again and they were moving down a narrow street lined with stores and restaurants.

A short while later, the limousine came to a stop on the Via dei Condotti and Renzo's driver hopped out to open the door. Renzo stepped onto the pavement and Faith followed, coming up short when all she saw were high-end fashion stores. Renzo's security emerged from another car, and then Renzo was propelling her toward the nearest shop.

"What are we doing?" she asked as the door swung open to let them into a salon. An expensively dressed woman behind the counter looked up and greeted them in Italian.

Renzo said something to her, and then her eyes slid toward Faith. To the woman's credit, her expression did not change.

"What is going on?" Faith demanded as the woman picked up a phone and made a call.

"You are getting your hair done," Renzo said.

Faith's hand came up to pat her bun. "My hair is fine," she hissed under her breath.

Renzo looked unconvinced. "And I say it is not, *cara*. We are in Italia now, and you are the personal assistant to a very rich man. I cannot have you managing my appointments and greeting my business associates like this."

Faith spluttered. "I look professional. There's nothing wrong with what I'm wearing. Or how I've styled my hair. Your business associates won't care. You are making that up."

"They *will* care. Even my grandmother had more style than you, *piccolo*." He took her briefcase from her numb fingers while her heart throbbed with hurt. "Consider this a part of your salary for accompanying me."

"I like my hair the way it is," she insisted.

He quirked an eyebrow. "Do you realize that in all the time you have worked for me, I've never seen your hair down?"

"I wanted to look professional."

"And you still shall. But with style, *cara mia*."

"I'm not happy with you," Faith said, seething inside and more than a little curious, as well. What would it be like to have a style she could actually manage? Something that gave her more versatility than she had now? She'd always been afraid to let a stylist touch her hair because she didn't know how to communicate what she wanted. What if they cut too much off, or gave her a look she hated?

It wasn't like she could afford the expensive places on Park Avenue where the rich went. No, she was more likely to use the local chop shop equivalent—and did when she got her annual trim. In fairness to Renzo, she had to admit that she made enough money to spring for a nicer salon than a discount place—but she never knew how to find someone she trusted, and therefore she never took the plunge.

Not to mention she saved every dime she could for the down payment on her future home.

Now, however, he was presenting her with the opportunity to use the kind of salon she could never have afforded on her own. The kind of salon the elite frequented.

Renzo gave her that smile that had the power to tilt her world sideways. "You will be happy with me when you are finished. Trust me."

"Fine," she said, arms crossed defensively. "But if I hate it, you're never going to hear the end of it."

Renzo laughed before nodding at the woman who then escorted Faith into the salon and handed her over to a smiling stylist named Giovanna. Thankfully, Giovanna spoke English and put Faith at ease. Before Giovanna made the first cut, Faith discussed her wishes that she be able to keep her hair long. Giovanna listened intently, and then told Faith exactly what she proposed to do.

She didn't cut much length, but she added plenty of layers to make Faith's hair more manageable. An hour later, Faith was staring in the mirror at a woman who had the sleekest, most gorgeously touchable hair imaginable.

"It's amazing," Faith said.

"You have great hair, *signorina*. You only needed a little cut, a little product to make it so." Giovanna spun the chair away from the mirror. "And now a little bit of makeup, *si*? I will teach you how to do a smoky eye, and you will be ready in moments. It is all you will need to drive the men wild."

Ten minutes later, Faith was walking out of the salon and into the reception area where Renzo sat making notes on his tablet. When he looked up and saw her, a little thrill of pleasure shot through her at the shock on his face. He quickly masked it, however, and stood to greet her as if salon appointments were an ordinary part of his day.

"*Fabuloso,* Faith. You look lovely."

Faith was feeling far too happy over her hair to harbor any resentment that he'd basically hauled her into a salon and told her to cut her hair. No, in fact, she was feeling grateful. For the first time, her hair was elegant and chic— but it still felt like her, not like someone else's idea of her.

Her happy feelings began to ebb, however, when Renzo dragged her into a clothing store and arranged an impromptu fashion show in which she was to be the leading lady.

"No," she said as a saleswoman stood patiently by and a group of others hauled clothing into a dressing area. "This is too much, Renzo. I can't accept clothes from you."

His expression was implacable. "Consider it a perk of the job, Faith. I require you to be stylish when you are at my side."

"You never cared before."

He didn't look in the least bit apologetic. "We were in the States. Things were different there. Here, you will be traveling at my side quite frequently and I require you to look the part."

"Look the part of what?" she demanded. "Your latest mistress?"

His gaze grew heated. "Would that be so bad?" he murmured so that no one else could hear.

"Yes," she said automatically, though a part of her was saying no. *Please, yes, now.*

No.

"You will do this, Faith, or you will be on the next flight back to the United States. But think carefully on your answer," he said silkily. "Because, should you choose to go, you will also be without a job."

Fury rolled through her, followed by frustration and a sense that she was in over her head. "That's blackmail."

She wasn't going to give up her job over a wardrobe, and he knew it. That would be a stupid move, no matter how she might wish to see the look of surprise on his face when she said no. A fresh tide of anger rose within her that he would force her into obeying his will.

She had a moment's ugly thought of her father standing over her and telling her she would continue to go to school as before, no matter what people said or did to her, but no matter how angry it made her, she knew this wasn't the same thing. Her father hadn't cared that she would be emotionally scarred by the experience; Renzo was being stubborn over clothing. Not the same at all.

But Renzo was unrepentant. "It is indeed. Now, choose."

Faith's heart throbbed, and her ears were hot with embarrassment. She'd never been the sort of person to draw attention to herself with clothing, but were her clothes really that bad? The gray suit she wore was perfectly serviceable. The skirt hit right below her knees, the jacket hung to midhip, and her shirt was a daring pink. Her heels were black, low and comfortable.

"This isn't necessary," she said. "We could just go to a

department store and spend a lot less money. I only need a few things off-the-rack—"

"Not a chance, *cara*. You represent me, and you will represent me the way I wish you to."

In the end, there was no choice. Faith succumbed to the will of Renzo and the overwhelming force of the saleswomen, who dressed her in outfit after outfit until she actually started to look forward to the next combination they would present her. She'd always worn her suits because she felt comfortable and professional in them. They were off-the-rack, and they fit just fine, but she was redefining what the meaning of a good fit meant as she tried on clothes that seemed tailor-made for her.

The skirts were shorter, but not too much so—right above the knee instead of below it, and fitted to the curve of her hips rather than hanging straight down. The jackets were nipped in at the waist, rounded on the bottom, and cut to right below the waistband of the skirts. There were silky undergarments, belts, trousers, sweaters, dresses, shoes, handbags, scarves and jewelry that went with each outfit. The fabrics were natural, luxurious, rich.

Renzo bore it all with his usual cool efficiency, looking up from his tablet when she emerged each time. He didn't say a word unless there was a disagreement, and he didn't try to force her to choose anything she didn't like. He gave his opinion when asked, and didn't contradict her when she expressed a preference or a dislike of anything in particular.

It wasn't much, but the fact he left her alone to make her choices made her feel somewhat better. It was as if he was telling her that he believed in her judgment, and she appreciated that more than she could say.

After what seemed like hours, the parade came to an end. Renzo said something in Italian, all the saleswomen melted away except for one, and Faith was left standing in the final outfit, a soft, pale green silk dress, belted at the waist, and a pair of sky-high designer heels in a rich cream color. She had to admit she loved the outfit, and hoped it was one they could buy. She felt sophisticated and pretty, like a princess instead of a secretary.

"We are finished here," Renzo said, and she blinked at him.

"But I need to change back into my clothes—"

"Those are your clothes," he told her. "The rest will be sent along."

"The rest?"

"Everything you chose."

"*Everything*?" If she'd had any idea, she would have been more careful. She'd liked so many things. So many *expensive* things. She shook her head. "It's too much. I can never repay you."

Renzo came over and put his hands on her shoulders. In the heels, she didn't have to tilt her head back to look at his expression. His gaze slid down her body, to the buttons on her dress that came together just over her cleavage, and then met her eyes once more while her insides began to melt. "*Mia bella,* it gives me pleasure to do this for you. I have told you before to consider this as a part of your compensation for accompanying me. It is not easy to leave behind one's friends and home, now is it?"

It was when you didn't really have any friends, and the home didn't belong to you, but Faith didn't say that. "I feel like it's too much," she said.

"And I feel like it's not enough. Which of us is right?"

"I'm pretty sure I am. My sense of what things cost is probably more realistic than yours."

Renzo laughed even as he looped her arm in his. "You

are a refreshing woman, Faith. You speak your mind without care for what I might think. I like it."

"You have enough women feeding your ego," she grumbled, and he laughed again.

They exited the shop and got into the waiting car. Faith turned her head to look out the window at the shops opposite, suddenly uncomfortable to be alone with him again. She didn't know why she should be, but she was.

Not because she was afraid of him, but because she was afraid of herself, she realized. The entire time she'd been trying on clothes, she'd been thinking of how he would look at her when she walked out in each outfit. What would Renzo think? What would he do? Would he look at her like he wanted to take her in his arms and kiss her again, the way he had in her apartment?

It was dangerous to think of him like that. Dangerous to think for even a moment that she wanted him to kiss her. There was nothing but heartbreak in allowing herself to think of a man like Renzo wanting her. She was his PA, not his girlfriend.

"I do understand the value of money, *cara*," he said, his voice breaking the silence between them as the car rolled through the streets of Rome. "I was not born rich."

She turned to look at him. She knew that, of course, because she'd read all about him when she'd joined the company. He'd started competing in motorcycle races at seventeen, had been picked up by a major manufacturer and ridden their motorcycles for a few years before coming up with his own designs. He'd poured every euro he had into building his first motorcycle, gotten sponsorship and investors and built D'Angeli Motors into a powerhouse in the industry while others had looked on in shock.

Renzo was formidable, both in his industry and in life, she thought. No wonder he'd maneuvered her so smoothly into changing her hair and buying clothes today. He did not accept defeat. Ever. "Did you grow up in Rome?" she asked.

His gaze was blank. "No. A small town on the Amalfi Coast. My mother was a waitress in a hotel there."

"And your father?"

The corners of his mouth tightened, and a throb of premonition squeezed her heart. "I do not have a father, *cara.*"

She didn't quite know what to say to that. She felt like she'd tripped into a minefield, and there was nothing to do now but finish the journey and hope for the best. "I'm sorry, Renzo."

He shrugged. "It has been this way my whole life. I am not bothered by it."

But he was. She could tell by the bleak look on his face, the way his voice was carefully controlled. Whatever it was, it bothered him a great deal.

"My father is a preacher," she said, and then wondered why she'd admitted that to him. But he'd seemed so lost, and she'd found herself wanting to confess that while she had a father, their relationship wasn't perfect.

He looked at her with interest. "A preacher? What is this?"

Faith twisted her fingers together. She didn't like talking about her family. It inevitably brought up painful memories, but she'd started the conversation and had to finish it. "He's a minister. In a church."

"Ah, I see." His gaze was suddenly keen. "Perhaps this explains much about you."

It explained a lot, actually, but she was far too embarrassed to tell him all of it. "He was a hard man to live with," she said softly. "He expected much out of his children. I was the disappointment. My brother Albert was an Eagle Scout, and I…"

She swallowed. Renzo reached for her hand. She let him take it, a little tingle of awareness beginning to sizzle up her spine as he threaded his fingers in hers.

"All children think they are a disappointment at one time or another. It is rarely true, I believe."

"It is definitely true in my case," Faith said. "I haven't spoken to my father in eight years."

His eyes searched hers, their blue depths full of dark emotion. "I'm sorry, Faith. I can tell this upsets you."

She shrugged. But yes, it hurt, even after all this time. She'd been so stupid. So naive and innocent and gullible. And she'd paid the price. Jason hadn't. He was a male, and males stuck together.

"I, um, I shouldn't have said anything," she replied, her gaze firmly fixed on their linked hands. "It makes me uncomfortable to talk about it."

He brought her hand to his mouth and feathered his lips across her skin. His breath was hot as he spoke. "Then we will not speak of it again."

Tears pricked her eyes. She really didn't want to like him, and yet she couldn't quite help it at the moment. "Thank you."

"It is nothing," he said. And then his voice grew firm, determined. "You are a good woman, Faith. Never believe otherwise."

"You don't really know me," she said. "I might be nothing more than a very good actress."

At that he laughed. "Actually, you aren't an actress at all," he told her. "Your every emotion is written across your face. Would you like to know what I see there now?"

She met his gaze evenly. His eyes glittered with heat and promise, and she could feel her nipples responding, tightening, her breasts growing heavy and firm. Her sex throbbed with need, her body growing tight and achy.

"What do you see?" she asked, surprised at the husky turn of her voice.

He lifted his hand to her face, traced his thumb across her bottom lip. She bit back the moan that wanted to escape as he did so. "I see a woman who wants me…but who is terribly afraid to admit it."

CHAPTER SIX

"You are mistaken, Renzo," Faith said once she found her voice again. Her heart, in the meantime, was pounding at light speed. "You really should see a doctor about that ego, you know. It must be such a burden carrying that thing around."

One corner of his mouth lifted in a grin. "You amuse me, and yet I recognize this tactic. It's not working, by the way."

"Tactic? What tactic? I assure you I'm only speaking the truth."

He leaned toward her, his eyes gleaming hotly. "Then prove it to me, *cara mia*. Kiss me and prove to me that you are unaffected."

Faith sat stiffly beside him, lacing her fingers together in her lap. "That would be unprofessional, Mr. D'Angeli."

He lounged back on the seat, watching her with dark humor sparking in his gaze. "Another tactic, lovely Faith. First you insult me. Then you wish to distance me with your formality."

"I'm your PA," she said. "It's perfectly appropriate."

"But aren't you curious?"

Her heart thumped at the wicked sparkle in his gaze. Of course she was curious. "Not at all." She smoothed the fabric of the green dress. "Honestly, does this usually work for you? I'd have thought you had much more complex methods to employ."

He laughed. And then he leaned toward her and it was everything she could do not to scoot away and cling to the door like a frightened virgin. "You try to push me away with your thorniness, but it doesn't work the way you suppose it does, *cara mia.*"

She drew her body upright, holding herself rigid in the seat. "Then you are not as smart as I thought you were. A shame, considering how many people depend upon you."

His eyes narrowed. "Do you know what you need, Faith?"

"Sleep," she ventured. "I didn't get a lot of it last night."

One eyebrow lifted. "What I propose does involve a bed, but sleep isn't part of the equation. At least not immediately."

She turned her head away to hide the blush that she knew was creeping up her neck and spreading over her cheeks. A moment later Renzo gasped. She turned, her heart tumbling at the anguish tightening his features. He clenched his fists at his sides, and his lips were white with pain.

"Renzo, are you all right? Is it your leg?"

He nodded once, and she sidled toward him, suddenly uncaring about keeping her distance. "Stretch your leg out if you can. Let me massage it."

His head fell back against the seat, his skin turning ashen as he stretched the leg. She had no doubt he was in agony. "*Dio*, it hurts," he said.

"Do you have any pain pills?"

"I do, but I took one last night. I can't take another for a few days yet."

His muscles were so tight. Faith massaged rhythmically, trying to ease the cramp. "Why not?"

His blue gaze pierced into her, the depths filled with pain and even perhaps a little bit of fear. "They are addictive, Faith. I can't allow that to happen."

No, a man like Renzo would not wish to be addicted to painkillers. She admired his willpower even though she feared he might be a bit too strict with parceling out the pills. "What about anti-inflammatories? Surely you can take those."

"*Si.*"

Faith grabbed her purse and dug through it until she found a bottle. "Here, I have something. They're over the counter and completely safe."

He blinked at her. "And why do you need these?" he asked, accepting the two pills she shook into his palm.

"My wrists sometimes hurt at the end of a long work day. Typing," she added when he continued to look perplexed. She poured water into one of the crystal goblets set against one wall of the limousine and handed it to him. He put the pills in his mouth and drank, and Faith continued to massage his leg until he grasped her hands and pulled her against him, wedging her into the curve of his body where he lay back against the seat.

"Just sit with me," he said softly, his breath ruffling her hair. "That is all I want."

"But your leg—"

"The spasm is easing. It does not always last long. Thankfully, this is one of those times."

Faith thought she should move away from him, but she couldn't do it. She could feel the tension in his body and knew he still hurt, so she leaned against him and sat very still. The heat of his body slid beneath her skin, the sensation both thrilling and comforting. His hand came up to stroke her hair, and goose bumps prickled along the back of her neck.

This was wrong, so wrong. And yet it felt too good.

They didn't speak, and eventually her eyes started to feel heavy, her body languid. Soon, in spite of her attempts otherwise, she fell asleep against Renzo. When she awoke, the car had stopped and Renzo was gently shaking her.

Faith pushed upright, horrified with herself for falling asleep on him. "I'm sorry."

Renzo was smiling. "For what? Being tired? I rather enjoyed it, *cara*. You are incapable of being prickly when you are asleep."

Faith smoothed her hair, certain it must be a wild mess, and dug through her purse for her mirror, praying to God she hadn't drooled in her sleep. Or that she wasn't now sporting raccoon eyes. A quick check in her compact assured her that she still looked presentable, once she slid her fingers through her hair to tame any flyaways.

Renzo exited the vehicle and stood waiting for her while a bevy of uniformed staff swarmed around the car, sorting luggage and packages and carting them into the house. Faith blinked at the facade in front of her. The stone house had that timeworn ocher color that only seemed to exist in Italy. It was less ornate than she'd expected it would be, and she stood with her head tilted back, taking in the wooden shutters and twining bougainvillea and climbing roses that graced both corners of the home. Spilling from each window was a profusion of bright red blooms.

"Do you like it?" Renzo asked.

"It's lovely."

"Then look this way," he said, turning her until she was facing a long slope of garden that butted up against a stone wall—beyond which was a beautiful valley dotted with tall cypresses, yellow fields, purple flowers, green grass and lush vineyards as far as the eye could see.

"We aren't in Rome?" she asked dumbly. How long had she slept anyway?

Renzo laughed. "No. This is my home in Tuscany. We are closer to Florence than Rome now."

"I…I missed it all," she said. Disappointment ate at her.

"You were tired, *cara*. Besides, there will be plenty of opportunities to see the countryside again." He tucked her arm in his and led her toward the house. "Now, however, you will wish to rest and freshen up. There is a party to-night."

Her heart fell. "Tonight?"

"You are nervous?" he asked gently, stopping to face her.

Yes, but she wouldn't admit that. Faith swallowed. What if there were photographers? What if someone back in Cottonwood saw her in a tabloid? Would they recognize her? She thought of her past coming back to haunt her now, after she'd run so far and done so much to change who she was, and felt sick.

"I—I was thinking you might want to rest," she said, letting her gaze drop briefly to his leg.

His expression shuttered when she met his eyes again. "I appreciate the concern, *cara*, but it is not necessary. There is much to be done in the next few weeks and little time to waste."

She wanted to tell him that looking after his health wasn't a waste of time, but she knew he didn't want to hear it. Renzo was determined to ride the Viper even if it killed him. She shoved down the feeling of panic that seemed determined to wrap around her throat and faced him squarely. She wasn't sure if the panic came from her fear of discovery or her fear for him—or both, more likely—but she didn't want to think about it any longer.

"Then perhaps we should work on your schedule for a

while," she said briskly, attempting to be all business and hoping he didn't see that she was upset.

He studied her for a moment before his sexy mouth curved into a smile that made her heart skip a beat. "*Si*, this is a very good idea. Next week, I take the Viper onto the track to begin training. I will have little time for business meetings then."

Faith's heart thumped in slow motion. "Next week? Is it ready so soon?"

Excitement danced in his eyes while her stomach twisted in fear. "It is."

And Renzo would be flying around a track at speeds approaching, perhaps exceeding, two hundred miles per hour. With a leg that could cramp at any moment and render him incapable of controlling the motorcycle.

Faith didn't want to think about the consequences of that scenario. Instead, she threw herself into her work once they reached Renzo's home office. They worked for a couple of hours, and then Renzo pushed back from his desk and told her to go get some rest.

"I'm fine," she said.

"Your eyes keep closing. You can hardly keep them open."

It was true, but he'd shown no signs of being tired and so she'd kept on working. "It's called blinking," she said stubbornly.

Renzo laughed. "Indeed." He got to his feet and stretched. "Nevertheless, go to your room and blink there. I am going to do the same. Come, I will show you where you are staying."

Faith followed him up the wide marble staircase that sat imposingly at the center of the house. She could hardly keep from gawking as they'd walked through the villa. It was lovely, with marble floors, Oriental rugs, old oil paint-

ings and tapestries on the walls, and vases of flowers filling every surface. There were antiques mixed with modern
furnishings, giving it all an eclectic and lush feeling.

It was as sumptuous as the Stein's penthouse, and yet it
was more livable. The kind of place where you could actually put your feet on a table and not be too worried that
you were mistaking some sort of modern art piece for a
footstool.

Renzo led her down a long hallway with tall doors that
opened to bedrooms filled with light. The last one was
hers, he told her, and she stepped into the room, certain
he'd made a mistake. This was the kind of room you gave
to guests, not employees. There was a huge tester bed covered in white linen, antique wardrobes for her clothing, a
delicate writing desk by a window, and silk chairs and a
couch where she could lounge in the evenings. There was
even a television, and three sets of tall windows, which
opened onto a balcony with a table and chairs.

Perfect for morning coffee, she thought.

"Do you approve?" he asked as she stood with her back
to him and gaped. It was like something out of a travel
fairy tale—the kind of thing you dreamed of when you
read about Tuscany and imagined yourself living there.

Faith turned to him. "It's lovely, Renzo. Thank you."

"I am glad you are pleased." He came over and put his
hands on her shoulders, skimmed them down her arms.
"I am across the hall, *cara*, should you require anything."

Faith bit the inside of her lip. "I—I'm sure I'll be fine.
But thank you."

His smile was wickedly sensual. "Nevertheless," he said
as he bent and kissed her on both cheeks while a tidal wave
of flame rolled through her, "I am there."

The party, it turned out, was being held in a villa nearby.
Faith slept for a couple of hours, and then dressed in a fig-

ure-skimming red cocktail dress with a halter top that kept her modest and a pair of silver strappy heels that made her feel like a princess. She'd asked Renzo why she needed to go along earlier when they were working, and he'd looked at her with that gorgeous broody look he got and told her she was going because he'd realized after the Stein's party that she was good repellant.

"Repellant?" she'd asked, certain her puzzled frown must have amused him.

"Female repellant," he'd deadpanned before going on to explain that he did not need the distractions of women in his life right now.

"And what am I?" Faith murmured as she studied herself in the mirror. Especially when she considered the way he'd told her that he was across the hall if she needed anything.

Anything, he'd stressed. Faith shivered as she remembered the feel of his lips on her cheeks, the imprint of his fingers on her arms.

Renzo D'Angeli was a very confusing man, she decided. And very sexy, a little voice added.

Faith ran the brush through her hair one last time. She didn't look half-bad, though she still wasn't in the same league as the Katie Palmers of the world. Her hair was smooth and golden, hanging down her back in a lustrous fall, and her eyes really stood out with the addition of eye shadow, liner and mascara.

It was her in the mirror, and not her. Her as she'd never been, she amended. She hadn't been allowed to wear makeup when she was growing up, and she'd never been allowed to do anything with her hair other than leave it long. As the daughter of a preacher, she'd been required to be as plain and circumspect as possible.

Until the day she hadn't been.

Faith turned away from the mirror and grabbed her

wrap and tiny purse. Then she hurried downstairs to meet Renzo. As she reached the bottom of the stairs, the butler came forward to greet her in impeccable English.

"Signorina," he began, "Signore D'Angeli had business to attend to in town. He asked me to let you know that he would meet you at the party."

"Grazie," Faith replied, her heart sinking.

She wasn't thrilled with the idea of going alone, but she went outside to get into the waiting car. The ride didn't last long, but since it was dark she didn't see anything along the way, until they arrived at a grand villa with lights spilling out of the windows and people mingling on the grounds and inside the house.

Faith exited the car and stood with her purse clutched to her body like a shield while the chauffeur drove away. Her pulse was tripping along recklessly and she took deep breaths, telling herself not to freak out. There was no sign of a photographer anyhow, was there? Perhaps arriving alone was a good thing, since Renzo was the main attraction for paparazzi. If she just stayed in the background, she would be fine.

"Buona notte," a voice said before a man strolled toward her from the garden.

"H-hello," she said as he stepped into the light. If Renzo was the most handsome man on the planet, then this man was surely second. He was tall, broad and lean—and she knew who he was. She'd seen his picture in the same motorcycle magazines in which she'd seen Renzo's.

"Ah, English," he said. "You are American, no?"

Faith swallowed. "Yes."

The man held out his hand. "Niccolo Gavretti. But you can call me Nico."

"I know who you are," Faith said as she accepted his handshake. "I'm Faith Black."

Nico's handsome face split in a grin. "Ah, Faith, I have heard of you. Renzo's prized secretary, yes?" His dark gaze slid down her body. "I see why he keeps you hidden away in America. *Bella.*"

Faith extracted her hand when he tried to hold it for longer than necessary. "No one keeps me hidden. I've only worked for Mr. D'Angeli for six months."

Nico didn't stop smiling. "Better and better," he said. "And yet I am glad you are here now."

"I don't see why you should be," she said. He was incredibly handsome, but he didn't make her heart throb the way Renzo did. He was, like Renzo, a player of the worst sort. Women flowed in and out of his bed like water from a faucet.

He laughed. "You are a beautiful woman. Why should I not be? Unless, of course, you are spoken for already?"

Faith felt herself reddening, though she knew he was only flattering her because it was second nature to him as breathing. "If you will excuse me, I need to find my boss."

"I will take you to him," Nico said, offering his arm. "You will never find him in this crush without help."

Faith hesitated. It was true the place was overrun with elegantly dressed people. And she spoke no Italian. She'd found a man who spoke English, and who knew Renzo. But she seemed to remember reading that Nico and Renzo were rivals on the track. And she knew for a fact that Renzo was determined to bring out his latest production bike before Gavretti Manufacturing could unveil theirs.

"Afraid of what Renzo will say?" Nico asked.

Faith lifted her chin. "No, of course not."

"Then come with me, *bella*, and we will find him."

Renzo arrived at the party later than he'd thought he would. But he'd gotten a call from one of his investors and he'd needed to go into Florence for a meeting. He'd fully intended to be back by the time Faith left, but he was nearly an hour late. She would, no doubt, be furious with him. He'd sent her into this gathering alone when he should have gone back for her and to hell with the time.

Now, he stood at the edge of the glittering crowd congregating in the garden and scanned it for a sighting of her. He knew she was here because Ennio had still been out front with the car when he'd arrived. Since Renzo had driven his own car, he'd sent Ennio home and then come to look for Faith. He'd tried calling her mobile phone, but she was not answering.

The hostess smiled when she saw him. "Renzo, darling, we're so glad you've returned to Italia," Filomena Mazzaro said. "How is the new motorbike coming along?"

Renzo didn't feel like talking to anyone until he found Faith, but he chatted for a moment before asking if Filomena had seen her. Filomena's brows drew together. "I don't remember greeting her, no. But I am sure she is here, darling. We have so many people tonight."

Renzo excused himself after a few more moments and continued the search. He should have asked Faith what she was planning to wear tonight, but how well would that have worked? She was a woman, and no doubt had changed her dress at least three times before deciding.

He drew up short when he spotted Niccolo Gavretti. He'd known Gavretti would be here, but he didn't particularly feel like dealing with the man tonight.

Perhaps he wouldn't have to. Gavretti was standing with a blonde in a red dress, and he seemed engrossed in her. He had his hand on her shoulder as he smiled down at her. He looked as if he wanted to kiss her, but she took a step to the side the moment his head dipped. Renzo laughed to himself. He couldn't see the blonde's face because the instant she'd stepped aside, a light had shone straight into his eyes, silhouetting her form.

She was, of course, voluptuous. He could tell that much. She had full, lush breasts and a nipped-in waist that flared out again in generous hips. Her legs were long and lovely, her feet encased in delicate shoes with glittery silver straps. Everything a woman ought to be, he decided. Gavretti had excellent taste, as he well knew from the days when they used to prowl the bars of Florence together, drinking and having a good time.

The blonde might be gorgeous, but Renzo wasn't interested in her. He had to find Faith. He started to walk past the two of them, but the woman cried out as he did so.

The voice was painfully familiar. Renzo stiffened as if he'd been struck by lightning. Slowly, he turned. The voluptuous blonde stared back at him, her green eyes wide, her lips red and luscious and kissable.

Kissable. Maldedizone.

Faith sashayed over to him while Gavretti smirked. The bastard.

"I've been looking for you, Faith," Renzo said calmly. He was proud of himself for how calm he sounded. How reasonable.

She was beautiful. Utterly gorgeous, and he was a fool for allowing her to come alone.

"I've been looking for you, too," she said. "Nico was helping me."

Renzo's lips peeled back from his teeth in a smile. He'd seen how Gavretti was helping her. The hard bite of acid flooded his throat as he thought of Gavretti's hand on her—of his attempt to kiss her. Kiss *his* Faith. It wasn't the first time Gavretti had tried to take something from Renzo that did not belong to him. "Was he? How wonderfully chivalrous of him."

Renzo slipped an arm around her lush form, anchored her to him. She gasped, the smallest intake of breath, and his body responded, tightening, hardening. He wanted her beneath him, making those noises while he took her to heaven and back. While he got her out of his system so he could concentrate again.

Because he'd been thinking of little else but getting her naked since this afternoon, when she'd transformed before his eyes. He should have known better. He'd already been attracted to her, inexplicably perhaps, but now? Now he wanted to mark her as his and kill any man who dared to touch her.

Gavretti's eyes narrowed as his gaze slipped back and forth between them. "If I had known she was yours, Renzo—"

"She is," he stated with finality.

He could feel Faith stiffening in outrage. Because she did not yet realize the truth. "Renzo, I am not—"

He cupped her jaw and slanted his mouth over hers, silencing her.

CHAPTER SEVEN

FAITH was furious. She sat in Renzo's sports car, her arms folded over her breasts and her head turned toward the window, seething. Renzo shifted smoothly, the engine revving into the night as the car raced along the Tuscan roads toward his villa.

How dared he? First, Niccolo Gavretti had thought he could have his way with her, and then Renzo had come along—hot, furious and broody as hell—and the standoff had begun. It wasn't about her—it was about who was in control, about who got what he wanted.

Renzo had kissed her in front of all those people while cameras flashed and caught the moment forever. Her heart did a long slide into the bottom of her stomach. It had only been a matter of time before she was photographed with Renzo, so she could hardly be surprised about it.

And yet the panic that clawed into her now wouldn't go away. She'd done nothing wrong. Not now, and not eight years ago. But she dreaded the attention if that old photograph was brought to light. The shame and helpless rage.

What angered her most about tonight was that Renzo hadn't kissed her because he'd wanted to, but because he'd wanted to prove something to Nico. He'd been marking her as his, but only because he knew it would irritate the other man.

The moment he'd let her go, she'd turned on her heel and marched for the door. It was the calmest, most rational response she'd been capable of, since staying there would have necessitated her slapping the both of them.

Renzo hadn't argued when she'd told him she wanted to go. He'd simply led the way to his car and roared out of the driveway without saying another word.

Now, the car ate up the roadway until Faith's heart began to beat hard for a different reason. "Renzo, you're scaring me. This isn't the track."

He swore, but the car throttled back to a more-reasonable speed. His hands flexed on the wheel, and his handsome face was harsh in the lights from the dash. He looked furious, which only fueled her anger.

"I don't know why you're angry," she said. "I'm not the one who embarrassed you by kissing you in front of all those people."

He shot her a disbelieving glance. "You're embarrassed? Over what?"

She turned toward him, arms still crossed, her heart racing. It was merely a game to him, while to her it could mean being the subject of public scrutiny again. "I realize that you may think you're God's gift—heaven knows enough women have told you so—but not everyone wants their private life put on display for the world to see. Not only that, but we *have* no private life! You did it just to prove a point to Nico."

His eyes flashed. "Do not call that man Nico," he growled. "He only wanted to use you so he could get to me."

Another spike of anger launched her blood pressure into the danger zone. "Do you think I don't know that? I'm not stupid, Renzo. Two of Italy's most famous bachelors fighting over me? I hardly think so. I just happened to be the bone that both dogs decided they wanted to control tonight. If there had been a juicy steak nearby, they'd have fought over that instead."

Renzo swore again. And then he jerked the car off the road and onto a narrow dirt track she hadn't seen before he turned. The car jolted to a stop and then he unsnapped her seat belt and reached for her before she knew what he was planning.

He crushed her mouth beneath his, his fingers sliding into her hair, his tongue demanding entrance. She opened to him, too shocked by the onslaught to protest. She should be angry. She should push him away. She should do anything but let him kiss her as if he were a dying man and she the last hope he had for salvation.

But, shockingly, she was turned on. Her body was on fire. Her nerve endings were zinging with sparks and her sex ached for his possession. She was throbbing, aching, melting—needing things she'd never needed before.

His tongue delved deep, demanding that she meet him, that she give him everything.

She did.

He slid one hand up her thigh, beneath the hem of her dress. Part of her wanted to clamp her legs together, to tell him no, but that was her father talking. Her damned childhood talking.

She was a woman, and she was capable of wanting a man, of choosing the man who would be her first. It wasn't wrong or ugly to feel this way. It was a revelation.

A glorious, exciting, shattering revelation.

Renzo's fingers spread along her hip, shaped her as she tried to get closer to him. When his hand slid over her panties, she had to force herself to keep breathing. She did not know what he would do, but she found herself hoping he would touch her. Dying for him to touch her.

And frightened, too.

And then he slid one finger across the thin silk, and then down…down over the damp heat of her. The groan that emanated from his throat vibrated into her. Thrilled her.

His finger stroked over her again, eliciting a moan. Every thought in her head flew out the window. All she wanted was to feel more of this delicious sensation, this wicked pleasure. He kissed her hard, and she shuddered and arched against his hand, wanting the barrier gone, wanting to feel everything.

She wanted more. *More.*

He skimmed his mouth down her throat, leaving a trail of hot kisses as the temperature in the car spiked. Faith closed her eyes, gasping at the sensual onslaught.

"I want you, Faith. I *want* you. It has nothing to do with Gavretti, nothing to do with anyone but you. I want to take you to my bed and spend the night lost in your body. I've been imagining all the things I want to do to you for the past week. All the ways in which I want to explore you."

His voice was deep, his Italian accent thicker than usual, and his words so sexy she could die. His words shocked her. Turned her on. She wanted to know what sort of things he'd imagined. Wanted to know what he would do if she said yes.

But she was cautious. Scared. She wasn't sophisticated enough to know how this worked or what tomorrow would bring if she said the yes he wanted her to say. The yes she was dying to say.

"I—I'm not sure this is a good idea," she said quickly. "This isn't part of my job—"

He pulled away from her suddenly. And then he swore in Italian, the words hot and sharp and nothing like the sexy words he'd just said to her. Faith wanted to cry at the loss of his heat.

He pounded the steering wheel once, a sharp, violent move that made her jump. And then he shoved a hand through his hair before turning the key. The car roared to life again, the dash lights illuminating the harsh lines of his jaw. Disappointment rolled through her, along with a healthy dose of regret. Why had she spoken? Why had she pierced the happiness that had been racing through her body like a nuclear explosion?

He turned to look at her, his blue eyes penetrating even in the darkness. "I would never pay a woman—*any* woman—to have sex with me, Faith. Do you understand that?"

"I wasn't suggesting—"

"You were," he snapped. "You keep throwing your job at me, as if I have no idea what it is I pay you for."

Her heart throbbed because she knew he was right.

He reversed onto the roadway and popped the car into gear before turning to her again. "I assure you that I know exactly what I pay you for. And I want you because you are beautiful and fascinating, not because you're convenient. If you believe that, then by all means go to bed alone tonight."

Faith couldn't sleep. Partly, it was the jetlag. And, partly, it was the adrenaline still coursing through her body after the way Renzo had kissed her in his car. She'd been so close to heaven, and so far at the same time.

It shocked her to admit it, but she'd wanted him with a fierceness that she would never have believed possible only a week ago. That was the power of Renzo D'Angeli, she thought sourly. He was gorgeous, compelling and utterly amazing. When he turned all that male power on you, you wanted to let him continue until the very end. Until you were a sobbing mess begging him for another chance.

What else explained the way women kept throwing

themselves at him, despite his reputation for never staying with one woman longer than a couple of months?

Nothing. And she was little different, apparently. Renzo was a flame that she wanted to immolate herself in—even though she knew she shouldn't. Pitiful. For all her professionalism, for all her belief that she alone would be immune to him, she was no different from the rest.

Faith threw the covers back and yanked on her robe. She owed him an explanation for the way she'd behaved, but it would have to wait until morning. She'd insulted him, and she hadn't meant to do so. But she'd been confused, scared, and she'd said the first thing that had popped into her head.

The wrong thing.

From the beginning, Renzo had made it clear that the decisions about what she did were hers to make. The decision to go to the party at the Stein's, though he'd cajoled pretty hard. The decision to come to Italy. Even the decisions about how to style her hair and what to wear, though he'd forced her into making the choices in the first place. He had not once told her how things would be, though he'd certainly pushed her into action.

Renzo might be her employer, but he would not ever expect it to give him access to her body. She knew better, and yet she'd implied he'd believed it did.

Faith's stomach growled, and she realized she'd failed to eat at the party. She'd been nervous, waiting for Renzo to arrive, trying to hold her own with Niccolo Gavretti—who had refused to let her search for Renzo by herself. Well, now she knew why. No doubt he'd orchestrated that moment when he'd tried to kiss her precisely because he knew Renzo was watching.

Clearly, there was something more between them than simple rivalry—and she'd been the one caught in the middle of their feud tonight, the collateral damage as they waged their war against each other.

Faith slipped from her room, hesitating at Renzo's door when she saw a light coming from underneath it, but continued down the hall and then down the marble staircase to the large kitchen at the back of the house.

She found a loaf of bread on the counter and some cheese in the fridge, and then dug around for a knife with which to slice them. Once she'd fixed a small plate, she turned to go back to her room, but stopped when a shadow moved outside the door. Her heart lodged in her throat and she wondered for a moment if she should scream, but then the door opened and a man stepped inside.

A man with a tiny, mewling bundle in his arms.

"Renzo?"

He looked up as if he'd just realized she was there. The kitten mewed again, such a sad, pitiful little sound, and Faith's heart squeezed tight.

Renzo came toward her and set the kitten on the large island, blocking the tiny thing from escaping. "I kept hearing something outside my window," he said. "I couldn't find the mother, or any trace of other kittens. I think maybe she moved the litter and forgot one."

"It's so little. It can't be more than a month old."

Renzo picked the creature up again and held it out to her. "You know what to do with cats, *si*?"

She took the kitten, a lump forming in her throat as it shivered hard. "He—or she—probably needs milk," Faith said. "But we have to warm it up. Cold milk won't do. It'll make his belly ache."

Renzo moved to the refrigerator and took out the milk. Then he found a saucepan and poured some in before setting it on the stove and turning on the burner. His hair was disheveled, and she realized for the first time that he wasn't wearing a shirt. His broad chest was muscled, firm, and she found her breath shortening as she watched him move.

He wore a pair of sleep pants with a drawstring tie that hung low on his hips, revealing the tight ridges of his abdomen and the arrow of dark hair that disappeared beneath the waist of his pants.

"He must have been terribly loud if you could hear him in your room," she said, hugging the kitten close and stroking the silky fur. She'd missed having a cat since Mr. Darcy had died last year. The little body began to rumble with a purr instead of a shiver, and tears filled Faith's eyes as she thought of the kitten lost and scared.

Renzo turned from the stove and leaned against the counter, crossing one leg over another as he stood there looking at her. "*Si*. I did not realize it was a cat at first, the whine was so high-pitched. He was in the bougainvillea beneath my windows. If I had not been standing on the balcony, I would not have heard him."

"He's lucky you went looking for him," she said.

"I could not leave him there."

"No."

After a moment, Renzo turned and rummaged in a cabinet for a small bowl. Then he stuck his finger into the milk on the stove, testing it. Faith's heart did a little skip at that sign of tenderness in such a hard man.

"It is ready," he said, pouring the milk and bringing the bowl over to the island. Faith set the kitten down and he immediately began to drink. His purr grew louder, and she glanced at Renzo. They laughed together.

"He is as loud as the Viper," Renzo said. "Perhaps we should call him that."

Faith felt heat curling through her stomach, her limbs. "We don't actually know it's a he," she pointed out. "He might be a she."

"Ah, then we will have to call her Miss Viper."

"You would keep this cat?" she asked.

"No," he said softly. "I would give him—or her—to you. Because you miss having a cat."

Her eyes were stinging. "I don't have time for a pet," she said. "I'm away from home too much, working...." She let her voice trail off as the word brought back memories of earlier.

"I'm sorry," he said, and she looked up again, met his gaze.

"For what?"

He shrugged. "For what happened in the car. I was... angry. I should not have kissed you like that."

"I didn't mind the kiss," she said softly, dropping her gaze again as her blood fizzed in her veins at the memory of all that heat and passion. "Renzo, I..."

She stroked the kitten's soft fur, unsure she could say the words she needed to say.

Renzo reached out and put his hand over hers, oh so lightly, and stroked the kitten with her for a moment. Then his hand dropped away, rested on the counter. "What is it, Faith?"

"I'm sorry, too," she said, forcing herself to meet his gaze. "I shouldn't have mentioned work. I know you wouldn't—" She stopped, swallowed. "I know that you don't expect me to sleep with you simply because I'm your PA."

"No," he said, "I don't. If you sleep with me, Faith, it will be because you want to. Because you cannot imagine another day without giving in to this passion between us."

"I don't know what passion is," she said hurriedly, before she lost her nerve. "I—I've never..." Her voice trailed off as her courage fizzled.

He tilted her chin up until she was looking at him, his

blue gaze searching hers. "You have never what, Faith? Slept with someone you worked with?"

Her laugh was strangled. "No, that's not it. I've never, um…slept…with anyone."

He was utterly silent. The only sound in the room was the kitten purring and lapping milk. Her heart was thrumming hard, and a rush of heat climbed into her cheeks, bloomed between her breasts. She was hot, so hot, and she wanted to take off her robe and slip beneath a cool spray of water.

"You are untouched?"

Untouched. It was such a quaint word, and yet it was less shocking than the other word he could have used. *Virgin.*

Faith nodded.

Renzo slid a hand through his hair and swore softly. "You have stunned me, Faith Black, and I am not easily stunned."

She tried to laugh it off. "I'm a preacher's daughter. What did you expect?"

"Yes, but you've been away from home for, presumably, eight years now. In all this time, you did not find someone you wanted to be with?"

Not until now.

Faith sighed. She was in so much trouble here. And not just because she was alone with a man she desperately wanted. No, it was worse. Much worse. Because she was at least half in love with him already.

He was kinder than she'd expected, more considerate, and he cared about tiny, helpless animals. It was more than she'd thought he was capable of just two weeks ago when she'd watched him leave the office with Katie Palmer on his arm. He'd been so remote then, so perfect and untouchable and polished. Not at all the kind of man who would warm milk for a kitten in the middle of the night.

Faith bit down on the inside of her lip. She wasn't *really* in love with him—but she could be if he kept doing things that made her heart tighten in her chest.

"It's not that simple," she said.

"I don't see why not."

She picked the kitten up again because it had finished drinking and was starting to wander. "Because it's different for a woman."

He reached out, stroked the kitten's head. "Do you know how to tell if it is a boy or a girl?"

Faith carried the kitten over to the window where a shaft of moonlight pooled over the kitchen sink. "Looks like a girl," she said after she held it up to the light, relieved that Renzo had decided to talk about something else.

"Ah, so Miss Viper it is. But that is not so pretty, is it?" he said, frowning.

"It is a bit much for such a little one," Faith replied.

"We could call her *Piccolo*."

"What does that mean?" He'd said that word to her earlier today, and she'd wondered then.

"Little one."

It was certainly appropriate, at least for the kitten. But still not quite right. Faith frowned, thinking. And then it hit her. "I think she is a Lola."

Renzo smiled. "*Si,* Lola is perfect. What do you recommend we do with her now that she has eaten?"

"She'll need a place to sleep," Faith said. "She'll need something to burrow into, and a small space where she can't get into trouble."

"Then we will find something for her."

They hunted through the kitchen until Renzo found an empty wine crate in the pantry. Then he retrieved a blanket from a closet and mounded it in the center. After they found another small box to make into a litter pan, Renzo helped her carry everything up to her room. They put Lola into a small walk-in closet off the bathroom and closed the door.

She mewed for a few moments while they stood there looking at each other in silence, hoping she would settle down. She did, and they crept from the bathroom, closing the door behind them.

Moonlight slanted through the long windows, illuminating Renzo's form as he stood in the center of her room. His skin looked warm, silky, and she realized with a jolt that she ached to touch him. To press her lips to his skin and see if he tasted as delicious as he looked.

"A virgin shouldn't look at a man the way you're looking at me," he said, an edge of strain in his voice.

"I'm sorry," she said automatically, ducking her head in embarrassment.

He closed the distance between them until he was standing so close that his heat enveloped her and her body began to soften and melt. It was novel. Her nipples were tingling, tightening, her sex aching with renewed want. If he spread her robe and slipped her gown off, she would be incapable of protest.

She wanted him to do it, and she feared he would at the same time.

Renzo lifted his fingers to her cheek, skimmed lightly over her flesh. "I'm sorry, too," he said. "It seems as if I am filled with nothing but apologies tonight. But, Faith, I see now that it would be wrong to take you to my bed. If you were experienced…"

Disappointment filled her. And a thread of anger snagged through the disappointment, pulling the fabric of it taut. "I see," she said primly, because she couldn't make herself say anything else. How could she be angry when only a moment before she'd been afraid?

"You are angry," he said. "I understand. But you've

saved yourself for a reason, Faith, and you shouldn't take that next step lightly."

She hadn't exactly saved herself so much as she'd had no opportunities. She hadn't dated very much, because she didn't trust men after Jason—and when she had dated, she'd inevitably broken the relationship off before they ever reached a point at which she might consider having sex. How did she know, if she got that far, that a man wouldn't violate her trust again?

Maybe it was a good thing this was happening. Because she wouldn't have to deal with the inevitable embarrassment and broken heart when Renzo grew tired of her.

"You're wrong," she said coolly, because she refused to let him see that he'd hurt her. "I'm not angry. I'm just tired. I think you've misread the situation entirely. I was not inviting you into my bed at all."

His hand dropped away. Somehow, she managed not to whimper. Not to beg him to touch her again.

"Then I will leave you to your rest," he said, his voice so cool it chilled her. Then he strode past her without another word and walked out the door.

After he was gone, Faith threw herself onto the bed in a dramatic maneuver worthy of generations of Southern women, and cried into her pillow. Angry tears, she told herself. Angry, frustrated, bitter tears.

CHAPTER EIGHT

RENZO could hardly wrap his head around the fact that his sexy PA was still a virgin. How was this possible when she was so passionate beneath the prim exterior? This was a woman who kissed with her whole body. She focused every bit of concentration she had on the meeting of lips and tongues, and the effect was exquisite.

Renzo shifted at his desk as his body began to react to the memory of kissing her last night in his car. She'd been like a living flame in his arms, and he'd wanted to burn himself up in her. When he'd encountered the damp evidence of her desire for him, it had been all he could do not to rip the thin silk from her body and bury himself inside her then and there.

Thankfully he had not, since she was a virgin. Not only would she likely not have appreciated such an introduction to lovemaking, but what if she took it too seriously? What if she thought that because they'd had sex, they had a future together?

Faith was serious, proper, a preacher's daughter. She'd probably want to get married, have babies, do charity work, hostess parties and drag him to school functions.

He did not know that for a fact, but if it was true, he did not want to hurt her when she learned he wanted none of those things. He wasn't against marriage or babies in principle, but he wasn't quite sure he would ever take that step.

He liked his life the way it was. He liked the excitement of the track, the excitement of a new lover in his bed whenever he chose, and the excitement of creating something that would make him richer than he'd ever dreamed possible when he'd still been an angry teenager with a grudge against the world.

In short, he liked the freedom to do what he wished. He always made it clear to the women who got involved with him there was no future with him, and he didn't see that changing anytime soon.

Faith said he'd misread her last night, but he was certain he had not. She'd wanted him, and if he'd swept her into his arms and carried her to the bed, he was fairly certain she would not have objected. If he'd done so, he could be buried inside her right now instead of sitting at his desk and fighting an erection that wouldn't go away.

Renzo glanced down at the report that she'd handed him an hour ago, and then back up at where Faith sat at a desk nearby, clicking keys on her computer and generally ignoring him. He couldn't seem to concentrate on anything other than her. It was quite annoying.

If he had sex with her, she would leave him—but perhaps that was the lesser of two evils at this point since he needed to turn his attention to the next few months on the circuit and couldn't seem to do so.

He let his eyes skim down her form. Her hair was perfectly coiffed this morning, and she wore a cinnamon-colored jacket and skirt that showed off her legs. Gone were the unfashionable short black heels; in their place was a pair of platform pumps in brown suede. Faith had her legs tucked to one side of her chair, one lovely leg crossed over the other.

Thank God she had not looked like this in New York.

He'd been insane to take her to a salon, even more insane to take her shopping afterward. He'd known she was beautiful beneath the ill-fitting suits and glasses and severe buns, but he'd made a mistake in showcasing that beauty for others to see.

For Niccolo Gavretti to see. Renzo's grip tightened on the pen he was holding until he threw it down in disgust before it cracked. Gavretti had tried to kiss her and it had made him crazy. Crazy enough to mark her as his at a party attended by everyone who was anyone. Soon, the story would appear in the tabloids that regularly reported on his life. He had a feeling that Faith wouldn't like that, but there wasn't much he could do about it now.

She must have sensed he was looking at her because her head snapped up, her eyes meeting his evenly. But then she glanced down, just for a moment, and he knew she was still thinking about it, too.

"How is Lola this morning?" he asked, thinking of the tiny ball of fur that he'd found in the bougainvillea. The little thing had clawed him something fierce until she'd realized he wasn't going to hurt her. He had scratch marks on his arms this morning, and one on his chest.

"She's fine," Faith said. "I think she'll be able to eat kitten food if I can go and buy her some today."

Renzo waved a hand. "Consider it done," he said, picking up his mobile phone and calling Fabrizio, the household butler. "Anything else?" he asked while he still had the man on the phone.

"A proper litter box, litter, a playhouse—maybe I should just make a list."

"I will wait," he said, and Faith began to scribble on a piece of paper. She handed it over and Renzo read off the items to Fabrizio, who took everything in his stride. *Dio,* who knew one tiny creature needed so many things?

When he hung up again, she was watching him. "I forget sometimes just how exalted a life you lead," she said. "When was the last time you shopped for yourself?"

Renzo laughed. "I can't remember, *cara*. When I want something, I make a call. It is much more preferable to the way I used to live."

"And how was that? Like the rest of us mortals?" She was teasing him, and he found he liked it. She was trying so hard to make everything seem normal again. Did he want to give that up by taking her to his bed? He was very afraid he did.

"There was a time," he said, "when I didn't always have enough money to buy food for the day. It's amazing what you will do when you're hungry."

Her eyes filled with sadness, and he realized he'd said more than he'd meant to say. That was what he got for only having half his mind on the question and the other half on her legs.

"I'm sorry, Renzo. I know what it's like to worry about where your next meal is coming from. I wouldn't wish that on anyone."

His senses sharpened at the unhappy note in her voice. "When did this happen to you, Faith?"

She pushed back from her desk and folded her arms. The movement pressed her already lush breasts even higher. Renzo stifled a groan.

"I left home without much of a plan. It was inevitable there would be some difficulties along the way." She shook her head. "But I don't really want to talk about it. I shouldn't have brought it up."

"You never want to talk about it," he said, suddenly wanting to know more about her. What did he know, other than she was from Georgia, that she didn't speak to her family, and that she had a cat that'd died last year?

Her eyes flashed. "Neither do you," she accused. "We both tap-dance around the difficult parts of our lives. And maybe that's best. You're my boss, not my boyfriend."

At that moment, he wanted to be more. He wanted to be the man she told her problems to. The one whose arms she lay in at night before going to sleep.

Dio, this was insane. Renzo shoved back from the desk and stood. There was only one place he was going to stop thinking about her, at least for a little while. It would only be temporary, but temporary was better than nothing.

"If you're finished with your work for the morning, it's time to go to the track, *cara*."

Something else flashed in her eyes then—fear? Inexplicably, it made him angry. There was nothing to be frightened of. He knew what he was doing. He was Lorenzo D'Angeli. He'd won nine world titles, broken records—and shattered his leg.

He tightened his fingers into fists at his side. Yes, he'd shattered his leg. And yes, it was bothering him more and more lately. But it was time to take the Viper out and see how it rode now that they'd made the modifications. He wouldn't push it today, but he had to get a feel for it before training began in earnest.

"You want me to go with you?" she asked in disbelief.

"*Si*, I need you there."

She swallowed and turned around to log off her computer. Then she gathered her purse and stood. She didn't ask why he needed her to come with him and for that he was grateful. Because he couldn't give her a reason, other than he simply wanted her to be there.

He turned to go but she stopped him with a word.

"Renzo," she said, and he turned back to her. Her green

eyes were wide, her cheeks flushed. "I want you to promise me that if your leg starts to bother you, you won't push
yourself," she said, clutching her purse in front of her like
a shield. "It's not worth the risk."

He took a step closer to her, stopped. "Would you be
upset if something happened to me, *cara*?"

"A lot of people would," she said, her lashes dipping to
cover her eyes. "A lot of people depend on you."

"But would *you* be upset?"

He wasn't sure she would look at him, but she lifted her
chin and met his gaze. "Yes, of course I would."

Some feeling he couldn't name curled inside him, warm-
ing him. "Then I suppose I will have to be careful."

If this was his idea of careful, then Faith wanted to scream.
He'd taken her to a test track near the D'Angeli factory
where she'd accompanied him as he'd inspected the Viper
before suiting up and taking the beast out.

The motorcycle was wicked, with its cool carbon frame
and cherry-red paint. It was wide in the front and narrow
in the back, and didn't look at all like something any sane
person would want to ride at the speeds Grand Prix racers
rode. While the men had oohed and ahhed, she'd chewed
the inside of her lip until it was nearly raw.

What if his leg cramped? What if he had an accident?
What if, what if, what if?

Renzo had spent time conferring with his team before
he'd gone to change. When he'd returned, he was clad head
to toe in dark leather. It wasn't the leather he wore when
racing, which was covered with logos and advertising, but
it was still familiar from the photos she'd seen of him in
his gear. He was wearing the knee sliders, the gloves, the
lightweight boots and, when he turned to the side, the hump
of the back protector was clearly visible.

She'd stood quietly by until he'd told someone to take her to the observation box. She'd stared at him, wanting to say something, until she'd finally had to turn and follow the man who was taking her away.

Now, she sat in the box and clenched her hands into tight fists as Renzo raced along a track that curved up high on the sides and contained at least one switchback, which he regularly took at lightning speed.

The motorcycle roared into the curves—and that's when Faith couldn't breathe. She'd watched footage of the races previously, because she'd felt it necessary if she was working at D'Angeli Motors, but she'd never before thought she was going to scream each time the motorcycle lay flat on its side, Renzo's knee and elbow skimming the ground before it came out on the other side and he throttled it higher, zooming into hyper speeds.

It was, without doubt, the most insane thing she'd ever witnessed—and that was going some, considering she was from the American South and car racing was a favored sport of many people there. But no car race she'd ever been forced to watch with her family could compare to the outright insanity of this.

When Renzo finally finished his run in what seemed like a century later, she wilted in relief. He brought the motorcycle to a stop, though not until after doing a series of wheelies, and climbed off as someone prepared to take the bike from him.

What happened next brought a gasp from her companions in the box—and sent her racing down the stairs as fast as she could go in her high heels.

The instant Renzo's right foot had touched the tarmac, he'd buckled into a heap.

By the time she reached ground level and burst out onto the track, he was standing and shaking his head as someone said something to him. He'd raised the visor on his helmet, but now he removed it and laid it on the seat as she barreled toward him.

Faith stopped short as several pairs of eyes turned toward her, questioning. But it was the look in Renzo's eyes that most concerned her. There was pain, she could clearly see that, but he was doing his best to hide it. Not only that, but he glared daggers at her. A warning.

"I beg your pardon," she said, even though her heart raced and a fine sheen of sweat broke out between her breasts. She had to salvage this somehow, had to help him out of the situation. "But, uh, you have an important conference call scheduled quite soon, Mr. D'Angeli. I thought you might have forgotten it in the excitement of testing the, uh, the Viper."

He stared at her for a long moment. "Thank you, Miss Black."

He turned back to the men and said a few things in Italian, and then he was moving toward her, no trace of a limp as he strode with the confidence and surety that she was accustomed to seeing in him.

But she could tell he was hurting. The corners of his mouth were tight and there was a groove in his forehead as he concentrated hard on walking without letting the pain show. They swept into the factory and then took an elevator up to his office. Once inside, he still didn't give in to the agony he was surely feeling. He walked over to his desk and sat down, his body still encased in racing leather.

And then he folded over until his head was on his arms and she could hear him breathing deeply.

"Renzo," she said, choking back tears as she went to his side and sank down beside him. "What can I do?"

"Nothing," he said. "There is nothing."

She reached up with shaking fingers and touched his

sweat-soaked hair. "I'm sorry. I seem to say that quite a lot, but I don't know what else to say." She let her hand drop to his shoulder, squeezed. "I think you should take a pain pill. And then you should call your doctor."

"No doctors," he said. "No pills."

Frustration pounded into her. "You can't just endure it," she said, trying to reason with him. "At least take a pill."

He pushed himself upright and her heart twisted as she got a look at him. His eyes were glazed, as if he'd been on the edge of tears.

"Does it hurt that badly?"

He gave a poor imitation of a laugh. "Worse."

Faith swallowed the lump in her throat. "Please consider taking a pain pill."

"Give me some of those pills from your purse," he said. "Maybe that will do the trick."

She didn't think so, but she dutifully complied, finding bottled water in the refrigerator built into the sleek counter on one wall. He'd removed his gloves by the time she returned to him, and he took the pills, draining half the water, then leaned back in his chair, one hand spanning his forehead as he sat with his eyes closed.

"How was the Viper to ride?" she asked. "Was it everything you'd hoped?"

He actually smiled. "It was glorious, *cara mia*. Almost perfect. There are a few tweaks required, but she'll be ready to go when it's time."

"I'm glad to hear it." Except, of course, Renzo would insist on riding the motorcycle himself instead of giving it to one of the racing team to ride. "What happened when you got off the Viper, Renzo?"

She wasn't sure he would tell her, but then he sighed. "My leg started to cramp on the final few laps. And that last turn was a bit hard on the knee. The pain was…surprising, I suppose."

"You promised not to push it," she said tightly. "I wish you would at least see a doctor. He might be able to help."

His blue eyes were piercing when they snapped open. "No. I've seen doctors. There is nothing they can tell me that I do not already know."

"Do you really think you can ride the Viper for an entire season? How will you explain it if you can't stand up when they hand you the trophy?" She could think of far worse scenarios, but she couldn't bring herself to say them. He knew the possibilities as well as she did.

His voice was as hard as diamonds. "I can ride, Faith. There is no other choice."

She swallowed the fear and bitterness roiling in her belly. "I don't understand that, Renzo. You have an entire racing team at your disposal. Men who know how this is done as well as you do."

"They don't know," he snapped, before muttering something in Italian. "I am one of the top-ranked riders in the world. And I know my motorcycles. It has to be me. This is the Viper's debut. It has to succeed, and for that to happen, I must be the one riding. The sponsors are counting on it. The company is counting on it. Do you wish to find yourself downsized because the Viper fails?"

She knew how much it meant to him, how proud he was, and yet she didn't believe it was as dire as he made it out to be. Yes, they might lose sponsors and, yes, the newest production model might not sell as well as hoped if the Viper was a disaster. Gavretti Manufacturing might even gain the upper hand on them, which would no doubt anger Renzo a great deal.

But so what? He would be alive and able to bring the company back from the edge of whatever misfortune they might teeter upon. "D'Angeli isn't going to go broke if the Viper doesn't smash records," Faith said firmly.

He looked at her darkly for several moments. And then he stood, his face whitening briefly as he clutched the edge of the desk. "I'll shower and change and then we can go back to the villa."

Faith ground her teeth in frustration. Typical man. He didn't want to talk about it when she pointed out the flaws in his logic.

He started to limp toward the adjoining bath, but she hurried over and slid an arm around his waist. He might be stubborn, but she couldn't watch him suffer.

"*Grazie*," he said, leaning on her as she helped him into the bathroom. It was a luxurious room, outfitted in exotic African hardwoods and sleek chrome fixtures. There was a huge shower at one end, entirely encased in glass, complete with a bench and several nozzles up and down the walls on three sides, as well as one overhead.

"Sit," she told him when they reached the leather couch in the dressing area off to one side.

He did as she said, and then she bent to take his boots off even though he had not asked her to. But how could he manage it when his leg still hurt? She got one boot off, and then the other before tackling the knee sliders, which were separate from the leathers because they had to be replaced so often. These were scraped pretty badly from his contact with the track, and it made her shudder to think again of how he lay almost flat on his side every time he went around a curve.

The barest slip of control and he and the bike would go their separate ways. At two hundred miles an hour.

Faith shuddered again. The leathers were made for protection, with Kevlar and titanium in the most vulnerable spots, but the last thing she wanted was to see firsthand how good the protection they provided was.

How was it that one of the other talented riders on the D'Angeli team couldn't ride the Viper? She didn't believe it for a moment, no matter how good Renzo was. With Renzo as a teacher, how could his team fail? He was simply too proud, too stubborn, to admit he couldn't do this any longer.

She got the sliders off and then lifted her head to look at him. The last thing she expected to see was the jut of an impressive arousal against the leather. Her gaze flew to his.

He smiled crookedly. "I could see down your shirt," he said, not the least bit apologetic. "It's a nice view."

"You're in no shape to be thinking about my breasts," she told him somewhat prudishly, her cheeks flaring with heat.

He laughed. "*Cara*, I'd have to be dead not to think about your breasts. I assure you I'm quite capable of thinking about them. Of thinking of every centimeter of your body, I should add."

Faith got to her feet and stood stiffly, in spite of the fact her body was doing that softening-melting-aching thing again. "I think you can do the rest yourself," she said. "I'll wait in the office."

He stood, his face less tight now, and tugged at the zipper that held the leathers in place. It was like having that magazine ad come to life, she thought, as her breath caught and held while the zipper slid downward. Unlike in the magazine, there was a tight shirt beneath the leather, but it was still one of the sexiest things she'd ever seen.

"I'll be, um, in the office," she said, turning away as he laughed.

"You could stay, Faith. Wash my back."

She spun to face him again just as he shrugged out of

the top half of the leathers and then peeled the shirt up and off. She'd seen his naked chest last night, but it had been dark. Now he stood before her in all his hard-bodied glory, muscles rippling and flexing beneath bronzed skin—and then she noticed a three-pronged scratch skating over one pectoral muscle.

Faith frowned even as her heart did that funny little skip thing again. She thought of him last night with a tiny mewing bundle in his arms. "Lola did that?"

He glanced down. "*Si*—but it is nothing."

And then he was staring at her again, blue eyes daring her. Only a few minutes ago, he'd been in enough pain to bring tears to his eyes, and now he was standing there like some sexy demigod and tempting her into the kind of behavior that ought to make her turn and run right this instant. Instead, she was imagining it. Considering it.

Wanting it.

"How about it, Faith?" he said, his voice a sexy rumble. "Do you want to wash my back?"

"I—I—" She closed her eyes, darted her tongue over her lips. She was not doing this. She was not stripping her clothing and stepping into that shower with him when he'd probably done the same thing a million times before with a million different women. She couldn't. "I'll be in the office, Renzo."

Before he could say another word, she hurried out the door and shut it firmly behind her. But his laughter echoed after her until she almost turned around and went back just so she could look at him one more time. Instead, she retreated to a chair by the window and forced herself to sit with her hands in her lap and stare at the Tuscan hills.

He emerged twenty minutes later, dressed in the trousers and button-down shirt he'd worn earlier, his hair still damp and curling sexily over his collar. Faith stood, clasping her hands together to hide their trembling. Her heart was still racing, and her body still ached, no matter that she'd sat and tried to will the feelings away.

It didn't work that way, apparently. She wanted things she'd never wanted before, and she didn't quite know how to get them. How to take that plunge that would mean the difference between continuing the way she had been, and knowing what it meant to be a sensual creature focused on her own pleasure.

Renzo stopped when he saw her. His gaze met hers, heat flaring anew in the blue depths, and she knew that he could see her struggle with herself. He was far too perceptive when it came to women. She tried to remind herself why that was a bad thing, but she just didn't seem to care.

"Come here, Faith," he said, and she obeyed without once asking herself why she was doing so. He smelled delicious, clean and fresh and male, and she itched to touch him. But she kept her arms rigid at her sides as she stood before him and waited for something to happen.

Until he reached for her and tugged her into his embrace. One hand came up to cup her jaw while the other spread across the small of her back, pressing her to him. Faith gripped the powerful muscles of his biceps, her breath shortening in her chest.

"I've been thinking about something," he said as she blinked up at him and wondered how any man could be so absolutely stunning. "I can't stop thinking about it, in fact."

"What's that?" she asked, trying not to devolve into a stammering idiot.

He smiled, and her stomach flipped. "I want to be your first, Faith."

She blinked. "M-my first?"

First what? She couldn't think, simply couldn't form a thought in her head when he held her so close, his body warm and hard against hers, his mouth so close, so sexy that she wanted to bite him, kiss him, lick him.

He dipped his head until those perfect lips were only a whisper away from hers.

"Yes, *cara mia,* I want to be your first lover."

She would never be certain who moved first, but then his lips were on hers and she was lost.

CHAPTER NINE

FAITH melted into his kiss as if she'd been born to do so. No man had ever kissed her the way Renzo had, she thought crazily. He kissed the way he rode motorcycles: expertly, passionately, and with a combination of control and recklessness that slayed her ability to think rationally about anything.

She was lost, helpless, powerless to resist when he held her so close, his mouth slanting over hers, his tongue sliding and teasing and tormenting.

He kissed her until she moaned, kissed her until she wrapped her arms around him and arched her body against his. Until she forgot who she was or where she was or why this might possibly turn out badly for her in the end.

His hand slid down her body, brought her hips in contact with his, and she gasped at the evidence of his need for her.

"I want you, Faith," he said in her ear. "But I want you to make the choice. It has nothing to do with who we are, and everything to do with this raw need we both feel when we touch. I want to explore this feeling, and I want to show you how good it can be between us when we do."

She could no longer deny that she wanted it, too. "Not here," she said quickly. "I don't want to do it here."

He lifted his head until he could look down at her, stroked his fingers over her cheek before tucking her hair behind her ear. "Of course not," he said. "Tell me what your fantasy is, *cara*. A castle? A desert tent? A tropical island? Name it, and it's yours."

Her pulse thrummed in her throat until she felt dizzy, drunk with passion and happiness and fear all at once.

"I—I've never quite thought about it." My God, what was she agreeing to? Was she really going to be this man's lover? Was she really negotiating the terms of her surrender in a sunlit office in Tuscany?

"What about Venice?" he said. "A gorgeous palazzo on the Grand Canal. I will do this for you, Faith, if it's what you want."

He looked so serious, and she knew that no matter what she named, no matter how far-fetched, he would move heaven and earth to get it for her. To make her first time special. She was touched that he would go to such trouble, and yet at this moment she wanted none of those things.

She only wanted him. In a bed. In his villa, with the scents of the flowers on the breeze and his taste on her tongue. That was all she needed to make it special, memorable.

But she felt unsophisticated for wanting something so simple when he was offering her the world. Would he think her too sentimental if she told him? Too unimaginative?

"I can see that you've thought of something," he said. "But you do not want to tell me. What is it, *cara*? Do you wish to refuse my offer? It is your choice, as I have said."

Faith sighed and lifted her hand to trace her fingers across his full lower lip. She was beyond hope now. She couldn't refuse even if her life depended on it. She knew that her heart probably depended on it, but that couldn't stop her, either.

Her fingers moved back and forth while he held completely still. She'd never done anything so sensual or bold to a man in her life, and yet the darkening of his eyes told her he liked it. She liked it, too. She felt as if there was a thread running from her fingers to her core, and when she touched him, her sex tightened with need.

"I want to go back to the villa, Renzo."

He captured her fingers in his and kissed them. "Then that is where we shall go."

The villa was only a short car ride away, but by the time they arrived, her bravado was fading and nerves were taking over. She was about to let a famous heartbreaker make love to her for the first time in her life. What if he didn't enjoy it? What if he was disappointed?

Because this wasn't about love. It was about desire and heat, about sexual gratification. Things that she knew nothing about, or at least not yet. What if she was terrible at it?

They left the car in the drive and passed into the house through the kitchen door, which was open to the breeze and the bright afternoon sunshine. The cook, Lucia, was busy making something that smelled wonderful. She looked up when they entered, and smiled. Renzo spoke to her for a few moments before Faith followed him into the long hallway leading toward the grand staircase, butterflies swirling in her belly until she was nearly sick with it.

When they were almost at the stairs, Renzo caught her to him and her blood began to sing once again. If he would just hold her, she could do anything.

"I want you desperately, *cara mia*," he said, his blue eyes serious as he studied her face, "but I want you to be certain. And I want to do this right. You should be wined and dined and seduced, not taken upstairs and stripped naked simply for my pleasure."

She clutched his sleeves as he cupped her face. She waited for the perfect storm of his kiss, that melding of lips and tongues that drove her insane with need, but his lips only skimmed hers, the kiss chaste and soft. When she would have wrapped her arms around his neck and pulled him to her, he lifted his head.

"Go, before I lose the will to send you away. We will dine together at eight. What happens then is entirely up to you."

It was nearly ten minutes after eight when she walked into the dining room. Renzo turned at the sound of her entrance. He'd been convinced she'd changed her mind when she hadn't been prompt—Faith had never been late even a single day at work, so it was inconceivable that she could be late now unless she wasn't joining him on purpose.

But she was here, and his blood began to hum at the sight of her. It was true he didn't know if she'd changed her mind or not, but the way she was dressed gave him hope. She wore a body-skimming blue wrap dress that was more daring than anything he'd yet seen her wear. It was still modest—Faith would always be modest—but the dress dipped in a V that showed the barest hint of cleavage while clinging to her curves.

Curves he wanted to explore in thorough detail.

Her color was high, he noted, her green eyes wide. Her blond hair spilled freely down her back, silky and shining in the lights from the Murano chandelier overhead. He had a sudden visceral reaction: he wanted to bury his fingers in her hair while he thrust into her body again and again.

Santo cielo.

He'd been determined not to do this, not to give in to his desire for her now that he knew she was a virgin. But he'd realized today, when she'd bent down to remove his boots, that she was a fire in his blood he wasn't going to quench any other way. Hell, she'd even invaded his ride on the Viper. At a time when he most needed his concentration, she'd been in his head, her pretty eyes and flushed cheeks, her beautiful full breasts, her hot little tongue as he'd kissed her in the car last night.

Faith was in his blood, in his body, and he knew of no other way to drive her out than to immerse himself in her. But the choice was hers. Only hers. He would not take advantage of her innocence. If she told him to go to hell, then he would find another woman tomorrow and take care of this burning sexual need at the least.

"I'm sorry I'm late," she said a touch breathlessly. "Lola wouldn't settle down."

"And how is our tiny tyrant?" he asked, going over and pulling out her chair like a gentleman instead of staring at her like the slavering beast he was. She skimmed past him, her hair brushing his arm, her sweet scent wrapping around his senses. She smelled like vanilla, he realized. Soft, warm vanilla.

It reminded him of home. Of his early home, when he was still a small child and his mother had plenty of work—and plenty of male attention, though he'd not known or cared how important that was to her then. They'd had a nice apartment with a sliver of a sea view. It had been tiny, but his memories of it were warm and happy.

Faith laughed as she sat down, though the sound was a bit high and nervous. Not the sound of a woman who planned to say no. Possessive heat coiled in his belly even as he felt a twinge of guilt.

"She is very tiny, and very tyrannical," Faith said, and he remembered that they had been talking of Lola. "But so adorable."

He took his seat, determined to do this right. To make this night special for her. "You love her already."

She smiled. "I do. It's hard not to. That's why Mother Nature makes babies so cute."

"Then I did the right thing in giving her to you." It gave him pleasure to see her smile. He'd rarely seen her smile in all the time she'd worked for him. She was always so serious, so proper.

She met his gaze then, and he could see the worry in her expression. "How is your leg, Renzo? Was it just a cramp, or did you reinjure it on the track today?"

Something inside him tightened. "I did not injure myself, *cara*."

She let out a sigh. "I'm glad."

A lot of people would be glad he wasn't injured—his team, his stockholders, his mother and sister—but somehow it seemed more important that she was relieved. That the worry lining her face was even now smoothing out and disappearing.

The meal arrived then, and their talk was confined to things like the kitten, his run on the track today—without any further mention of a doctor or his difficulty at the end of the ride, *grazie a Dio*—and the beauty of the Tuscan countryside.

"I will take you to Florence soon," he told her, and she smiled so genuinely that it actually hurt. She was so sweet and innocent, and he had no right to take her for his own when he did not intend to keep her.

He should get up now, get into his car and go to his apartment in Florence. Alone.

But he would not. He wasn't that selfless.

"Can we see *David?*" she asked excitedly.

"Of course. He is quite magnificent. I am an Italian male, and yet the first time I saw him, even I was moved by the beauty of the sculpture."

She sighed. "There is so much beauty in Italy."

"*Si*," he said meaningfully. "There is."

Her lashes dropped. She reached for her wineglass, her fingers trembling. It nearly undid him.

"Faith."

She looked up. "Yes?"

"You can say no." He drew in a deep breath. He couldn't believe what he was about to say. "You probably should say no, *cara*. I offer you nothing except pleasure. And you can wait for that when the time—and the man—is right."

She dipped her head to study the wine in her glass, tucking a lock of hair behind her ear as she did so. "If you don't want me, it's okay. I understand. I'm not sophisticated or experienced enough for a man like you, and maybe it is better if we continue to be professional after all."

He reached across the table to tip her chin up. She tried to keep her eyes from meeting his. "Look at me," he commanded.

Her lashes lifted until he was staring into the deepest, greenest eyes he'd ever seen. He felt a jolt in his gut, a visceral need for her that stunned him with its intensity.

"What I want is you beneath me. Naked, *cara mia*. Right now would not be soon enough."

There was an electrical current in the air, sliding between them on invisible pathways that sparked and sizzled with each look, each touch, that flowed between them. Faith's blood felt hot, thick, and her chest ached as if she couldn't quite breathe properly.

Anticipation coiled in her belly. *Naked.* She tried to imagine it, tried to imagine what he said he wanted, and her vision swam as she did so.

She could hear Renzo's soft laugh, and then he was standing and pulling her to her feet, holding her close. "Breathe, Faith. Don't pass out on me."

She clutched her fingers into the expensive silk of his

shirt and sucked air into her lungs. Air that smelled like him, spicy and male and clean.

"You must think me ridiculous," she said, her voice muffled against his chest.

He stroked her hair. "Not at all. I think you're refreshing. Lovely."

"This is not quite how I imagined my first time would go."

His voice was smooth, warm. "And what did you imagine, *cara*?"

She shrugged. She'd imagined love, though she wouldn't tell him that. She wasn't naive—she was a grown woman who'd had to take care of herself for the past eight years. She'd had roommates, she'd watched movies and she'd listened to bedroom tales when her roommates wanted to share. But, through it all, she'd imagined some sort of special moment when Faith Black—Faith Winston—met her Prince Charming. The man who would love her the way she loved him, and who would pledge his soul to hers when he made love to her for the first time.

It was a crazy fantasy, a girlish fantasy. She knew better. Relationships were messy and imperfect, and you kissed a lot of frogs before you found Prince Charming.

"I'm not sure," she said softly. "Music, dancing, candles. Romantic nonsense."

"It's not nonsense if it's what you want." He took her hand and led her into the living area. The room was beautiful, she thought wistfully, as she sat on the plush couch at his direction and let her eyes roam over the wood beams and the original artwork that graced the stuccoed walls. Renzo picked up a remote control, and then the soft strains of smooth jazz filled the background.

There were candles clustered in the hearth, she realized, when he struck a long match and lit them. Then he returned to the couch and sat beside her. She thought he might pull her into his arms, kiss her, but he simply sat back and put his arm around her. After a moment's hesitation, she curled into him and watched the flames.

"Do you want me to tell you about my first time?" he asked.

Faith nodded. She could feel his smile against her temple. "This is top secret information, *cara*. It would surely ruin me if it got out."

"I doubt that."

He laughed at the sarcasm in her voice. "I was seventeen," he said. "And very green. She was older than I, so sexy and experienced that I could not believe she wanted me."

"I can," Faith said, and meant it.

"Nevertheless, I fumbled quite badly. She was very patient."

Faith pushed back until she could see his face. "What do you mean, fumbled?"

His blue eyes were sharp. Sexy. She could drown in those eyes. "I mean that I failed. That I lasted about as long as it takes the Viper to go from zero to one hundred."

Faith could only blink.

"Don't look so surprised," he said.

"But you did it right the second time."

He nodded. "The second time was about fifteen minutes later. It was quite an improvement."

"You're only saying this to make me feel better. You didn't really, um…"

"Come too quickly? I did." He dipped his head and kissed her, his voice a soft, sensual growl when next he spoke. "I assure you this is no longer a problem."

Faith strained toward him, even though she was already close. She wanted him to kiss her again, to kiss her the way he had in his office, to make her forget everything but him and this moment together. Her body hummed with excitement, with anticipation and nerves and a zillion other feelings that were sparking and zapping inside her.

So long as he kissed her, the fear was submersed beneath the need.

One hand spanned her jaw, and then his mouth slanted over hers again, taking her roughly. She was shocked—and aroused. She wanted this kiss, wanted it just like this. Because it reminded her of last night, in the car, when he'd seemed so barely controlled that she'd thought he would tear her clothes off and make her his in a too-small sports car parked in the Tuscan countryside.

"Faith," he murmured. "You are so sweet. So intoxicating. Why did I not realize this before?"

"Renzo." His name was a sigh.

His lips touched hers again, and then his tongue slid against hers like silk and she moaned. She knew the rhythm so well now. Knew it as if she'd been born to kiss this one particular man for eternity.

She expected that he would quickly tire of the kissing and try to move on to the main event. That's what Jason had done on the fateful night when she'd refused him. She'd felt so badly afterward that she'd committed the single biggest error of her life.

Tonight, however, was not an error. She was twenty-six, more than responsible for herself—and more than ready to experience lovemaking.

Renzo kissed her endlessly, tirelessly, as if he had all night to do so. The tension in her body wound tighter and tighter until she throbbed with it. She wanted him so badly that it hurt—physically hurt—not to have him.

She was on fire. She wanted her clothes off, wanted to feel the cool air wafting over her sweat-sheened skin.

Renzo must have sensed it, because he stood then and pulled her with him. Without a word, they climbed the stairs to the second floor, where he tugged her into his arms and kissed her even while he moved her inexorably toward her bedroom.

A moment later, he scooped her up and carried her into the room—not hers, she realized, but his. This room was even bigger than the one she was staying in, and furnished with antiques, priceless art and a large bed with white linens that he laid her on before coming down over top of her.

Faith wrapped her arms around his neck, arched her body toward his. His arousal came as no surprise, considering the way she felt. He was big, hard, and he moved his hips against hers until she caught fire. Her body spiraled toward the peak, but he did not let her reach it. Before she fell over the edge, he stopped, moved down her body, kissed her throat, the exposed skin at the top of her dress.

Then he lifted himself onto his knees and shrugged out of his shirt while she bit her lip and stared. His eyes were so hot, so full of promise, as he gazed down on her.

"You could not have chosen a sexier dress, Faith," he said, his voice rough. His fingers strayed to the tie at her waist. "You wrapped yourself up for me, and I've been looking forward to the unwrapping all night."

CHAPTER TEN

RENZO tugged at the knot at her waist until it came free. Faith held her breath as he undid the inner knot—and then he opened the dress as if he were opening a present, his eyes gleaming appreciatively as they slid over her.

She'd never been so open to a man in her life, and yet she didn't feel exposed. She felt beautiful, desirable. She didn't envy the Katie Palmers of the world at this moment. No, it was they who should envy her. Because this gorgeous, gorgeous man was looking at her like she was the only one in the world who could satisfy him.

It might only be temporary, might only be for this one moment in time, but she didn't care. Right now, he was hers. She could see it in his eyes, in his beautiful masculine body. His entire focus was on her, and she knew she wouldn't be the same after tonight.

Renzo shook his head slowly. "What have you been hiding from me, Faith? For six long months, you've been hiding this sexy body."

He made her blush. "At this point, I'm a sure thing," she said, her heart beating hard. "You don't have to flatter me to get your way."

He looked so serious. "It is not flattery, Faith. It's truth. You are incredibly sexy." He spread his hand over her belly.

It wasn't a flat belly, not like his, and she bit her lip as embarrassment sliced through her.

"Renzo—"

"I love your skin," he told her, as if she hadn't spoken. "So creamy and pale. And your curves." He sucked in a breath. "*Dio*, Faith, your curves could kill a man if he weren't careful."

His hand slid down over her hip, skimmed over the silk of her panties, and then back up to cup a breast. His other hand went behind her back, unsnapped her bra, and then he was lifting it off her arms—along with the dress—and tossing it aside.

"They aren't perfect," Faith blurted. "They aren't round and perky and firm."

Renzo put a finger over her lips. "Don't talk, *cara mia.* Feel."

He bent until his mouth hovered over one stiff nipple. "I love your breasts. They are real. Round and firm, as you say, is usually made of silicone."

He licked the tip of her nipple, and her sex tightened. "Renzo," she gasped.

"Yes, *amore, feel.*"

He made love to her nipples then, licking and sucking the stiff little points until she wanted to scream. She'd never known that arousal could be painful until tonight. Because she burned for more than this, exquisite as it was. She burned for his body inside hers, for the sweetness of a shattering climax. She was gasping with need, writhing beneath him, and still he wouldn't put her out of her misery.

When he moved down her body, his mouth skimming her flesh, she cried out. If this was what making love felt like, why had she waited so long?

Because this was what making love with *Renzo* felt like. It would not have been the same with another man.

He tugged her panties from her hips, sliding them from her legs, and then he brought her to his mouth and slid his tongue along the seam of her sex. She arched up off the bed when he did so, her entire body on fire in a way she'd never before experienced. Of course she'd had self-induced orgasms before, but she'd never felt this kind of *excitement* in the buildup.

Renzo spread her with his thumbs. The instant his tongue touched her soft, sensitive core, she came apart with a cry. The sensations had been building for so long, her body growing so tight with it, that she needed nothing else to send her plunging over the edge. He didn't take his mouth off her as she shattered. Instead, he pushed her harder over the edge, kept the pressure focused on that one spot, his tongue darting and swirling long after she would have thought she had nothing left.

When it was over, she closed her eyes and turned her head into the pillow. Embarrassment echoed through her. And something else. Something hot and dark and ecstatic.

And yet she was surprised to realize that she wasn't completely satisfied. She felt boneless, liquid—and edgy. There was more, so much more that she'd not yet experienced.

"*Dio*, you are sexy," Renzo said, his voice roughened with passion. "The things I want to do to you, Faith. You tempt me beyond what is reasonable."

She couldn't speak as he stood and stripped off his trousers. She could only watch as his body was revealed inch by delicious inch, her breath catching in her chest at the sight of Renzo D'Angeli finally in the very naked and very hot flesh.

He knelt between her legs. He was big and hard and beautiful, and her heart thrummed so fast it made her dizzy. She reached for him, wanting to touch that part of him she knew nothing about. She'd never seen a man naked in the flesh before, and he fascinated her.

His breath hissed in as she tentatively stroked her fingers along his erection. He *was* hot. And very hard.

"Wrap your hand around me," he said, and she obeyed. She could feel him pulsing beneath her palm. It made her feel powerful, sexy, to know she'd caused this reaction. He put his hand over hers, showed her how to stroke him. When he let her go, she didn't stop. Boldly, she continued to stroke him, loving the way he groaned. A second later, he pulled her hand away, kissing her fingertips.

"Much more of that," he told her, "and it will be like *my* first time again."

He was far too experienced to lose control that easily, and yet it made her heart soar to think she could excite him that much.

He grabbed a condom from the nightstand and sheathed himself. Still kneeling, he lifted her hips and positioned himself at her entrance.

"If it hurts too much, you must tell me," he said.

She nodded, and then the hot, hard head of him was pushing into her. It was a tight fit, but it didn't hurt quite the way she'd expected it would.

"You are so ready for me," he said, his voice unexpectedly raw, his eyes closing tight as the muscles in his neck corded.

He didn't move for a long minute, and then he lowered himself on top of her. His mouth slanted over hers as he thrust completely inside her. Faith gasped at the fullness of his possession, at the heat and light shimmering through her, at this feeling of finally being joined with him. But there was no tearing, no pain.

Renzo lifted his head to look at her curiously.

"It happened at the doctor's office," she blurted, suddenly worried he might think she'd lied about being a virgin when there was no hymen. "My first exam."

His thumbs glided over her cheeks as he held himself still while she got used to the feel of him inside her. "You are the most surprising woman, Faith...."

"You believe me," she said softly, her body trembling from nerves and excitement. She hadn't much considered how he might react until the moment came. That he believed her without hesitation made her chest ache. It was more than her family had done for her when the picture she'd sent Jason went viral. They'd believed the worst from that moment onward.

"Of course I do," he said, dipping his head to run his tongue along her lower lip. "Why wouldn't I?"

Something inside her twisted. Faith glided her palms along the muscles of his arms, arching her body against him, shuddering as sensation rolled through her when he moved his hips just the tiniest bit. It was the most beautiful feeling.

And she wanted more of it. She wanted the physical so she could take her mind off the emotional, off the way he smashed all her misconceptions about him.

"Now," she said—begged, really, "please, now."

With a growl, he began to move, slowly at first, and then faster as she wrapped her legs around his waist and lifted her hips to meet him with every thrust.

It was a bold move, very unlike her in many ways, and yet she couldn't help herself. Because it was a revelation, this feeling of having a man inside her for the first time.

It was raw and sexy and primal, but it was also beautiful. Faith closed her eyes. She'd never felt so close to another person in her life, never felt so cherished and special.

Renzo bracketed her face in his hands and kissed her, a hot, wet kiss that excited her almost as much as his body possessing hers so completely did. She was spiraling higher, her body catching fire with feelings she'd never experienced.

When his mouth moved to her nipples, she couldn't keep her moans of pleasure locked inside any longer. She was losing control of herself—and she didn't care.

Her hips thrust up to meet his, her body accepting—demanding—the exquisite torment of his lovemaking. He answered her with an intensity she hadn't imagined possible. Their bodies moved together, lifting and sinking and soaring, until stars exploded behind her eyes and she cried out.

He kept moving, kept thrusting, wringing every last moment of pleasure from her until a ragged groan tore from his throat. And then he sank down on top of her, his mouth taking hers again, before he rolled to the side and pulled her with him.

Faith lay against him, panting, her body still tingling and shuddering in the aftermath.

My God, what had just happened to her? She'd never flown so completely apart, nor wanted the feeling so desperately that she would have done anything to get it.

Renzo's breathing was as hard as hers as his fingers skimmed down her naked back. A few moments later, he got up and walked into the attached bathroom, and her skin began to cool when he was no longer lying next to her. She lay sprawled on the bed, her body flushed and quivering and moist, and a sudden sensation of guilt pricked at her conscience.

She reached for the covers, suddenly acutely aware of her own nakedness. The room wasn't brightly lit, but a lamp was on, spilling soft light over the rumpled bed.

She was not like Renzo, she thought. He was so beautiful, so perfectly made, muscles bunching and rippling as he moved.

And she was softer than she should be, padded. She was definitely not underwear model material. She yanked the covers to her chin as the heat of embarrassment infused her. Renzo had been too preoccupied before to really notice the flaws in her body—but now? Now he would notice everything.

Faith would have shot from the bed and grabbed her clothes, but he returned too quickly. As he strode toward the bed, she got her first good look at his injured leg. There was a long scar down one side of his thigh and along the side of his knee. The scar was faded, but still noticeable.

He stopped and glanced down at his leg, and she realized she must have been frowning. She tried to wipe the look from her face, but he wasn't fooled.

"It was a long time ago," he said. "And yes, it was bad. So bad they said I would never race again."

Faith bit her lip. She hated to think of him in so much pain, being told he couldn't do the one thing he loved to do, the thing he had been the best in the world at. For the first time ever, she had an idea of just how hard he must have fought to prove them wrong. And how much it frustrated him to be dealing with it again now when he thought he'd conquered it.

"But that is unimportant at this moment," he said, joining her in the bed again. His fingers hooked into the covers and tugged gently. "Let me see you, Faith."

"You already saw me."

He laughed. "It's a little late for modesty, don't you think?"

Her ears burned. It was a little late for *everything*. Where was her decorum, her sense? Her self-respect? She'd tumbled headlong into carnality. If she was sorry now, it was no less than she deserved.

Except that she wasn't sorry. Not for what they'd done.

If she was sorry for anything, it was that she'd given herself to him and erased the mystery. How soon before he tired of her? How soon before she was looking for another job?

She'd done the one thing that she'd sworn she would never, ever do. She'd had sex with her billionaire boss, and become one of *those* women who seemed to think they could sleep their way to a better job or a better life. She knew women like that, women she'd met who worked for powerful men and thought that sleeping with them would lead to love.

Elaine had never admitted it, but Faith was convinced that's why her roommate left the city and returned to Ohio. She'd had an affair with a man in her office who, while not her boss, was in senior management and quite wealthy. And married, it turned out. The affair had been over for a while, but Elaine had never quite gotten over it.

Renzo leaned down and kissed her, and Faith's body started to melt. It surprised her, how she could respond so instantly after what they'd just done. She should be replete, too satisfied to react.

And yet she wasn't. It was a shock to realize that if he wanted her again, right now, she'd happily wrap herself around him and go along for the ride.

And it was terrifying, too. If she couldn't control herself now, what would happen later, when she was so accustomed to his lovemaking that the inevitable breakup would crush her? She'd be one of those pitiful women who kept calling his office—except that *she* was the gatekeeper.

Faith wanted to whimper and wail—and surrender to his touch.

Renzo was oblivious to the feelings crashing through her as he kissed her, and the covers inched down until she could feel the air sliding over her breasts, her torso.

"Beautiful," he said, his hot mouth kissing a trail to her breasts. "I think I should keep you naked at all times."

"It would make getting work done a little difficult," she said, trying hard to be sophisticated and cool.

He propped himself on an elbow, his gaze smoldering. "Not if you worked in here."

She reached for the covers again, and this time he did not stop her. "I—I think I should go back to my room now."

His brows lifted in surprise. And then drew down as his features clouded. "Why would you want to do that?"

She couldn't look at him. Her heart was pounding, her stomach flipping. What was she doing? "Thank you for showing me what it was like. For being my f-first. But I still work for you, and if I'm going to do my job properly, then I should go back to my own room now."

His face was a thundercloud. She didn't think she'd ever seen him so angry. Not even when Niccolo Gavretti had tried to kiss her. He swore in Italian—and then in English, shocking her with the coarseness of his words.

He shot from the bed and stood there in all his naked glory. "Fine. Go then."

Misery sliced into her. They'd been so close, and now she'd done this. She'd alienated him when all she wanted to do was turn into his arms and sleep the night away. "You need to turn around."

"No." His voice was hard, cruel. "We just had sex, Faith. I think I know what you look like. What you feel like. If you want to leave, get out of the bed and get dressed right now. I'm not going anywhere."

She hesitated a minute before climbing from the bed and dragging the top cover with her. Renzo wrapped his fists in it and stripped it away, forcing her to stand there naked and exposed.

Like he was.

She wrapped her arms around her torso, turning in a circle while she searched for her dress. It was on the other side of the bed. She went to get it but before she could bend down, he was there, jerking her into his arms, pressing the full length of her naked body against his.

"You don't want to go," he said harshly. "You're only doing this because you think you have to. Because you think I won't want you anymore. But I do, Faith. I *do*."

Faith shivered. Her hands were fists against his pectoral muscles, her forearms resting against his chest. And she was softening inside, aching and wanting and needing. When he held her, she wasn't embarrassed or afraid. She simply wanted him, wanted this man she cared for more than she should.

It was already too late to protect her heart, she realized. She was falling, falling hard, and there was nothing she could do, short of leaving now. Leaving, going to the airport, climbing on a plane, and flying back to New York, where she would get another job and never, ever see Renzo again.

She should run away now, but she didn't have the strength.

"I don't understand this," she said, her voice full of anguish. "Because you shouldn't, shouldn't…"

He gripped her shoulders and forced her to look at him. "Stop trying to tell me what I should and shouldn't want." He took her hand, dragged it down his torso, to the evidence of his desire for her. Already, he was hard again, and she gasped as she wrapped her hand around him.

His breath hitched in, and her bones dissolved. How could she walk away from this?

She couldn't. It was impossible. And he knew it, too.

He pressed her back on the bed, turning her until she was on her knees. And then he showed her another way to tumble headlong into pleasure, entering her from behind so that she gasped at the erotic fullness of his possession. His fingers skimmed over the sensitive heart of her even as he moved so exquisitely inside her. When she flew apart this time, he gave her no quarter, gripping her hips and thrusting into her until he came with a ragged cry and they collapsed together onto the bed.

Then he pulled her into the curve of his body and anchored her to him with a hand firmly on her hip. Once more she tumbled, only this time it was into the sweet oblivion of sleep.

CHAPTER ELEVEN

THERE was a rumbling in Faith's ear. Someone was mowing grass and the sound of the mower was filtering into her consciousness, waking her slowly. But, no, the sound was warmer than a mower. And then a cold, wet nose tickled her ear and Faith's eyes snapped open.

Lola lay curled on the pillow next to her, purring happily. Faith turned her head. Renzo was standing near the window, naked except for the towel wrapped around his waist, coffee cup in one hand, other hand propped against the window frame above his head.

He turned when she stirred. And then he moved toward the bed and her heart squeezed so tight she couldn't get her next breath out. Lola lifted her head and mewed, then bounded toward Renzo as he perched on the side of the bed. He laughed and scooped her up, nuzzling his cheek against her fur before putting her down again.

Faith's heart thumped hard. The thin ice beneath her cracked just a little more, threatening her with a headlong plunge into emotions she wasn't prepared to deal with just yet.

Renzo looked up at her, his eyes clouding over. "What is wrong, Faith? Did I hurt you last night?"

Yes. Because it was beautiful and magical—and it wouldn't last. He wasn't hers, and she was just another in a long line of women who'd fallen into his bed and under his spell. Even though she'd known better.

"No, of course not," she said, shifting herself higher in the bed until she was sitting back against the pillows.

He didn't look convinced. "I'm sorry if I was…rough," he said. "I should not have taken you like that when this is still so new to you."

Her ears were hot. She couldn't meet his gaze. Lola wandered over and stretched her little paws against Faith's leg. Faith stroked the silky head, her heart so full of feeling for man and beast that she thought she would burst with it.

"There is nothing you did to me that I did not want," she admitted, her gaze firmly fixed on the gray-striped kitten. She was afraid to look at him, not because she was embarrassed, but because she was afraid he would see what was in her heart.

But he wouldn't allow her that kind of evasion. He tilted her chin up with a finger, forced her to look at him. Neither of them said anything for a long moment. Her blood rushed through her veins, swirled in her head and heart until she felt dizzy.

"How do you feel this morning?" he asked.

Like I'm in deep, deep trouble. "Fabulous," she said. "Slightly sore, but not unpleasantly so."

"Regrets?"

"No."

His expression was doubtful, but he didn't say anything. She could tell him that she had no regrets now, but she knew she would eventually—when he left her for someone else and her heart shattered into a million pieces.

She tickled Lola's chin. The kitten swatted at her and she laughed. "I'm glad you went and got her." She pictured him crossing over to her room and scooping Lola from her nest in the bathroom. That he even remembered the tiny kitten made her heart swell.

"She needs you as well as I."

Needs. She told herself not to read anything into that word, but she couldn't help it if it made her feel as though she'd swallowed sunshine.

There was something else she'd been thinking about, too. "Thank you for believing me last night, Renzo. It means a lot."

His blue eyes seemed to see inside to her soul as he sat and watched her. "You don't trust people, do you?"

Lola curled against her leg and Faith rested a hand on the tiny purring body. "I—I'm just cautious."

"Why? Who hurt you, Faith?"

"I don't know what you mean." It was evasion, pure and simple. And it wasn't working, because he was looking at her like he knew better. He *did* know better, she realized. Something about that knowledge pricked her to her core. He could see right through her, and she still knew nothing about him. Other than he had a big heart and a stubborn streak a mile wide.

And that his reputation as a lover wasn't in the least bit exaggerated, she thought with a twinge of heat.

"I think you do," he said softly. "Something happened to you. Something that made you leave home and never want to go back. Something that made you unwilling to trust."

Faith's shoulders sagged beneath the weight of his words. She was tired of being cautious, of carrying her burdens alone. It wasn't tragic, what had happened—though she'd certainly thought so at the time.

No, with the perspective of years and distance, it was simply humiliating. Once she'd left Cottonwood behind, she'd never told anyone. She'd been terrified to tell anyone, as if it would bring the whole ugly business up again.

"Yes," she said softly. "You're right. But it's not what you think. It's just, um, embarrassing."

"As embarrassing as my first sexual experience?" he said, one corner of his mouth turning up in a grin.

Faith smiled. "Worse, actually." She toyed with the edge of the coverlet. "I had a boyfriend I thought I was terribly in love with in high school. It was assumed we would get married once school was over."

"But you did not."

"No." She sighed as she let herself remember the ugly events of her senior year. "His name was Jason, and my parents adored him. He wanted to, uh, go all the way—and I didn't. It almost happened, on my parents couch when they were out one night. But it didn't, and Jason was angry with me.

"He texted me later, telling me it was over between us. Unless I proved I loved him." Faith sucked in a breath, remembering how naive she'd been. How trusting and gullible and downright stupid. "I sent him a picture I took with my phone."

"A picture?"

Faith closed her eyes. Even now, the humiliation was intense. "A naked picture, Renzo. I wasn't smart enough to cut my head out of the picture when I took it. It was clearly me—and Jason sent it to a friend. Who sent it to another friend, and on and on. You get the idea. My parents were furious. I made my father look bad, you see, since he was a minister."

Renzo reached over and squeezed her hand. "This is why you haven't spoken to them in eight years?"

The lump in her throat ached. Her family hadn't stood beside her at all. They'd thrown her to the wolves, and all because of her father's self-righteousness. "Yes. It was hell, absolute hell, going to that school for the rest of the year. Everyone laughed at me. Everyone pointed and talked about me. I lost all my friends. I was mortified."

She took a deep breath, determined to hold her angry tears at bay. It was cathartic to tell someone, and so very hard at the same time. "But my parents wouldn't take me out of school or let me go to another school. They made me keep going until I graduated—which I barely did since I stopped studying and getting good grades. My dad thought it was a fitting punishment for my sins. When I graduated, I left town and I've never looked back. I even changed my last name so I could feel like someone new."

She'd had to change her name because the thought of being Faith Winston made her physically ill. It was so much easier to become someone else, another Faith who had never done something as stupid as send a naked photo to a boy. Reinventing herself had been the only way to survive.

Renzo looked furious, but he leaned back against the headboard and pulled her into the curve of his arm. "You were young," he said fiercely. "You didn't do anything wrong."

"I was stupid," she said. "And because I was eighteen, the authorities did nothing about it. I imagine you could still find the picture if you typed Faith Winston into a search engine."

Renzo swore softly. "I'm sure you were absolutely beautiful, but I have no desire to see this photo when I have the real Faith warm and naked in my bed. And you were not stupid, *cara mia*. You were young. And in love with someone who did not deserve you."

He handed her his cup of coffee. She took it silently, sipped. It was such an intimate gesture, but she was determined not to think it meant more than it did. No doubt he was always this solicitous with his lovers. And, right now, he felt sorry for her.

"Why don't we get dressed and go into Florence?" he said a few moments later. "We'll have lunch there, and I'll take you to see the *David*."

"I'd love that," she said wistfully. "But you have a meeting this afternoon. I remember because I went over your calendar when we returned from the factory."

And as much as she wanted to go to Florence with him, to pretend they were a normal couple on a date, she couldn't let him down when it was her duty to manage his appointments. They might have spent one night together, but she was still his PA. The job came first.

He took the coffee from her and placed it on the bedside table. And then he tilted her head back, kissing her until she squirmed with the sizzling tension coiling inside her body.

"Cancel it," he murmured a few minutes later. "In fact, cancel getting dressed, too. At least for another hour…"

Renzo was on edge in a way he couldn't recall ever feeling before.

He trailed after Faith, who walked through the Accademia Gallery and oohed and ahhed at everything like a child at her first carnival. She was so lovely and sweet that he couldn't imagine the sort of family who would be cruel to her. How could anyone want to hurt Faith?

She strolled along, oblivious to his dark thoughts. She'd temporarily forgotten him, and it made him oddly jealous. He wanted her to look at him the way she was looking at the art, wanted her to turn and slip her arm around his waist and stroll beside him, her warmth pressing into him.

He'd loved the expression on her face when they'd first entered the long Galleria del David where Michelangelo's *Prisoners* lined the walls. Her soft pink mouth had dropped open, her eyes growing wide. She'd studied each of the *Prisoners* before making her way to the David, who stood on his pedestal beneath the dome at one end of the long gallery.

Voices echoed throughout the chamber, but it was also solemn, thanks to the guards stationed nearby who refused to allow shouting or running—or camera flashes. Faith stopped and stood with her head tilted back and her jaw loose as she let her gaze skim the perfect form of the sculpture.

Faith studied the statue, but Renzo studied her. He'd often heard about a woman glowing—when she'd had fabulous sex, when she was in love, when she was pregnant— but he'd never noticed that glow until today.

There was something about her that drew his eye and wouldn't let him look away. She moved with a grace that was far more sensual than he'd realized before. He didn't usually pay attention to women's fashion, other than to note how a woman looked in her clothes, but he'd found himself analyzing Faith's clothing and wishing he could remove it. Not because she looked dowdy or boxy or unattractive, but because she looked chic and put together and it annoyed him when men turned to look at her.

And plenty of them had turned to look at her.

She'd worn a casual dress with sandals. The dress accented her waist, her breasts, and flared over her hips into a swingy skirt that fluttered and swirled when she moved. Her legs were bare, and he found himself thinking of how they'd felt wrapped around his waist as he'd taken her body into sweet oblivion.

She'd been so innocent, and so carnal at the same time. He thought back to the moment he'd unwrapped her like a present, and his body grew as hard as the Carrara marble on the pedestal.

"It's wonderful," she said, turning to him and reaching for his hand, her eyes shining with unshed tears that caused his chest to ache.

"*Si*, it is quite magnificent."

"Thank you for bringing me."

He tugged her into the circle of his arms, uncaring that others moved around them like water flowing around a rock in the stream. "I can think of a few ways you can show your appreciation later," he told her.

Her eyes widened as she felt the strength of his desire for her. "How can you possibly be…?"

He grinned at the word she did not say. *Aroused. Ready?* "Aren't you?"

The heat of a blush spread over her cheeks. "Yes, I have to confess that I am." She put her forehead against his chest. "I can't believe you've managed to turn me into the kind of woman who would rather spend the day in bed with you than do just about anything else."

He threaded his fingers into the silk of her hair. "I would have been happy to oblige had I known."

She looked up at him again. "If I weren't starving, I'd suggest we leave right now and go back to the villa."

Possessiveness, hot and sharp, flared inside him. "Ah, but there is no need, *cara*. I have an apartment nearby. But first, lunch."

He took her hand and led her from the gallery. They emerged onto the street and walked a few blocks to one of his favorite Florentine restaurants. They were greeted like old friends and shown to a table on the terrace with a lovely view of the Duomo. Usually, Renzo liked a bit more privacy, but since it was Faith's first time in Italy, he wanted to indulge her appetite for adventure.

They started with a beef Carpaccio that was so thin and tender it melted in the mouth, a *mozzarella di bufala* and tomato salad, and then moved on to a luscious spaghetti carbonara before finishing with *panna cotta* and espresso. Faith ate everything with gusto, her eyes closing from time to time while she sighed and licked her lips.

It was refreshing to see a woman eat something other than a salad for a change. American women—especially the ones like Katie Palmer and Lissa Stein—seemed to subsist on nothing but lettuce and water for the most part.

But then he had to acknowledge that it was more the *sort* of woman he'd dated rather than a cultural trait. The Faith Blacks of the world seemed to have no trouble enjoying a good meal. Faith was so refreshing, so different—so real. Why had he avoided real women in his life? Why had he always chosen the ones who, deep down, repelled him?

In spite of his desire to get Faith alone again, he was also enjoying her company. They lingered over their coffee, talking about things like how he got started building motorcycles, what had made him want to race and how she'd ended up in New York. For the first time ever, he found himself wanting to share more about himself with her than he had with anyone else.

Faith knew what it was like to be ostracized from her family. Knew how it felt to have a father care more for himself and his reputation than he did for you. She would understand—and yet he couldn't quite bring himself to tell her. He wasn't golden like Niccolo Gavretti, who came from a supremely wealthy family with pedigree and influence, and who'd grown up with every privilege.

He was a mongrel in comparison, a cur slipping into back alleys and stealing food and clothing. He couldn't tell Faith that, couldn't bear the pity or the disgust in her eyes if he did.

So he said nothing.

The sun dipped lower in the sky and golden light bathed the square, turning everything he'd always taken for granted into something magical. Or perhaps that was because he was seeing it through her eyes.

Nothing that good could last, however. Soon, he began to notice camera flashes. At first, he thought it was tourists—but then the flashes became more numerous, and directed toward them. Renzo swore, and Faith turned to look, her expression falling after the picture snapped.

He knew what she was afraid of, and he wanted to leap over the railing and rip the cameras away from the paparazzi. He wanted to smash them into a million pieces and protect her from any fear of her old photo coming to light again.

But an action like that would only inflame their curiosity, so instead he took her hand and tugged her toward the back of the restaurant. He laid a handful of bills on the counter for the owner, who apologized profusely, and then they exited the restaurant into the alley behind it and hurried toward another alley.

Renzo took her on a crisscross trip through the city, but the photographers never caught up to them. Soon, he slowed their pace until they were strolling pleasantly along as if everything was normal.

"I'm sorry, Faith. I had hoped that wouldn't happen."

"You're a public person. It was inevitable." She seemed troubled and he stopped, turned to face her. She didn't look at him at first, but when she did, he could see the worry in her eyes.

His heart squeezed at the look on her face. He knew how much that impulsive nude photo had affected her, how much it had shaped her life. It would have been hell to endure what she'd endured. "You are concerned that if you appear in the paper with me, someone will find that old picture of you, aren't you?"

She shrugged, and he knew she was trying to put a brave

face on it. "It's silly. I'm no one. Who's going to care about an old nude photo that isn't even all that good? It would take an extraordinary effort to find it, and then to connect it to the woman I am today."

Yet with the press, anything was possible. Especially where it concerned his life. They'd dug up just about everything he'd ever done. The only thing they didn't know was who his father was. He didn't protect the *conte*'s identity for the man's family—or even for his own, since the *conte* no longer had the power to harm them—but because he didn't want the old man to have any credit for who Renzo had become.

"I wish I could tell you it won't happen, but the truth is that I don't know." He put his hands on her shoulders and bent until he was looking her in the eye. "I promise you that I will do everything in my power to find and destroy that photo before it can happen."

She shook her head. "It's out there, Renzo. I don't think even you can make it go away for good." She sighed. "I knew if I were seen with you, there was a good chance I'd end up in the papers. And I was willing to take the risk. So whatever happens next, I'll deal with it."

She looked determined, strong, even though he knew she was afraid. But that was Faith: practical and brave, and convinced she had to look after herself because no one else would. He pulled her into his arms and hugged her tight. "*We* will deal with it, *cara*, should it come to pass."

"It's sure to thrill Cottonwood if it gets that far," she grumbled. "I think I was the most excitement they'd had since Sherman marched to the sea and burned the town down around their ears."

Renzo blinked. Her voice was syrupy and sweet with that slow drawl he loved, but he didn't understand the reference. "What is Sherman?"

She laughed softly. "A Civil war general typically reviled in the South. It happened over one hundred years ago. It was very exciting, according to Miss Minnie Blaine, who's nearly one hundred herself and remembers her grandmama talking about it when she was a child."

"I should like to visit this South someday," he said truthfully. "It sounds fascinating."

She pushed back and arched an eyebrow. "I can see you there, Renzo. Eating barbecued ribs and drinking sweet tea. You'd be the third most exciting thing to happen to Cottonwood."

"Only the third?" he teased. "Perhaps I should do something a bit more scandalous first."

She laughed. "Perhaps you'd care to text a nude photo of yourself to the town elders? That would surely get some blood pumping."

"Happily, *cara*, if it meant they would forget about your photo."

She looked wistful, and he reached out to push a strand of hair from her face. "They will never forget it. I am persona non grata in Cottonwood."

"I doubt that," he said. "But I understand why you think so. It was a long time ago, and you are a very successful career woman now. Would they truly not welcome you back if you wanted to go?"

She frowned. "I don't want to go. Ever."

He understood her conviction. They were more alike than she knew, but instead of telling her so he took her hand and pressed it to his lips. Then they continued down the street, threading their way back toward the apartment and talking about the differences between Georgia and Italy. He was so lost in the conversation that he didn't realize where they were until it was too late. They emerged from a narrow alley between buildings, out onto a wider thoroughfare, and he realized his mistake. He'd come here as if on autopilot, and he stiffened even as Faith gasped at the magnificent villa before them.

"Oh, it's gorgeous," she exclaimed. "Does someone actually live there, or is it open to tourists?"

The wrought iron fence surrounding the Villa de Lucano was imposing, but the house that sat back from the street was ornate, part of its facade carved from Carrara marble and carefully timeworn in that way that only houses in the Old World could be.

The gardens were vast, lush, manicured. A fountain gurgled somewhere out of sight. Renzo imagined children playing there, imagined a father coming outside to greet them after time away, bending to hug them all as they flew into his open arms. It was an old fantasy, and not a particularly welcome one.

"No, it is a private residence," he said, unable to hide the bitterness in his voice.

She turned to him, her soft eyes questioning. And, in spite of everything she'd shared with him, he still couldn't seem tell her the shameful truth of his life before he'd become Lorenzo D'Angeli, tycoon, Grand Prix bad boy, superstar.

He wasn't ready for that. Didn't know if he would ever be ready for it. He would never, ever allow his life to sink to that level again. Anger surged through him.

He had to win the championship. *Had to.*

Success was everything. Renzo wanted his father to choke on his success, to regret every single day that he had not found a way to be a part of his son's life. The *conte* was proud, and Renzo was the richest, the most successful of his children. And no one knew.

"Is everything okay, Renzo? Does your leg hurt?"

"A bit," he said, seizing on the excuse. His leg did hurt, but it was a mild discomfort more than anything.

She looked contrite, and for that he felt a pinprick of guilt. He knew she blamed herself, as if the walking was her fault.

"It's not far now," he said, guiding her away from the Villa de Lucano. "Just a few minutes more."

Once they reached the apartment, Renzo laid his keys on a table and went to look out the huge plate window fronting the living area. He'd picked this apartment because of the city view, and because it was the best money could buy. He could see the rooftop of the Villa de Lucano, but that didn't usually bother him.

Now, however, it irritated him.

He stood with his hands in his pockets and stared at nothing in particular. Faith came to his side and quietly studied the view with him.

"What is it, Renzo?" she finally said when he didn't move or speak. "I know something is bothering you, and I know it's not your leg."

He closed his eyes for a moment. Of course she knew. She was attuned to him somehow. He didn't understand the connection between them, but he knew there was one. It was odd, and yet somehow necessary, too.

The words he didn't want to say burned at the back of his throat until he had to let them out or choke on them. "It's that place. The Villa de Lucano."

She pulled him around to face her, her green eyes wide and full of concern. "What is it about that place that bothers you so much?"

He studied her for the longest time—the sheen of moisture in her eyes, the determined set to her jaw, the high color in her cheeks. She'd endured much humiliation, and she'd survived it. She'd reinvented herself, the same as he had. She understood what it took to do so.

"The Conte de Lucano is my father," he found himself saying. And once he'd said that much, he told her the rest. What did it matter? "He does not want to know me. He never has."

He watched the emotions play over her face: confusion, anger, sadness and worry.

"Oh Renzo, I'm sorry," she finally said, her voice barely more than a whisper. A moment later, a single tear spilled down her cheek. It stunned him that she would cry for him. He caught the droplet with his thumb, smoothed it away.

"Tears, *cara*?" he asked.

She closed her eyes and shook her head, as if shaking the tears away. "I'm just emotional. It's part of being a girl."

He laughed in spite of himself. In spite of the vise squeezing his chest. She made him laugh, even when he did not want to. He pulled her closer and dipped to nuzzle her hair. He ached inside, but for once it was almost bearable.

"I like very much that you're a girl."

And then, because he didn't want to talk anymore—because he didn't think he *could* talk anymore—he swept her off her feet and carried her into the bedroom.

CHAPTER TWELVE

FAITH looked up from her computer, her heart doing that funny little flip thing it always did as the door to Renzo's office opened. They were spending days at the factory now while he went over the details for the Viper and for the next production launch. The launch was timed to coincide with the Viper's debut on the Grand Prix circuit, and everyone was working long hours to make it happen smoothly.

She'd never been so happy and so miserable at the same time. She was happy because she enjoyed being Renzo's lover, and miserable because she felt as if she'd done everything wrong. The other office staff kept their distance. She knew why. It wasn't a language barrier, as everyone spoke English, but more of a perception barrier. She was the boss's girlfriend, and everyone knew it.

It was, in some respects, a nightmare. She felt their censure, and it felt far too much like the censure she'd gotten at home when the photo of her began to circulate. People were distant, judgmental. They whispered behind her back.

She hated the way it made her feel. As if she were different. Damaged.

It had been inevitable, she supposed. The pictures of the two of them had finally appeared in the paper after the night in Florence when they'd been photographed together at the restaurant. Those photos were innocuous, but when you added in the photo of the kiss at the party, it didn't take a genius to put two and two together.

Her heart had beat so hard when she'd seen that picture that she'd thought she would pass out. Renzo had hugged her to him and told her not to worry. So far, he'd been right. There'd been nothing about her real name or the photograph that had caused her so much pain.

Still, she feared the feelings it would dredge up once the photo was public knowledge again. She'd thought she could handle it, but now, with the office staff treating her like she was a leper, she wasn't quite so confident.

She smiled as Renzo approached. He was as mind-numbingly delicious as always as he came over to her desk, clad in a custom suit and loafers, his dark hair curling over his collar. His blue eyes were sharp, but she could see the strain in them. He'd been pushing himself relentlessly, riding the Viper, working on the details for the launch—and making love to her at night in his bed.

A tendril of heat coiled in her belly and her body responded with a surge. Those nights were the hottest, most incredible she'd ever known. Renzo had taught her things she'd have blushed at only a few weeks ago, but things that she now did hungrily, greedily, as if she couldn't get enough of him.

Which, she acknowledged, she couldn't.

But she wanted more than just the physical from him. She wanted his heart, his trust. She'd thought perhaps she was starting to get those things that night in Florence when he'd told her who his father was, but they'd not spoken of it since. They'd spoken of nothing so deeply emotional again. It was as if he regretted letting her see inside his life.

"Did that fax from Robert Stein arrive?" he asked.

"It just came through," she replied, handing him the papers she'd taken from the machine only a moment before he'd opened the door.

He took it, frowning as he looked it over, and her heart squeezed tight with all the emotions she had to keep bottled inside. She felt hot and achy and needy every time she looked at him.

But it was more than that.

Whenever he touched her, whenever he played with Lola, everything inside her hurt. In a good way. She knew what it was, even if she'd never felt quite this way before. She was in love with him, but she didn't dare tell him.

He'd shown absolutely no signs of returning her feelings, and she wasn't about to commit the mistake that she was certain other women had committed in the past.

And yet it made her angry, too. Why couldn't she be herself? Why couldn't she speak up and tell him how she felt? Why was she afraid to do so? If he threw her out, then at least she would know where she stood, wouldn't she? Why waste time loving someone who didn't love you back?

There was another side to her despair, as well. Every time Renzo went onto the track, she could hardly breathe. He'd been training hard, riding the Viper and icing his leg at night. She'd tried to convince him to see a doctor, to hire a masseuse, but he was stubborn and wouldn't do it.

So she massaged his leg, praying that it was enough, that today would not be the day his leg would cramp up at two hundred miles an hour. She could stand it when he was alone on the track—but when he entered the circuit, and there were other screaming motorcycles all around him?

How could he stop if something happened? How could he possibly get out of the way in time?

He looked up then and caught her watching him. The answering heat in his eyes sent a surge of relief rushing through her. For now, at least, he was hers.

He glanced toward the open hallway that led to his suite of offices. No one was in sight, so he bent and fitted his lips to hers. She knew she should push him away, but she couldn't do it. It had been hours since she'd kissed him.

He smelled delicious, and so very sinful. She wanted to strip away his clothes and lick her way down his body. And then she wanted to take him in her mouth and feel the power she had over him as he gasped and groaned his pleasure.

"Come into the office with me," he said. "We'll lock the door and—"

She put a hand over his mouth to silence him. "You know I can't do that. Your people already dislike me enough. Especially that secretary you shuffled to another office."

He darted his tongue out to lick her palm, then straightened again. "No one dislikes you, *cara mia.* And it was time for Signora Leoni to go. She never kept my appointments straight. But if you feel people don't like you, you can work from home."

Home. It was his home, not hers, but she loved it anyway. She was happy there, and not because it was beautiful and far more lush than she was accustomed to in her life, but because Renzo was there. And Lola, her sweet little kitten who was growing in leaps and bounds. Lola owned the place now. Even stodgy Fabrizio couldn't resist her kitten antics.

Faith lowered her lashes. "I think you underestimate the benevolence of your staff, Renzo. They dislike me because they know we're together. But I won't leave. I'll be fine working here."

His hand ghosted over her hair. "You never give up, do you, Faith?"

She met his curious gaze. "I believe in working hard

to get what I want. And I'm not going to let what anyone else thinks stop me."

He bent and kissed her swiftly. "This is why I like you so much," he said. "We are exactly alike, *cara*."

Like? Her mind focused on that one word and wouldn't let it go. Like. He liked her. After everything they'd shared, he *liked* her.

It stung. She turned back to her computer, angry that sudden tears pricked the backs of her eyes. Well, honestly, what had she expected? She'd known she shouldn't get involved with him, but she'd gone down that road with very little hesitation when it came right to it.

"Have I said something?" he asked from behind her.

She shook her head. "Of course not. But I have a lot of correspondence to get through before the day is over. And you have a conference call in half an hour."

"Ah, *si*, I do." He sounded tired, and she turned to look at him. He ran the fingers of one hand through his hair.

Worry pricked her. "You need to rest, Renzo. Nothing good will come of it if you keep burning the candle at both ends."

Fatigue lines bracketed his mouth and eyes. "It is always this way before the season starts."

"I can't imagine it's good for you when you need your strength."

"There are a lot of things that aren't good for me. But they must be done."

"But your leg—"

"I'm fine, *cara*," he snapped suddenly.

Faith gaped at him. It was as if she'd reached out to pet sweet little Lola and been bitten for her trouble. His expression was a mix of rage, bitterness and despair. She knew that he was tired, that he was worried, and that he was angry over the hand fate had dealt him.

But he would not share any of it with her. He would not tell her how he felt, or how scared he was. It hurt. After all she thought they'd shared together, he would not open up to her now. Instead, he lashed out, pushed her away.

She was no different to him than Katie Palmer. And that made her angry.

"I think we both know better," she said, her heart throbbing. "You might deny it to everyone else, but you aren't denying it to me."

His jaw worked, his eyes flashing with a different kind of heat than they had a moment ago. "Type your letters, Faith," he said. And then he turned and walked back into his office, shutting the door firmly behind him. Shutting her out.

Renzo went back to his desk and collapsed in the chair. He felt like an ass for snapping at Faith. But he'd been feeling edgier than ever lately. He was tired, and his leg throbbed almost nonstop these days. The pain was bearable, but only just.

Yet he knew if he told her the truth, she'd beg him not to ride the Viper. And he simply did not want to have that conversation with her.

With anyone.

Since the night a little over a week ago when they'd stumbled onto the *via* opposite the Villa de Lucano, he'd been more determined than ever to make the Viper a success. And the only way that was happening was if he kept the reins for a little while longer. His team was good, but a victory didn't mean as much to them as it did to him.

He'd thought about pulling out. He really had. But the media expected him to ride. His investors expected him to do so, as well. The whole world was waiting for Renzo D'Angeli, the Iron Prince, to zoom onto the track and claim the ultimate victory for the tenth time. It would be a great feat, and everyone was watching.

Some were hoping he would fail. Niccolo Gavretti, of course. And quite possibly his father. They had never spoken, but Renzo knew his father followed the sport. He'd even seen the *conte* in the paddock once before. Backing Gavretti, naturally. The De Lucanos and the Gavrettis were old friends, blue bloods who stuck together in business and in life.

Renzo tossed down the papers that he'd been trying to concentrate on and leaned back in his chair, propping his leg on a low table that he'd pulled over for the purpose.

Dio. He rubbed the knotted muscles hard, hoping to ease the pain. He thought of calling Faith, but she was angry with him. Besides, he didn't want to admit that she'd been right. He couldn't admit it.

He slipped open a desk drawer and pulled out a bottle of over-the-counter painkillers. He shook two pills into his hand—and then shook out two more. He had to remain focused on the goal. Everything else was secondary.

He took the pills, and then picked up the phone and punched in a number. When a familiar voice answered on the third ring, he knew he was doing the right thing. For her, he would win again. For her, he would rub victory in the *conte*'s face once more.

"Renzo," his mother said. "*Ciao,* darling!"

They were at the factory late. Renzo rode the Viper again, zooming around the track at speeds Faith was certain were somehow faster than he'd ever ridden before. When he dismounted, there was no hitch in his gate, no weakness that she could detect. He'd had a great few days, though she knew it was only a matter of time before the pain got to be too much for him.

He kept a bottle of painkillers on the nightstand, rationing them out as if they were the last, most precious pills on earth. She admired his strength of will even while she cursed his stubbornness. If he would take them more regularly, or see a doctor, perhaps something could be done. Something that would ensure his safety on the track.

After he showered and dressed, they drove into Florence where they went to his apartment and changed for the evening. There was another party tonight, another gathering of investors and people who followed the MotoGP circuit. The season would start soon and all the teams would be heading to Qatar for the first race.

Eighteen races in thirteen countries. It was a grueling circuit, with two or three races each month, plus all the travel that was required to move from country to country. The logistics of it were a nightmare. Now that she knew what Renzo actually did, it was no wonder she'd worked at D'Angeli's New York factory for months before she'd ever seen him in person.

She loved being here with him, but she almost wished she'd remained in the financial office of the company. If she had, she wouldn't be so desperately in love with him now. She wouldn't be here, praying that every time he took that beast of a motorcycle on the track, he'd make it out alive.

Faith looked at the dress she'd selected for tonight and felt her heart thump hard. It was more daring than anything she'd yet worn. Black, made of clingy jersey, and figure hugging from the strapless bosom to her ankles. There was a slit up one side that went as high as midthigh.

She finished her hair and slipped into the dress, then slid her feet into glittery peep-toe platforms. She studied her appearance in the mirror, pleased with the elegant sensuality portrayed before her. Yes, it was a long way from the preacher's daughter to this, but she was comfortable, confident in the way she looked.

When she joined Renzo in the foyer, his gaze glided over her approvingly. But then his expression clouded.

"I'm not sure I want you going out like that, *cara*." He kissed her on the cheek and she inhaled his clean, fresh scent, closing her eyes for a brief second as she did so. "You look…too sexy for your own good."

Faith reached for her wrap, her pulse thrumming. "Nevertheless, it's what I'm wearing. I brought nothing else with me."

She hadn't forgotten that he'd dismissed her earlier, though it seemed as if he had. She thought for a minute he might pull her close and kiss her properly, but she was glad he did not. She couldn't quite bear it right now, when she was fighting with herself over what she meant to his life.

They arrived at the party, held at one of Florence's museums, fashionably late. Reporters and photographers were stationed outside the exclusive location, snapping pics and shouting questions to everyone who arrived. Faith hesitated before exiting the car. Renzo squeezed her hand, and she found the strength to join him on the red carpet. She always felt as if she didn't belong, and yet while he held on to her, she could do anything.

Faith pasted a smile on her face as they moved down the line. Renzo stopped every so often, smiling for the cameras as he anchored her to his side like a pretty ornament.

Finally, they passed inside. The host and hostess greeted them, fawning over Renzo before he extracted himself from their grip. The next guest came in, and the routine started all over again.

Faith accepted a glass of champagne from a waiter passing by with a tray. Between the paparazzi just now and Renzo's reaction to her concerns earlier, her nerves were frayed tonight. She sipped the liquid, hoping it would at least take the edge off.

She couldn't stop thinking about the way Renzo had shut down when she'd mentioned his leg. It bothered her a great deal that he would cut her from the important parts of his life, that he would refuse to discuss something so elemental as his fitness to do the job he intended to do. Was she just supposed to accept his edict and hope for the best?

Yes, clearly, she was. Faith tried not to frown as they moved through the gathering. Renzo introduced her to so many people she would never remember them all. She noted that while he did not say she was his PA, he also did not say she was his girlfriend. He introduced her simply as Faith.

It was a silly thing to focus on, but it was yet one more piece of evidence piled onto all the rest that had her wondering about her place in his life. Was this how it began for the other women he'd been with? Did they all start searching for signs that they meant more to him than just a warm body in his bed?

You knew, she told herself. *You knew what this was, and you did it anyway.*

She didn't say much, but then she wasn't expected to. Renzo stayed by her side for the longest time, but then he got caught in a crowd of men who wanted to talk motorcycles and ended up drifting away from her. In a way, she was relieved. She wasn't in the mood for a party, and it meant she could escape somewhere quiet for a few moments.

Faith glided through the rooms of the museum, studying the art, enjoying the rarity of having a gallery to herself while she was dressed up and sipping champagne. This certainly wasn't the kind of life she'd led before becoming Renzo's lover, and it would not be the kind she led after. If her old friends in Cottonwood could see her now, wouldn't they be surprised?

"Abandoned, *bella*?"

Faith gasped at the voice as she spun to find Niccolo Gavretti watching her from the entrance. He looked sinful in his tuxedo and white shirt, but he did not move her. For a moment, she wished he did. How easy would it be if she could just cast off her current lover for a new one?

"I am not abandoned," she said coolly. "Renzo is busy."

"I noticed," he said, his lips curving in a smile. "And he will only get busier once the season starts. There will be no time at all for lovely distractions when he is so focused on winning."

Ice dripped down her spine as she gripped the glass hard and tried not to react. "I'm sure I'll survive," she said.

He smiled his cool predator's smile. "I am sure you will, *bella*."

He crossed the room to her side, tilted his head back to study the painting of a weeping Madonna. It was a beautiful picture, dark and lovely, with the most vibrant blues and golds that made Mary stand out from the rest of the scene.

"If you wish for a change, lovely Faith, I am certain we could have a good time together. I promise I would not leave you to amuse yourself while I caroused with my buddies." His silvery eyes fixed on her and she shivered. There was nothing but coldness behind that gaze. Ruthlessness.

Another time, before she'd fallen in love with Renzo, she might have been flattered. But she knew Niccolo's goal in approaching her now that she'd been caught between them once before. He only wanted to annoy Renzo. It had nothing at all to do with her.

And she wasn't tempted anyway. Far from it.

"I don't like change," she said, her voice a touch sharp. "If you will excuse me."

He laughed. "You have only to let me know if you change your mind."

"I won't."

Her pulse raced as she brushed past him, but he didn't try to stop her. She headed for the noise of the more-populated areas of the museum. As soon as she stepped out of the gallery, she ran into Renzo. Her heart thumped.

He was frowning. "I've been looking for you, *cara mia*."

"And now you've found me," she said brightly. Too brightly, because his gaze sharpened. Damn Niccolo Gavretti.

"What have you been doing all alone, Faith?"

"Looking at paintings," she said. "They are really quite amazing."

She heard footsteps behind her, and knew precisely who it was. Knew what Renzo would see and what he would think. And she suddenly didn't feel like pretending anymore. She'd done nothing wrong, and if he couldn't trust that she hadn't, then she wanted to know it.

"*Ciao,* Renzo."

He stiffened. She could see his entire body go rigid, his eyes flashing fire. "Nico," he replied, his voice cold in spite of the angry heat in his gaze.

"I'm looking forward to our match in Qatar."

Renzo vibrated with anger. "I'm not sure why. The Viper is far better than anything you've designed lately—assuming you haven't stolen anything that does not belong to you."

Niccolo's eyes flashed. "Still banging that drum, Renzo?"

"We both know the motorcycles are not your true passion. It's simply another way to spend your father's money and stay out of the way doing it, *si?* You could not design an original bike if your life depended upon it."

Niccolo smiled, but it was a flat, lethal curving of the lips that didn't quite reach his eyes. "Arrogant as always, Renzo. I'll enjoy watching you fail."

Renzo's jaw could have been carved from granite. "I won't fail."

"You might." Niccolo strolled toward them, his hands thrust casually into his pockets. Then he stopped and let his gaze slide to Renzo's thigh. "If your leg continues to give you trouble, who knows what will happen?"

CHAPTER THIRTEEN

THEY left the party soon after and returned to Renzo's apartment. Renzo did not speak during the short car ride, and Faith didn't quite know what to say. She wanted to defend herself, to say that she hadn't told Niccolo Gavretti anything, but she couldn't speak. Every time the words formed on her tongue, they wouldn't come out.

Because if she spoke, if she denied it, she sounded guilty. She looked guilty, considering that she'd been alone with the man he hated—the man he'd accused of stealing from him—and she was the only one who knew he'd been having trouble. Except, clearly, she was *not* the only one. Someone else knew, or had at least guessed.

She wanted Renzo to trust her, to believe that she wouldn't tell anyone his secrets.

And yet he was silent.

She waited for him to say something, to ask her to explain, until she couldn't wait anymore. Until they climbed from the car and stood in the darkened street with the cool Tuscan air making her shiver and pull her wrap tighter.

"I didn't tell him, Renzo."

He looked at her over the roof of the sports car. "I did not say you did."

But he sounded cold.

Her heart burned and she felt hot, in spite of the chill. "No, you didn't say anything."

His gaze pinned her, and she knew that he was fighting with himself, that he did in fact think she might have betrayed him.

It hurt more than she'd ever realized it could. How could he possibly think such a thing of her?

They climbed the stairs to his apartment and went inside. Faith removed her wrap and draped it over a chair. Then she kicked her heels off and waited.

"Niccolo Gavretti is not to be trusted, Faith," he finally said. "He will do anything to win, including cheat. He will tell any lie, use any grain of information. You should not talk to him. Ever."

Her stomach twisted. There was certainly more to the story than he'd ever told her before. And if he was going to accuse her of betraying him, then she felt she deserved to know. "What happened between you?"

She wasn't sure he would speak. She watched a hint of sadness chase across his features. But then it was gone, and in its place was the usual fury she saw whenever he spoke of Niccolo.

"We were friends once. Long ago. He knew what my dreams were, what I was planning to do with my designs. Instead of backing me as he promised, he started his own business—with designs remarkably similar to mine."

"He stole from you." It made her sick, and angry. She wanted to punch Niccolo Gavretti's handsome face herself.

"He would love nothing better than to destroy me. I think it would soothe his guilty conscience to know he'd won in the end. Which is why you should not talk to him."

She touched his arm. "I didn't tell him anything, Renzo. Anyone who saw you that first day on the track could have surmised what was happening. You fell to your knees. A lot of people saw it."

His expression grew hard. "You accuse one of my people of spying on me?"

Pain squeezed her belly tight. "Why not? Or am I the only suspect?"

He shoved a hand through his hair and swore. Then he ripped off his bow tie and shrugged out of the bespoke tuxedo jacket. "I know you wouldn't say anything deliberately, Faith. Nico is quite good at extracting what he wants to know."

If he'd stabbed her in the heart with a rusty knife, he couldn't have hurt her more. "I'm not an idiot, Renzo! I didn't say anything to anyone. Ever. Not even accidentally!"

"You could have implied—"

"I implied nothing," she shouted. Fury held her in its cold grip. How could he think she would betray him, even unintentionally? She wouldn't, not ever. Her body shook with the adrenaline pulsing through it.

Renzo stared at her for a long moment. She didn't know what he would do, what he would say—but then he came over and gathered her to him. She stood stiffly in his embrace and refused to soften even while she swallowed angry tears.

"I'm sorry," he said, his lips against her hair. "I'm sorry. I know you would not have said anything."

She put her arms around him and buried her face in his chest. She loved him so much it hurt. And she feared for him.

"I didn't tell him—but maybe you should consider that he's right. You don't know what's going to happen when you get out there."

"It's always been that way on the track, Faith. You never know what will happen. It's part of the challenge."

She clutched his shirt. She was afraid for him, especially now that she knew how much Niccolo Gavretti hated him. "But it's too dangerous now. Maybe you should retire from the circuit. Let someone else do this."

She felt him stiffen and knew she'd said the wrong thing. He pushed her back, holding her at arm's length, and glared at her.

"I'm not retiring, *cara*. Not until I've won."

Her vision was growing blurry, but she no longer cared if she cried or not. "Why do you have to be so stubborn? It's your *life* we're talking about. How many times do you need to win before you'll be satisfied? How many times do you need to prove yourself?"

He turned and went over to the liquor cabinet, poured brandy into a glass. Then he set it down without drinking it, put both his hands on the cabinet, and stood with his back to her for a long moment.

Faith wrapped her arms around herself. She'd gone so far now, way over the line maybe, but for the first time since she'd started to fall for him, she felt as if she'd done the right thing. As if she'd been herself instead of who she thought he wanted her to be. It felt good—and frightening at the same time.

"One more time, Faith," he said. He turned and faced her, his eyes glittering hot. "I need to win one more time."

She sniffled. "Is that one more race or one more championship?"

"You know what it is."

She did. He meant he wanted to win another championship. Eighteen grueling races against a field of competitors who might be just as determined as he was. And who were certainly healthier.

"I'm not sure I can take it," she said softly, truthfully. How could she sit in those stands and watch him each time, her heart in her throat while she waited for something to go wrong?

"I've crashed before. I'll probably crash again. It's part of the sport, *cara*." He picked up the brandy and took a sip. "The goal is not to crash badly. To get up and walk away."

She bit her trembling lip. "And just how are you supposed to do that when you can't even walk without pain most of the time?"

His head snapped up, his nostrils flaring. "I'm fine, Faith. My leg only hurts when the muscles knot. Which is *not* most of the time."

Faith swore. "That's a lie, Renzo, and you know it. I massage it nightly for you. You practically live with an ice pack in the evenings. You're hurting and you're too stubborn to admit you have a problem. You might lie to everyone else, but don't lie to me."

"You go too far," he bit out.

"Do I? I sometimes think I don't go far enough!"

"That's enough, Miss Black," he snapped.

She recoiled as if he'd hit her. And then she gathered herself up, stood straight and tall and glared at him. She knew where she stood with him. Where she would always stand.

"You told me that I didn't trust people, and you were right. But you're a hypocrite, you know that? You don't trust anyone, either. You refuse to let anyone get close to you. You keep everyone at a distance. You cycle through relationships like you cycle through racing leathers. I knew it," she said angrily. "And I was still dumb enough to fall for you."

"We are lovers, not soul mates," he said coolly. "If you expected this from me, I am sorry."

"You aren't," she snapped. "You're only sorry you didn't get the chance to throw me out before I walked away."

He took a step toward her, stopped. Faith's heart was breaking. She'd gone much further over the edge than she'd intended, but it was too late to stop now.

"We'll go to bed," he told her. "Sleep. Tomorrow, everything will look different."

She shook her head. "It won't. Nothing will change the facts. You are injured and you won't admit it, and you intend to kill yourself on the track. I can't stand by and watch you, Renzo. I won't."

"Are you threatening to quit, Faith?"

She snorted. "Quit? Is that how you see this? That I'm quitting my job?"

His jaw tightened. "You can't abandon me right before the season starts. I need you."

Those three words punctured her heart. He didn't need her. He only needed the efficient PA by his side, nothing more. They'd had sex and he'd enjoyed her, but he didn't love her. And he never would.

"My God, my stupidity never ends," she said, half to herself. "I didn't learn my lesson with Jason. I'm just as gullible and needy as I was then. And I want to believe that the man asking me to give him a piece of myself cares for me when I know he doesn't."

"We're good together," he said. "This doesn't need to end."

She laughed, the sound broken and bitter. "Doesn't it? I won't watch you crash and burn, Renzo. I won't be there waiting for something to happen, waiting for them to haul you away in an ambulance because you're too proud to admit you can't do this any longer." She reached for her wrap, shrugged into it blindly. "I'm done. I can't do this."

She fled toward the door, intending to escape into the

Florentine night, to get as far away as she could, but he caught her before she could, turned her with rough hands.

His face was livid. "You aren't leaving me, Faith. I won't let you leave me."

"Then tell me you'll quit," she begged. "Tell me you'll stop this insanity and let someone else race the Viper."

He let her go abruptly and she shot a hand out to steady herself against the wall.

"I won't play this game with you," he said harshly.

"It's not a game," she cried. "I love you, and I don't want to lose you—" She stopped speaking when she realized what she'd said. What she'd revealed.

Renzo stood there before her, looking so cold and cruel. So removed, as if he'd already detached himself from the situation. Which, of course, he had. He'd had a lot of practice, hadn't he?

"I won't stop, Faith." His eyes glittered hot. "If you truly loved me, you wouldn't ask me to."

She could feel the tears trickling down her cheeks. She'd just told him she loved him, and he didn't say anything. Or, he did say something, but something designed to use that love against her.

She wiped the tears away with the back of her hand. "Jason said the same thing, did you know that? He said that if I loved him, I would do what he wanted me to do."

She hadn't had sex with him because she'd been young and scared, but she'd felt the pressure of those words. Felt them so deeply that she made the stupid decision to take that picture for him. To try and appease him.

She would never allow herself to cave in to that kind of pressure again, no matter the cost.

Renzo looked furious. "You can't compare this to what happened eight years ago. I've never asked you to do anything you didn't want to do. I've never threatened you if you didn't. You've made your own choices."

"And I have to keep making them," she said. "I can't stay and watch you go on that track and worry every time that it will be the last."

He shoved his hands in his pockets. "Think carefully, *cara*. If you are asking me to choose between you and riding the Viper, you will lose."

She shook her head sadly. "Don't you think I already know that?"

CHAPTER FOURTEEN

THEY raced at night in Qatar because it was too hot during the day. Renzo stood in the paddock in full leathers, wearing a baseball cap until it was time to put on the helmet and climb onto the shining red-and-white Viper, and talked with the press. Paddock girls pranced around in tight dresses and heels, carrying big umbrellas, but he barely noticed them even when one or two of them purposely came near and shot him coy smiles.

They were sexy and alluring, but they were not Faith. *Dio*, how he missed her. It had been a week since she'd left him, and he'd been miserable just about every moment since then.

She'd told him she loved him, but she'd lied. If she had truly loved him, she wouldn't have left him. And she wouldn't have given him an ultimatum.

His leg ached today, but it ached every day. She was right that he'd kept that from her, just like he'd kept it from everyone. But he was used to the aching. Aching was nothing. Muscle cramps, on the other hand, were a bit more problematic.

He'd been training hard, working the muscles, and he hadn't had an issue in any of the test runs. He would not have an issue today, either.

Faith did not understand that he had to do this. He appreciated that she'd been concerned for him, but if she'd truly loved him, she would have supported him. She would be here with him instead of back in New York, working for one of the other officers in D'Angeli Motors. She'd said she would leave the company and find another job, but he wouldn't let her do it. He'd sent her back with a glowing recommendation, and had heard that she'd been put to work in one of the senior vice president's offices.

He would see her again someday, when he returned to New York to oversee the U.S. operations, but that day would not be anytime soon. Perhaps she would have found someone else by then, a man who could appreciate her and love her for the remarkable woman she was.

His gut twisted hard at the thought of another man loving her. Loving his Faith. He held up his hand to signal the end of the interview and turned and walked away.

He had to get his head into the game today. He could not keep thinking about Faith, about her silky blond hair and her sexy curves, about the way she smiled at him, and the way she hugged that silly cat and said the most ridiculous things to it.

She'd left Lola behind, and he thought it had probably broken her heart more than leaving him had done. But she'd told him, while she stood there with tears in her eyes and hugged the cat close, that Lola would be happier in Tuscany. She had a big house to run and play in, and people there to take care of her. In New York, she'd live in an apartment and be alone most of the day while Faith worked.

Renzo had promised that Lola would have the best care and that she would always have a home with him. Faith had seemed satisfied by that, though she'd quickly put the cat down and walked away after he'd said it.

Out of his life and into the car that would take her to the airport.

He'd been glad he still had Lola after she was gone. The cat slept with him, curled next to his body like a fuzzy rumbling heater, and he sometimes reached over and stroked her soft fur and thought of Faith lying in bed with him and doing the same thing.

Dio, what was wrong with him? Was he a man? Or was he a toothless beast who'd enjoyed cuddling up to a woman and a cat in the middle of the night?

"And where's the lovely Faith today? I had thought she would be by your side, hovering over you like a mother hen until the start."

Renzo looked up to find Niccolo Gavretti sneering at him.

"Faith is not here," he said shortly. He would always despise this man, but he somehow couldn't find the energy to care much today.

"Ah, I see."

Annoyance slid through him at the other man's tone. "Do you?"

Niccolo shrugged. "We are alike, Renzo. We enjoy women, and when we are finished enjoying them, we move on."

Renzo ground his teeth together. "Faith is not just any woman," he said. "And if you ever touch her, I will destroy you."

Gavretti laughed. "If you've discarded her, Renzo, I can hardly see why you'd care."

Renzo took a step toward him, and then stopped, fists clenched at his sides. Gavretti just smiled a slick smile, eyes gleaming in challenge.

"You aren't worth it, Nico." He pulled in a deep breath that was filled with the scents of motor oil and fumes, heard the roar of the crowd in the stands and the growl-

ing whine of engines being tweaked and tuned—and he
felt empty.

It didn't fill him with elation the way it once had. His
blood wasn't pumping hard in his veins, adrenaline wasn't
rushing through his body, and he wasn't eager to climb
onto the back of the Viper and roar around the track with
a pack of other men who were also determined to win.

His lungs filled again with the scents he loved, but again
he felt empty. He didn't care. If he rode the Viper to victory or not, he didn't care. It didn't matter what anyone
else thought. It only mattered what he thought. What he
felt. He had nine world titles, a thriving company and a
woman who loved him.

A woman who loved him.

He cared what Faith thought, he realized. He cared a
great deal what she thought. It was a revelation to him, a
sudden parting of the clouds so that the sun could shine
down fully upon him and show him what a fool he'd been.
What an utter idiot he was still being if he didn't go after
her and beg her to forgive him.

Renzo spun from Gavretti without another word and
stalked toward the exit. He had to get out of here, and he
had to find Faith and tell her how he felt before he lost
her forever.

Faith was frantic. She'd been flying for hours and now she
was rushing through the crowd at the Losail Circuit, trying
to get to the paddock before the race started.

She'd had to come. She'd been in New York, working
and trying to forget that the first race of the season was
about to happen. But she'd realized as she sat at her desk
and refreshed her computer for the zillionth time, learning the layout of Losail and studying the course, that she'd
made a mistake.

She needed to be with Renzo, no matter what happened. No matter what her fears were, it hadn't been fair to ask him to choose between her and the races. She understood that now, and she needed to tell him.

"Matteo," she screamed when she saw the D'Angeli crew chief. She was almost there, but hands were barring her way, stopping her from reaching the D'Angeli team. She'd gotten this far because she still had the cell phone numbers of some of Renzo's team on her phone. She'd called Matteo from the airport in Doha, praying it wasn't too late. He'd promised to get her through to the staging area.

The noise was deafening. The crowd was screaming, the motorcycles were being tuned, and the paddock teemed with reporters and women in tight dresses who paraded around and smiled for the cameras.

"Matteo," she screamed again—and miraculously, his head popped up, his eyes meeting hers across the distance separating them. He spoke to someone, who came rushing over to extract her from the people holding her back. After a hurried conversation over her credentials, she was free and rushing toward the staging area.

"Where is he?" she asked when she reached Matteo's side. The gleaming Viper was gorgeous, its red-and-white paint scheme shiny, the sponsor decals prominent against the surface. She expected Renzo to be standing proudly near the beast, but he was not.

Matteo shrugged. "Not sure, *signorina*. He was here a minute ago."

She turned in a circle, looking for the familiar racing leathers. But there were so many racing leathers, so many bright spots of color that caught her eye that she didn't think she would ever find him.

Her heart hammered in her breast and panic threaded

through her belly. Where was Renzo? Would he ever forgive her? Would she ever have the right to wrap her arms around him again?

And then she saw him, walking through the crowd toward the Viper, and her heart filled to bursting with love. She sprinted toward him, calling his name. He looked confused as he stopped. But then his eyes widened as he saw her, and his arms opened a split second before she crashed into them.

He smelled like leather and gasoline and she closed her eyes and hugged him tight. But then he pushed her back until he could see her, and she nearly burst into tears at the look on his face. He seemed…happy.

"Renzo, I—"

"Faith, I love you," he said, and her heart stopped. Literally stopped right there in the middle of the paddock with all the noise and craziness going on around them.

But it kicked hard again, lurching forward at double speed. She was dizzy. Dizzy and drunk with happiness and love.

"Did—did you just say…?"

He tugged her to him and captured her mouth, kissing her until her toes curled, kissing her until she could hear cheering and clapping all around them. She could see the flashes of cameras from behind her closed lids, but she didn't care. She didn't care what they reported about her anymore. So long as Renzo loved her, they could say any damn thing they wished and print any picture they wanted. She would never be ashamed again.

When he finally lifted his head, she clutched his arms for balance, her heart careening out of control with all she felt. But she still hadn't said what she'd come to say.

"Renzo, I want you to go out there and win. Do you understand? I want you to win."

He only smiled and slid his thumbs against her cheeks. "I don't care, *amore mia*. It's over, and I don't care. I'm not racing."

She blinked. "Is it—" She couldn't finish, so she glanced down to his leg, back up again.

He shook his head. "No. But you were right. I need to end it now. I need to retire and let someone else take the team to victory. I've had my time in the spotlight."

Her eyes filled with tears. "Please don't do this because of me. If you want to race, I want you to race. You've worked so hard." She tipped her head toward the men in cherry-red uniforms who were standing and watching them. "They've worked hard. If you want to take the Viper out, then don't stop because of me."

"I don't need the success anymore," he said. "I craved it because it was all I had, the only way to prove I was worthy...."

He didn't say anything for a long moment and she squeezed him tight. "*Cara*, everything I've done has been to prove that I was good enough to be my father's son. He may not acknowledge me, but by God he will know who I am and be sorry. I've let it rule me for far too long, and I no longer need it to validate my life." He smiled crookedly, and her heart broke for him. "I only need you."

"Oh Renzo, I understand."

"I know you do. We're alike, you and I. I know you've struggled with your feelings about your father. You've taught me that you just have to let it go at a certain point. It will always haunt me, but it doesn't have to rule me."

She squeezed him tight, her eyes flooding with tears. "Your father's a fool. A stupid, blind, ridiculous man who doesn't deserve you."

He laughed at her fierceness, but she meant it. "I know that, *cara*. Thanks to you."

There was an announcement of some kind, and then the teams began to move the motorcycles toward the starting grids. Matteo glanced over at them as he gave the order to move the Viper.

Renzo turned his head to watch them. She could see the spark in his eyes, the glint that said he was proud of the motorcycle and knew it would be amazing. And she wanted him to have this moment more than she wanted anything else. Because that's what you did when you loved someone.

She smiled at him through her tears. "Go, Renzo. It's okay. I swear it's okay. Just come back to me in forty-five minutes, you hear?"

He hesitated for a moment more. And then he bent and kissed her swiftly. "I will, Faith. I promise you I will."

EPILOGUE

THEY were married in the Duomo in Florence with one thousand of their friends and colleagues—as well as Renzo's mother and sister—packed inside the church. Outside in the square, thousands more gathered for the wedding of their favorite champion and his former PA. When Faith and Renzo emerged from the church, the crowd cheered in a loud, thundering rumble.

It sounded the same as when Renzo had been standing on top of that podium in Qatar, Faith thought. He'd won the race that day, and then he'd announced his retirement from MotoGP while a shocked crowd gasped and groaned.

But they'd forgiven him quickly, and the D'Angeli team was even now traveling the circuit and racking up wins on the Viper. The new production motorcycles had hit the dealerships, and business was booming.

Renzo tugged her into his arms and kissed her on the steps of the church, and then they were hurrying to the car that would take them back to the villa. Of all the places they could have honeymooned, that's where Faith wanted to be. Lola was there, and Fabrizio and Lucia. The vines were heavy with grapes that were ripening, the olive trees were bearing fruit, and the countryside was green during the day and golden in the evening. It was the most perfect place on earth, and she couldn't imagine another place in the world she would rather be.

They retreated to the bedroom where Renzo gave up patiently trying to divest her of her wedding gown and instead bunched the beautiful white taffeta around her hips as he held her against the wall and thrust into her urgently. It was the first time they'd made love without a barrier between them, and the sensation was exquisite.

They managed to undress, and then they fell into bed and lost themselves in each other's arms for the next few hours. Lucia brought dinner to the room, leaving it outside the door on a serving cart, and they sat on the private terrace overlooking the valley and ate. Faith was wearing a sheet and Renzo had slipped into a pair of briefs. It was as dressed as they would be for the next few days.

Renzo looked over from where he sat across from her in the evening light and smiled. "I love you, Signora D'Angeli," he said. "This is how I want to spend the rest of my life with you."

Faith laughed. "I love you too, Renzo. But you do have a very successful company to run."

He sighed. "And I need a new PA. I am not looking forward to finding one to replace you."

Faith bristled. "Replace me? I hardly think so, mister. You can't live without me, remember?"

"No," he said, smiling. "I can't. But you are my wife, not my PA. You won't always want to schedule my appointments and type my correspondence."

"I'm not particularly fond of typing correspondence," she admitted.

He grasped her hand and tugged her into his lap. The sheet slipped down her bosom, but she hardly cared, especially when his eyes flared with heat.

"You can be my PA as long as you want," he said. "And

when it's time to quit, you can interview the candidates if you like."

She put her arms around his neck and pressed herself closer to him. Oh, she was shameless when it came to wanting her gorgeous husband. "Since I'm the expert, yes. I would like that."

"There is only one condition," he said.

She reared back to look down at him. "What?"

"If I want you naked in my office, you have to comply."

Faith laughed. "What if I want *you* naked in your office? Does that work, too?"

She could feel him growing hard beneath her, and her body answered with a surge of heat between her thighs.

"What do you think?" he asked.

She wrapped her arms around his neck. "I think I'm going to enjoy working with you."

He kissed her hard, and then carried her into the bedroom. When they were entwined on the mattress, when he was deep inside her and she was begging him for more, he stopped and held still until her eyes opened.

"What is wrong, Renzo?"

He smiled. It was so full of tenderness and love that it made her heart ache. "Nothing is wrong," he said. "In fact, everything is right."

And it was. Faith knew that their lives together would be full and complete. They had each other, they had Lola— and several other stray cats that ended up making their way to the villa—and, nine months later, they had a screaming baby who refused to sleep through the night for at least a year.

It was chaos, but it was their chaos. And they wouldn't have it any other way.

* * * * *

AT THE COUNT'S BIDDING

CAITLIN CREWS

CHAPTER ONE

"I MUST BE hallucinating. And may God have mercy on you if I am not."

Paige Fielding hadn't heard that voice in ten years. It wrapped around her even as it sliced through her, making the breezy Southern California afternoon fade away. Making the email she'd been writing disappear from her mind in full. Making her forget what year it was, what day it was. Rocketing her right back into the murky, painful past.

That voice. *His voice.*

Uncompromisingly male. As imperious as it was incredulous. The faint hint of sex and Italy in his voice even with all that temper besides, and it rolled over Paige like a flattening heat. It pressed into her from behind, making her want to squirm in her seat. Or simply melt where she sat. Or come apart—easily and instantly—the way she always had at the sound of it.

She swiveled around in her chair in instant, unconscious obedience, knowing exactly who she'd see in the archway that led into the sprawling Bel Air mansion high in the Hollywood Hills called La Bellissima in honor of its famous owner, the screen legend Violet Sutherlin. She knew who it was, and still, something like a premonition washed over her and made her skin prickle in the scant seconds before her gaze found him there in the arched, open door, scowling at her with what looked like a healthy mix of contempt and pure, electric hatred.

Giancarlo Alessi. The only man she'd ever loved with every inch of her doomed and naive heart, however little good that had done either one of them. The only man who'd made her scream and sob and beg for more, until she was hoarse and mute with longing. The only man who still haunted her, and who she suspected always would, despite everything.

Because he was also the only man she'd ever betrayed. Thoroughly. Indisputably. Her stomach twisted hard, reminding her of what she'd done with a sick lurch. As if she'd forgotten. As if she ever could.

She hadn't thought she'd had a choice. But she doubted he'd appreciate that any more now than he had then.

"I can explain," she said. Too quickly, too nervously. She didn't remember pushing back from the table where she'd been sitting, doing her work out in the pretty sunshine as was her custom during the lazy afternoons, but she was standing then, somehow, feeling as unsteady on her own legs as she had in the chair. As lost in his dark, furious gaze as she'd been ten years ago.

"You can explain to security," he grated at her, each word a crisp slap. She felt red and obvious. Marked. As if he could see straight through her to that squalid past of hers that had ruined them both. "I don't care what you're doing here, Nicola. I want you gone."

She winced at that name. That hated name she hadn't used since the day she'd lost him. Hearing it again, after all this time and in that voice of his was physically upsetting. Deeply repellant. Her stomach twisted again, harder, and then knotted.

"I don't—" Paige didn't know what to say, how to say

it. How to explain what had happened since that awful day ten years ago when she'd sold him out and destroyed them both. What was there to say? She'd never told him the whole truth, when she could have. She'd never been able to bear the thought of him knowing how polluted she was or the kind of place, the kind of people, she'd come from. And they'd fallen in love so fast, their physical connection a white-hot explosion that had consumed them for those two short months they'd been together—there hadn't seemed to be any time to get to know each other. Not really. "I don't go by Nicola anymore."

He froze solid in the doorway, a kind of furious astonishment rolling over him and then out from him like a thunderclap, deafening and wild, echoing inside of her like a shout.

It hurt. It all hurt.

"I never—" This was terrible. Worse than she'd imagined, and she'd imagined it often. She felt an awful heat at the back of her eyes and a warning sort of ache between her breasts, as if a sob was gathering force and threatening to spill over, and she knew better than to let it out. She knew he wouldn't react well. She was lucky he was speaking to her at all now instead of having Violet's security guards toss her bodily from the estate without so much as a word. But she kept talking anyway, as if that might help. "It's my middle name, actually. It was a— my name is Paige."

"Curiously, Paige is also the name of my mother's personal assistant."

But she could tell by the way his voice grew ominously quiet that he knew. That he wasn't confused or asking her to explain herself. That he'd figured it out the moment he'd seen her—that she'd been the name on all those emails from his mother over the past few years.

And she could also tell exactly how he felt about that revelation. It was written into every stiffly furious line of his athletic form.

"Who cannot be you." He shifted and her breath caught, as if the movement of his perfect body was a blow. "Assure me, please, that you are no more than an unpleasant apparition from the darkest hour of my past. That you have not insinuated yourself into my family. Do it now and I might let you walk out of here without calling the police."

Ten years ago she'd have thought he was bluffing. *That* Giancarlo would no more have called the police on her than he would have thrown himself off the nearest bridge. But this was a different man. *This* was the Giancarlo she'd made, and she had no one to blame for that but herself.

Well. Almost no one. But there was no point bringing *her* mother into this, Paige knew. It was his he was concerned about—and besides, Paige hadn't spoken to her own in a decade.

"Yes," she said, and she felt shaky and vulnerable, as if it had only just occurred to her that her presence here was questionable, at best. "I've been working for Violet for almost three years now, but Giancarlo, you have to believe that I never—"

"Stai zitto."

And Paige didn't have to speak Italian to understand that harsh command, or the way he slashed his hand through the air, gruffly ordering her silence. She obeyed. What else could she do? And she watched him warily as if, at any moment, he might bare his fangs and sink them in her neck.

She'd deserve that, too.

Paige had always known this day would come. That this quiet new life she'd crafted for herself almost by accident was built on the shakiest of foundations and that all it would take was this man's reappearance to upend the whole of it. Giancarlo was Violet's son, her only child. The product of her fabled second marriage to an Italian count that the entire world had viewed as its own, personal, real-life fairy tale. Had Paige imagined this would end in any other manner? She'd been living on borrowed time from the moment she'd taken that interview and answered all the questions Violet's managers had asked in the way she'd known—thanks to her insider's take on Violet's actual life away from the cameras, courtesy of her brief, brilliant affair with Giancarlo all those years ago—would get her the job.

Some people might view that harshly, she was aware. Particularly Giancarlo himself. But she'd had good intentions. Surely that counted for something? *You know perfectly well that it doesn't,* the harsh voice in her head that was her last link to her mother grated at her. *You know exactly what intentions are worth.*

And it had been so long. She'd started to believe that this might never happen. That Giancarlo might stay in Europe forever, hidden away in the hills of Tuscany building his überprivate luxury hotel and associated cottages the way he had for the past decade, ever since she'd set him up and those sordid, intimate photographs had been splashed across every tabloid imaginable. She'd lulled herself into a false sense of security.

Because he was here now, and nothing was safe any longer, and yet all she wanted to do was lose herself in looking at him. Reacquainting herself with him. Reminding herself what she'd given up. What she'd ruined.

She'd seen pictures of him all over this house in the years she'd worked here. Always dark and forbiddingly elegant in his particularly sleek way, it took no more than a glance to understand Giancarlo was decidedly not American. Even ten years ago and despite having spent so much time in Los Angeles, he'd had that air. That *thing* about him that whispered that he was the product of long centuries of European blue bloods. It was something in the way he held himself, distant and disapproving, the hint of ancient places and old gods stamped into his aristocratic bones and lurking behind his cool dark gaze.

Paige had expected Giancarlo would still be attractive, of course, should she ever encounter him again. What she hadn't expected—or what she'd allowed herself to forget—was that he was so *raw.* Seeing him was like a hard, stunning blow to the side of her head, leaving her ears ringing and her heart thumping erratically inside her chest. As if he knew it, his head canted to one side as he regarded her, as if daring her to keep talking when he'd ordered her to stop.

But she couldn't seem to do anything but stare. As if the past decade had been one long slide of gray and here he was again, all of him in bold color and bright lights. So glaring and hot she could hardly bear to look at him. But she did. She couldn't help herself.

He stood as if he was used to accolades, or simply commanding the full and rapt attention of every room he entered. It was partly the clothes he wore, the fabrics fitting him so perfectly, almost reverently, in a manner Paige knew came only at astronomical expense. But it was more than that. His body was lean and powerful, a symphony of whipcord strength tightly leashed, the crackle of his temper and that blazing sensuality that felt like a touch from ten feet away, carnal and wild. Even though she knew he'd never willingly touch her again. He'd made that clear.

Giancarlo was still so beautiful, yes, but there was

something so *male* about him, so rampantly masculine, that it made Paige's throat go dry. It was worse now, ten years later. Much worse. He stood in the open doorway in a pair of dark trousers, boots, and the kind of jacket Paige associated with sexy Ducati motorcycles and mystical places a girl like her from a ramshackle desert town in Nowhere, Arizona, only fantasized about, like the Amalfi Coast. Yet somehow he looked as effortlessly refined as if he could walk straight into a black-tie gala as he was—or climb into a bed for a long, hot, blisteringly feral weekend of no-holds-barred sex.

But it did her no good to remember that kind of thing. For her body to ready itself for his possession as if it had been ten minutes since they'd last touched instead of ten years. As if it knew him, recognized him, wanted him— as deeply and irrevocably as she always had. As if *wanting him* was some kind of virus that had only ever been in remission, for which there was no cure.

The kind of virus that made her breasts heavy and her belly too taut and shivery at once. The kind of virus that made her wish she still danced the way she had in high school and those few years after, obsessively and constantly, as if that kind of extended, heedless movement might be the only way to survive it. *Him.* His marvelous mouth tightened as the silence dragged on and she sent up a prayer of thanks that he hadn't thought to remove his mirrored sunglasses yet. She didn't want to know what his dark gaze would feel like when she could actually see his eyes again. She didn't want to know what that would do to her now. She still remembered what it had been like that last time, that short and harsh conversation on the doorstep of her apartment building that final morning, where he'd confronted her with those pictures and had truly understood what she'd done to him. When he'd looked at her as if he'd only then, in that moment, seen her true face—and it had been evil.

Pull yourself together, she ordered herself fiercely. There was no going back. There were no do-overs. She knew that too well.

"I'm sorry," she managed to get out before he cut her off again. Before she melted into the tears she knew she'd cry later, in private. Before the loss and grief she'd pretended she was over for years now swamped her. "Giancarlo, I'm so sorry."

He went so rigid it was as if she'd slapped him, and yet she felt slapped. She hurt everywhere.

"I don't care why you're here." His voice was rough. A scrape that tore her open, ripping her right down her middle. "I don't care what game you're playing this time. You have five minutes to leave the premises."

But all Paige could hear was what swirled there beneath his words. Rage. Betrayal, as if it was new. Hot and furious, like a fire that still burned bright between them. And she was sick, she understood, because instead of being as frightened of that as she should have been, something in her rejoiced that he wasn't indifferent. After all this time.

"If you do not do this of your own accord," Giancarlo continued with a certain vicious deliberation, and she knew he *wanted* that to hurt her, "I will take great pleasure in dumping you on the other side of the gates myself."

"Giancarlo—" she began, trying to sound calm, though her hands nervously smoothed at the soft blouse and the pencil skirt she wore. And even though she couldn't see his eyes, she felt them there, tracing the curve of her hips and her legs beneath, as if she'd deliberately directed his gaze to parts of her body he'd once claimed he worshipped. Had she meant to do that? How could she not know?

But he interrupted her again.

"You may call me Count Alessi in the remaining four minutes before I kick you out of here," he told her harshly. "But if you know what's good for you, whatever name you're using and whatever con you're running today and have been running for years, I'd suggest you stay silent."

"I'm not running a con. I'm not—" Paige cut herself off, because this was all too complicated and she should have planned for this, shouldn't she? She should have figured out what to say to someone who had no reason on earth to listen to her. And who wouldn't believe a word she said even if he did. Why hadn't she prepared herself? "I know you don't want to hear a single thing I have to say, but none of this is what you think. It wasn't back then, either. Not really."

He seemed to *expand* then, like a great wave. As if the force of his temper soared out from him and crashed over the whole of the grand terrace, the sloping lawn, the canyons all around, the complicated mess of Los Angeles stretched out below. It crackled as it cascaded over her, making every hair on her body seem to stand on end. That mouth of his flattened and he swept his sunglasses from his face at last—which was not an improvement. Because his eyes were dark and hot and gleamed a commanding sort of gold, and as he fastened them on her he made no attempt at all to hide the blistering light of his fury.

It made her want to sit down, hard, before she fell. It made her worry her legs might give out. It made her want to cry the way she had ten years ago, so hard and so long she'd made herself sick, for all the good that had done. She felt dangerously, dizzyingly hollow.

"Enlighten me," he suggested, all silken threat and that humming sort of violence *right there* beneath his elegant surface. Or maybe not really *beneath* it, she thought, now that she could see his beautiful, terrible face in all its furious perfection. "Which part was not what I thought? The fact that you arranged to have photographs taken of us while we were having sex, though I am certain I told you how much I hated public exposure after a lifetime in the glare of my mother's spotlight? Or the fact that you sold those photos to the tabloids?" He took a step toward her; his hands were in fists at his side, and she didn't understand how she could simultaneously want to run for her life and run *toward* him. He was a suicide waiting to happen. She should know that better than anyone. "Or perhaps I am misunderstanding the fact that you have now infiltrated my mother's house to further prey on my family?" He shook his head. "What kind of monster *are* you?"

"Giancarlo—"

"I will tell you exactly what kind." His nostrils flared and she knew that look that flashed over his face then. She knew it far too well. It was stamped into her memories and it made her stomach heave with the same shame and regret. It made her flush with terrible heat. "You are a mercenary bitch and I believe I was perfectly clear about this ten years ago. I never, ever wanted to see your face again."

And Paige was running out of ways to rank which part of this was the worst part, but she couldn't argue. Not with any of what he'd said. Yet rather than making her shrink down and curl up into the fetal position right there on the terra-cotta pavers beneath their feet, the way she'd done the last time he'd looked at her like that and called her names she'd richly deserved, it made something else shiver into being inside her. Something that made her straighten instead of shrink. Something that gave her the strength to meet his terrible glare, to lift her chin despite all of that furious, condemning gold.

"I love her."

That hung there between them, stark and heavy. And, she realized belatedly, an echo of what she'd said ten years ago, when it had been much too late. When he'd believed her even less than he did now. When she'd known full well that saying it would only hurt him, and she'd done it anyway. *I'm so sorry, Giancarlo. I love you.*

"What did you say?" His voice was too quiet. So soft and deliberately menacing it made her shake inside, though she didn't give in to it. She forced her spine even straighter. "What did you *dare* say to me?"

"This has nothing to do with you." That was true, in its way. Paige wasn't a lunatic, no matter what he might think. She'd simply understood a long time ago that she'd lost him and it was irrevocable. She'd accepted it. This wasn't about getting him back. It was about paying a debt in the only way she could. "It never did have anything to do with you," she continued when she was certain the shaking inside her wouldn't bleed over into her voice. "Not the way you're thinking. Not really."

He shook his head slightly, as if he was reeling, and he muttered something in a stream of silken, shaken Italian that she shouldn't have felt like that, all over her skin. Because it wasn't a caress. It was its opposite.

"This is a nightmare." He returned his furious glare to her and it was harder. Fiercer. Gold fury and that darkness inside it. "But nightmares end. You keep on, all these years later. It was two short months and too many explicit pictures. I knew better than to trust a woman like you in the first place, but this ought to be behind me." His lips thinned. "Why won't you go away, Nicola?"

"Paige." She couldn't tolerate that name. Never again. It was the emblem of all the things she'd lost, all the terrible choices she'd been forced to make, all the sacrifices she'd made for someone so unworthy it made her mouth taste acrid now, like ash and regret. "I'd rather you call me nothing but *mercenary bitch* instead of that."

"I don't care what you call yourself." Not quite a shout. Not quite. But his voice thudded into her like a hail of bullets anyway, and she couldn't disguise the way she winced. "I want you gone. I want this poison of yours out of my life, away from my mother. It disgusts me that you've been here all this time without my knowing it. Like a malignant cancer hiding in plain sight."

And she should go. Paige knew she should. This was twisted and wrong and sick besides, no matter the purity of her intentions. All her rationalizations, all her excuses, what did any of them matter when she was standing here causing *more* pain to this man? He'd never deserved it. She really was a cancer, she thought. Her own mother had always thought so, too.

"I'm sorry," she said, yet again, and she heard the bleakness in her own voice that went far beyond an apology. And his dark, hot eyes were on hers. Demanding. Furious. Still broken, and she knew she'd done that. It stirred up sensations inside of her that felt too much like ghosts, an ache and a fire at once. But Paige held his gaze. "More than you'll ever know. But I can't leave Violet. I promised her."

Giancarlo's dark gaze blazed into a brilliant fury then, and it took every bit of backbone and bravado Paige had not to fall a step back when he advanced on her. Or to turn tail and start running the way she'd wanted to do since she'd heard his voice, down the expansive lawn, through the garden and out into the wild canyon below, as far as she could get from this man. She wanted to flee. She wanted to run and never stop running. The urge to do it beat in her blood.

But she hadn't done it ten years ago, when she should have, and from far scarier people than Giancarlo Alessi. She wouldn't do it now. No matter how hard her heart catapulted itself against her chest. No matter how great and painful the sobs she refused to let loose from inside.

"You seem to be under the impression I am playing a game with you," Giancarlo said softly, so very softly, the menace in it like his hand around her throat. What was the matter with her that the notion moved in her like a dark thrill instead of a threat? "I am not."

"I understand that this is difficult for you, and that it's unlikely you'll believe that was never my intention." Paige tried to sound conciliatory. She did. But she thought it came out sounding a whole lot more like panic, and panic was as useless as regret. She had no space for either. This was the life she'd made. This was what she'd sown. "But I'm afraid my loyalty is to your mother, not to you."

"I apologize." It was a snide snap, not an apology. "But the irony rendered me temporarily deaf. Did you—*you*—just utter the word *loyalty?*"

Paige gritted her teeth. She didn't bow her head. "You didn't hire me. She did."

"A point that will be moot if I kill you with my bare hands," he snarled at her, and she should have been afraid of him, but she wasn't. She had no doubt that he'd throw her off the estate, that if he could tear her to shreds with his words he would, and gladly, but he wouldn't hurt her. Not physically. Not Giancarlo.

Maybe that was the last remnant of the girl she'd been,

she thought then. That foolish, unbearably naive girl, who'd imagined that a bright and brand-new love could fix anything. That it was the only thing that mattered. She knew better now; she'd learned her lessons well and truly and in the harshest of ways, but she still believed Giancarlo was a good man. No matter what her betrayal had done to him.

"Yes," she said, and her voice was rough with all the emotion she knew she couldn't show him. He'd only hate her more. "But you won't."

"Please," he all but whispered, and she saw too much on his face then, the agony and the fury and the darkness between, "do not tell me you are so delusional as to imagine I wouldn't rip you apart if I could."

"Of course," she agreed, and it was hard to tell what hurt when everything did. When she was sure she would leave this encounter with visible bruises. "If you could. But that's not who you are."

"The man you thought you knew is dead, *Nicola*," he said, that hated name a deliberate blow, and Paige finally did step back then, it was so brutal. "He died ten years ago and there will be no breathing him back to life with your sad tales of loyalty and your pretty little lies. There will be no resurrection. I might look like the man you knew, for two profoundly stupid months a lifetime ago, but mark my words. He is gone as if he never was."

It shouldn't be so sad, when it was nothing more than a simple truth. Not a surprise. Not a slap, even, despite his harsh tone. There was absolutely no reason she should feel swollen anew with all that useless, unwieldy, impossible grief, as if it had never faded, never so much as shifted an inch, in all this time. As if it had only been waiting to flatten her all over again.

"I accept both responsibility and blame for what happened ten years ago," she said as matter-of-factly as she could, and he would never know how hard that was. How exposed she felt, how off balance. Just as he would never know that those two months she'd lost herself in him had been the best of her life, worth whatever had come after. Worth anything, even this. "I can't do anything else. But I promised Violet I wouldn't leave her. Punish me if you have to, Giancarlo. Don't punish her."

Giancarlo Alessi was a man made almost entirely of faults, a fact he was all too familiar with after the bleakness of the past decade and the price he'd paid for his own foolishness, but he loved his mother. His complicated, grandiose, larger-than-life idol of a mother, who he knew adored him in her own, particular way. It didn't matter how many times Violet had sold him out for her own purposes—to combat tales of her crumbling marriage, to give the tabloids something to talk about other than her romantic life, to serve this or that career purpose over the years.

He'd come to accept that having one's private moments exposed to the public was par for the course when one was related to a Hollywood star of Violet's magnitude—which was why he had vowed never, ever to have children that she could use for her own ends. No happy grandchildren to grace magazine articles about her *surprising depths*. No babies she could coo over in front of carefully selected cameras to shore up her image when necessary. He'd never condemn a child of his to that life, no matter how much he might love Violet himself. He'd pass on his Italian title to a distant cousin of his father's and let the sharp brutality of all that Hollywood attention end with him.

He forgave his mother. It was who she was. It was *this* woman he wanted to hurt, not Violet.

This woman who could call herself any name she wanted, but who was still Nicola to him. The architect of his downfall. The agent of his deepest shame.

The too-pretty dancer he'd lost his head over like a thousand shameful clichés, staining his ancient title, his relationship with his late father, and himself in the process. The grasping, conniving creature who had led him around by his groin and made him a stranger to himself in the process. The woman who had made him complicit in the very thing he hated above all others: his presence in the damned tabloids, his most private life on parade.

He'd yet to forgive himself. He'd never planned on forgiving her.

Standing here in this house he'd vowed he'd never enter again, the woman he'd been determined he'd cut from his memory if it killed him within his reach once more, he told himself the edgy thing that surged in him, making him feel something like drunk—dangerously unsteady, a little too close to dizzy—was a cold, clear, measured hatred. No more and no less than she deserved.

It had to be cold. Controlled. He wouldn't permit it to be anything else. He wouldn't let it run hot, burn within him the way loving her had, take charge of him and ruin him anew. He wasn't that trusting, gullible fool any longer, not as he'd been then—so sure he'd been the experienced one, the calloused and jaded one, that no one could take advantage of. She'd made certain he'd never be that idiot again.

He would save that kind of heated, brooding dislike for the sprawling, sunbaked city of Los Angeles itself. For California, brown and gold with only its manufactured, moneyed swaths of green as relief in another breathless summer. For the elegant monstrosity that was La Bellissima. For his heedless, callow twenties playing silly playboy games with films and a parade of famous and beautiful lovers, which *this woman* had brought to a screeching, excruciatingly public halt. For that dry blast of relentless heat on the wind, spiced with smoke from far-off brushfires and the hint of the Pacific Ocean that never cooled it, that made him feel too edgy, too undone. For his mother's recklessness in lovers and husbands and assistants, in all her personal relationships to the endless delight of the predatory press, a trait of hers Giancarlo had long despaired of and had shared but once.

Once.

Once had been enough.

He studied Nicola—*Paige*—as she stood there before him, gazing back at him from her liar's eyes that were neither blue nor green, that fall of thick, dark hair with a hint of auburn that she'd tamed into a side plait falling over one bare, exquisitely formed shoulder. Back then her hair had been redder, longer. Less ink, more fire, and he wished he found the darker shade unpleasant, unattractive. She was still as tall as he remembered but had gone skinny in that way they all did here, as if the denial of every pleasure in the world might bring them the fame they wanted more than anything. More than breath, more than food. Much, much more than love, as he knew all too well.

Don't even think that word, he snarled at himself.

She stiffened as he let his gaze roam all over her, so he kept doing it, telling himself he didn't care what this woman, whatever the hell she called herself now, thought or felt. Because she'd made it clear that the only things she'd ever seen when she'd looked at him—no matter how many times he'd made her scream his name, no matter how many ways they'd torn each other up and turned each other inside out, no matter how deeply he'd fallen for her or how enthusiastically he'd upended his life for her in those two months they'd spent almost entirely in his bed—were Violet's fame and a paycheck to match.

It wasn't only his heart she'd broken. She'd ground his pride, his belief that he could read anyone's intentions at a glance and keep himself safe from the kind of grasping predators who teemed over this city like ants, under her heel. She'd completely altered the way he'd seen himself, who he was, as surely as if she'd severed one of his limbs.

Yet she still held herself well, which irritated him. She still had that dancer's easy grace and the supple muscle tone to match. He took in her small, high breasts beneath that sleeveless white shirt with the draped neck, then the efficient pencil skirt that clung to the swell of her hips, and his hands remembered the lush feel of both. The slick perfection of her curves beneath his palms, always such a marvel of femininity in such a lean frame. The exquisite way she fit in his hands and tasted against his tongue. She'd left her legs bare, toned and pretty, and all he could think about was the way she'd wrapped them around his hips or draped them over his shoulders while he'd thrust hard and deep inside of her.

Stop, a voice inside him ordered, *or you will shame yourself anew.*

Her disguise—if that was what it was—did nothing to hide her particular, unusual beauty. She'd never looked like all the other girls who'd flocked around him back then. It was that fire in her that had called to him from that first, stunning clash of glances across the set of the music video where they'd met. She'd been a backup dancer in formfitting tights and a sport bra. He'd been the high-and-mighty pseudo director who shouldn't have noticed her with a band full of pop stars hanging on his every word. And yet that single look had singed him alive.

He could still feel the same bright flames, even though she'd darkened her hair and wore sensible, professional clothes today that covered her mouthwatering midriff and failed to outline every last line of her thighs. Like the efficient secretary to his mother that he knew she'd proved herself to be over these past years, for some reason—and Giancarlo refused to let himself think about that. About her motives and intentions. Why she'd spent so long playing this game and why she'd bothered to excel in her position here while doing it. Why he couldn't look at her without wanting her, even with all of this time between them. Even knowing exactly what she'd done.

"Is this where you tell me your sob story?" he asked coldly, taking a grim pleasure in the way she reacted to his voice. That little jump, as if she couldn't control this crazy thing between them any more than he could. "There's always one in these situations, is there not? So many reasons. So many excuses."

"I'm not sobbing." He couldn't read that lovely oval of a face, with cheekbones made for a man to cradle between his palms and that wide mouth that begged to be tasted. Plundered. "And I don't think I've made any excuses. I only apologized. It's not the same thing."

"No." He let his gaze move over her mouth. That damned mouth. He could still feel the slide of it against his, or wrapped hot and warm around his hardness, trailing fire and oblivion wherever she used it. *And nothing but lies when she spoke.* "I'll have to see what I can do about that."

She actually sighed, as if he tried her patience, and he didn't know whether he wanted to laugh or throttle her. He remembered that, too. From before. When she'd

broken over his life like a hurricane and hadn't stopped
tearing up the trees and rearranging the earth until she
was gone the same way she'd come, leaving nothing but
scandal and the debris of her lies in her wake.

And yet she was still so pretty. He found that made
him angrier than the rest of it.

"Glaring ferociously at me isn't going to make me
cry," she said, and he wanted to *see things* in those chameleon eyes of hers. He wanted something, anything, to
get to her—but he knew better, didn't he? She hadn't simply destroyed him, this time. She'd targeted his mother
and she'd done it right under his nose. How could he
imagine she was anything but evil? "It only makes the
moment that much more uncomfortable." She inclined her
head slightly. "But if it makes you feel better, Giancarlo,
you should go right ahead and try."

He did laugh then. A short, humorless little sound.

"I am marveling at the sight of you," he said, sounding cruel to his own ears, but she didn't so much as blink.
"You deserve to look like the person you really are, not
the person you pretended you were." He felt his mouth
thin. "But I suppose this is Hollywood magic in action,
no? The nastiest, most narcissistic things wrapped up
tight in the prettiest packages. Of course you look as
good as you did then." He laughed softly, wanting it to
hurt. Wanting something he said or did to have *some* effect on her—which told him a bit more than he wanted
to know about his unresolved feelings about this woman.
"That's all you really have, is it not?"

CHAPTER TWO

GIANCARLO HAD FANCIED himself madly in love with her. That was the thing he couldn't forgive, much less permit himself to forget, especially when she was *right here* before him once again. The scandal that had ruined his budding film career, that had cast that deep, dark shadow over what had been left of his intensely private, deeply proper father's life, that had made him question everything he'd thought he'd known about himself, that had made him finally leave this damned city and all its demons behind him within a day of the photos going live—that had been something a few shades worse than terrible and it remained a deep, indelible mark on Giancarlo's soul. But however he might have deplored it, he supposed he could have eventually understood a pampered, thoughtless young man's typical recklessness over a pretty girl. It was one of the oldest stories in the world.

It was his own parents' story, come to that.

It was the fact that he'd been so deceived that he'd wanted to *marry* this creature despite his lifelong aversion to the institution, make her his countess, bring her to his ancestral home in Italy—he, who had vowed he'd never marry after witnessing the fallout from his parents' tempestuous union—that made his blood boil even all these years later. He'd been plotting out weddings in his head while she'd been negotiating the price of his disgrace. The fury of it still made him feel much too close to wild.

She only inclined her head again, as if she was perfectly happy to accept any and all blame he heaped on her, and Giancarlo didn't understand why that made him even more enraged.

"Have you nothing to say?" he taunted her. "I don't believe it. You must have lost your touch in all these years, Nicola." He saw her jerk, as if she really did hate that name, and filed that away as ammunition. "I beg your pardon. *Paige.* You can call yourself whatever you want. You've obviously spent too much time with a lonely old woman if this is the best you can do."

"She *is* lonely," Paige agreed, and he thought that was temper that lit up her cheeks, staining them, though her voice was calm. "This was never meant to be a long-term situation, Giancarlo. I assumed you'd come home and recognize me within the month. Of course, that was three years ago."

It took him a moment to understand what it was he was feeling then, and he didn't like it when he did. *Shame.* Hot and new and unacceptable.

"The world will collide with the sun before I explain myself to you," he bit out. Like how he'd managed to let so much time slip by—always so busy, always a crisis on the estate in Italy, always *something.* How he'd avoided coming here and hurt his mother in the process. Those things might have been true—they were why he'd finally forced himself to come after an entire eighteen months without seeing Violet on one of her usual press junkets around the globe—but they certainly weren't *this* woman's business.

"I didn't ask you to explain anything." She lifted one

shoulder, still both delicate and toned, he was annoyed to notice, and then dropped it. "It's simply the truth."

"Please," he scoffed, and rubbed his hand over his face to keep from reacting like the animal he seemed to become in her presence. Ten years ago he'd thought that compulsion—that need—was passion. Fate. He knew better now. It was sheer, unadulterated madness. "Do not use words you cannot possibly know the meaning of. It only makes you look even more grasping and base than we both know you are already."

She blinked, then squared her shoulders, her chin rising as she held his gaze. "Do I have time to get a list of approved vocabulary words in what remains of my five minutes? Before you have me thrown over Violet's walls and onto the street?"

Giancarlo looked at her, the breeze playing in her inky dark hair with its auburn accents, the sun shifting through the vines that stretched lazily above them in a fragrant canopy, and understood with a painful surge of clarity that this was an opportunity. This woman had been like a dark, grim shadow stretching over his life, but that was over now. And he was so different from the man he'd been when she'd sunk her claws in him that he might as well have been a stranger.

She had never been the woman she'd convinced him she was. Because *that* woman, he had loved. *That* woman had been like a missing piece to his own soul that he'd never known he lacked and yet had recognized instantly the moment he'd seen her.

But that was nothing but a performance, a stern voice whispered in his head.

And this was the second act.

"Does my mother know that you are the woman who starred in all those photos a decade ago?" he asked, sounding almost idle, though he felt anything but. He slid his hands into his pockets and regarded her closely, noting how pale she went, and how her lips pressed hard together.

"Of course not," she whispered, and there was a part of him that wondered why she wanted so badly to maintain his mother's good opinion. Why should that matter? But he reminded himself this was the way she played her games. She was good—so good—at pretending to care. It was just another lie and this time, he'd be damned if he believed any part of it.

"Then this is what will happen." He said it calmly. Quietly. Because the shock of seeing her had finally faded and now there was only this. His revenge, served nice and cold all these years later. "I wouldn't want to trouble my mother with the truth about her favorite assistant yet. I don't think she'd like it."

"She would hate it, and me," Nicola—*Paige* threw at him. "But it would also break her heart. If that's your goal here, it's certainly an easy way to achieve it."

"Am I the villain in this scenario?" He laughed again, but this time, he really was amused, and he saw a complex wash of emotion move over her face. He didn't want to know why. He knew exactly what he did want, he reminded himself. His own back, in a way best suited to please him, for a change. This was merely the dance necessary to get it. "You must have become even more delusional than your presence here already suggests."

"Giancarlo—"

"You will resign and leave of your own volition. Today. Now."

She lifted her hands, which he saw were in tight fists, then dropped them back to her sides, and he admired the act. It almost looked real. "I can't do that."

"You will." He decided he was enjoying himself. He couldn't remember the last time that had happened. "This isn't a debate, *Paige*."

Her pretty face twisted into a convincing rendition of misery. "I can't."

"Because you haven't managed to rewrite her will to leave it all to you yet?" he asked drily. "Or are you swapping out all the art on the walls for fakes? I thought the Rembrandt looked a bit odd in the front hall, but I imagined it was the light."

"Because whatever you might think about me, and I'm not saying I don't understand why you think it," she rasped, "I care about her. And I don't mean this to be insulting, Giancarlo, but I'm all she has." Her eyes widened at the dark look he leveled at her, and she hurried on. "You haven't visited her in years. She's surrounded by acolytes and users the moment she steps off this property. I'm the only person she trusts."

"Again, the irony is nearly edible." He shrugged. "And you are wasting your breath. You should thank me for my mercy in letting you call this a resignation. If I were less benevolent, I'd have you arrested."

She held his gaze for a moment too long. "Don't make me call your bluff," she said quietly. "I doubt very much you want the scandal."

"Don't make me call *your* bluff," he hurled back at her. "Do you think I haven't looked for the woman who ruined my life over the years? Hoping against hope she'd be locked up in prison where she belongs?" He smiled thinly when she stiffened. "Nicola Fielding fell off the face of the planet after those pictures went viral. That suggests to me that you aren't any more keen to have history reveal itself in the tabloids than I am." He lifted his brows. "Stalemate, *cara*. If I were you, I'd start packing."

She took a deep breath and then let it out, long and slow, and there was no reason that should have bothered him the way it did, sneaking under his skin and making him feel edgy and annoyed, as if it was tangling up his intentions or bending the present into the past.

"I genuinely love Violet," she said, her eyes big and pleading on his, and he ignored the *tangling* because he knew he had her. He could all but taste it. "This might have started as a misguided attempt to reach you after you disappeared, I'll admit, but it stopped being that a long time ago. I don't want to hurt her. Please. There must be a way we can work this out."

He let himself enjoy the moment. Savor it.

This wasn't temper, hot and wild, making him act out his passions in different ways, the line between it and grief too finely drawn to tell the difference. Too much time had passed. There was too much water under that particular bridge.

And she should never have come here. She should never have involved his mother. She should never have risked this.

"Giancarlo," she said, the way she'd said it that bright and terrible morning a decade ago when he'd finally understood the truth about her—and had seen it in full color pictures splashed across the entirety of the goddamned planet. When he'd showed up at the apartment she'd never let him enter and had that short, awful, final conversation on her doorstep. Before he'd walked away from her and Los Angeles and all the rest of these Hollywood machinations he hated so deeply. Five painful minutes to end an entire phase of his life and so many of his dreams. "Please."

He closed the distance between them with a single step, then reached over to pull on the end of that dark, glossy hair of hers, watching the auburn sheen in it glow and shift in the light. He felt more than heard her quick intake of breath and he wanted her in a thousand ways. That hadn't dimmed.

It was time to indulge himself. He was certain that whatever her angle was, her self-interest would win out over self-preservation. Which meant he could work out what remained of his issues in the best way imaginable. Whatever else she was, she was supple. *He had her.*

"Oh, we can work it out," he murmured, shifting so he could smell the lotion she used on her soft skin, a hint of eucalyptus and something far darker. *Victory,* he thought. His, this time. "It requires only that you get beneath me. And stay there until I'm done with you."

She went still for a hot, searing moment.

"What did you say?"

"You heard me."

Her changeable eyes were blue with distress then, and he might have loathed himself for that if he hadn't known what a liar she was. And what an actress she could be when it suited her. So he only tugged on her plait again and watched her tipped-up face closely as comprehension moved across it, that same electric heat he felt inside him on its heels.

That, Giancarlo told himself, was why he would win this game this time. Because she couldn't control the heat between them any more than he could. And he was no longer fool enough to imagine that meant a damned thing. He knew it was a game, this time.

"I want to make sure I'm understanding you." She swallowed, hard, and he was certain she'd understood him just fine. "You want me to sleep with you to keep my job."

He smiled, and watched goose bumps rise on her

smooth skin. "I do. Often and enthusiastically. Wherever and however I choose."

"You can't be serious."

"I assure you, I am. But by all means, test me. See what happens."

Her lips trembled slightly and he admired it. It looked so real. But he was close enough to see the hard, needy press of her nipples against the silk of her blouse, and he knew better. He knew she was as helpless before this *thing* between them as he was. Maybe she always had been. Maybe that was why it had all got so confused— she'd chosen him because he was Hollywood royalty by virtue of his parents and thus made a good mark, but then there'd been all of *this* to complicate things. But he didn't want to sympathize with her. Not even at such a remove.

"Giancarlo…" He didn't interrupt her but she didn't finish anyway, and her words trailed off into the afternoon breeze. He saw her eyes fill with a wet heat and he had to hand it to her, she was still too good at this. She made it so *believable*.

But he would never believe her again, no matter the provocation. No matter how many tears she shed, or *almost* shed. No matter how convincingly she could make her lips tremble. This was Hollywood.

This time, he wouldn't be taken by surprise. He knew it was all an act from the start.

"Your choices are diminishing by the minute," he told her softly. It was a warning. And one of the last he'd give her. "Now you have but two. Leave now, knowing I will tell my mother exactly why you've left and how you've spent these past years deceiving her. It might break her heart, but that will be one more black mark on your soul, not mine. And I'd be very surprised if she didn't find some way to make you pay for it herself. She didn't become who she is by accident, you must realize. She's a great deal tougher than she looks."

"I know she is." Her gaze still shimmered with that heat, but none of it spilled over—and he reminded himself that was *acting talent,* not force of will. "And what's the second choice?"

He shrugged. "Stay. And do exactly as I tell you."

"Sexually." She threw that at him, her voice unsteady but her gaze direct. "You mean do as you tell me *sexually.*"

If she thought her directness would shame him into altering his course here, she was far stupider than he remembered. Giancarlo smiled.

"I mean do as I tell you, full stop." He indulged himself then, and touched her. He traced the remarkable line of her jaw, letting the sharp delight of it charge through his bones, then held her chin there, right where he could stare her down with all the ruthlessness he carried within him. "You will work for me, *Paige.* On your back. On your knees. At your desk. Whatever I want, whenever I want, however I want."

He could feel her shaking and he exulted in it.

"Why?" she whispered. "This is *me,* remember? Why would you want to...?"

Again, she couldn't finish, and he took pleasure in these signs of her weakness. These cracks in her slick, pretty armor. Giancarlo leaned in close and brushed his mouth over hers, a little hint of what was to come. A little test.

It was just as he remembered it.

All that fire, arcing in him and in her, too, from the shocked sound she made. All that misery. Shame and fury and ten years of that terrible longing. He'd never quite got past it, and this was why. This thrumming, pounding excitement that had only ever happened here, with her. This unmatched hunger. This beautiful lie that would not wreck him this time. Not this time.

He needed to work it all out on that delectable body she'd wielded like a weapon, enslaving him and destroying him before she'd finally got around to killing him, too. He needed to make her pay the price for her betrayal in the most intimate way possible. He needed to work out his goddamned issues in the very place they'd started, and then, only then, would he finally be free of her. It had only been two months back then. It would have burned out on its own—he was sure of it, but they hadn't had time. He wanted time to glut himself, because only then would he get past this.

Giancarlo had to believe that.

"I know exactly who you are," he told her then, and he didn't pretend he wasn't enjoying this. That now that the shock had passed, he wasn't thrilled she'd proved herself as deceitful as he remembered. That he wasn't looking forward to this in a way he hoped scared her straight down into her bones—because it should. "It's long past time you paid for what you did to me, and believe me when I tell you I have a very, very detailed memory."

"You'll regret it." Her voice was like gauze and had as much effect.

"I've already regretted you for a decade, *cara*," he growled. "What does it matter to me if I add a little more?"

He leaned in closer, felt her quiver against him and thrilled to it. To her, because he knew her true face this time. He knew *her*. There would be no losing himself. There would be no fanciful dreaming of marriage and happy-ever-afters in the Tuscan countryside, deep in all the sweet golden fields that were his heritage. There would only be penance. Hers. Hard, hot, bone-melting penance, until he was satisfied.

Which he anticipated might take some time.

"This doesn't make sense." Did she sound desperate or did he want her to? Giancarlo didn't care. "You hate me!"

"This isn't hate," he said, and his smile deepened. Darkened. "Let's be clear, shall we? This is revenge."

Paige thought he would leap on her the moment she agreed.

And of course she agreed, how could she do anything *but* agree when Violet Sutherlin had become the mother her own had been far too addicted and selfish and hateful to pretend to be? How could she walk away from that when Violet was therefore the only family she had left?

But Giancarlo had only smiled that hard, deeply disconcerting smile of his that had skittered over her skin like electricity.

Then he'd dropped his hand, stepped away from her and left her alone.

For days. Three days, in fact. Three long days and much longer nights.

Paige had to carry on as if everything was perfectly normal, doing her usual work for Violet and pretending to be as thrilled as the older woman was about the return of her prodigal son. She'd had to maintain her poise and professionalism, insofar as there *was* any professionalism in this particular sort of job that was as much about handling Violet's personal whims as anything else. She'd had to try not to give herself away every time she was in the same room with Giancarlo, when all she wanted to do was scream at him to end this tension—a tension *he* did not appear to feel, as he lounged about, swam laps in the pool and laughed with his mother.

And every night she locked herself into the little cottage down near the edge of the canyon that was her home on Violet's property and tortured herself until dawn.

It was as if her brain had recorded every single moment of every single encounter she'd ever had with Giancarlo and could play it all back in excruciating detail. Every touch. Every kiss. That slick, hard thrust of his possession. The sexy noise he'd made against her neck each time he'd come. The sobs echoing back from this or that wall that she knew were hers, while she writhed in mindless pleasure, his in every possible way.

By the morning of the fourth day she was a mess.

"Sleep well?" he asked in that taunting way of his, his dark brows rising high when he met her on the back steps on her way into the big house to start her day. Violet took her breakfast and the trades on a tray in her room each morning and she expected to see Paige there, too, before she was finished.

Giancarlo stood on the wide steps that led up to the terrace, not precisely blocking her way, but Paige didn't rate her chances for slipping past him, either. Had she not been lost in her own scorching world of regret and too many vivid memories as she'd walked up the hill from her cottage, she'd have seen him here, lying in wait. She'd have avoided him.

Would you? that sly voice inside her asked.

A smart woman would have left Los Angeles ten years ago, never to return to the scene of so much pain and betrayal and heartache. A smart woman certainly wouldn't have got herself tangled up with her ex-lover's mother, and even if she had, she would have rejected Giancarlo's devil's bargain outright. So Paige supposed that ship had sailed a long time ago.

"I slept like a baby," she replied, because her memories were her business.

"I take it you mean that in the literal sense," he said drily. "Up every two hours wailing down the walls and making life a misery, then?"

Paige gritted her teeth. He, of course, glowed with health and that irritating masculine vigor of his. He wore an athletic T-shirt in a technical fabric and a pair of running shorts, and was clearly headed out to get himself into even better shape on the surrounding trails that scored the mountains, if that were even possible. No wonder he maintained that lean, rangy body of his that appeared to scoff at the very notion of fat. She wished she could hate him. She wished that pounding thing in her chest, and much lower, was *hate*.

"I've never slept better in my life," she said staunchly.

Her mistake was that she'd drifted too close to him as she said it, as if he was a magnet and she was powerless to resist the pull. She remembered that, too. It had been like a tractor beam, that terrible compulsion. As if they were drawn together no matter what. Across the cavernous warehouse where she'd met him on that shoot. Across rooms, beds, showers. Wherever, whenever.

Ten years ago she'd thought that meant they were made for each other. She knew better now. Yet she still felt that draw.

Paige only flinched a little bit when he reached over and ran one of his elegant fingers in a soft crescent shape beneath her eye. It was such a gentle touch it made her head spin, especially when it was at such odds with that harsh look on his face, that ever-present gleam of furious gold in his gaze.

It took her one shaky breath, then another, to realize

he'd traced the dark circle beneath her eye. That it wasn't a caress at all.

It was an accusation.

"Liar," he murmured, as if he was reciting an old poem, and there was no reason it should feel like a sharp blade stuck hard beneath her ribs. "But I expect nothing else from you."

Bite your tongue, she ordered herself when she started to reply. Because she might have got herself into this mess, twice, but that didn't mean she had to make it worse. She poured her feelings into the way she looked at him, and one corner of that hard, uncompromising mouth of his kicked up. Resignation, she thought. If they'd been different people she might have called it a kind of rueful admiration.

But this was Giancarlo, who despised her.

"Be ready at eight," he told her gruffly.

"That could cover a multitude of sins." So much for her vow of silence. Paige smiled thinly when his brows edged higher. "Be ready for what?"

Giancarlo moved slightly then on the wide marble step, making her acutely aware of him. Of the width of his muscled shoulders, the long sweep of his chiseled torso. Of his strength, his heat. Reminding her how deadly he was, how skilled. How he'd been the only man she'd ever met, before or since, who had known exactly what buttons to push to turn her to jelly, and had. Again and again. He'd simply looked at her, everything else had disappeared and he'd known.

He still knew. She could see it in that heat that made his dark eyes gleam. She could feel it the way her body prickled with that same lick of fire, the way the worst of the flames tangled together deep in her belly.

She felt her breath desert her, and she thought she saw

the man she remembered in his dark gaze, the man as lost in this as she always had been, but it was gone almost at once as if it had never been. As if that had been nothing but wishful thinking on her part.

"Wear something I can get my hands under," he told her, and there was a cruel cast to his desperately sensual mouth then that should have made her want to cry—but that wasn't the sensation that tripped through her blood, making her feel dizzy with something she'd die before she'd call excitement.

And as if he knew that too, he smiled.

Then he left her there—trying to sort out all the conflicting sensations inside of her right there in the glare of another California summer morning, trying not to fall apart when she suspected that was what he wanted her to do—without a backward glance.

"I think he must be a terribly lonely man," Violet said.

They were sitting in one of the great legend's favorite rooms in this vast house, the sunny, book-lined and French-doored affair she called her office, located steps from her personal garden and festooned with her many awards.

Violet lounged back on the chaise she liked to sit on while tending to her empire—"because what, pray, is the point of being an international movie star if I can't conduct business on a chaise?" Violet had retorted when asked why by some interviewer or another during awards season some time back—with her eyes on the city that preened before her beneath the ever-blue California sky and sighed. She was no doubt perfectly aware of the way the gentle light caught the face she'd allowed age to encroach upon, if only slightly. She looked wise and gorgeous at once, her fine blond hair brushed back from her face and only hinting at her sixty-plus years, dressed in her preferred "at home" outfit of butter-soft jeans that had cost her a small fortune and a bespoke emerald-green blouse that played up the remarkable eyes only a keen observer would note were enhanced by cosmetics.

This was the star in her natural habitat.

Sitting in her usual place at the elegant French secretary on the far side of the room, her laptop open before her and all of Violet's cell phones in a row on the glossy wood surface in case any of them should ring, Paige frowned and named the very famous director they'd just been discussing.

"You think *he's* lonely?" she asked, startled.

Violet let out that trademark throaty laugh of hers that had been wowing audiences and bringing whole rooms to a standstill since she'd appeared in her first film in the seventies.

"No doubt he is," she said after a moment, "despite the parade of ever-younger starlets who he clearly doesn't realize make him look that much older and more decrepit, but I meant Giancarlo."

Of course she did.

"Is he?" Paige affected a vague tone. The sort of tone any employee would use when discussing the boss's son.

"He was a very lonely child," Violet said, in the same sort of curious, faraway voice she used when she was puzzling out a new character. "It is my single regret. His father and I loved each other wildly and often quite badly, and there was little room for anyone else."

Everyone knew the story, of course. The doomed love affair with its separations and heartbreaks. The tempestuous, often short-lived reunions. The fact they'd lived separately for years at a time with many rumored affairs, but had never divorced. Violet's bent head and flowing tears at the old count's funeral, her refusal to speak of him publicly afterward.

Possibly, Paige thought ruefully as she turned every last part of the story over in her head, she had studied that Hollywood fairy tale with a little more focus and attention than most.

"He doesn't seem particularly lonely," Paige said when she felt Violet's expectant gaze on her. She sat very still in her chair, aware that while a great movie star might *seem* to be too narcissistic to notice anyone but herself, the truth was that Violet was an excellent judge of character. She had to be, to inhabit so many. She read people the way others read street signs. Fidgeting would tell her much, much more than Paige wanted her to know. "He seems as if he's the sort of man who's used to being in complete and possibly ruthless control. Of everything."

The other woman's smile then seemed sad. "I agree. And I can't think of anything more lonely," she said softly. "Can you?"

And perhaps that conversation was how Paige found herself touching up what she could only call defensive eyeliner in the mirror in the small foyer of her cozy little cottage when she heard a heavy hand at her door at precisely eight o'clock that night.

She didn't bother to ask who it was. The cartwheels her stomach turned at the sound were identification enough.

Paige swung open the door and he was there, larger than life and infinitely more dangerous, looking aristocratic and lethal in one of the suits he favored that made him seem a far cry indeed from the more casual man she'd known before. *This* man looked as if he'd sooner spit nails than partake of the Californian pastime of surfing, much less lounge about like an affluent Malibu beach bum in torn jeans and no shirt. *This* man looked as forbidding and unreachable and haughtily blue-blooded as the Italian count he was.

Giancarlo stood on the path that led to her door and let his dark eyes sweep over her, from the high ponytail she'd fashioned to the heavy eye makeup she'd used because it was the only mask she thought he'd allow her to wear. His sensual mouth crooked slightly at that, as if he knew exactly what she'd been thinking when she'd lined her eyes so dramatically, and then moved lower. To the dress that hugged her breasts tight, with only delicate straps above, then cascaded all the way to the floor in a loose, flowing style that suggested the kind of casual elegance she'd imagined he'd require no matter where he planned to take her.

"Very good, *cara*," he said, and that wasn't quite *approval* she heard in his voice. It was much closer to *satisfaction,* and that distinction made her pulse short-circuit, then start to drum wildly. Erratically. "It appears you are capable of following simple instructions, when it suits you."

"Everyone can follow instructions when it suits them," she retorted despite the fact she'd spent hours cautioning herself not to engage with him, not to give him any further ammunition. Especially not when he called her that name—*cara*—he'd once told her he reserved for the many indistinguishable women who flung themselves at him. *Better that than "Nicola,"* she thought fiercely. "It's called survival."

"I can think of other things to call it," he murmured in that dark, silken way of his that hurt more for its insinuations than any directness would have. "But why start the night off with name-calling?" That crook of his mouth became harder, deadlier. "You'll need your strength, I suspect. Best to conserve it while you can."

He's only messing with you, she cautioned herself as she stepped through the door and delivered herself into his clutches, the way she'd promised him she would. *He wants to see if you'll really go through with this.*

So did she, she could admit, as she made a show of locking the front door, mostly to hide her nerves from that coolly assessing dark gaze of his. But it was done too fast, and then Giancarlo was urging her into a walk with that hand of his at the small of her back, and their history seemed particularly alive then in the velvety night that was still edged with deep blues as the summer evening took hold around them.

Everything felt perilous. Even her own breath.

He didn't speak. He handed her into the kind of low-slung sports car she should have expected he'd drive, and as he rounded the hood to lower himself into the driver's seat she could still feel his hand on that spot on her back, the heat of it pulsing into her skin like a brand, making the finest of tremors snake over her skin.

Paige didn't know what she expected as he got in and started to drive, guiding them out of Violet's high gates and higher into the hills. A restaurant so he could humiliate her in public? One of the dive motels that rented by the hour in the sketchier neighborhoods so he could treat her like the whore he believed she was? But it certainly wasn't the sharp turn he eventually took off the winding road that traced the top of the Santa Monica Mountains bisecting Los Angeles, bringing the powerful car to a stop in a shower of dirt right at the edge of a cliff. There was an old wooden railing, she noted in a sudden panic. But still.

"Get out," he said.

"I, uh, really don't want to," she said, and she heard the sheer terror in her own voice. He must have heard it too, because while his grim expression didn't alter, she thought she saw amusement in the dark eyes he fixed on her.

"I'm not going to throw you off the side of the mountain, however appealing the notion," he told her. "That would kill you almost instantly."

"It's the 'almost' part I'm worried about," she pointed out, sounding as nervous as she felt suddenly. "It encompasses a lot of screaming and sharp rocks."

"I want you to suffer, *Paige*," he said softly, still with that emphasis on her name, as if it was another lie. "Remember that."

It told her all manner of things about herself she'd have preferred not knowing that she found that some kind of comfort. She could have walked away, ten years ago or three days ago, and she hadn't. He'd been the one to leave. He'd hurled his accusations at her, she'd told him she loved him and he'd walked away—from her and from his entire life here. This was the bed she'd made, wasn't it?

So she climbed from the car when he did, and then followed him over to that rail, wary and worried. Giancarlo didn't look at her. He stared out at the ferocious sparkle, the chaos of light that was this city. It was dark where they stood, no streetlamps to relieve the night sky and almost supernaturally quiet so high in the hills, but she could see the intent look on his face in the reflected sheen of the mad city below, and it made her shake down deep inside.

"Come here."

She didn't want to do that either, but she'd promised to obey him, so Paige trusted that this was about shaming her, not hurting her—at least not physically—and drifted closer. She shuddered when he looped an arm around her neck and pulled her hard against the rock-hard wall of his chest. The world seemed to spin and lights flashed, but that was only the beaming headlights of a passing car.

Giancarlo stroked his fingers down the side of her face, then traced the seam of her lips.

Everything was hot. Too hot. He was still as hard and male as she remembered, and his torso was like a brand beside her, the arm over her shoulders deliciously heavy, and she felt that same old fire explode inside of her again, as if this was new. As if this was the first time he'd touched her.

He didn't order her to open her mouth but she did anyway at the insistent movement, and then he thrust his thumb inside. It was hotter than it should have been, sexy and strange at once, and his dark eyes glittered as they met hers with all of Los Angeles at their feet.

"Remind me how exactly it was I lost my head over you," he told her, all that fury and vengeance in his voice, challenging her to defy him. "Use your tongue."

Paige didn't know what demon it was that rose in her then, some painful mixture of long lost hopes and current regrets, not to mention that anger she tried to hide because it was unlikely to help her here, but she did as she was told. She grabbed his invading hand with both of hers and she worshipped his thumb as if it were another part of his anatomy entirely, and she didn't break away from him while she did it.

She didn't know how long it went on.

His eyes were darker than the night around them, and the same hectic gold lit them, even as it burned within her. She felt molten and wild, reckless and lost, and none of that mattered, because she could taste *him*. He might hate her, he might want nothing more than to hurt her, but Paige had never thought she'd taste him again. She'd never dreamed this could happen.

She told herself it didn't matter, those things she felt deep inside her that she didn't want to acknowledge. Only that this was a gift. It didn't matter what else it was.

He pulled his thumb out then and shifted her so they were facing each other, and the space between them seemed dense. Electric.

"I'm glad to see you haven't lost your touch," he said, and though his tone was cruel his voice was rougher than it had been, and she told herself that meant something. It meant the same thing her breathlessness did, or that manic tightening deep in her belly, that restlessness she'd only ever felt with him and knew only he could cure.

He smiled, and it was so beautiful it made her throat feel tight, and she should have known better. Because he wasn't finished.

"Get on your knees, *Paige,*" he ordered her. "And do it right."

CHAPTER THREE

FOR A MOMENT Paige thought she really had pitched over the side of the hill, and this taut, terrible noise in her head was her own scream. But she blinked and she was still standing there before Giancarlo, he was still waiting and she didn't want him to repeat himself.

She could see from that faintly mocking lift to his dark brows and that twist to his lips that he knew full well she'd heard him.

"Not *here*, surely," she said, and her voice sounded thin and faraway.

"Where I want. How I want. Was I unclear?"

"But I—" She cleared her throat. "I mean, I don't—"

"You appear to be confused." His hands were still on her, and that didn't help. The offhanded sweep of his thumbs against the tender skin of her bare shoulders made her want to scream, but she didn't think she'd stop if she started. "*I* this, *I* that. This isn't about you. This is about me."

"Giancarlo."

"I told you what to do," he said coolly. "And what will happen if you don't."

She jerked back out of his grip, furious in a sudden jolt, and not only because she knew he could have held her there if he liked. But because he hated her and she hated that he did. Because he was back in her life but not really, not in the way she'd refused to admit to herself she'd wanted him to be.

God, in those first months, those first years, she'd expected him to appear, hadn't she? She'd expected him to seek her out once his initial anger passed, once the last of the scandal had died down. To continue that conversation they'd had outside her apartment the morning the pictures had run, so swift and terrible. Because they might have been together only a short time, but he'd known her better than anyone else ever had. *Or ever would.* Maybe not the details of her life, because she'd never wanted anyone to know those, but the truth of her heart. She'd been so sure that somehow, he'd understand that there had to have been extenuating circumstances....

But he'd never come.

So perhaps it was a very old grief that added to the fury and made her forget herself completely.

"Is this really what you want?" she demanded, forgetting to hold her tongue, the taste of his skin still a rich sort of wine in her mouth, making her feel something like drunk. "Is this what a decade did to you, Giancarlo?"

"This is what you did to me." He didn't use that name then, but she was sure they could both hear it, *Nicola* hanging in the air and weaving in and out of the scent of the night-blooming jasmine and rosemary all around them. "And this is exactly what I want."

"To force me. To make me do things I don't want to do. To—" She found she couldn't say it. Not to the man who was the reason she knew that love could be beautiful instead of dark and twisted and sick. Not to the man who had made her feel so alive, so powerful, so perfect beneath his touch. "There are words, you know. Terrible words."

"None of which apply." He thrust his hands in the pockets of that suit, and she wondered if he found it hard to keep them to himself. Was she as sick as he was if that made her feel better instead of worse? How could she tell anymore—what was the barometer? "You don't *have* to do anything. I have no desire to force you. Quite the opposite."

"You told me I had to do this—to—to—"

"Don't stutter like the vestal virgin we both know you are not," he said silkily, and she wondered if he'd forgotten that she'd been exactly that when she'd come to him ten years ago. If he thought that was another lie. "I told you that you had to obey me. In and out of bed."

"That I had to have sex with you *at your command* or leave," she gritted out.

He didn't quite shrug, or smile. "Yes."

"So then I do, in fact, have to do something. You *are* perfectly happy to use force."

"Not at all." He shrugged as if he didn't care what happened next, but there was a tension to those muscled shoulders, around his eyes, that told her otherwise. And it wasn't in the least bit comforting. "You're welcome to leave. To say no at any time and go about your life, such as it is, using whatever name appeals to you. I won't stop you."

It was as if her heart was in her mouth and she felt dizzy again, but she couldn't look away from that terrible face of his, so sensual and impassive and cruel.

"But if I do that, you'll tell Violet who I am. You'll tell her I…what? Stalked you? Deliberately hunted her down and befriended her to get to you?"

"I will." His face hardened and his voice did, too. "It has the added benefit of being the truth."

But Paige knew better, however little she could seem

to express it to him. She knew what had grown between her and Violet in these past years, and how deeply it would wound the other woman to learn that Paige was yet one more leech. One more user, trying to suck Violet dry for her own purposes. It made her feel sick to imagine it.

"That's no choice at all."

"It's a choice, *Paige*," he said with lethal bite. "You don't like it, perhaps, but that doesn't make it any less of a choice, which is a good deal more than you offered me."

"I can't hurt her. Don't you care about that? *Shouldn't* you?"

"There are consequences to the choices you make," he said with a certain ruthless patience. "Don't you understand yet? This is a lesson. It's not supposed to be fun." That smile of his was a sharp blade she was certain drew blood. "For you."

For a moment she thought she'd bolt, though it was a long walk to anywhere from high up on this hill. She didn't know how she kept herself still, how she stayed in one piece. She didn't know how she wasn't already in a thousand shattered bits all over this little pull out on the side of the deserted road, like a busted-out car window.

"Tell me, then," she managed after a moment, keeping her head high, though her eyes burned, "how does this lesson plan work, exactly? You say you don't want to force me, but you're okay with me forcing myself? When it's the last thing I want?"

"Is it?" He shook his head at her, that smile of his no less painful. "Surely you must realize how little patience I have for lies, *Paige*." He let out a small sound that was too lethal to be a laugh. "If I were to lift your dress and stroke my way inside your panties, what would I find? Disinterest?"

Damn him.

"That's not the point. That's biology, which isn't the same thing as will."

"Are you wet?"

It wasn't really a question, and her silence answered it anyway. Her bright red cheeks that she was sure were like a flare against the night. A beacon. Her shame and fury and agony, and none of that mattered because she was molten between her legs, too hot and too slippery, and he knew it.

He knew it by looking at her, and she didn't know which one of them she hated more then. Only that she was caught tight in the grip of this thing and she had no idea how either one of them could survive it. How anything could survive it.

"Please," she said. It was a whisper. She hardly knew she spoke.

And the worst part was that she had no idea what she was asking for.

"We'll get to the begging," he promised her.

Giancarlo looked as ruthless as she'd ever seen him then, and it only made that pulsing wet heat worse. It made her ache and hunger and *want*, and what the hell did that make her? *Exactly what he thinks you are already,* a voice inside her answered.

And he wasn't finished. "But first, I want you on your knees. Right here. Right now. Don't make me tell you again."

He didn't think she'd do it.

They stood together in the dark, close enough that any observer would think them lovers a scant inch away from a touch, and Giancarlo realized in a sudden flash that he didn't want her to do it—that there was a part of him that wanted her to refuse. To walk away from this thing before it consumed them both whole and then wrecked them all over again.

To stop him, because he didn't think he could—or would—stop himself.

Seeing her had taken the brakes off whatever passed for his self-control and he was careening down the side of a too-steep mountain now, heedless and reckless, and he didn't care what he destroyed on the way down. He didn't care about anything but exploring the phrase *a pound of flesh* in every possible way he could.

She didn't blink. He didn't think either one of them breathed. He saw her clench her hands into fists, saw her stiffen her spine. He wanted to stop her from running. From not running. From whatever was about to happen next in this too-close, too-dark night, where the only thing that moved was that long dress of hers, rippling slightly against the faint breeze from the far-off sea.

Then she moved, in a simple slide of pure grace that was worse, somehow, than all the rest. It reminded him of so many things. The supple strength and flexibility of her body, her lean curves, and all the ways he'd worshipped her back before he'd known who she really was. With his hands. His mouth. His whole body. She was his memory in lovely action, a stark and pretty slap across his face, and when she was finished she was settled there on her knees before him.

Just as he'd asked. *Demanded.*

Giancarlo stared down at her, willing back all of his self-righteous fury and the armor it provided, but it was hard to remember much of anything when she was staring up at him, her eyes wide and mysterious and her lips slightly parted, making the carnal way she'd taken his thumb inside her mouth seem to explode through him all over again.

Making him realize he was kidding himself if he thought he was in control of this.

As long as *she* didn't realize that, Giancarlo thought, he'd manage. So he waited, watching her as he did. The night seemed much darker than it was, heavy on all sides and far fewer stars above than in the skies over his home in Tuscany, and he *felt* the ragged breath she took. That same old destructive need for her poured through him, rocketing through his veins and into his sex, making him clench his jaw too tight to keep from acting on it.

He felt like granite—everywhere—when she tilted herself forward and propped herself against his thighs, her palms like fire, her mouth much too close to the part of him that burned the hottest for her.

"Your mother thinks you're lonely," she said.

It took him a moment to understand the words she spoke in that husky tone of voice, and when he did, something he didn't care to identify coursed through him. He told himself it was yet more anger. He had an endless well where this woman was concerned, surely.

Giancarlo reached down and took her jaw in his hand, tugging her face up so he could look down into it, and it was the hardest thing he'd done in a long, long time to keep himself in check. In control. To crush the roaring thing that wanted only to *take her, possess her* and force himself to *think*, instead.

"That's not going to work," he told her softly. He was so hard it very nearly hurt, but he stood there as if he could do this all night, and he felt the faintest shiver move through her, making it all worthwhile.

"What do you mean? That's what she said."

"It doesn't matter if she hauled out her photo albums and wept over pictures of me as a fat, drooling infant," he said mildly, though his hand was hard against her jaw and he could feel how much she wanted to yank herself back, away from him. He could feel the flat press of her hands on his thighs, and the heat there that neither one of them had ever been any good at harnessing. "You're not bringing it up now, on your knees in the dirt because I ordered it, because you have a sudden interest in my emotional well-being."

"I could be interested in nothing *but* your emotional well-being and you'd tell me I was only running a con," Nicola—*Paige* said, with more bravado than he might have displayed were he the one kneeling there in the dark. "I don't know why I bother to speak."

"In this case," he said silkily, moving his hand along the sweet line of her jaw, her cheek, cradling her head with a softness completely belied by the lash in his words, "it is because you hope to shame me into stopping this. Why else bring up my mother when you're about to take me into your mouth at last?"

Her mouth fell open slightly more, as if in stunned astonishment, and he laughed, though it wasn't a very nice sound.

"Fine," she said, though her voice sounded like a stranger's. "Whatever you want."

"That is the point I am trying to make to you, *Paige,*" he bit out then, holding her immobile, so she had no choice but to gaze back at him, and he was a terrible man indeed, to revel in the temper he saw in her changeable eyes. "'Whatever I want' isn't an empty phrase. It could mean pleasuring me by the side of the road without any consultation whatsoever about your feelings on the subject. It is what *I* want. Are you beginning to understand me? How many object lessons do you think you will require before this sinks in?"

She said something in reply but the night stole her

words away, and she cleared her throat. She was trembling fully then, and he might have felt like the monster all that accusation in her gaze named him, but he could see the rest of it, too. The stain of color on her cheeks. That glassy heat in her eyes. And beneath the hand he still held to her face and against her neck, the wild drumming of her pulse, pounding out her arousal in an unmistakable beat.

He knew that rhythm better than he knew himself. He thought it might have been the only honest thing about her, then and now.

"How long?" she whispered.

"Until what?"

"Until this is done." She moistened her lips and he felt it like her wicked mouth, wet and soft and deep, and nearly groaned where he stood.

"Until I'm bored."

"A few hours, then," she said, with a remnant of her usual fire, and he smiled.

"I don't imagine you'll be that lucky." He traced a pattern from that stubborn chin of hers to the delicate shell of her ear, then back. "I've had a long time to think about all the ways I'd like to make you crawl. Then pay. Then crawl some more. There's no telling how long it could take."

"And yet when you had the chance, you talked to me for three seconds and then disappeared for a decade," she pointed out.

He felt that same wash of betrayal, that same kick in the gut he'd felt that long-ago day when he'd realized she'd used him the way his own mother always had—and it had been far more shattering, because Violet had only sold him out when he was clothed.

"I don't want to *talk* to you," he said, as harshly as he

could in that same soft voice. "I didn't then. I don't now. I thought I'd made that clear."

A car passed by on the winding mountain drive, the headlights dancing over them, and he saw something bleak in her eyes, across her lovely face. He told himself there was no echo at all inside him, no hollow thing in his chest.

"Then we'd better get started with the humiliation and sexual favors, hadn't we?" she said with a cheerfulness that was as pointed as it was feigned, and he felt her hands tighten against his thighs. She moved them up toward his belt and he didn't know he meant to stop her until he did.

He watched her face as he helped her rise to her feet, and he didn't let go of her arm when she was standing, the way he should have done.

"And here I thought we were right on target to get arrested for public indecency," she whispered, her voice still sharp but something raw in her chameleon gaze. "They could throw me in jail and charge me for solicitation and it would be like all your dreams come true in one evening."

"This is my dream," he growled at her, his hand wrapped tight around her arm and that fever in his blood. His revenge, he thought. At last. "It's not the act itself that matters, *cara*. That's a privilege you haven't earned. It's the surrender. It's all about the surrender." He laughed then, a dark sound he felt in every part of him, as if it was a part of the night and as dangerous, and then he let her go. It was harder than it should have been. "You'll learn."

It became clear to Paige in the week that followed that it wasn't Giancarlo's intention to *actually* make her have sex with him whenever and wherever he chose, no matter what provocative things he might say to the contrary.

That would have been easy, in its way. He was far more diabolical than that.

He wanted her in a constant state of panic, with no idea what he might do next. He wanted her to think of nothing at all but him and the little things he made her do to prove her obedience that were slowly driving her insane.

It's all about the surrender, he'd said. Her surrender. And she was learning what he'd meant.

One day—after nearly a week filled with anticipation and the faintest of touches, always in passing and always unexpected, all of which still felt like a metal collar around her neck that he tightened at will—he found her in Violet's expansive closet, putting together a selection of outfits with appropriate accessories for Violet to choose between for the event the star was scheduled to attend that evening.

"Pull up your skirt, take off your panties—if you are foolish enough to be wearing any—and hand them to me," Giancarlo said without preamble, making Paige jump and shiver into a bright red awareness of him, especially because her mind had been a long way away.

Ten years ago away, in fact, and treating her to a play-by-play, Technicolor and surround-sound replay of one of their more adventurous evenings in the Malibu house down on the beach she had no idea if he still owned.

"What?" she stammered out, but her body wasn't in any doubt about his instructions. Her breasts bloomed into an aching heaviness, making her bra feel too tight and too scratchy against her skin. Her stomach flipped over, and below, that shimmering heat became scalding.

And that was only at the sound of his voice. What would happen if he touched her this time?

"Is this your strategy, *cara*? To feign ignorance every time I speak to you?" He loomed in the doorway, looking untamed and edgy, furious and male. He'd forgone the exquisite suits and running apparel today and looked more like the Giancarlo she remembered in casual trousers and a top that was more like a devotional poem extolling the perfection of his torso than anything so prosaic as a *T-shirt*. "It's already tiresome."

She was standing too straight, too still, on the other side of the central island that housed Violet's extensive jewelry collection, entirely too aware that she resembled a deer stuck fast in the glare of oncoming headlights. But she couldn't seem to move.

Anything besides her mouth, that was. "I did try to warn you that this would get boring."

Giancarlo's mouth crooked slightly and made hers water. His eyes were so dark the gold in them felt as much like a caress as a warning, and she was terribly afraid she could no longer tell the difference.

"Show me that you know how to follow directions." He folded his arms over that chest of his and propped a shoulder against the doorjamb, but Paige wasn't the least bit fooled. He looked about as casual and relaxed as a predator three seconds before launching an attack. "And I'd think twice before making me wait, if I were you."

"It's all the threats," she grated at him. "They make me dizzy with fear. It's hard to hear the instructions over all the heart palpitations."

"I'm certain that's true." That crook in his mouth deepened. She was fascinated. "But I think we both know it isn't fear."

Paige couldn't really argue with that, and she certainly didn't want him to wander any closer and prove his point—did she? She glanced down at her outfit, the short, flirty little skirt with nothing on beneath it, and realized that she'd obeyed him without thinking about it when she'd dressed this morning. *Make sure that I have access to you, should I desire it,* he'd told her two nights ago, a harsh whisper in the hallway outside Violet's office. She'd obeyed him and in so doing, she'd revealed herself completely.

When she raised her gaze to his again, he was smiling, a fierce satisfaction in his dark gold eyes and stamped across that impossibly elegant face of his. He jerked his chin at her, wordlessly ordering her to show him, and her hands moved convulsively, as if her body wanted nothing more than to prove itself to him. To prove *herself* trustworthy again, to jump through any hoop he set before her—

But that wasn't where this was headed. This wasn't a love story. No matter how many memories she used to torture herself into imagining otherwise.

"Come over here and find out for yourself, if you want to know," she heard herself say. Suicidally.

Giancarlo only shook his head at her, as if saddened. "You seem to miss the point. Again. This is not a game that lovers play, *cara*. This is not some delightful entertainment en route to a blissful afternoon in bed. This is—"

"Penance," she finished for him, with far more bitterness than she should have allowed him to hear. "Punishment. I know."

"Then stop stalling. Show me."

Paige could see he meant it.

She told herself it didn't matter. That he'd seen all of her before, and in a far more intimate setting than this. That more than that, he'd had his mouth and his hands on every single inch of her skin, in ways so devastating and intense that she could still feel it ten years later. So what did it matter now? He was all the way across the room and he *wanted* her to balk. To hate him. That was why he was doing this, she was sure.

So instead, she laughed, like the carefree girl she'd never been. Paige stepped out from behind the center island so there could be no accusations of hiding. She watched his hard, hard face and then, slowly, she reached down and pulled her skirt up to her hips.

"Satisfied?" she asked when she was fully bared to his view—because she was.

She'd been so lost in her guilt, her shame, her own anger at everything that had happened and Giancarlo too, that she'd forgotten one very important fact about this thing between them that Giancarlo had been using to such great effect.

It ran both ways.

He stared at her—too hard and too long—and she saw the faintest hint of color high on those gorgeous cheeks of his. And that hectic glitter in his dark eyes that she recognized. Oh yes, she recognized it. She remembered it.

She knew as much about him as he did about her, after all. She knew every inch of *his* body. She knew his arousal when she saw it. She knew he'd be so hard he ached and that his control would be stretched to the breaking point. The chemistry between them wasn't only his to exploit.

She stood there with her skirt at her waist, supposedly debasing herself before the only man she'd ever loved, and Paige felt better than she had in years. Powerful. *Right*, somehow.

"Looked your fill?" she asked sweetly when the silence stretched on, taut and nearly humming. He swallowed as if it hurt him, and she felt like a goddess as he dragged his gaze back to hers.

"Come here." His voice was a rasp, thick and hot, and it moved in her like joy.

She obeyed him and this time, she was happy to do it. She walked toward him, reveling in the way her blood pounded through her and her skin seemed to shrink a size, too tight across her bones. Because he could call this revenge. He could talk about hatred and penance. But it was still the same thick madness that felt like a rope around her neck. It was still the same inexorable pull.

It was still *them*.

Paige stopped in front of him and let out a surprised breath when he moved, reaching down to gather her wrists in his big hands and then pull them behind her, securing them in one of his at the small of her back. Her skirt fell back into place against the sensitized skin of her thighs, her back arched almost of its own accord, and Giancarlo stared down at her, a hard wildness blazing from his eyes.

Paige remembered that, too.

She didn't know what he looked for, much less what he saw. He stared at her for a moment that dragged out to forever and she felt it like panic beneath the surface of her skin. Like an itch.

And then he jerked her close, her hands still held immobile behind her back, and slammed his mouth to hers.

It wasn't a brush of his mouth, a tease, like before. It wasn't an introduction.

He took her mouth as if he was already deep inside of her. As if he was thrusting hard and driving them both toward that glimmering edge. It was more than wild, more than carnal. He bent her back over her own arms, pressing her breasts into the flat planes of his chest, and he simply possessed her with a ruthless sort of fury that set every part of her aflame.

She thrilled to his boldness, his shocking mastery. The glorious taste of him she'd pined for all these years. The sheer *rightness*.

Paige kissed him back desperately, deeply, forgetting about the games they played. Forgetting about penance, about trust. Forgetting her betrayal and his fury. She didn't care what he wanted from her, or how he planned to hurt her, or anything at all but this.

This.

There was too much noise in her head and too much heat inside of her and she actually moaned in disappointment when he pulled back, holding her away from him with that iron strength of his that reminded her how gentle he was with it. How truly demanding, because he knew—as he'd always known—exactly what she wanted. How far away from *force* all of this really was.

"You kiss like a whore," he said, and she could see it was meant to be an insult, but it came out sounding somehow reverent, instead.

She laughed. "Have you kissed many whores, then? You, the exalted Count Alessi, who could surely have any proper woman he wished?"

"Just the one."

She should be wounded by that, Paige thought as she studied him. She should feel slapped down, put in her place, but she didn't. She cocked her head to one side and saw the fever in his dark gaze, and she knew that whatever power he had over her, she had it over him, too. And more, he was as aware of that as she was.

"Then how would you know?" she asked him, her voice like a stranger's, breathy and inviting. Nothing like hurt at all. "Maybe the whore is you."

"Watch your mouth." But he'd moved closer again, his shoulders filling her vision, her need expanding to swallow the whole world. Or maybe it was his need. Both of theirs, twined together and too big to fit beneath the sky.

"Make me," she dared him, and he muttered something in Italian.

And then he did.

He let go of her hands to take her face between his hard palms, holding her where he wanted her as he plundered her mouth. As he took and took and then took even more, as if there was no end and no beginning and only the madness of their mouths, slick and hot and perfect. The fire between them danced high and roared louder, and he didn't stop her when Paige melted against him. When she wound her arms around his neck and clung to him, kissing him back as if this was the reunion she'd always dreamed of. As if this was a solution, not another one of his clever little power games.

And she didn't know when it changed. When it stopped being about fury and started to taste like heat. When it started to feel like the people they'd been long ago, before everything had gone so wrong.

He felt it, too. She felt him stiffen, and then he thrust her aside.

And for a long moment they only stared at each other, both of them breathing too fast, too hard. Paige tried to step back and her legs wobbled, and Giancarlo scowled at her even as his hand shot out to steady her.

"Thank you," she said, because she couldn't help herself. Her mouth felt marked, soft and plundered, and Giancarlo was looking at her as if she was a ghost. "That certainly taught me my place. All that punitive kissing."

She didn't know what moved across his face then, but it scraped at her. It hurt far worse than any of his words had. She had to bite her own tongue to keep from making the small sound of pain that welled up in her at the sight of it.

"It will," he promised her, a bleakness in his voice that settled in her bones like a winter chill. Like the fate she'd been running from since the day she'd met him, loath as she was to admit it. "I can promise you that. Sooner or later, it will."

Kissing her had been a terrible mistake.

Giancarlo ran until he thought his lungs might burst and his legs might collapse beneath him, and it was useless. The Southern California sun was unforgiving, the blue sky harsh and high and cloudless, and he couldn't get her taste out of his mouth. He couldn't get the feel of her out of his skin.

It was exactly as it had been a decade ago, all over again, except this time he couldn't pretend he'd been blindsided. This time, he'd walked right into it. He'd been the one to kiss her.

He cursed himself in two languages and at last he stopped running, bending over to prop his hands on his knees and stare down the side of the mountain toward his mother's estate and the sprawl of the city below it in the shimmering heat of high summer. It was too hot here. It was too familiar.

Too dangerous.

It was much too tempting to simply forget himself, to pick up where he'd left off with her. With the woman who was no longer Nicola. As if she hadn't engineered his ruin, deliberately, ten years ago. As if she hadn't then tricked her way to her place at his mother's side with a new name and God only knew what agenda.

As if, were he to bury himself in her body the way he wanted to do more than was wise and more than he cared to admit to himself, she might transform into the woman she'd already proved she wasn't in the most spectacular way imaginable.

He was already slipping back into those old habits he'd thought he'd eradicated. The work he'd left in Italy was piling up high, and yet here he was, running off steam in the Bel Air hills the way he'd done when he was a six-teen-year-old. She was the first thing he thought of when he woke. She was what he dreamed about. She was tak-ing over his life as surely as she ever had, very much as if this was *her* revenge, not his.

He was an addict. There was no other explanation for the state he was in, hard and ready and yearning, and he didn't want that. He wanted her humbled, brought low, destroyed. He wanted her to feel how he'd felt when he'd woken that terrible morning to find his naked body splashed everywhere for the entire world to pick over, parse, comment upon, like every other time his private life been exploited for Violet's gain—but much worse, because he hadn't seen the betrayal coming. He hadn't thought to brace himself for impact.

He wanted this to hurt.

Giancarlo straightened and shoved his hair back from his forehead, the past seeming to press against him too tightly. He remembered it all too well. Not just the af-fair with Nicola—*Paige,* he reminded himself darkly—in all its blistering, sensual perfection, as if their bodies had been created purely to drive each other wild. But the parts of that affair he'd preferred to pretend he didn't re-member, all these years later. Like the way he'd always found himself smiling when they'd spoken on the phone, wide and hopeful and giddy, as if she was sunshine in a bottle and only his. Or the way his heart had always thudded hard when she'd entered a room, in the moment before she'd seen him and had treated him to that dazzling smile of hers that had blotted out the rest of the world. The way she'd held his hand as if that connection alone would save them both from darkness, or dragons, or something far worse.

Oh yes, he remembered.

And he remembered the aftermath, too. After the pictures ran in all those papers. After those final, horrible moments with this woman he had loved so deeply and known not at all. After he'd done the best he could to clear his head and then made his way back to Italy. To face, at last, his elderly father.

His father, who had felt denim was for commoners and had thought the only thing more tawdry than Europe's aristocracy was the British royals, with their divorces and dirty laundry and *jeans*. His father, Count Alessi, who could have taught propriety and manners to whole nunneries and probably had, in his day. His father, who had been as gentle and nobly well-meaning as he was blue-blooded. Truly the last of his kind.

"It is not your fault," he'd told Giancarlo that first night in the wake of the scandal. He'd hugged his errant son and greeted him warmly, his body so frail it had moved in Giancarlo like a winter wind, a herald of the coming season he hadn't wanted to face. Not then. Not yet. "When I married your mother I knew precisely who she was, Giancarlo. It was foolish to imagine she and I could raise a son untainted by that world. It was only a matter of time before something like this happened."

Perhaps his father's disappointment in him had cut all the deeper because it had been so matter-of-fact. Untouched by any hint of anger or vanity or sadness. There was nothing to fight against, and Giancarlo had understood that there had been no one to blame but himself for his poor judgment. His father might have been antiquated, a relic of another time, but he'd instilled his values in his only son and heir.

Strive to do good no matter what, he'd told Giancarlo again and again. *Never make a spectacle of oneself. And avoid the base and the dishonorable, lest one become the same by association.*

Giancarlo had failed on all counts. It was why he knew that the vows he'd made when he was younger were solid. Right. No marriage, because how could he ever be certain that someone wanted *him*? And no heirs of his own, because he'd never, ever, subject a child to the things he'd survived. He might not be able to save himself from his own father's disappointment, he might find his life trotted out into public every time his mother starred in something new and needed to remind the world of her once upon an Italian count fairy-tale marriage, but it would end with him.

Damn Nicola—*Paige*—for making him think otherwise, even if it had only been for two mostly naked months a lifetime ago.

It was that, he thought as he broke into a run again, his pace harder and faster than before as he hurtled down the hill, that he found the most difficult to get past. He hated that she had betrayed him, yes. But far worse was this *thing* in him, dark and brooding, that yearned only for her surrender no matter how painful, and that he very much feared made him no different than she was.

He thought he hated that most of all.

CHAPTER FOUR

AFTER A LONG shower and the application of his own hand to the part of him that least listened to reason, Giancarlo prowled through the house, his fury at a dull simmer. An improvement, he was aware.

La Bellissima was the same as it ever was, as it had been throughout his life, he thought as he moved quietly through its hushed halls, gleaming with Violet's wealth and consequence in all its details. The glorious art she'd collected from all over the planet. The specially sourced artisan touches here and there that gave little hints of the true Violet Sutherlin, who had been born under another name and raised in bohemian Berkeley, California. Old Hollywood glamor mixed with contemporary charm, the house managed to feel light and airy rather than overfed, somehow, on its own affluence.

Much like Violet herself, all these years after her pouty, sex kitten beginnings in the mid-seventies. He should know, having been trotted out at key moments during her transition from kitten to lion of the industry, as a kind of proof, perhaps, that Violet could do more than wear a bikini.

There was the time she'd released a selection of cards he'd written her as a small child, filled with declarations of love that the other kids at school had teased him about all the way up until his high school graduation. There was the time she'd spent five minutes of her appearance in a famous actor's studio interview telling a long, involved anecdote about catching him and his first girlfriend in bed that had humiliated fourteen-year-old Giancarlo and made his then-girlfriend's parents remove her to a far-off boarding school. He knew every inch of this house and none of it had ever been his; none of it had ever been safe. He was as much a prop as any of the other things Violet surrounded herself with—only unlike the vases, he loved her despite knowing how easily and unrepentantly she'd use him.

He followed the bright hall toward Violet's quarters, knowing how much she liked to spend her days in the office there with its views of the city she'd conquered. He had memories of catapulting himself down this same hallway as a child, careening off the walls and coming to a skidding halt in that room, only to climb up on the chaise and lie at his mother's feet as she'd run her lines and practiced her voices, her various accents, the postures that made her body into someone else's. He'd found her fascinating, back then. He supposed he still did, and Giancarlo couldn't remember, then, at what age he'd realized that Violet was better admired than depended upon. That her love was a distantly beautiful thing, better experienced as a fan than a family member. The first time she'd released a photo of him he'd found embarrassing? Or the tenth, with as little remorse?

He only knew they'd both been far happier once he'd accepted it.

Giancarlo paused in the doorway, hearing his mother's famous laugh before he saw her. She wasn't in her usual place today, reclining on her chaise like the Empress of Hollywood. She was standing at the French doors instead, bathed in soft light from the summer day beyond with a mobile phone in her hand, and even though there was no denying her celebrated beauty, his gaze went straight to the other woman in the room as if Violet wasn't there at all.

Paige sat at the fussy little desk in the corner, typing something as a male voice responded to whatever Violet had said from her mobile phone, obviously on speaker. Paige was frowning down at her laptop as her fingers flew over the keys, and when Violet turned toward her to roll her eyes at her assistant, Giancarlo could see the face Paige made in immediate response.

Sympathetic. Fully on Violet's side. Staunch and true, he'd have said, if he didn't know better.

He'd seen that expression before. *That* was the woman he'd loved in all the passionate fury of those two months of madness. Stalwart. Loyal. Not in any way the kind of woman who would sell a man out and print it all up in the tabloids. He'd have sworn on that. He'd have gambled everything.

Giancarlo still couldn't believe how wrong he'd been.

His stomach twisted, and it took everything he had not to make a noise, not to bellow out his fury at all of this—but mostly at himself.

Because he wanted to believe, still. Despite everything. He wanted there to be an explanation for what had happened ten years ago. He wanted Paige—and when had he started thinking about her by that name, without stumbling over it at all?—to be who she appeared to be. Dedicated to his mother. Deeply sorry for what had gone before, and with some *reason* for what she'd done. And not the kind of self-serving reason Violet always had...

He wanted her back.

And that was when Giancarlo woke up with a jolt and recognized the danger he was in. History could not repeat itself. Not with her. Not ever.

"Darling," Violet said when she ended her call, turning from the window and smiling at him. "Don't lurk in the hallway. It was only my agent. A whinier, more demanding fool I have yet to meet, and yet I'm fairly certain he's the best there is."

But what Giancarlo noticed was the way Paige straightened in her chair, her eyes wide and blue when they flew to him, then quickly shuttered when she looked back to her keyboard.

He could think of a greater fool than his mother's parasitical agent. It was something about finding himself back in Los Angeles, he thought as he fought back his own temper, as well as seeing Paige again. It would have been different if he'd encountered her in some other city. Somewhere that held no trace of who they'd been together. But here, their history curled around everything, like a thick, encroaching smog, and made it impossible to inhale without confronting it every time.

With every goddamned breath.

"I must return to Italy," he said shortly. Almost as if he wasn't certain he'd say it at all if he didn't say it quickly and that, of course, made him despise himself all the more.

"You can't leave," Violet said at once. Giancarlo noticed Paige seemed to type even more furiously and failed to raise her head at all. "You've only just arrived."

"I came because it had been an unconscionably long time, Mother," he said softly. "It was never my intention to stay away so long. But I have a solution."

"You are moving back to Los Angeles," Violet said, a curve to her mouth that suggested she didn't believe it even as she said it. "I'm delighted. That Malibu house is far too nice to waste on all those renters."

"Not at all." He wanted to study Paige instead of his mother but he didn't dare. Still, he was as aware of her as if she was triple her own size. As if she loomed there in his peripheral vision, a great dark cloud, consuming everything. "You must come to Italy. Bring your assistant. Stay for the rest of the summer."

Violet looked startled for a moment, but then in the next her face smoothed out, and he recognized the mask she wore then. As impenetrable as it was graceful. A vision of loveliness that showed only what she wanted seen, and nothing else. Violet Sutherlin, the star. Giancarlo didn't know what it said about him that he found this version of her easier to handle than the one who pretended motherhood was her primary concern.

"Darling, you know my feelings about Italy," she murmured, and a stranger might have believed her wry, easy tone. "I love it with all my heart. But I'm afraid I buried that heart with your father."

"Not that Italy," he said. He smiled, though he understood he was speaking as much to the silent woman in the corner of his eye as to his mother. "My Italy."

"Do you have your own?" Violet asked. She laughed again. "You have been busy indeed."

"I've completely transformed the estate," Giancarlo said quietly. "I know we've discussed all these changes over the years, but I'd like you to see them for yourself. I think Father would be proud."

"I know he would," Violet said with a glimmer of something raw in her gaze and the sound of it in her voice, and Giancarlo knew he had her. Paige knew it too, he could tell. He felt more than saw her stiffen at her desk, and it took everything he had to keep the triumph from his voice, the sheer victory from his face. "Of course, Giancarlo. I'd love to see Tuscany again."

He only let himself look at Paige again when he was certain he had himself under complete control. *Like iron,* he thought fiercely. Like the old houses he'd rebuilt on the ancestral estate in Tuscany, stone by ancient stone, forcing his will and vision onto every acre.

He would take her away from Los Angeles, where history seemed to infuse every moment between them with meaning he didn't want. He didn't know why he hadn't thought of this sooner.

In the far reaches of Tuscany, as remote as it was possible to get in one of the most famous and beloved regions of the world, she would be entirely dependent on him. Violet could relax in the hands of his world-class staff, her every need anticipated and met, and he would have all the time in the world to vanquish this demon from his past, for good. All the time he needed to truly make her pay.

Because that was what he wanted, he reminded himself. To make her pay. Everything else was memory and fantasy and better suited to a long night's dream than reality.

"Wonderful." Giancarlo tried not to gloat, and knew he failed when Paige frowned. And it was still a victory. It was still a plan. And it would work, he was sure of it. Because it had to. "We leave tonight."

Paige had dreamed of Italy her whole life.

When she was a child, she'd sneaked library books into her mother's bleak trailer in the blistering heat of the rocky Arizona desert. She'd waited for Arleen to pass out before she'd lost herself in them, and she'd dreamed. Fierce dreams of cypress trees in stern columns marching across a deep green undulation of ancient fields. Monuments to long lost gods and civilizations gone centuries before her birth, red-roofed towns clustered on gentle hills beneath a soft, Italian sun.

Then she'd met Giancarlo, who carried the lilt of Italy in every word he spoke, and her dreams had taken on a more specific shape. Even back then, when he'd wanted to play around in Hollywood more than he'd wanted to tend to his heritage, he'd spoken of the thousands of rural acres that his father had only just started to reclaim from the encroaching wilderness of a generation or two of neglect. They were his birthright and in those giddy days ten years ago she'd dared to imagine that she was, too.

And now she was finally here, and it turned out it was extraordinarily painful to visit a place that she'd once imagined might be her home and now knew never, ever would be. More than painful—but she told herself it was the jet lag that made her ache like that. Nothing a good night's sleep on solid ground wouldn't cure.

Even if it was *this* solid ground.

The vast estate sprawled across a part of Tuscany that had been in the Alessi family in one form or another since the Middle Ages. It was dotted with old farmhouses Giancarlo had spent the past decade painstakingly renovating for a very special class of clientele: people as wealthy as his mother and as allergic to invasions of their privacy as his father had been. As Paige supposed he must be himself now, after his too-public shaming at her own hands.

Here at Castello Alessi and all across its hilly lands, thick with olive groves and vineyards, lavender bushes and timeless forests of oak trees—according to the splashy website Paige had accessed a hundred times before and once again from the plane when she'd accepted she was really, truly coming here at last—such privacy-minded people could relax, secure in the knowledge that the "cottages" they'd paid dearly either to rent or to buy outright and fashion to their liking were as private and remote as it was possible to get while still enjoying world-class service akin to that of the finest hotels, thanks to Giancarlo's private, around-the-clock staff.

But none of that applied to Paige, she was well aware.

They'd landed on a private airstrip in a nearby valley after flying all night. It had been a bright, somehow distinctly Italian summer morning, filled with yellow flowers and too-blue skies, and a waiting driver had whisked them off to the estate some forty minutes away. It was a long, gorgeous drive, winding in and around the hills of Tuscany that looked exactly as Paige had imagined them while also being somehow so much *more* than she'd anticipated. Violet had been installed in the lavishly remodeled *castello* itself, arrayed around a welcoming stone courtyard with heart-stopping views and her own private spa with waiting staff to pamper her at once, as if she was truly the High Queen of Italy.

Paige, on the other hand, Giancarlo ushered into a Jeep and then personally drove far out into the heart of the property, until all she could see in all directions was the gently rolling countryside and one lone house at the top of the nearest hill. All of it so gorgeous and yet so *familiar*, as if she'd been here before and recognized it like a homecoming, and yet, she was forced to keep telling herself, none of this was hers. Not the perfect sky, the charming lane, the pretty little houses on this or that ridge. *Not hers.* The man beside her least of all.

"Are you deliberately stranding me out here as some kind of punishment?" she asked him, when it became clear that a smaller cottage down in the valley beneath that lone house was where he was headed. She was doing her best not to look at him, braced beside her in the smaller-by-the-moment front of his Jeep as they bumped along the lazy dirt road that meandered toward the little stone house, because she was afraid it might make all these raw emotions inside of her spill over into tears. Or worse. "Don't you think that looks a little bit strange?"

"My mother will be waited on hand and foot in the *castello*," he said, his gruff voice either impatient or triumphant, and Paige couldn't tell which. She wasn't sure she wanted to know. "And if by some chance she needs you while undergoing a battalion of spa treatments, never fear, the Wi-Fi is excellent. I trust she can manage to send out an email should she require your presence."

"So the answer is yes," Paige said stiffly as he pulled up in front of the cottage. He turned the key in the ignition and the sudden quiet seemed to pour in through the open windows, as terrifying as it was sweet. "This is a punishment."

"Yes," he said in that low way of his that wrapped around her and made her yearn, then made her question her own sanity. "I am punishing you with Tuscany. It is a fate worse than death, obviously. Just look around."

She didn't want to look around, for a thousand complicated reasons and none she'd dare admit. It made her feel scraped to the bone and weak. So very weak. So she looked at him instead, which wasn't really any better.

"You think I don't know why you brought me here, but of course I do." She laughed, though it was a hollow little sound and seemed to make that scraped sensation expand inside of her. "You're making sure I have nowhere to run. I think that counts as the most basic of torture methods, doesn't it?"

"Correction." He aimed a smile at her that didn't quite

reach the storm in his eyes, but made her feel edgy all the same. "I don't care if you know. It isn't the same thing."

Paige pushed her way out of the Jeep, not surprised when he climbed out himself. Was this all a prologue to another one of these scenes with him—as damaging as it was irresistible? She tucked her hands into the pockets of the jeans she'd worn on the long flight and wished she felt like herself. *It's only jet lag,* she assured herself. Or so she hoped. *You've read about jet lag. Everyone says it passes or no one would ever go anywhere, would they?* But she didn't feel particularly tired. She felt stripped to the bone instead. Flayed wide-open.

And the way he looked at her didn't help.

"How long?" she asked, her voice not quite sounding like her own. "How long do you think you can keep me here?"

Giancarlo pulled her bags from the back and carried them to the door of the cottage, shouldering it open and disappearing inside. But Paige stayed where she was, next to the Jeep with her eyes on the rolling green horizon. The sweet blue of the summer sky was packed with fluffy white clouds that looked as if they were made of meringue and were far more beautiful than all of her dreams put together, and she tried her best not to cry, because this was a prison—she knew it was—and yet she couldn't escape the notion that it was *home.*

"I'll keep you as long as I like," he said from the doorway, his voice another rolling thing through the morning's stillness, like a dark shadow beneath all that shine. "This is about my satisfaction, *cara.* Not your feelings. Or it wouldn't be torture, would it? It would be a holiday."

"By your account, I imagine I don't have any feelings anyway, isn't that right?" She hadn't meant to say that, and certainly not in that challenging tone. She scowled at the stunning view, and reminded herself that she'd never really had a home and never would. Longing for a place like this was nothing more than masochistic, no matter how familiar it felt. "I'm nothing but a mercenary bitch who set out to destroy you once and is now, what? A delusional stalker who has insinuated herself into the middle of your family? For my own nefarious purposes, none of which have been in evidence at all over the past three years?"

"I find *parasite* covers all the bases." Giancarlo drawled that out, and it was worse, somehow, here in the midst of so much prettiness. Like a creeping black thing in the center of all that green, worse than a mere shadow. "No need to succumb to theatrics when you can merely call it what it is."

She shook her head, that same old anguish moving inside of her, making her shake deep in her gut, making her wish for things she knew better than to want. A home, at last. Love to fill it. A place to belong and a person to share it with—

Paige had always *known better*. Dreams were one thing. They were harmless. No one could have survived the hard, barren place where she'd grown up, first her embittered mother's teenage mistake and then her meal ticket, without a few dreams to keep them going. Much less what had happened ten years ago. What her mother had become. What Paige had nearly had to do in a vain attempt to save her.

But *wishes* were nothing but borrowed trouble. And she supposed, looking back, that had been the issue from the start—being with Giancarlo had made her imagine she could dare to want things she knew, *she knew,* could never be hers. Never.

You won't make that mistake again in a hurry, her mother's caustic voice jeered at her.

Paige risked a look at Giancarlo then, despairing at the way her heart squeezed tight at the sight of him the way it always had, at that dark look on his face that was half hunger and half dislike, at the way she had always loved him and understood she always would, and to what end? He would have his revenge and she would endure it and somehow, somehow, she would survive him, too.

It hurts a little bit more today than it usually does because you're here and you're tired, she tried to tell herself. *But you're fine. You're always fine. Or you will be.*

"I know you don't want to believe me," she said, because she had always been such an idiot where this man was concerned. She had never had the slightest idea how to protect herself. Giancarlo had been the kind of man who had blistering affairs the way other people had dinner plans, but *she* had fallen head over heels in love with him at first glance and destroyed them both in the process. And now she wanted, so desperately, for him to *see* her, just for a moment. The real her. "But I would do anything for your mother. For a hundred different reasons. Chief among them that she's been better to me than my own mother ever was."

"And here I thought you emerged fully grown from a bed of lies," he said silkily. He paused, his dark eyes on her, as if recognizing how rare it was that Paige mentioned her own mother—but she watched him shrug it off instead of pursuing it and told herself it was for the best. "I was avoiding the city my mother lived in all these years and the kind of people who lived in it, not my mother. A crucial distinction, because believe me, *Paige*, I would also do anything for my mother. And I will."

There was a threat in the last three words. A promise. And there was no particular reason it should thud into her so hard, as if it might have taken her from her feet if she hadn't already been braced against all of this. The pretty place, the sense of homecoming, the knowledge he was even more lost to her when he stood in front of her than he had been in all their years apart.

"I loved my mother, too, Giancarlo," Paige said, and she understood it was that scraped raw feeling that made her say such a thing. Giancarlo would never understand the kind of broken, terrible excuse for love that was the only kind Paige had ever known, before him. The sharp, scarring toll it exacted. How it festered inside and taught a person how to see the world only through the lens of it, no matter how blurred or cracked or deeply twisted. "And that never got me anything but bruises and a broken heart." And then had taken the only things that had ever mattered to her. She swallowed. "I know the difference."

He moved out of the doorway of the cottage then, closing the distance between them with a few sure steps, and Paige couldn't tell if that was worse or better. Everything seemed too mixed up and impossible and somehow *right*, too; the gentle green trees and the soft, lavender-scented breeze, and his dark gold eyes in the center of the world, making her heart beat loud and slow inside her chest.

Stop it, she ordered herself. *This is not your home. Neither is he.*

"Is this an appeal to my better nature?" Giancarlo asked softly. Dangerously. "I keep telling you, that man is dead. Killed by your own hand. Surely you must realize this by now."

"I know." She tilted up her chin and hoped he couldn't see how lost she felt. How utterly out of place. How hideously dislocated if it seemed that *he* was the only steady thing here, this man who detested her. "And here I am. Isolated and at your beck and call. Just think of all the ways you can make me pay for your untimely death."

She couldn't read the shadow that moved over his face then. His hand moved as if it was outside his control and he ran the backs of his fingers over the line of her jaw, softly, so softly, and yet she knew better than to mistake his gentleness for kindness. She knew better than to trust her body's interpretations of things when it came to this man and the things he could do to it with so seemingly careless a touch.

The truth was in that fierce look in his eyes, that flat line of his delectable mouth. The painful truth that nothing she said could change, or would.

He wanted to hurt her. He wanted all of this to *hurt*.

"Believe me," he said quietly. Thickly, as if that scraped raw thing was in him, too. "I have thought of little else."

Paige thought he might kiss her then, and that masochist in her *yearned* for it, no matter what came after. No matter how he made her pay for wanting him, which she knew he would. She swayed forward and lifted her mouth toward his and for a moment his attention seemed to drift toward her lips—

But then he muttered one of those curses that sounded almost pretty because it was in Italian. And he stepped back, staring at her as if she was a ghost. A demon, more like. Sent to destroy him when it was clear to her that if there was going to be any destruction here, it would be at his hands.

It was going to be her in pieces, not him. And Paige didn't understand why she didn't care about that the way she should. When he looked at her, she didn't care about anything but him and all these terrible, pointless wishes that had wrecked her once already. She should have learned her lesson a long time ago. She'd thought she had.

"I suggest you rest," he said in a clipped tone, stalking back toward the driver's side of the Jeep. "Dinner will be served at sunset and you'll wake up starving sometime before then. That's always the way with international flights."

As if he knew she'd never left the country before, when she'd thought she'd hidden it well today. His knowing anyway seemed too intimate, somehow. The sort of detail a lover might know, or perhaps a friend, and he was neither. She told herself she was being ridiculous, but it was hard to keep looking at him when she felt there had to be far too much written across her face then. Too much of that Arizona white trash dust, showing him all the things about her she'd gone to such lengths to keep him from ever knowing.

"At the *castello*?" she asked, after the moment stretched on too long and his expression had begun to edge into impatience as he stood there, the Jeep in between them and his hand on the driver's door. "That seems like a bit of a walk. It was a twenty-minute drive, at least."

"At the house on the hill," he said, and jerked his head toward the farmhouse that squatted at the top of the nearest swell of pretty green, looking sturdy and complacent in the sunlight, all light stones and an impressive loggia. "Right there. Unless that's too much of a hike for you these days, now that you live on a Bel Air estate and are neck deep in opulence day and night. None of it earned. Or yours."

Paige ignored the slap. "That really all depends on who lives there," she replied, and it was remarkably hard to make her voice sound anything approximating *light*.

"A troll? The Italian bogeyman? The big, bad wolf with his terrible fangs?"

His mouth moved into that crooked thing that made her stomach flip over and her heart ache. More. Again. *Always.*

"That would be me," he said softly, and she thought he took a certain pleasure in it. "So that's all of the above, I'd think. For your sins."

A long nap and a very hot shower after she woke made Paige feel like a new person. Or herself again, at last. She had been too weary and inexplicably sad to explore the cottage when Giancarlo had driven away, so she did it now, with the whisper-soft robe she'd found in the master bathroom wrapped around her and her feet bare against the reclaimed stone floors, her wet hair feeling indulgent against her shoulders as she moved through the charming space.

It was a two-story affair in what had looked from the outside like a very old stone outbuilding. Inside, it was filled with the early-evening light thanks to the tall windows everywhere, the exposed beams high above, and the fact the interior was wholly open to best take advantage of what would otherwise have felt like a small space. Stairs led from the stone ground floor to the loft above, which featured a large, extraordinarily comfortable bed in the airy room nestled in the eaves, a small sitting area with a balcony beyond, and the luxurious master bath Paige had just enjoyed.

The main floor was divided into an efficient, cheerful kitchen with a happily stocked refrigerator, a cozy sitting area with deep sofas arranged around a wide stone fireplace, a small dining area that led out to a patio that spanned the length of the cottage and led into a small, well-tended garden. And everywhere she looked, behind everything and hovering near and far and more beautiful by the moment, the Tuscan view.

Home, she thought, despite herself.

Evening had crept in with long, deep shadows that settled in the valley and made art out of the soft green trees, the cypress sentries and the rounded hills on all sides. The road that had felt torturously remote when Giancarlo had driven her here looked like something from one of her beloved old books now, winding off into the distance or off into dreams. Paige stood there in the window until the air cooled around her, and realized only when she started back up the stairs that she hadn't breathed like that—deeply and fully, all the way down to her feet, the way she had when she'd danced—in a very long time.

Almost as if she was comfortable here. As if she belonged. She'd felt that way in only one other place in her whole life, and had been as wrong. Giancarlo's Malibu home, all wood and glass, angled to best let the sea in, had only been a pretty house. This was a pretty place.

And when you leave here, she told herself harshly, *you will never come back. The same as that house in Malibu. Everyone feels at home in affluent places. That's what they're built to do.*

Paige dressed slowly and carefully, her nerves prickling into a new awareness as she rifled through her suitcase. Should she wear the sort of thing she would wear if this was a vacation in Italy she happened to be taking by herself? Or should she wear something she suspected Giancarlo would prefer, so he could better enact his revenge? On the one hand, jeans and a slouchy sweatshirt, all comfort and very little style. On the other, a flirty little dress he could *get his hands under,* like before. She didn't have the slightest idea which way to go.

"What do *you* want?" she asked her sleepy-eyed reflection in the bathroom mirror, her voice throaty from all that sleep.

But that was the trouble. She still wanted the same things she'd always wanted. She could admit that, here and now, with Giancarlo's Italy pressing in on her from all sides. The difference was that this time, she knew better than to imagine she'd get it.

Paige dried her hair slowly, her mind oddly empty even as the rest of her felt tight with all the things she didn't want to think about directly. Taut and on edge. She pulled on a pair of soft white trousers and a loose sort of tunic on top, a compromise between the jeans she'd have preferred and what she assumed Giancarlo would likely want to see her wear, given the circumstances.

"What he'd really like is me, as naked as the day I was born and crawling up that hillside on my hands and knees," she muttered out loud and then laughed at the image, the sound creaky and strange in the quiet of the cottage. She kept laughing until a wet heat pricked at the back of her eyes and she had to pull in a ragged breath to keep the tears from pouring over. Then another.

Paige frowned as she slipped her feet into a pair of thonged flat sandals. When was the last time she'd laughed like that? About anything?

What a sad creature you've become, she scolded herself as she dug out her smartphone from her bag and scrolled through her messages. But the truth was, she had always been a fairly sad thing, when she looked back at the progression of her life. Sad and studious or determined and stubborn, from the start. It had been the only way to survive the chaos that had been her mother. There had only been one two-month stretch of laughter in her life, gleaming and overflowing and dizzy with joy, and she'd ruined it ten years ago.

"My goodness," Violet said in her grand way when she picked up her private line, after Paige apologized for disappearing and then sleeping for hours, "this is *Italia*, Paige. One must soak in *la dolce vita*, especially when jet-lagged. I plan to spend the night in my lovely little castle, getting fat on all the *marvelous* local cuisine! I suggest you do the same."

And Paige would have loved to do the same, she thought when she finally stepped out of her cottage into the cool evening, the Tuscan sky turning to gold above her. But she had a date with her sins instead.

Sins that felt like wishes granted, and what was wrong with her that she didn't want to tell the difference between the two?

She took her time and yet the walk was still too short. Much too short.

And Giancarlo waited there at the crest of the hill, his eyes as hard as his body appeared loose and relaxed, in linen trousers and the sort of camel-colored sport coat that made her think of his aristocratic roots and her lack of them. And Paige was suddenly as wide-awake as if she'd drowned herself in a vat of espresso.

He looked like something more than a man as he waited there, at first a shadow next to the bold upright thrust of a thick cypress tree, then, as she drew closer, very distinctly himself. He'd clearly watched her come all the way up the side of his hill, and she wasn't sure if she'd seen him from afar without realizing it or if it was that odd magnetic pull inside of her that had done it, pointing her toward him as unerringly as if she'd been headed straight to him all along.

Home, that thing in her whispered, and she didn't have

the strength to pretend she didn't feel it when she did. Not tonight.

She stopped when she was still some distance away and looked back the way she'd come, unable to keep the small sigh of pleasure from escaping her lips. There was the hint of mist in the valley the lower the sun inched toward the hills, adding an elegant sort of haunting to the shadows that danced between them, and far off in the distance the *castello* stood tall and proud, lights blazing against the coming night. It was so quiet and perfect and deeply satisfying in a way Paige hadn't known anything could be. Gooseflesh prickled up and down her arms and she felt it all like a heavy sob in her chest, rolling through her, threatening her very foundations.

Or maybe that was him. Maybe it had always been him.

"It's gorgeous here," she said, which felt deeply inadequate. "It doesn't seem real."

"My father believed that the land is our bones," Giancarlo said. "Protect it, and we strengthen ourselves. Conserve it and care for it, and we become greater in its glory. Sometimes I think he was a madman, a farmer hiding in an aristocrat's body." His gaze moved over her face, then beyond her, toward the setting sun. "And then another sunset reminds me that he was right. Beauty is always worth it. It feeds the soul."

"He sounds like some kind of poet."

"Not my father. Poets and artists were to be championed, as one must always support art and culture for the same reason one tends the land, but Alessis had a higher calling." He shook his head. "Endless debt and responsibility, apparently. I might have been better off as an artist, come to that."

"If I had a home like this, I don't think I'd mind doing

whatever it took to keep it," Paige said then. She remembered herself. "I don't think anyone would."

She thought Giancarlo smiled, though his face was obscured in the falling dark and then she knew she must have imagined it, because this wasn't that kind of evening no matter how lovely it was. He wasn't that kind of man. Not anymore. Not for her.

"Come," he said. He reached out his hand and held it there in the last gasp of golden light, and Paige knew, somehow, that everything would be divided into before and after she took it. The world. Her life. This *thing* that was still between them. And that precarious, wildly beating creature inside her chest that was the battered ruins of her heart.

His mouth crooked slightly as the moment stretched out. She made no move; she was frozen into place and wasn't sure she could do anything about it, but he didn't drop his hand.

"Did you make me dinner?" she asked, her voice shockingly light when there was nothing but heaviness and their history and her treacherous heart inside of her, and she thought neither one of them was fooled. "Because food poisoning really would be a punishment, all joking aside."

"I am Italian," he said, with a note of amused outrage in his voice, which reminded her too strongly of all that laughter they'd shared a lifetime ago. As if the only things that had mattered in the whole world had been there in his smile. She'd thought so then. She thought maybe she still did, for all the good that would do her here. "Of course I can cook." He paused, as if noticing how friendly he sounded and remembering how inappropriate that was tonight. As if he, too, was finding it hard to recall the battle lines he'd drawn. "But even if I couldn't, the estate has a fleet of chefs on call. Meals are always gourmet here, no matter who prepares them."

"Careful," she said softly, more to her memories and her silly heart than the man who stood there before her, still reaching out to her, still her greatest temptation made flesh. Still the perfect embodiment of all the things she'd always wanted and couldn't have. "I might forget to be suitably intimidated and start enjoying myself. And then what would happen?"

He definitely smiled that time, and Paige felt it like a deep, golden fire, lighting her up from the inside out. Making her shiver.

"Surrender takes many forms," he replied into the indigo twilight that cloaked them both, now that the sun had finally sunk beneath the furthest hill. "I want yours every way I can get it."

"I can surrender to *la dolce vita*," she said, as airily as possible, as if her tone of voice might make it so. "I understand that's the point of Italy."

He still stood there, his hand out, as if he could stand like that forever. "That's as good a place to start as any."

And there was no real decision, in the end. There had been so many choices along the way, hadn't there? Paige could have got a different job three years ago. She could have left Violet's house and employ the moment Giancarlo had appeared, or anytime since. She could have declined the offer of that "date" that night, she could have stayed standing up instead of sinking to her knees by the side of that road, she could have shown him nothing in Violet's closet that day but her back as she walked away from him. She could have refused to board his plane, refused to leave her cottage tonight, locked herself inside rather than climb this hill to stand before him like this.

He hadn't *happened* to her, like the weather. She'd

chosen this, every step of the way, and even here, even stranded in the countryside with this man who thought so ill of her, she felt more at home than she had in years. Maybe ever. She supposed that meant she'd made her decision a long time ago.

So Paige reached out her hand and slid it into his. She let the heat of him wash through her at that faintly rough touch, his palm warm and strong and perfect, and told herself it didn't matter what happened next.

That she'd surrendered herself to Giancarlo a long time ago, whether he understood that or not.

CHAPTER FIVE

"IF THIS IS your revenge," Paige said, a current of laughter in her voice though her expression was mild, "I think I should confess to you that it tastes a whole lot like red wine."

He should do something about that, Giancarlo thought, watching her move through the refurbished ground floor of his renovated house. She was still so graceful, so light on her feet. Like poetry in motion, and he'd never been able to reconcile how she could flow like that and have turned out so rotten within. He'd never understood it.

It doesn't matter what you understand, he snapped at himself. *Only what you do to make this* thing *for her go away—*

But something had happened out there as the sun set. Something had shifted inside him, though he couldn't quite identify it. He wasn't certain he'd want to name it if he could.

"It may prove to be a long night, *cara,*" he told her darkly, pouring himself a glass of the wine they made here from Alessi grapes. "This is merely the beginning."

"The civilized version of revenge, then," she murmured, almost as if to herself, running her fingers along the length of the reclaimed wood table that marked his dining area in the great, open space he'd done himself.

In soothing yet bright colors and historically contextual pieces, all of which dimmed next to that effortless, off-handed beauty of hers. "I'll keep that in mind."

This didn't feel like revenge. This felt like a memory. Giancarlo didn't want to think too closely about that, but the truth of it slapped at him all the same. It could have been any one of the long, lush evenings they'd shared in Malibu a decade back that still shimmered in his recollection, as if the two of them had been lit from within. It shimmered in him now, too. Again. As if this was the culmination of all the dreams he'd lied and told himself he'd never had, in all those years since he'd left Los Angeles and started bringing the estate back to life.

There was too much history between them, too much that had gone wrong to ever fix, and yet he still caught himself watching her as if this was a new beginning. But then, he had always been such a damned fool where this woman was concerned, hadn't he?

Earlier he'd stood in the courtyard of the *castello* with Violet, toasting her first night back in Italy since his father's funeral eight years ago, and he'd felt a sense of deep rightness. Of homecoming, long overdue. These hills held his happiest childhood memories, after all. When his parents had both been alive, and in those early years, so much in love it had colored the air around them.

"You've done a marvelous thing here, darling," Violet had said, smiling as much at him as at the achingly perfect view.

"I remember the days when we couldn't drive out the gates in Bel Air without having to fight our way through packs of photographers," he'd said, gazing out at the slumbering hills, all of them his now, his birthright and his future. His responsibility. And not a single paparazzo in a thousand miles or more. No lies. No stories. Only the enduring beauty of the earth. "Just to get to school in the morning."

"The tabloids giveth and the tabloids taketh away," Violet had said drily, looking as chic and elegant as ever though she wore her version of lounge wear and what was, for her, a practically cosmetic-free face. "It's never been particularly easy to navigate, I grant you, but there did used to be a line. Or perhaps I'm kidding myself."

"I want this place to be a refuge," he'd told her then. "It's nearly fifteen miles to the nearest main road. Everything is private. It's the perfect retreat for people who can't hide anywhere else."

Violet had tasted her wine and she'd taken her time looking at him again, and he'd still been unsure if she was pausing for dramatic effect or if that was simply how she processed emotion. She was still a mystery to him and he'd long since accepted she always would be. Or anyway, he'd been telling himself he'd accepted it. It might even have been true.

"Yes," she'd said, "and it's very beautiful. It's always been beautiful. I imagine I could live here quite happily and transform myself into one of those portly, Italy-maddened expatriates who are forever writing those merry little Tuscan memoirs and waxing rhapsodic about the *light*." Her brows had lifted. "But which one of us is it that feels they need a hiding place, Giancarlo? Is that meant to be you or me?"

"Never fear, Mother," he'd replied evenly. "I have no intention of having children of my own. I won't have any cause to hide away, the better to protect them from prying eyes and a judgmental world. Perhaps I, too, will flourish in the heat of so many spotlights."

She'd only smiled, enigmatic as ever, seemingly not in the least bit chastised by what he'd said. Had he expected otherwise? "Privacy can be overrated, my darling boy. Particularly when it better resembles a jail."

And now he stood in the cheerful lounge of the house he'd taken apart and put back together with his own two hands, and watched the woman he'd once loved more than any other walk through the monument—he wouldn't call it a *jail*—he'd built to his own unhappiness, his lonely, broken, betrayed heart.

How had he failed to realize, until this moment, that he'd built it for her? That he'd been hiding here these past ten years—deliberately keeping himself some kind of hermit, tucked away on this property and in this very cottage? That it was as much his refuge *for* her as it was *from* her?

That notion made something like a storm howl in him, deep and long. And as if she could read his mind, Paige turned, a small smile on that distracting mouth of hers.

"I always liked your films," she said, her voice the perfect complement to the carefully decorated great room, the furnishings a mix of masculine ease and his Italian heritage, as if he'd planned for her to stand there in its center and make it all work. "I suppose it shouldn't surprise me that that kind of attention to detail should spill over into all the things you do."

"My films were laughable vanity projects at best," he told her, that storm in his voice and clawing at the walls of his chest. "I should never have taken myself seriously, much less allowed anyone else to do the same. It's an embarrassment."

Paige wrinkled her nose and he thought that might kill him, because finding her *adorable* was far more dangerous than simply wanting her. One was about sex, which was simple. The other had consequences. Terrible consequences he refused to pay.

"I liked them."

"Shall we talk about the things you like?" Giancarlo asked, and he sounded overbearingly brooding to his own ears. As if he was performing a role because he thought the moment needed a villain, not because he truly wanted to put her back in her place. "Your interest in photography and amateur porn, for instance?"

Some revenge, he thought darkly. *Next you'll try to cuddle her to death with your words.*

But she only smiled in that enigmatic way of hers, and moved closer to one of the paintings on the wall, her hands cupped around her glass of wine and that inky black hair of hers falling in abandon down her back, and it wasn't cuddling he thought about as he watched her move. Then bite her lower lip as she peered up at the painting. It wasn't *cuddling* that made his blood heat and his mouth dry.

"I don't understand why I'm here," Paige said, so softly that it took him a moment to realize she'd spoken. She swiveled back to look at him, framed there like a snapshot, the woman who had destroyed him before the great, bright canvas that stretched high behind her, all shapes and emotion and a swirl of color, that he hadn't understood until tonight had reminded him of her.

Giancarlo told himself it was a sour realization, but his sex felt heavy and the air between them tasted thick. Like desire. Like need.

Like fate.

"It seems as if you've achieved what you set out to do," she continued as if she couldn't feel the thickness, though he knew, somehow, that she could. "You've separated me from Violet without seeming to do so deliberately, which I'm assuming was your purpose from the start. But why bring me all the way here? Why not leave me

in California and spirit Violet away? And having made
me come all the way here," Paige continued, something
he couldn't identify making her eyes gleam green in the
mellow light, "why not simply leave me to rot in my little
cottage? It's pretty as prison cells go, I grant you. Very
pretty. It might take me weeks to realize I'm well and
truly trapped there."

He let his gaze roam over her the way his hands itched
to do. "You've forgotten the most important part."

"The sex, yes," Paige supplied, and she didn't sound
particularly cowed by the idea, or even as outraged as
she'd been back in Los Angeles. Her tone was bland. Perhaps too bland. "On command."

"I was going to say obedience," he said, and he didn't
feel as if he was playing a game any longer. He was too
busy letting his eyes trace over her curves, letting his
hands relish the tactile memory of her face between them
as if she'd burned her way into his flesh. He could still
taste her, damn it. And he wanted more.

"Obedience," she repeated, as if testing each syllable
of the word as she said it. "Does that include feeding
me a gourmet dinner in this perfect little mansion only
a *count* would call a cottage? Are you entirely sure you
know what *obedience* involves?"

Giancarlo smiled, or anyway, his mouth moved.
"That's the point. It involves whatever I say it involves."

He took a sip of his wine as he walked over to the open
glass doors that led out to the loggia, nodding for her to
join him outside. Stiffly, carefully—as if she was more
shaken by their encounter than she appeared, and God
help him, he wanted that to be true—she did.

Because the truth was so pathetic, wasn't it? He still
so badly wanted her to be real. To have meant some part
of the things that had happened between them. All these

years later, he still wanted that. Giancarlo despaired of himself.

A table waited out in the soft night air, bright with candles and laden with local produce and delicacies prepared on-site, while a rolling cart sat next to it with even more tempting dishes beneath silver covers. It was achingly romantic, precisely as he'd ordered. The hills and valleys of the estate rolled out beneath the stars, with lights winking here and there in the distance, making their isolation high up on this terrace at a remove from all the world seem profound.

That, too, was the point.

He moved to pull her chair out for her like the parody of the perfect gentleman he had never quite been and waited as she settled in, taking a moment to inhale her scent. Tonight she smelled of the high-end bath products he had his staff stock in the cottages, vanilla and apricots, and that hint of pure woman beneath.

"This house was a ruin when I started working on it," he told her, still standing behind her, because he didn't know what his face might show and he didn't want her to see it. To see *him*. He succumbed to a whim and ran his fingers through her hair, reveling in the heavy weight of the dark strands even as he remembered all the other times she'd wrapped him in the heat and sweetness of it. When she'd crawled over him in that wide bed in Malibu and let her hair slip and tumble all over his skin as she tortured him with that sweet mouth of hers, driving them both wild. Giancarlo hardened, remembering it, and her hair was thick silk in his hands. "It sits on its original foundation, but everything else is changed. Perhaps the walls still stand, but everything inside is new, reclaimed, or altered entirely. It might look the same from a distance, but it isn't."

"I appreciate the metaphor," Paige said, with a certain grittiness to her voice that he suspected meant her teeth were clenched. He smiled.

"Then I hope you'll appreciate this, too," he said as he rounded the table and sat down across from her, stretching out his legs before him as he did. "This is the Italian countryside and everything you can see in every direction is mine. You could scream for days and no one would hear you. You could try to escape and, unless you've taken up marathon running in your spare time, you'd run out of energy long before you found the road. You claimed to be obedient in Los Angeles because it suited you. You wanted your job more than you minded the loss of your self-respect, such as it is. Here?" He shrugged as he topped up their wineglasses with a bottle crafted from grapes he'd grown himself and then sat back, watching her closely, as she visibly fought not to react to his cool tone, his calmly belligerent words. "You have no other choice."

"That's not at all creepy," Paige said, though he could have sworn that gleam of green in her chameleon gaze was amusement, however beleaguered. "I'm definitely the terrifying stalker in this scenario, not you."

Giancarlo laughed. "Not that I would care if it really was creepy, but I don't think you really think so, do you? Shall we put it to the test?"

He wanted her to push him, he understood. He wanted to see for himself. He wanted to peel those crisp white trousers from her slim hips and lick his way into her wetness and heat and know it was all for him, the way he'd once believed it was. The way he'd once believed *she* was.

Soon, he assured himself as his body reacted to that image with predictable enthusiasm. *Soon enough.*

"Again," Paige said tightly, taking a healthy gulp of

her wine, "it seems to me that there are more effective forms of payback than a romantic dinner for two, served beneath the starry night sky on what might be the most intimate terrace on the entire planet." She looked out at the view as the heavens sparkled back at her, as if they were performing for her pleasure. "I suspect you might be doing it wrong."

"Ah, Paige," Giancarlo said softly. "You lack imagination." Her eyes swung back to his and he smiled again, wider, pleased when that seemed to alarm her. "The romantic setting will only make it more poignant, will it not, when I order you to strip and sit there naked as we eat. Or when I demand that you please me with your mouth while I soak in the view. Or when I bend you over the serving table and make you scream out my name until I'm done." He let his smile deepen as her eyes went very green, and very round. "The more civilized the setting, the more debauched the act," he said mildly. "I find there is very little more effective."

She looked stunned, and then something like wistful, and he almost broke and hauled her into his arms—but somehow, *somehow*, he reined himself in. *Just a little bit longer,* he promised himself. She blinked, then coughed, and then she folded her hands together in her lap with such precision that Giancarlo knew she was torturing *herself* with all those images he'd put in her head.

Va bene.

"You say that as if this isn't the first time you've done this." Her voice was his own little victory, so raspy was it then, with that stunned heat in her gaze and that band of color high on her cheeks. "Do you spend a lot of time enacting complicated revenge fantasies, Giancarlo? Is that another one of your heretofore hidden talents—like architecture and interior design, apparently?"

"I went to architecture school after university," he said, and something about the fact she didn't know that bothered him. Had he never told her his own story? Had he been as guilty of wearing a false persona ten years ago as she had been? Had it simply been the rush, the need that had kept them in bed and focused on other things? Had it been by her design—or had it been his own selfishness at play? He shoved that disconcerting thought aside. "But when I was finished, I decided I wanted to leverage my position as Violet's son, instead. That didn't work out very well for either one of us, did it?" He reached over and removed the silver cover from the plate of antipasti in front of her, then from his own, and smiled at her when she looked confused. "The *salsicce di cinghiale* is particularly good," he told her. "And you should be certain to eat well. We have a very long night ahead of us."

He expected her to do as she was told. It took a moment or two for him to realize that she hadn't moved. That she appeared to have frozen solid where she sat and was staring at him with a stricken sort of expression on her face.

Giancarlo lifted a brow. "Was I unclear?"

"I appreciate all the tension and drama," Paige said after a moment. "I don't think I realized how very much you take after your mother until now. That's a compliment," she added in a hurry when he frowned at her. "But I'll pass."

"That is not an option you have." He shrugged. "You persist in thinking what you want comes into play here. It doesn't."

"What will you do?" she asked softly, so softly it took a moment for him to hear the challenge beneath the words, and then to see it there in her chameleon eyes.

"Make me scream for people who won't hear me? Make me walk for days in search of a road that's still hours from anywhere? Force me to stay in that gorgeous little cottage down the hill like a bird in a cage?"

"Or, alternatively, merely call my mother and tell her exactly who you are," he suggested. "A fate you felt was worse than death and far more terrible than anything I might do a week ago."

But tonight she only shook her head and she didn't avert her gaze, reminding him of that moment in his mother's closet across the world. Reminding him he'd never controlled this woman, not even when she'd agreed to let him.

"I think if you were going to do that, Giancarlo, you would have. You wouldn't have dragged me across the planet and then presented me with wine and a four-course meal."

He laughed, a smoky little sound against the night. It did nothing to ease the mounting tension. "Do you really want to test that theory?"

She leaned forward, holding his gaze, and his laughter dried up as if it had never been. He was aware of everything at once. The stars above them, the faint breeze that teased him with the intoxicating scent of her. The rich food before them, the dancing candlelight. The way she sat now, the wide neck of her brightly patterned tunic falling open as she leaned toward him, hinting at the soft curves beneath.

And all that fire, as bright as it had ever been, burning them both where they sat.

Her gaze was like a touch on his, and he felt it everywhere. "I have a different theory."

"I'm all ears, of course. Every inmate is innocent, every killer was merely misunderstood, every con man an

artist in his soul, et cetera. Tell me your sob story, *cara*."
He felt his mouth crook. "I knew you would, sooner or
later."

But Paige only smiled, and her eyes were so green tonight they rivaled his own lush fields. It moved in him
like summer, an exultation of all that boundless heat that
spiked the air between them.

"You don't want revenge. Not really. You want sex."

Her smile deepened when he only stared back at her,
that mouth of hers still an utter distraction, still his undoing. Her gaze proud and unwavering and he had no
defense against that, either.

"You don't want to admit it, given what happened the
last time we had sex, but look where we are." She lifted
a shoulder, somehow encompassing the whole of the estate in that simple little gesture. "You've made sure there
couldn't possibly be a camera here. You've cut us off
from the rest of the world. And you're calling it *revenge*
because you're furious that you still want me."

"Or because *wanting* you is only part of it," he replied,
stiffer than he should have sounded, because it was that
or let loose the wild thing in him that wanted nothing but
her however he could have her. That didn't give a toss
about the rest of it as long as he got his hands on her one
more time. Just one more time. "And not mutually exclusive with revenge, I assure you."

Her smile seemed to pierce straight through him
then, heat and fire and danger, and it sank straight to
his sex.

Making him nothing at all but that wildness within.

"Call it whatever you want," she suggested in that
rough voice of hers that hinted at her own dark excitement, that called to him like a song the way it always had.
That sang in him still, no matter how he tried to deny it.

"Call it *hate sex*. I don't care, Giancarlo." She shrugged. "Whatever it is, whatever you need to call it to feel better about it, I want it, too."

"I beg your pardon?" Giancarlo's voice was a rough whisper that somehow sounded in Paige like a bellow.

It was the wine, Paige told herself as she stared back at him, her own words seeming to cavort between them on the heavily laden tabletop, making it impossible to see or hear much of anything else. Of course it was the wine—though she'd only had a few sips—and the lingering jet lag besides, though she didn't feel anything like tired at the moment.

Nothing else could possibly have made her say such things, she was sure, much less throw down the gauntlet to a battle she very much feared might be the end of her.

She opened her mouth to take it back, to laugh and claim she'd been kidding, to break the strange, taut spell that stretched between them and wrapped them tight together, caught somewhere in that arrested expression that transformed his beautiful face. But Giancarlo lifted an aristocratic hand that stopped her as surely as if he'd placed it over her mouth, and she knew she really shouldn't have shivered in a rush of dark delight at the very image.

"I find I'm not as trusting as I used to be," he told her, though *untrusting* wasn't how she would have described the wolfish look in his dark eyes then. "It is a personality flaw, I am sure. But I'm afraid you'll have to offer proof."

She was watching his mouth as if it was a show, which was only part of the reason Paige didn't understand what he'd said. She blinked. "Proof?"

"That this is not another one of your dirty little games

that will end up painting the front page of every godfor-saken gossip rag in existence." He lounged back in his chair, but his eyes were hot, and she had the notion that he was coiled to strike. "You understand my reticence, I'm sure."

"And I'd offer you my word," she said, not sure how she kept her tone so light, as if *dirty little games* hadn't pricked at her and hurt while it did, because he had no idea what kind of dirt she'd been drowning in back then, "but somehow, I'm betting that won't be enough for you."

"Sadly, no," he agreed. He sounded anything but sad. "Though it pains me to cast such aspersions on your char-acter, even if only by insinuation."

"Oh, that's what that look on your face is." Her tone was arch and if she hadn't known better, if she hadn't known it was impossible, she might have thought she was enjoying herself here. "It looks a bit more like glee than pain from this side of the table, I should tell you."

Giancarlo smiled, dark and intent. "I can't imagine why."

The night air seemed to shimmer in the space between them, in the flickering light of the candles and in the vel-vety dark that surrounded the table like an embrace. He settled even farther back in his chair and stretched his legs out again, like an indolent god awaiting a sacrifice, and Paige knew she should put a stop to this before it got out of control—but she didn't. The truth was she didn't want to stop it. She didn't want to do anything but this.

"Strip." It was a hoarse command, rich and dark, like the finest chocolate poured over her skin, and she should have been outraged by his arrogance. Instead, she wanted to bathe in it. In him.

Wasn't that always what she'd wanted?

She didn't pretend she hadn't heard him or that she didn't understand. "Here?"

"Right here." His dark gaze burned, gold and onyx, daring her. "Unless there is some new reason you refuse to obey me this time?"

"You mean, besides the fact that we're sitting outside? Where anyone could see us engaged in all manner of shocking acts? I thought you had a horror of public displays of anything."

"How shocking could a simple strip show be?" he asked, and there was something else in his gaze then, sharp and hard. "It has slipped your mind, perhaps, that the entire world has already seen us having sex. I doubt anything we do could possibly shock them now. Unless you've learned new tricks since I last saw you?"

"Nothing but the same old tricks here," she said, keeping her tone the same as it was, as if that slap of history hadn't made her feel dizzy at all. It was too bad nothing seemed to keep her from wanting him. She was that masochistic. "I'm sorry to disappoint you. Should I keep my clothes on?"

Paige saw that flash of fury in his gaze once more, but it melted into molten heat in the space of a heartbeat, as if they were both masochists here. Somehow, that made her feel better.

"No," he said in a low voice. "You most certainly should not."

"Then it seems I have no choice but to obey you, as promised," she said quietly. "Despite your poor, apparently unshockable neighbors and the things they might see."

"The closest resident aside from my mother is over forty miles away tonight," Giancarlo said, as if impatient. But she could see the fire in his gaze. She could practically taste his need. "Your modesty is safe enough, such as it is. What other excuses do you have?" He let out a bark of something not quite laughter. "We might as well address them all now and be done with them."

"What happens after I strip for you?" Paige asked, almost idly, but she was already pushing her chair back with a too-loud scrape against the stones, then rising to her feet. "This is daring, indeed, to get me naked and then leave me standing here all alone. Is that the plan? It's something of a waste, I'd think."

"First we'll worry about whatever cameras you might have secreted on that body of yours," he told her, and if she hadn't known him she might have thought him cold. Unmoved by all of this. But that wild, uninhibited lover she'd known lurked there in the sensual curve of his lips, that gleaming thing deep in his gaze. Giancarlo might hate her, but he wanted her as much as she did him. And Paige clung to that, perhaps harder than she should have. She clung to it as if it was everything and opted not to listen to the alarms that rang out in her at the thought. "Then we'll worry about what to do with that body."

"Whatever you say, Count Alessi," she murmured, which was as close to obedient as she'd ever come. She saw a certain appreciation for that—or for her wry tone, more like—in his dark eyes, but then it was time to dance.

Because that was what this was. Paige didn't pretend otherwise. The only music was his breath and hers, the only audience the primeval explosion of stars above them. She hadn't danced in years. Ten years, in fact. But she could feel him in her feet, in her hips. In the glorious stretch of her arms over her head. Her pulse and her breath. She could feel him everywhere, better than any sound track with her own hopeful heartbeat like the kick of drums, and she danced.

She poured herself into each undulation of her hips, each exultant reach of her hands. She'd kicked off her shoes when she'd stood and she curled her toes down hard into the smooth stones beneath her, feeling what was left of the day's heat against her soles and that wildfire that only arced higher between the two of them as she moved. She tried her best to catch the sensation in the movement of her hips, her legs, her torso. She took her time peeling off her trousers, managing to kick them aside with a flourish, and then she moved closer to him as she rid herself of her shirt, as if his intent expression beckoned her to him.

She took her time with her bra, offering her breasts to him when she finally dropped it at her side, and she smiled at the way he moved in his chair, his gaze a wild touch on her skin, so fierce it made her nipples pull taut. And she wasn't done. She kept up the dance, the ecstatic dance, and she made it her apology, her regret. She told him all about her love and her silly, shattered hopes with every move she made, and when she stepped out of her panties she didn't know which one of them was breathing more heavily.

Paige only knew that he was standing, too. And that she was naked before him and she still wasn't done.

Naked in the Tuscan night, she danced for all those dreams she'd let carry her away as a girl. For the dream she'd destroyed with a single phone call and a cashed check ten years ago, and none of it worth the sacrifice, in the end. It was like skinny-dipping, warm and cool at once, the summer air a sensual caress against her flesh. She danced for the joy she'd only ever felt in this man's presence, the laughter she still missed, the love she'd squandered for good reasons that seemed nothing but sad in retrospect.

She danced and she danced, and she might have danced all night, but Giancarlo swept her into his arms instead, high against his chest, and that was like a much better dance. Hotter and more intense, and then his mouth came down on hers, claiming her and destroying her that easily.

He came down hard on top of her and she loved it. That lean, hard body of his crushing her with his delicious weight, his narrow hips keeping her legs apart, and it took her a moment to realize that he'd moved them over to one of the sun chaises that sat around the gleaming, sleek pool that jutted out from the loggia toward the vineyards. And that he'd lost his jacket in the move.

And he looked as gorgeously undone as she felt, and very nearly as wild.

"Giancarlo," she whispered, the dance still running madly in her veins, almost as addictive as he was. "Don't stop."

"I give the orders, not you," he growled, but his lips were curved when they took hers all over again.

And then everything slowed down. Turned to honey, thick and sweet.

Giancarlo feasted on her as if she were the gourmet meal his chefs had prepared for him, and beneath his talented mouth she felt almost that cherished, that perfect. She wanted his naked skin pressed to hers more than she could remember wanting anything else, ever, but he kept her too busy to peel his shirt back from his strong shoulders.

He kissed her until her head spun, and then he followed the line of her neck, tasting her and muttering dark things in Italian that she told herself she was happy she didn't understand.

Even if they moved in her like music, dark and compelling, sex and magic and *Giancarlo,* at long last.

He found her breasts and pulled one of the proud nipples deep into his hot mouth, and she didn't care what he *said.* Or in what language. She arched into him, mindless and needy, and he punished and praised her with his lips, his tongue, the scrape of his teeth. He played with her until she begged him to stop and then he only laughed and kept going, sending a catapult of pure wildfire straight down into her core.

She thought for a panicky, wondrous second that he might throw her straight over the edge with only this—

But he stopped, as diabolical as ever, raising his dark head to take in the flushed heat on her face and all down her neck. Her sensual distress. Her driving need.

"This punishment appears to be far more effective than you imagined it would be, *cara*," he murmured, his voice another sensual shiver against her sensitive skin, with its echoes of the playfully wicked lover she'd met so long ago. "It's almost as if you forgot what I can do to you."

"Thank you for the harsh lesson, Count Alessi," she whispered, not trying too hard to keep her tone anything approaching respectful when she was this close to the edge. "May I have another?"

He laughed, and she did too, and she didn't know if she'd been kidding or if she'd meant it when he returned his attention to her body, shifting to crawl down farther. If these were harsh lessons indeed, or gifts. He left a shimmering trail of fire from her breasts to her belly, and when he paused there, his breath fanning out over the hungriest part of her, Paige realized she was breathing as heavily as if she was running a race. The marathon he'd mentioned earlier, God help her.

"You'd better hold on," he warned her, dark and stirring and *right there* against her sex. "I'm going to stop when I'm done, not when you are."

And then he simply bent his head and licked his way into her.

Paige ignited.

She went from the mere sensation of burning straight into open flame. She couldn't seem to catch her breath. She arched against the exquisite torment of his wickedly clever mouth, or she tried to escape it, and either way, it didn't matter. He gripped her hips in his strong hands and he tasted her molten heat as if it was his own greatest pleasure, and before she knew it she was bucking against him, her hands buried deep in his thick, dark hair.

Calling out his name like a prayer into the night.

And he was as good as his word. He didn't stop. He didn't wait for her to come back down, to come back to herself. He simply kept on tasting her, settling in and taking his time, laughing against her tender flesh when she begged him to stop, laughing more when she begged him to keep on going.

The fire poured back into her, hotter and higher than before, and then he plunged two fingers deep inside of her and threw her over the side of the world. Again.

This time, when she shuddered her way back to earth, Giancarlo had moved off her to stand beside her, his hard hands impatient as he pulled her to her feet. It took her a moment to realize he'd finally stripped but she had no time to appreciate it, because he was lying back on the chaise and pulling her down to sit astride him.

"I want to watch," he told her, his voice dark and nearly grim with need, and it lit that flame inside of her all over again.

And then he simply curled his strong hands around her hips the way he had a thousand times before, the way she'd never dreamed he would again, and thrust home.

CHAPTER SIX

He was inside her again. At last.

Finally.

Giancarlo thought the sensation—far better than all his pale memories across these long years, far better than his own damned hand had ever been—might make him become a religious man.

She was so damned hot, molten and sweet and slick and *his,* and she still held him so tightly, so snugly, it was nearly his undoing. Her hair was that deep black ink with hints of fire and it tumbled all around her in a seductive tousle, falling to those breasts of hers, still high and pert, the tips already tight again and begging for his mouth.

Paige looked soft and stunned, exactly how he liked her best, exactly how he remembered her, and then she made everything better by reaching out to prop her hands against his chest. The shift in position made her sink down even farther on him, making them both groan.

He let his hands travel back to cup the twin globes of her delectable bottom, and tested the depth of her, the friction. God help him, but she was perfect. She had always been perfect. The perfect fit. The perfect fire.

Perfect for him.

Giancarlo had somehow forgotten that, in all the long years since he'd last been inside her. He'd convinced himself he'd exaggerated this as some kind of excuse for his own idiocy—that she'd been nothing more than a pretty girl with a dancer's body and all the rest had been a kind of madness that would make no sense if revisited.

But this was no exaggeration. This was pure, hot, bliss. This was that same true perfection he remembered, at last.

Paige looked down at him, her gaze unreadable. Bright and something like awed. And then she started to move.

He had watched her dance ten years ago, and he had wanted her desperately. He'd watched her dance tonight, that astonishing performance for him alone, equal parts sensual and inviting, and he'd thought he might die if he didn't find a way inside her. But nothing compared to *this* dance. Nothing came close.

She braced herself against him, her hands splayed wide over his pectoral muscles, while her hips set a lazy, shattering, insistent rhythm against his. And Giancarlo was lost.

He forgot about revenge. He forgot about their past. Her deceit, his foolish belief in her. All the terrible lies. The damned pictures themselves, grainy and humiliating. He lost his plans in the slide of her body against his, the sleek thrill that built in him with every rocking motion she made. Every life-altering stroke of the hardest part of him so deep, so very deep, in all of her soft heat.

"Make me come," he ordered her, in a stranger's deep growl. He saw her skin prickle at the sound of it, saw the way she pulled her lower lip between her teeth as if she was fighting back the same wave of sensation he was. "Make it good."

Not that it could be anything but good. Not that it ever had been. This was a magical thing, this wild, hot fire that was only theirs. He could feel it every time he sank within her. He knew it every time he pulled back. He felt it in the sure pace she set with her hips, the tight hold of her flesh against his. He wanted it to go on forever, the way he'd thought it would when he'd met her that first time.

The way it should have, that little voice that was still in love with her, that had never been anything but in love with her, whispered deep inside him.

But she was following his orders and this was no time for regrets. She moved against him, lush and lovely, her hips a sinuous dance, a well-cast spell of longing and lust and too many other things he refused to name. He'd thought he'd lost her forever and yet she was here, moving above him, her lovely body on display because he'd wanted it, holding him so deep inside her he couldn't tell where he ended and she began. He didn't want to know.

"Your wish is my command, my count," she teased him, her voice a husky little dream, and then she did something complicated with her hips and the world turned to flames all around them.

When he finally exploded, a bright rush of fire turned some kind of comet, rocketing over the edge of the night, he heard her call out his name.

And then follow him into bliss.

Giancarlo did not welcome reality when it reasserted itself.

Paige lay slumped over him, her face buried in his neck, while he was still deep inside of her. He opted not to think about how easy it was to hold her, or how she still seemed to have been crafted especially to fit in his arms, exactly this way. It took him much longer than it should have to get his breathing under control again. He held her the way a lover might, the way he always had before, and stared out over the top of her head at the faint lights on distant hills and the smear of starlight above.

He wished he didn't care about the past. More than that, he wished he could trust her the way he had once. He wished so many things, and yet all of the stars were fixed tonight, staring down at him from their cold positions, and he knew better.

Paige was an accident waiting to happen. He'd been caught up in that accident once—he wouldn't subject himself to it again. Even he wasn't foolish enough to walk into the same trap twice. No matter that it felt like glory made flesh to touch her again, like coming home after too long away.

He would learn to live without that, too. He had before.

She shifted against him, and he felt the brush of her lips over his skin and told himself it was calculated. That everything about her was calculated. There was no use remembering the afternoons they'd spent curled around each other in his huge bed surrounded by the Malibu sea. When she'd tasted him everywhere with her eyes closed, as if she couldn't help herself, as if her affection was as elemental as the ocean beyond his windows or the sky above and she had no choice but to sink into it with all of her senses.

That had been an act. This was an act. He needed to remember it.

But that didn't mean he couldn't enjoy the show.

"You've obviously been practicing," he said, to be horrible. To remind them both that this was here and now, not ten years back. "Quite a lot, I'd say, were I to hazard a guess."

He felt her tense against him, but almost thought he'd imagined it when she sat up a moment later, displaying her typical offhanded grace. And then she smiled slightly as she looked down at him.

"I was about to compliment you on the same thing," she said, a brittle sort of mischief and something else lighting up her gaze. "You must have slept with a thousand women to do that so well! My congratulations. Especially as I would have said there weren't ten women you could sleep with in a hundred miles, much less a thousand. The privileges of wealth, I presume?"

"You're hilarious." But he couldn't help the crook of his mouth. "I have them flown in from Rome, of course."

"Of course." She wrinkled her nose at him, and it was as dangerous as it had been earlier. It made him want things he knew he couldn't have. He couldn't have them, and more to the point, she couldn't give them. Hadn't he learned anything? "You realize, Giancarlo, that people might get the wrong idea. They might begin to think you're a playboy whore."

"They won't."

"Because you tell them so?" She shook her head, her expression serious though her mysterious eyes laughed at him. "I think that tactic only works with me. And not very well."

"Because," he said, his hands moving to her bottom again, then higher along the tempting indentation in her lovely back to tug her down to him, "a man is only a playboy whore when he appears to be having too much of a certain kind of uncontrolled fun in public. I can do all the same things in private and it doesn't count. Didn't you know?"

Her attention dropped to his mouth and he wanted it there. He was already hardening within her again and she shifted restlessly against him as if she encouraged it, making the fire inside him leap to new life that easily.

"It all counts," she breathed. "Or none of it does."

"Then I suppose that makes us all whores, doesn't

it?" he asked. He indulged himself and sank his hands deep into her hair, holding her head fast, as he tested the depth of her again and found her hotter around him. Wetter. Better, somehow, than before. That quickly, he was like steel. "But let's be clear. How many lovers have you taken in the last ten years?"

"Less than your thousand," she said, her voice a thin little thing, as her hips met his greedily. Deliciously. He grunted, and then pulled out to flip them around, coming down over her again and drawing her legs around his waist. He teased her heat with the tip of his hardness, and he didn't know what it was that drove him then, but he didn't let her pull him into her.

"How many?" he asked. He had no idea why he cared. He didn't care. He'd imagined it a thousand times and it scraped at him and it changed nothing either way. But he couldn't seem to stop. "Tell me."

Her eyes moved to his, then away, and they looked blue in the shadows. "What does it matter? Whatever number I pick, you'll think the worst of me."

"I already think the worst of you," he said, the way he might have crooned love words a lifetime ago, and he couldn't have said what he wanted here. To hurt her? Or himself? To make this all worse? Or was this simply his way of reminding them both who they were? "Why don't you try the truth?"

"None," she said, and there was an odd expression on her face as she said it. He might have called it vulnerable, were she someone else. "I told you there were no new tricks."

It took another beat for him to process that, and then something roared in him, a primal force that was like some kind of howl, and he thought he shook though he knew he held himself perfectly still.

"Is that a joke?" But he was whispering. He barely knew his own voice.

Her wide mouth twisted and her gaze was dark with something he didn't want to understand. Something that couldn't possibly be real.

"Yes," she said, her voice broken and fierce at once. "Ha ha, what a joke. I meant ten. Twenty. How many lovers do you imagine I've taken, Giancarlo? What number proves I'm who you think I am?"

He heard her voice break slightly as she asked the question, and a kind of ripple went through her lush body. He felt it. This time when she urged him into her, he went, slick and hard and even better than before, making him mutter a curse and press his forehead to hers. And he didn't have the slightest idea if this was his form of an apology, or hers.

"I don't care one way or the other," he lied, and he didn't want to talk about this any longer. He didn't want to revisit all those images he'd tortured himself with over the years. Because his sad little secret was that he'd never imagined her in prison, the way he'd told her he had. He'd imagined her wrapped around some other man exactly like this and he'd periodically searched the internet to see if he could find any evidence that she was out there somewhere, doing it with all that same joy and grace that had undone him.

And it had killed him, every time. It still killed him.

So he took it out on her instead, in the best way possible. He set a hard pace, throwing them headfirst into that raging thing that consumed them both, and he laughed against the side of her neck when she couldn't do anything but moan out her surrender.

He held on, building that perfect wildness all over again, making her thrash and keen, and when he thought he couldn't take it any longer he reached between them and pressed hard against the center of her need, making her shatter all around him.

And he rode her until he could throw himself into that shattering, too. Until he could forget the truth he'd heard in her voice when she'd told him there hadn't been anyone since him, because he couldn't handle that—or what he'd seen on her face that he refused to believe. *He refused.*

He rode her until he could forget everything but this. Everything but her. Everything they built between them in this marvelous fire.

Until he lost himself all over again.

"Violet is asking for you," Giancarlo said.

Paige had heard him coming from a long way off. First the Jeep, the engine announcing itself high on the hill and only getting louder as it wound its way down toward her cottage. Then the slam of the driver's door. The thud of the cottage's front door, and then, some minutes later, the slide of the glass doors that led out to where she sat, curled up beneath a graceful old oak tree with her book in her lap.

"That sounds like an accusation," she said mildly, putting her book aside. He stood on the terrace with his hands on his lean hips, frowning at her. "Of course she's asking for me. I'm her assistant. She might be on vacation here, but I'm not."

"She needs to learn how to relax and handle her own affairs," he replied, somewhat darkly. Paige climbed to her feet, brushing at the skirt she wore, and started toward him. It was impossible not feel that hunger at the sight of him, deep inside her, making her too warm, too soft.

"Possibly," she said, trying to concentrate on something, anything but the sensual spell he seemed to weave simply by existing. "But I'm not her therapist, I'm her personal assistant. When she learns how to relax and handle her own affairs, I'm out of a job."

Her heart set up its usual clatter at his proximity, worse the closer she got to him, and she didn't understand how that could still happen. They'd been here almost a week. It should have settled down by now. She should have started to grow immune to him, surely. After all, she already knew how this would end. Badly. Unlike the last time, when she'd been so blissfully certain it would be the one thing in her life that ended well, this time she knew better. Their history was like a crystal ball, allowing her to see the future clearly.

Maybe too clearly. Not that it seemed to matter.

She stopped when she was near him but not too near him, and felt that warm thing in the vicinity of her heart when he scowled. He reached over and tugged her closer, so he could land a hard kiss on her mouth. *Like a mark of possession,* she thought, *more than an indication of desire*—but she didn't care.

It deepened, the way it always deepened. Giancarlo muttered something and angled his head, and when he finally pulled back she was wound all around him and flushed and there was that deep male satisfaction stamped all over his face.

"Later," he told her, like a promise, as if she'd been the one to start this.

And in this past week, Paige had learned that she'd take this man any way she could have him. She imagined that said any number of unflattering things about her, but she didn't care.

"I might be busy later," she told him loftily.

He smiled that hard smile of his that made her ache,

and he didn't look particularly concerned. "I will take that chance."

And she would let him, she knew. Not because he told her to. Not because he was holding anything over her head. But because she was helpless before her own need, even though she knew perfectly well it would ruin her all over again....

Later, she told herself. *I'll worry about it later.*

Because *later* was going to be all the years she got to live through on the other side of this little interlude, when he was nothing but a memory all over again. And she wasn't delusional enough to imagine that there was any possibility that when this thing with Giancarlo ended he might permit her to remain with Violet, in any capacity. He was as likely to fall to his knees and propose marriage.

She moved around him and into the house then, not wanting him to read that epic bit of silliness on her face, when that notion failed to make her laugh at herself the way it should have. When it made everything inside of her clutch hopefully instead. *You are such a fool,* she chided herself.

But then again, that wasn't news.

Paige swept up her bag and hung it over her shoulder, then followed Giancarlo out to his Jeep. He climbed in and turned the key, and she clung to the handle on her side of the vehicle as he bumped his way up the old lane and then headed toward the *castello* in the distance.

It was another beautiful summer's day, bright and perfect with the olive trees a silvery presence on either side of the lane that wound through the hills toward Violet, and Paige told herself it was enough. This was enough. It was more than she'd ever imagined could happen with Giancarlo after what she'd done, and why did she want to ruin it with thoughts of *more*?

But the sad truth was, she didn't know how to be anything but greedy when it came to this man. She wanted all of him, not the parts of himself he doled out so carefully, so sparingly. Not when she could feel he kept so much of himself apart.

She'd woken the morning after that first night to find herself in his bed. Alone. He'd left her there without so much as a note, and she'd lectured herself about the foolishness of her hurt feelings. She'd told herself she should count herself lucky he hadn't tossed her out his front door at dawn, naked.

What she told herself and what she actually went right on feeling, of course, were not quite the same thing.

Modify your expectations, girl, she'd snapped at herself on the walk down the hill to her cottage. The birds had been singing joyfully, the sun had been cheerful against her face, she was in *Italy* of all places, and Giancarlo had made love to her again and again throughout the night. He could call it whatever he wanted. She would hold it in her battered little heart and call it what it had meant to her.

Because she hadn't lied to him. She hadn't touched another man since him, and she'd grown to accept the fact she never would. At first it had hurt too much. She'd seen nothing but Giancarlo—and more important, his back, on that last morning when he'd walked away from her rather than talk about what had happened, what she'd done. Then she'd started working for Violet and it had seemed as if Giancarlo was everywhere, in pictures, in emails, in conversation. Paige had had the very acute sense that so much as going out to dinner with another man was some kind of treason—which she'd known was absurd. Beyond absurd, given the way in which she'd betrayed him. She'd made certain he hated her. He'd walked away from her without a single backward glance. Why should he care what she did?

And yet somehow, each of these ten years had crept by and he was still the only man she'd ever slept with. She'd been unable to contain the small, humming thing inside her then as that thought had kept her company on her walk. It had felt a little bit too much like a kind of silly joy she ought to have known better than to indulge.

But he'd turned up that night, his face drawn as if he'd fought a great battle with himself, and he hadn't seemed interested in talking about whether he'd lost or won. He'd led her up her stairs, thrown her on her bed, and kept them up for another night—this time, she'd noted, with the condoms they'd failed to use before.

They hadn't talked about that first night and its lack of birth control. Just like ten years ago, they hadn't talked about a thing.

And that was how it had been since her arrival, Paige thought now, as they drew closer to the *castello*. She'd never spent much time wondering what it felt like to be a rich man's *kept woman* before now. What she thought people in this part of the world might call a *mistress*. But she imagined it must be something like this past week.

Nothing but the pleasures of their flesh. No unpleasant topics, save the odd bout of teasing that never quite landed a hard punch. Nothing but sex and food and sex again, until she felt glutted on it. Replete. Able to know him at a touch, taste him when he wasn't there, scent him on any breeze.

The last time she'd felt so deeply a part of her own body, her own physical space, she'd been dancing more hours of the day than she'd slept.

She didn't tell him that, either. That she filled these golden, blue-skied days with dancing, as if the first dancing she'd done on that initial night with him had freed her. Paige hadn't understood how lost she'd been until she found herself out in the field near her cottage, dancing in great, wide circles beneath the glorious Tuscan sky with tears running down her face and her arms stretched toward the sun. She wanted nothing more than to share that with him.

But Giancarlo drove the Jeep with the same ferocity he did everything else—except in bed, where he indulged every sense and took his sweet time—and with that same hard edge of his old dark fury beneath it.

Almost as if he, too, preferred the little fairy tale they'd been living this past week, where she existed purely to please him, and did, again and again.

Paige knew better than to ask him about it. Or to tell him the things that moved in her, sharp and sweet, in this place that felt more like home every day. This was a no-talking zone. This was a place of sun and sex and silence. It was the only possible way it could work.

Like all temporary things, all stolen moments, it could only be a secret, or it would implode.

"What have you been up to all this time?" Violet asked, peering at Paige from her position on one of the *castello*'s lovely couches, her iPad in her lap and her voice no more than mildly reproving. "I thought perhaps you'd been sucked into one of the olive groves, never to be seen again."

"You should have told me you needed me!" Paige exclaimed instead of answering the question. Because she didn't want to know what Violet would think about the help touching her son. She didn't want to risk her relationship with either one of them. "I thought I was giving you some much-needed time and space to yourself!"

"My dear girl," Violet said, sounding amused, "if I

wanted time and space to myself, I would have chosen a different life altogether."

Paige was too aware of Giancarlo's dark, brooding presence on the other side of the living room then, lounging there against the massive stone fireplace, supposedly scrolling through his phone's display. She was certain he was hanging on every word. Or did she simply want to be that important to him?

There was no answer to that. Not one that came without a good dose of pain in its wake.

"I'm here now," Paige said stoutly, trying to focus on the woman who had always been good to her, without all these complications and regrets. *Not that she'd give you the time of day if she knew who you really were,* that rough voice that was so much like her mother's snarled at her.

"Then I have two questions for you," Violet replied, snapping Paige back to the present. "Can you operate a manual transmission?"

That hadn't been what Paige was expecting, but that was Violet. Paige rolled with it. "I can."

It was, in fact, one of the few things she could say her mother had taught her. Even if it had been mostly so that Paige could drive the beat-up car she owned to pick her up, drunk and belligerent, from the rough bars down near the railroad tracks.

"And do you want to drive me to Lucca?" Violet smiled serenely when Giancarlo made an irritated sort of noise from the fireplace across the room and kept her eyes trained on Paige. "If memory serves, it has wonderful shopping. And I'm in the mood for an adventure."

"An adventure with attention or without?" Paige asked without missing a beat, though she was well aware it had been a long time since Violet had gone out on one of her excursions into the public without expecting attention from the people who would see her out and about.

"Without," Giancarlo snapped, from much closer by, and Paige had to control a little jump. She hadn't heard him move.

"With, of course," Violet said, as if he hadn't spoken. "No one has fawned over me in a whole week, and I require attention the way plants require sunlight, you know. It's how I maintain my youthful facade."

She said it as if she was joking, but in that way of hers that didn't actually allow for any argument. Not that it was Paige's place to argue. Her son, however, was a different story.

"You're one of the most famous women in the world," Giancarlo pointed out, and the dark thing Paige heard in his voice was a different animal than the one he used when he spoke to her. More exasperated, perhaps. Or more formal. "It's not safe for you to simply wander the streets alone."

"I won't be alone. I'll have Paige," Violet replied.

"And what, pray, will Paige do should you find yourself surrounded? Mobbed?" Giancarlo rolled his eyes. "Hold the crowd off with a smart remark or two?"

"I wouldn't underestimate the power of a smart remark," Paige retorted, glaring at him—but his gaze was on his mother.

"That was a long time ago," Violet said softly. With a wealth of compassion that made Paige stiffen in surprise and Giancarlo jerk back as if she'd slapped him. "I was a very foolish young woman. I underestimated the kind of interest there would be—not only in me, but in you. Your father was livid." She studied her son for a moment and then rose to her feet, smiling faintly at Paige. "We were in the south of France and I thought it would be a marvelous idea to go out and poke around the shops by myself. Giancarlo was four. And when the crowds surrounded us, he was terrified."

"The police were called," he said, furiously, Paige thought, though his voice was cold. "You had to be rescued by armed officials and you never went out without security again—and neither did I. I hope you haven't spent your life telling this story as if I was an overimaginative child who caused a fuss. It wasn't a monster in my closet. It was a pack of shouting cameramen and a mob of fans."

"The point is, my darling, you were four," Violet said quietly. "You are not four any longer. And while I flatter myself that I remain relevant, I am an old woman who has not commanded the attention of packs of paparazzi in a very long time. I'm perfectly capable of enjoying an afternoon with my assistant and, if you insist, *one* driver."

"And you wonder why I refuse to have children," he growled at her, and it took every shred of self-preservation Paige had to keep from reacting to that. To Giancarlo and the pain she could hear beneath the steel in his voice. "Why I would die before I'd subject another innocent to this absurd world of yours."

"I didn't wonder," Violet replied. "I knew. But I hoped you'd outgrow it."

"Mother—"

"I don't like being locked away in Italian castles, Giancarlo," she said, and there was steel in the way she said it, despite the smile she used. It was the famous star issuing a command, not a mother. "If you cast your memory back, you'll remember that I never have."

There was a strange tension in the room then. And though she knew better, though it would no doubt raise the suspicions of the woman who could read anyone,

standing right there beside her, Paige found herself looking to Giancarlo as if she could soothe him somehow. As
if he'd let her—

And she found that great darkness blazing in his eyes
as he slowly, slowly turned his attention from Violet to
her.

As if this was something she'd done, too.

Because, of course, she had. When he'd been far older
than four. And what she'd done to him hadn't been an
accident.

The truth of that almost knocked her sideways, and
she would never know how she remained standing. She
wanted to tell him everything, and who cared what Violet thought? She wanted to explain about her mother's
downward spiral. The money owed, the threats from the
horrible Denny, the fear and panic that she'd thought
were just the way life was. Because that was how it had
always been. Paige wanted him to understand—at last—
that she never, ever would have sacrificed him if she
hadn't believed she had no other choice. If she hadn't
been trapped and terrified herself, with only hideous
options on all sides.

But this wasn't the place and she knew—*she knew*—
he wouldn't want to hear it anyway. He didn't want to
know *why*. He only wanted her to pay.

He didn't realize that she had. That she still did. Every
moment since.

And so she stood there, she said nothing the way she'd
always said nothing and somehow she managed not to
fall to her knees. Somehow Paige managed not to break
into pieces. Somehow, she stared back at him as if she'd
never broken his heart and she wished, hard and fierce
and utterly pointless, that it were true.

"Don't worry," he said quietly, as if he was answering

his mother. All of that darkness in his gaze. All of the betrayal, the loss. The terrible grief. It made Paige's chest ache, so acutely that she forgot to worry that Violet would be able to sense it from a few feet away. So sharp and so deep she thought it might have been a mortal blow, and how could anyone hide that? "I remember everything."

CHAPTER SEVEN

LUCCA WAS A walled city, an old fortress turned pros-
perous market town, and it was enchanting. Paige dutifully followed Violet through the bustle of tiled red
roofs, sloped streets and the sheer tumult of such an ancient place, and told herself there was no reason at all
she should feel so unequal to the task she'd done so well
and well-nigh automatically for years.

But her heart wasn't with her in the colorful city. It
was back in the hills with the man she'd left there, with
that look on his face and too much dark grief in his gaze.

And the longer Violet lingered—going in and out of
every shop, pausing for cell phone photos every time she
was recognized, settling in for a long dinner in a restaurant where the chef came racing out to serenade her and
she was complimented theatrically for her few Italian
phrases, all while Paige looked on and/or assisted—the
more Paige wondered if the other woman was doing it
deliberately. As if she knew what was going on between
her son and her assistant.

But that was impossible, Paige kept telling herself.

This is called guilt, that caustic voice inside her snapped
as Violet flirted outrageously with the chef. *This is why
you're here. Why you work for his mother. Why you accept
how he treats you. You deserve it. You earned it.*

More than that, she missed him. One afternoon know-ing Giancarlo wasn't within reach, that there was no chance he'd simply appear and tumble her down onto the nearest flat surface, the way he'd done only yester-day with no advance warning, and she was a mess. If this was a preview of what her life was going to be like after this all ended, Paige thought as she handled Violet's bill and called for the car, she was screwed.

"Like that's anything new," she muttered under her breath as she climbed into the car behind Violet, nearly closing the heavy door on the still-grasping hands of the little crowd that had gathered outside the restaurant to adore her.

"Pardon?" Violet asked.

Paige summoned her smile. Her professional de-meanor, which she thought she'd last seen weeks ago in Los Angeles. "Did that do? Scratch the attention itch?"

"It did." Violet sat across from her in the dark, her gaze out the window as the car started out of the city. "Giancarlo is a solitary soul. He doesn't understand that some people recharge their batteries in different ways than he does. Not everyone can storm about a lonely field and feel recharged."

Said the woman who had never passed a crowd she couldn't turn into a fan base with a few sentences and a smile. Paige blinked, amazed at her churlishness even in her own head, and found Violet's calm gaze on hers.

"You're an extrovert." Paige said evenly. "I'm sure he knows that by now. Just as he likely knows that therefore, his own needs are different from yours."

"One would think," Violet agreed in her serene, untrou-bled way, which shouldn't have sent a little shiver of warn-ing down Paige's back. "But then, the most interesting men are not always in touch with what they need, are they?"

Violet didn't speak much after that, yet Paige didn't feel as if she could breathe normally until the car pulled off the country road and started along the winding drive into the estate. And she was impatient—the most impatient she'd ever been in Violet's presence, though she tried valiantly to disguise it—as she helped the older woman into the *castello* and oversaw the staff as they sorted out her purchases.

And only when she was finally in the car again and headed toward her cottage did Paige understand what had been beating at her all day, clutching at her chest and her throat and making her want to scream in the middle of ancient Italian piazzas. Guilt, yes, but that was a heavy thing, a spiked weight that hung on her. The rest of it was panic.

Because any opportunity Giancarlo had to reflect on what was happening between them—not revenge, not the comeuppance he'd obviously planned—was the beginning of the end. She knew it, deep inside. She'd seen it in his eyes this morning.

And when she got to her cottage and found not only it but the house above it dark, it confirmed her fears.

Paige stood there in the dark outside her cottage long after the driver's car disappeared into the night, staring up the hill, willing this shadow or that to separate from the rest and become Giancarlo. She was too afraid to think about what might happen if this was it. If that kiss he'd delivered in the garden was their last.

Too soon, she thought desperately, or perhaps that was the first prayer she'd dared make in years. *It's too soon.*

She stared up the side of the hill as if that would call him to her, somehow. But the only thing around her was the soft summer night, pretty and quiet. Still and empty, for miles around.

When she grew too cold and he still didn't appear, she made her way inside, feeling more punished by his absence than by anything else that had happened between them. Paige entertained visions of marching up the hill and taking what she wanted, or at least finding him and seeing for herself what had happened in her absence today, but the truth was, she didn't dare. She was still so uncertain of her welcome.

Would he throw back the covers and yank her into his arms if she appeared at his bedside? Or would he send her right back out into the night again, with a cruel word or two as her reward? Paige found she was too unsure of the answer to test it.

There were red flags everywhere, she acknowledged as she got ready for bed and crawled beneath her sheets. Red flags and dark corners, and nothing safe. But maybe what mattered was that she knew that, this time. She'd known the moment she'd decided to apply for that job with Violet. She'd always known.

She would have to learn to live with that, too.

Later that night, Paige woke with a sudden start when a lean male form crawled into her bed, hauling her into his arms.

Giancarlo. Of course.

But her heart was already crashing against her ribs as he rolled so she was beneath him. Excitement. Relief. The usual searing hunger, sharper than usual this time.

"Why didn't you come to me?" he gritted at her, temper and need and too many other dark and hungry things in his voice. Then the scrape of his teeth against the tender flesh of her neck, making her shudder.

Paige didn't want to think about the contours of her fears now, her certainty he'd finished with this. With her. Not now, while he was braced above her, his body so familiar and hot against hers, making the night blaze with the wild need that was never far beneath the surface. Never far at all.

Not even when she thought she'd lost him again.

"I thought you'd gone to bed already." *I didn't know if you'd want me to come find you,* she thought, but wisely kept to herself. "All of your lights were out."

She thought she saw a certain self-knowledge move over his face then, but it was gone so quickly she was sure she must have imagined it.

"Did you have a lovely day out with my mother?" he asked in a tone she wasn't foolish enough to imagine was friendly, his dark eyes glittering in the faint light from the rising moon outside her windows. "Filled with her admirers, exactly as she wished?"

"Of course." Paige ran her hands from his hard jaw to the steel column of his neck, as if trying to imprint the shape of him on her palms. Trying to make certain that if this was the last time, she'd remember it. That it couldn't be snatched from her, not entirely. "When Violet decrees we are to have fun, that is precisely what we have. No mere crowd would dare defy the crown jewel of the Hollywood establishment."

Giancarlo didn't laugh. He shifted his body so he was hard against her and she melted the way she always did, ready to welcome him no matter his mood or hers, no matter the strange energy that crackled from him tonight, no matter the darkness that seemed wrapped around him even as he wound himself around her.

There were other words for what she was with this man, she knew, words she hadn't heard in a long time but still remembered all too well. Words she'd dismissed as the unhealthy rantings of the worst person she'd ever known, the person who had taken everything she'd wanted from her—but it turned out dismissing them wasn't the same thing as erasing them.

Even so, the hollow, gnawing thing that had sat inside her all day and made her feel so panicked was gone, because he was here. She filled it with his scent, his touch, his bold possession.

Him. Giancarlo.

The only man she'd ever touched. The only man she'd ever loved.

And this was the only way she could tell him any of that. With her body. Paige shifted so he was flush against her entrance and hooked her legs over his hips, letting him in. Loving him in the only way she knew. In the only way he'd let her.

"Maybe that didn't always work out when you were a child," she whispered, hoping he couldn't read too much emotion in her eyes, across her face. "But my relationship with Violet is much easier. She pays, I agree, the end."

Giancarlo bent his head to press hot, open kisses along the ridge of her collarbone. Paige moved restlessly, hungrily against him, tilting her head back to give him greater access. To give him anything—everything—he wanted.

Because this won't last forever, that harsh voice that was too much an echo of her mother's reminded her. That was what today had taught her. There were no fairy tales. This situation had an expiration date, and every moment she had with him was one moment closer to the end.

"In a way," Giancarlo said, still too dark, still too rough, his mouth against her skin so Paige could feel the rumble of his words inside of her as he spoke, "that is every relationship that Violet has."

She heard that same tense grief that had been in him in the *castello* that morning and this time, no one was watching. She could soothe him, or try. She ran her fingers through his thick hair and smiled when he pressed into her touch, like a very large cat.

"I don't think it can be easy to be a great figure," Paige said after a moment, concentrating on the feel of his scalp beneath her fingertips, the drag of his thick hair as she moved her hands through it, the exquisite sensation of stroking him. "Too many expectations. Too much responsibility to something far bigger than oneself. The constant worry that it will be taken away. But it must be harder still to be that person's child."

He shifted away from her, propping himself up on his elbows, though he kept himself cradled there between her thighs, his arousal a delicious weight against her softness. A promise. The silence stretched out and his face was in shadow, so all she could see was the glitter of his dark gold eyes, and the echo of it deep inside her.

"It's not hard," he said, and she'd never heard that tone before, had she? Clipped and resigned at once. And yet somehow, that pit in her belly yawned open again as he spoke. "As long as you remember that she is always playing a role. The *grande dame* as benevolent mother. The living legend as compassionate parent. The great star whose favorite role of all is *mom*. When she was younger there were different roles threaded into the mix, but the same principle applied. You learn this as a child in a thousand painful ways and you vow, if you are at all wise, never to inflict it on another. To let it end with you."

Paige tried to imagine Giancarlo as a small boy, all stubborn chin and fathomless eyes, and ached for him, though that didn't explain her nervousness. It was something in the way he held himself apart from her, a certain danger rippling down the length of his body, as hard and as steel-hewn as he was. It was the way he watched her, too still, too focused.

"I'm sorry," she said, though she wanted to say so much more. She didn't dare. Just like before, when she'd stood outside and wanted him and had known better than to go and find him, she was too uncertain. "That can't have been easy."

"Is that sympathy for me, *cara*? Don't bother."

He wasn't quite scoffing at her. Not quite, though his face went fierce in the darkness, edging toward cruel the way he'd been in the beginning, and she found she was bracing herself—unable to open her mouth and stop him. Unable to defend herself at all. *Whatever he's about to say,* that hard voice reminded her, like another slap, *you deserve.*

"Here is what I learned from my mother, the great actress," Giancarlo said. "That she is a mystery, unknowable even to herself. That she prefers it that way. That intimacy is anathema to her because it cannot be controlled, it cannot be directed, it cannot cut to print when she is satisfied with her performance. It is one long take with no rehearsal and no do-overs, and she goes to great lengths indeed to avoid it."

Paige wasn't sure why she felt so stricken then, so stripped raw when he wasn't talking about her—but then he moved again, dropping his weight against her to whisper in her ear, hot and close and dark. So very dark.

You deserve this, she told herself. *Whatever it is.*

"I want a woman I can trust, *Paige*," he said with a ruthless inevitability. And it didn't even hurt. It was like a deep slice of a sharp blade. She knew he'd cut her and now there was only the wait for blood. For the pain that would surely follow. And he wasn't finished. "A woman I can know inside and out. A woman who carries no secrets, who does not hide herself away from me or from the world, who never plays a role. A woman who wants a partner, not an audience."

"Giancarlo." She felt torn apart even though he was holding her close. Wrecked as surely as if he'd thrown her from the roof of the towering *castello*. "Please."

But the worst part was, he knew what he was doing. She'd seen it in the cast of his sensual mouth. She'd felt it in the way he'd very nearly trembled as he'd held himself above her.

He knew he was hurting her. And he kept going.

"I want a woman I can believe when she tells me she loves me," he said, raw and fierce and she knew she deserved that, she knew she did, even though it felt a little bit like dying. And then he lifted his head to look her straight in the eyes, making it that much worse. "And that can never be you, can it? It never was. It never will be."

Later, she thought she might take that apart and live awhile in the misery he'd packed into those last two sentences. Later, she thought she might cry for days and check herself for scars, the way she'd done ten years ago. But that was later.

Tonight Paige thought the pain in him was far greater than the hurt he'd caused—that she deserved, that voice kept telling her, and she agreed no matter how it cut her up—and she couldn't bear it.

She didn't care if he still hated her, even now, after another week in his bed when he'd tasted every part of her and had to have recognized the sheer honesty in her response to him. She told herself she didn't care about that at all and some part of her believed it.

Or wanted to believe it.

But worrying about that was for later, too. Later, when she could put herself together again. Later, when she could think about something other than the man who stretched over her and broke her heart, again and again and again. Because he could.

"Giancarlo," she said again, with more force this time. "Stop talking."

And he surrendered with a groan, thrusting deep and hard inside of her where there was nothing but the two of them—that shimmering truth that was only theirs, wild and dizzying and hotter every time—and that perfect, wondrous fire that swept them both away in its glory.

And Paige did her best to make them both forget.

Two more weeks passed, slow and sweet. The Tuscan summer started to edge toward the coming fall. The air began to feel crisp in the mornings, and the sky seemed bluer. And if she'd allowed herself to think about such things, Paige might have believed that the tension between her and Giancarlo was easing, too—all that heavy grief mellowing, turning blue like the sky, gold like the fields, lighter and softer with age.

Or perhaps she'd taught them both how to forget.

Whatever it was, it worked. No more did she spend her days trapped in her isolated cottage, available only to him and only when he wanted—and she told herself she didn't miss it, all that forced proximity and breathlessness. Of course she didn't miss it.

Paige's days looked a great deal as they had back home. She met with Violet most mornings, and helped her plan out her leisure time. Violet was particularly fond of day trips to various Italian cities to soak in all the art and culture and fashion with a side helping of adulation from the locals, which she often expedited by taking Giancarlo's helicopter that left from the roof of the *castello* and kicked up such a ruckus when it returned it could be heard for miles around.

"I've always preferred a big entrance," Violet had murmured the first time, that famous smile of hers on her lips as the helicopter touched down.

But when Violet was in between her trips—which meant days of spa treatments and dedicated lounging beneath artfully placed umbrellas at the side of the *castello*'s private pool instead—Paige was left to her own devices, which usually meant she was left to Giancarlo's.

One day he stopped the Jeep the moment it was out of sight of the *castello*'s stout tower and knelt down beside the passenger door, pulling her hips to his mouth and licking his way into Paige right there—making her sob out his name into the quiet morning, so loud it startled the birds from the nearby trees. Another time he drove them out to one of the private lakes that dotted the property and they swam beneath the hot sun, then brought each other to a shuddering release in the shallow end, Giancarlo holding her to him as she took advantage of the water's buoyancy to make him groan.

Other times, they talked. He told her of his father's dreams for this land, its long history and his own plans to monetize it while conserving it, that it might last for many more generations. He showed her around the Etruscan ruins that cropped up in the oddest spots and demonstrated, as much as possible, that a man who knew the ins and outs of three thousand acres in such extraordinary detail seemed something like magical when the landscape in question was a woman's body. *Her* body.

Paige didn't know which she treasured more. His words or his body. But she held them to her like gifts, and she tried not to think about what she deserved, what she knew she had coming to her. She tried to focus on what she had in her hands, instead.

One lazy afternoon they lay together in the warm sun, the sweet breeze playing over their heated skin. Paige propped her chin against his chest and looked into his eyes and it was dizzying, the way it was always dizzying. And then he smiled at her without a single stray shadow in his gorgeous eyes, and it was as if the world slammed to a stop and then started in the other direction.

"I saw you dancing in the garden the other night," he said.

There was no reason to blush. She told herself the heat she felt move over her was the sun, the leftover fire of the way he'd torn her to pieces only moments before, and nothing more.

"I haven't danced in a long while," she said, and she wanted to tear her gaze away from his, but she didn't. Or she couldn't. He ran his hand through her hair, slow and sweet, and she was afraid of the things he could see in her. And so afraid of the things she wanted.

"Why not?"

And Paige didn't know how to answer that. How to tell him the why of it without blundering straight into all the land mines they'd spent these weeks avoiding. That they'd managed to avoid entirely after that night she'd come back late from Lucca.

I want a woman I can trust, he'd said, and she wanted him to trust her. She might not deserve his trust, but she wanted it.

"I was good," she said after a moment, because that was true enough, "but I wasn't *amazing.* And there were so many other dancers who were as good as I was, but wanted it way more than I did."

Especially after he'd left and she hadn't had the heart

for it any longer, or anything else involving the body she'd used to betray the one man she'd ever given it to. She'd auditioned for one more gig and her agent had told her they'd said it was like watching a marionette. That had been her last audition. Her last dance, period.

Because once she'd lost Giancarlo, she'd lost interest in the only other thing she'd had that'd ever had any meaning in her life. Her mother had descended even further into that abyss of hers and Paige had simply been *lost*. And when she'd run into a woman she'd met through Giancarlo on one of those Malibu weekends, who'd needed a personal assistant a few days a week and had kind of liked that Paige was a bit notorious, it had seemed like a good idea. And more, a way to escape, once and for all, the dark little world her mother lived in.

A year later, she'd been working for a longtime television star who had no idea that competent Paige Fielding was related to *that* Nicola Fielding. A few years after that, she had enough experience to sign with a very exclusive agency that catered to huge stars like Violet, and when Violet's previous assistant left her, to put herself forward as a replacement. All of those things had seemed so random back then, as they happened. But now, looking back, it seemed anything but. As if Paige's subconscious had plotted out the only course that could bring her back to Giancarlo.

But she didn't want to think about that now. Or about what she'd do when she was without him again. How would she re-create herself this time? Where would she go? It occurred to her then that she'd never really planned beyond Violet. Beyond the road she'd known would bring her back to him.

I want a partner, he'd said, and the problem was, she

was a liar. A deliberate amnesiac, desperate to keep their past at bay. That wasn't a partner. That was a problem.

Giancarlo was still smiling, as if this was an easy conversation, and Paige wished it was. For once, *just once,* she wanted something to be as easy as it should have been.

"I'm surprised," he said, and there was something very much like affection in his gaze, transforming his face until he looked like that younger version of himself again. She told herself that it didn't make her ache. That it didn't make her heart twist tight. "I would have said dancing was who you were, not something you did."

"I was twenty years old," she heard herself say, in a rueful sort of tone that suggested an amusement she didn't quite feel. "I had no idea who I was."

You're his toy, Nicola, her mother had screamed at her in those final, dark days, when Paige had believed she'd somehow navigate her way through it all unscathed— that she'd manage to keep Giancarlo, please her mother and her mother's terrible friends, and pay off all of that debt besides. *He'll play with you until he's done and then he'll leave you broken and useless when he moves on to the next dumb whore. Don't be so naive!*

Giancarlo's face changed then, and his hand froze in her hair. "I think I always forget you were so young," he said after a moment, as if remembering her age shocked him. "What the hell was I doing? You were a kid."

She laughed then. She couldn't help it.

"My life wasn't exactly pampered and easy before I came to Hollywood," she told him, knowing as she said it that she'd never talked about that part of her life. He had been so bright, so beautiful—why would she talk about dark, grim things? "And I did that about ten minutes after I graduated from high school. My mom had the car packed and waiting on the last day of classes."

She shook her head at him as her laughter faded. "I was never really much of a kid."

She hadn't had the opportunity to be a kid, which wasn't quite the same thing, but she didn't tell him that. Even though she had the strangest idea that his childhood hadn't been that different from hers, really. The trappings couldn't have been more opposite, but she'd spent her whole life tiptoeing around, trying to predict what mood her mother would be in, how much she might have drunk, and how bad she could expect it to get of an evening. She wasn't sure that was all that different from trying to gauge one of Violet's moods.

It had never occurred to her that she'd traded one demanding mother for another, far classier one—and she wasn't sure she liked the comparison. *At least Violet cares for you in return,* she told herself then. *Which is more than Arleen ever did.*

"I'm not sure that excuses me," Giancarlo was saying, but then he laughed, and everything else shot straight out of her head and disappeared into that happy sound. "But then, I never had any control where you were concerned."

"Neither did I," she said, smiling at him, and they both stilled then. Perhaps aware in the same instant that they were straying too close to the very things they couldn't let themselves talk about.

Or the words they couldn't say. Words he'd told her he wouldn't believe if she did dare speak them out loud.

But that didn't keep her from feeling them. Nothing could.

He studied her face for a long moment, until she began to feel the breeze too keenly on her exposed skin. Or maybe that was her vulnerability. Having sex was much easier, for all it stripped her bare and seemed to involve every last cell in her body. It required only feeling and action. *Doing.* It was this *talking* that was killing her, making her want too much, making her imagine too many happy endings when, God help her, she knew better.

Paige pushed away from him, not willing to ruin this with a conversation that could only lead to more hurt. Or worse, something good that would be that much harder to leave behind when the time came. She sat up and gathered her clothes to her, pulling the flirty little sundress over her head as if the light material was armor. But she only wished it was.

"Was it ever real?" he asked quietly.

Paige didn't ask him what he meant. She froze, her eyes on the rolling hills that spread out before her in the afternoon light, the glistening lake in the valley below. That stunning Tuscan sky studded with chubby white clouds, the vineyards and the flowers, and she didn't think he understood that he was holding her heart between his palms and squeezing tight. Too tight.

Maybe he wouldn't care if he did.

"It was for me," she said, and her voice was too rough. Too dark. Too much emotion in it. "It always was for me, even at the end."

She didn't know what might happen then. What Giancarlo might say. Do. She felt spread open and hung out in all the open space around them, as if she was stretched across some tightrope high in the sky, subject to the whims of any passing wind—

His hand reached out and covered hers and he squeezed. Once.

And then he pulled on his clothes and he got to his feet and he never mentioned it again.

Giancarlo watched her sleep, and he did not require the chorus of angry voices inside of him to remind him that this was a bad idea.

He didn't know what had woken him, only that he'd come alert in a rush and had turned to make sure she was still there beside him—the way he'd done for years after the photographs hit. He'd lost count long ago of the number of times he'd dreamed it all away, dreamed she'd never betrayed him, dreamed that things had been different. He'd grown uncomfortably well used to lying there in his empty bed, glaring at the ceiling and wishing her ill even as he'd wanted her back, wherever she was.

But this time, she was right here. She was curled up beside him and sound asleep, so that she didn't even murmur when he stretched out on his side, his front to her back, and held her there. The way he knew he wouldn't do if she was awake, lest it give her too many ideas…

So much for your revenge plot, he chided himself, but it all seemed so absurd when she was lying beside him, her features taking on an angelic cast in the faint light that poured in from the skylight above them, the stars themselves lighting her with that special glow.

He found himself tracing the line of her cheek with his finger, the memories of ten years ago so strong he could almost have sworn that no time had passed. That the pictures and the separation had been the bad dream. Because he might be wary of her, but every day it seemed that was only because he thought he should be, not because he truly was. And every day it seemed to make less and less sense.

She had been so young.

He didn't know how he'd forgotten that. How he'd failed to factor it in. When he'd been twenty he'd been a bona fide idiot, making an ass of himself at Stanford and enjoying every minute of it. He certainly hadn't been performing for a living, running from this audition to that gig with no guarantee he'd ever make his rent or make some money or even get cast. When Violet had been twenty years old she'd been famously divorcing the much, much older producer who had married her and made her when she'd been only seventeen. No one had called her a mercenary bitch, at least, not to her face. She'd been lauded for her powerful choices and the control she'd taken over her career.

Maybe that was why he'd spent a decade *this furious* with Paige. Because he loved his mother, he truly did, but he'd wanted something else for himself. He'd wanted a girl who wouldn't think of herself first, second, last and always. He'd wanted a girl who would put *him* first. Had he known Paige wouldn't stick with dancing? Had he assumed she would gravitate toward the life she had here in Tuscany, which was more or less arranged around pleasing him?

He'd told her he wanted a partner, but nothing he'd done supported that. Back in Malibu, he'd been jealous of the time she spent practicing and really anything else that took her away from him. This time around he was jealous of her devotion to his own mother. Did he want a partner? Or did he want her to *treat* him like a partner while he did whatever he liked?

Giancarlo didn't much care for the answers that came to him then, in the quiet night, the woman he couldn't seem to get over lying so sweetly beside him. All he knew was that he was tired of fighting this, of holding her at arm's length when he wanted her close. He was tired of the walls he put up. He hated himself more every time he hurt her—

We all must practice what we preach if we are to achieve anything in this life, his father had told him a long time ago as they'd walked the land together, plotting out the placement of vineyards the older man hadn't lived to see to completion. *The trouble is we're all much better at the preaching and not so good at the listening, even to ourselves.*

It had to stop. *He* had to stop. There was no point demanding her trust if he refused to give his own.

He shifted beside her, pulling her close and burying his face in the sweet heat of her neck.

It was time to admit what he'd known for years. She was the only woman he'd ever loved, no matter what she called herself. No matter what she'd done when she was little more than a kid. And he'd never stopped loving her.

"Come sei bella," he whispered into the dark. *How beautiful you are.* And, *"Mi manchi." I miss you.* And then, "I love you," in English, though he knew she couldn't hear him.

Giancarlo understood then, in the soft darkness, Paige snuggled close in his arms as if she'd been there all along, that he always had. He always would.

He just needed to tell her when she could hear him.

Paige woke up the next morning in her usual rush when the morning light danced over her face from the skylights above. Giancarlo was next to her, his big body wrapped around her, and she thought, *this is my favorite day.*

She thought that every day, lately. No matter what that voice in her head had to say about it.

And she continued to think it until her stomach went funny in a sudden, hideous lurch, and she had to pull away from him and race for the toilet.

"I must have eaten something strange," she said when she came out of the bathroom to find him frowning with concern, sitting on the side of his bed. She grimaced. "Your mother insisted we eat those weird sausages in Cinque Terre yesterday. One must not have agreed with me."

But Violet wasn't affected. "I have a stomach of steel, my dear girl," she proclaimed when Paige called her to check in, "which is handy when one is living off craft service carts for weeks at a time in all the corners of the earth." And it happened again the next morning. And then the morning after that.

And on the fourth morning, when Paige ran for the bathroom, Giancarlo came in after her and placed a package on the floor beside her as she knelt there, pale and sick and wishing for death. It took her a long moment to calm the wild, lurching beat of her heart. To force back the dizziness as that awful feeling in her stomach retreated again. To feel well enough to focus on what he'd put there in front of her.

Only to feel even more light-headed when she did.

It was a pregnancy test.

"Use it," Giancarlo said, his voice so clipped and stern she didn't dare look up at him to see if his expression matched. She didn't think her stomach could take it. She knew her heart couldn't. "Bring me the result. Then we'll talk."

CHAPTER EIGHT

PAIGE CLIMBED SHAKILY to her feet after his footsteps re-treated. She rinsed her mouth out with a scoop of water from the sink and then she followed the directions on the package. She waited the requisite amount of time—she timed it on her phone, to the second—and when the alarm chirped at her she let herself look.

And just like that, everything was forever altered. But all she could do was stare at the little stick with its un-mistakable plus sign and wish she wasn't naked.

That didn't merely say things about her character, she thought dimly. It said far more dire things about the kind of mother she'd be to the tiny little life that was somehow there inside her—

That was when it hit her. It was a tidal wave of raw *feeling,* impossible to categorize or separate or do any-thing but survive as it all tore through her. Terror. Joy. *Panic.* How could she be someone's mother when all she'd ever known of mothering was Arleen? How could she be someone's *mother*?

She was holding on to the sink in a death grip when it passed, tears in her eyes and her knees weak beneath her. It was hard to breathe, but Paige made herself do it. In, then out. Deep. Measured.

Then she remembered Giancarlo was waiting for her,

and worse, what he'd said before he'd gone downstairs. And Paige understood then. That this was her worst fear come to life, literally.

That this was the other shoe she'd spent all this time knowing would drop.

She dressed before she went downstairs, glad she'd worn something more substantial than a silly dress the night before. That meant she could truly wrap herself up in her clothes as if they would offer her protection from whatever was about to come. She pulled her hair back into a tight knot at the nape of her neck and she took longer than she should have, and she only went to find him when she understood that dragging this out was going to make it worse. *Was* making it worse.

This will be fine, she told herself as she walked down the wide, smooth stairs, aware that she was delivering herself to her own execution. But there was, despite everything, that teeny tiny sliver of hope deep inside of her that maybe, just maybe, she'd be wrong about this. That he'd surprise her.

We're both adults. These things happen...

Giancarlo waited for her in the open doors that led out to the loggia—which, she supposed with the faintest hint of the hysteria she fought to keep away for fear it might swamp her, was appropriate, given where this baby had likely been conceived. He didn't turn when she came up behind him, he merely held out his hand.

Demonstrating how little he trusted her, she realized, when she finally understood what he was doing and what he expected her to put in his palm. Not her hand, for comfort. The pregnancy test. For proof.

Because he expected tricks and lies from her, even now. Even about this.

She felt something topple over inside of her, some

foundation or other, but she couldn't concentrate on that now. There was only Giancarlo, scowling down at the slender stick in his hand before he bit out a curse and flung it aside.

A thousand smart responses to that moved through her, but she was still shaky from that immense emotional slap that had walloped her upstairs, and she kept them all to herself. He stood there, every muscle tight, even his jaw a hard, granite accusation, and he didn't look at her for a long time.

When he did, it was worse.

Paige waited for him to speak, even as something inside her protested that no, she did not deserve his anger here. That she hadn't done this alone. But she shoved that down, too.

"I thought you were on the pill."

She blinked at the ferocity in his tone. The bite.

"No, you didn't. You used condoms after the first night. Why would you do that if you thought I was on the pill?" He stared at her, and the truth of that rolled over her. For a moment, she couldn't breathe through it. Then she could, and it hurt. It more than hurt. Another foundation turned to dust in an instant. "Oh."

"Tell me," he said in that vicious, cruel way she hadn't heard in almost a month now, so long she'd forgotten how awful it was, how deeply it clawed into her, "what possible reason you could have for sleeping with a man without protection?"

"You did the same thing." But her tongue felt too thick and her head buzzed and she'd known this would happen. Maybe not *this*. Maybe not a pregnancy. But that look on his face. She'd always known she'd see that again. She hadn't understood, until now, how very much she'd wanted to be wrong. "You were right there with me."

"I thought you were on the pill."

She felt helpless. Terrified. Sick. "Why?"

He swore again, not in Italian this time, and she flinched. "What kind of question is that? Because you were before."

"That was different." She was too shaken to think about what she was saying, so she told him the truth without any varnishing. "My mother was terrified I'd end up pregnant at sixteen and forced to raise the baby, like she was with me, so she had me on the pill from the moment I hit puberty."

"And you stopped?" He sounded furious and disbelieving, and Paige didn't understand. How could he think she'd planned this? How could she have, even if she'd wanted to? *You knew he didn't use anything that first night. Why didn't you say something?* But she knew. She hadn't wanted him to stop. She'd wanted him more than anything. "Why the hell would you do something like that?"

"I told you."

Paige was whispering, and she'd backed up so her spine was against the far side of the open doorway as if the house might keep her from collapsing to the floor, but Giancarlo hadn't moved at all. He didn't have to move. His black fury took up all the air. It blocked out the sun.

This is what you deserve, her mother's voice said in her head, filled with a sick glee. *This is what happens to little whores like you, Nicola. You end up like me.*

"You're the only man I've slept with the past ten years," she told him, bald and unflinching. He let out a sound she couldn't interpret and so she kept going, because she was certain she could explain this to him so he would understand. He had to understand. They were going to be parents whether he liked it or not. "You're the only man I've ever slept with, Giancarlo."

"Do not try to sell me that nonsense, not now," he barked at her, as if the words were welling up from somewhere deep inside of him. "I didn't believe the story that you were a virgin then, not even when I thought I could trust you. I'll hand it to you, though. You really do remember all the tortured details of the lies you spin."

"What are you talking about?" Paige shook her head, trying to keep her panic at bay, trying to keep the tears from her voice, and not really succeeding at either. "Who lies about being a virgin at twenty?"

"I can't believe I fell for this twice," he spat, his gaze a molten fury of dark gold, his mouth grim. "I can't believe I walked straight into this. Let me guess. You've never given motherhood a moment's thought, but today, as you gazed upon the test that confirmed your pregnancy, something stirred within you that you'd never felt before." His laugh felt like acid. "Is that about right?"

"Why are you talking to me like I planned this?" she cried. "No one forced you to have sex with me! And no one forced you to do it without a condom!"

"You're good," he said, still in that horrible way that curled inside of her, oily and thick. "I'll give you that. I never saw this coming. I thought I was being too hard on you. I was falling in love with you all over again, but in the end, you're just like her. You always have been. *I'm such an idiot.*"

"For all you know I have no intention of keeping it," she threw at him, desperate to make him look at her like a person again, not like a scam with two legs. Exactly the way he had ten years ago, when he'd waved that magazine in the air outside her apartment and she'd almost wished he'd thrown it at her—because that would

be better, she'd thought then, and less violent than that
look on his face in that moment before he'd turned and
walked away.

But the look of contempt he gave her now was not an
improvement.

And his words finally penetrated. *I was falling in love
with you.*

"Am I to understand that this is your threat?" he asked
in that low, lethal way of his that made her shudder.
That made that hollow thing inside of her grow wide
and grow teeth. That made it perfectly clear any love he
might have felt for her was very much past tense. "I ap-
plaud you, *Nicola,*" and that name was worse than acid.
If he'd hauled off and hit her, he couldn't have hurt her
more. "Most women would dance around the issue. But
you, as ever, go right to the heart of it."

"I'm not threatening you," she said wildly, only realizing when her cheeks felt cool in the breeze that tears were
running down her face. "This wasn't planned. I don't
know why you insist on thinking the worst of me—"

"Stop." It was a command, harsh and cold. "I'm not
doing this with you again. I'm not pretending it matters
what you say. You'll do what you like, *Nicola.* You always do. And like a cockroach I have no doubt you'll
survive whatever happens and come back even stronger.
Violet's protégé in more ways than I realized."

"Why would I force a child on you?" she demanded.
"Why?"

"Perhaps you thought your payday last time wasn't
enough," he bit out. "Perhaps you want to make certain
you really will make it into Violet's will. Perhaps you're
looking forward to selling as many tabloid stories as you
can. It wouldn't take much effort to position yourself as
one of those celebrities for no apparent reason, not with

Violet's grandchild in your clutches. To say nothing of the Alessi estate. You must know by now I'd never keep my heritage from my own child." He was nearly white with fury. "Which are only a few of the reasons I never wanted one."

"Giancarlo—"

But he straightened, his expression changed, and it was as if he disappeared, right there in front of her. As if the man she knew was simply…gone.

"If you decide to have the baby, inform my lawyers," he told her with a hideous finality that shuddered through her like an earthquake. There was none of that bright gold fury in his eyes any longer when he looked at her. There was only emptiness. A dark, cold nothing that made everything inside her twist into blackness. "I will pay whatever child support you deem necessary, and I will pay more if you honor my wish for privacy and keep my name to yourself. But I don't expect that's in your nature, is it? How can you leverage my privacy to your best advantage?"

"Please," she said, pleading with him now, unable to stop the sobs that poured out of her, worse, perhaps, because she'd always known this was coming. But not today. Not like this. She still wasn't ready. "You can't—"

"Do not attempt to contact my mother again." His voice got dangerous then. Flint and fury, and still, he was a stranger. "I will have you arrested and thrown in jail and no judge in any country would ever grant a woman with mental problems and a prison record custody of a child over me. I want you to remember that. You so much as text Violet and you'll never see that child again."

"Stop," she threw at him, in a terrible whisper. "You can't think—"

"A driver will pick you up in an hour," he told her, and

he was merciless. Pitiless. As if he was made of marble and was that soft, that bendable. "I want you gone. And I never, ever want to see you again. Not in ten minutes. Not in another ten years. Is that clear?"

Paige couldn't reply. She was shaking so hard she was afraid she'd fall over, the tears were hot and endless, and he looked at her as if she was a stranger. As if he was. Crafted of marble, but far crueler. Marble might crush her. But he'd torn her into pieces first.

"Do you understand?" he asked, even harsher than before.

"Yes," Paige managed to say. "I understand." She scrubbed her hands over her face and sucked in a breath and tried one last time. "Giancarlo—"

But he was already gone.

It was over.

The slippery December roads were treacherous but the wind outside was even worse, rattling his SUV and shaking the skeletons of the trees on either side of the New England country roads.

And inside him, Giancarlo knew, it was colder and darker still.

He had not been in a good mood to begin with when he'd left Logan International Airport in Boston more than two hours earlier on this latest quest to find Paige. It was fair to say he'd been in a black mood for the past three months.

The tiny, lonely little Maine town a hundred miles from anywhere sat under a fresh coat of snow, lights twinkling as the December evening fell sudden and fast in the middle of what other places might still consider the afternoon, and he felt the stirrings of adrenaline as he navigated through the very few streets that comprised the village to the small, white clapboard house that was his destination.

He'd hired detectives. He'd scoured half of the West Coast and a good part of the East Coast himself. This was the last place on earth he'd have thought to look for her—which was, he could admit, why it had no doubt made such a perfect hiding place.

This time, he knew she was here. He'd seen the photo on his mobile when he'd landed in Boston from Italy, taken this very morning. But he wouldn't believe it until he saw her with his own eyes.

He could admit the place held a certain desolate charm, Giancarlo thought grimly as he climbed from the car, the boots he only ever wore at ski resorts in places like Vail or St. Moritz crunching into the snow beneath him. The drive from Boston into the remote state of Maine had reminded him of the books he'd had to read while in his American high school. Lonely barns in barren fields and the low winter sky pressing down, gray and sullen. Here and there a hint of the wild, rocky Atlantic coast, lighthouses the only bit of faint cheer against the coming dark.

It felt like living inside his own bleak soul, in the great mess he'd made.

Giancarlo navigated his way over the salted sidewalk and up the old front steps to the clapboard house's front door, able to hear the faint sound of piano music from inside. DANCE LESSONS, read the sign on the door, making his chest feel tight.

He stopped there, frozen on the porch with his hand on the doorknob, because he heard her voice. For the first time since that last, ugly morning in his Tuscan cottage. Counting off the beat.

Wedging its way into his heart like one of the vicious icicles that hung from the roof above him.

He wrenched the door open and walked inside, and then she was right there in front of him after all this time. *Right there.*

She took his breath away.

Giancarlo's heart thundered in his chest and he forced himself to take stock of his surroundings. The ground floor of this house was its dance studio, an open space with only a few pillars and a class in session. And the woman he'd accused of a thousand different scams was not lounging about being fed bonbons she'd bought with his mother's money or her own infamy, she was teaching the class. To what looked like a pack of very pink-faced, very uncoordinated young girls.

He was standing in what passed for the small studio's lobby and if the glares from the women sitting in the couches and chairs along the wall were anything to go by, he'd disrupted the class with his loud entrance.

Not that Giancarlo cared about them in the slightest.

Paige, he noted as he forced himself to breathe again and not do anything rash, did not look at him at all, which was a feat indeed, given the mirrors on every available wall. She merely carried on teaching as if he was nothing to her.

But he refused to accept that. Particularly if it were true.

The class continued. And Giancarlo studied her as she moved in front of the small collection of preadolescents, calling out instructions and corrections and encouragement in equal measure. She looked as if she hadn't slept much, but only when he studied her closely. Her hair was still that inky black, darker now than he remembered, and he wondered if it was the sun that brought out its auburn hints. She moved the way she did in all his dreams, all of that grace and ease, as if she flowed rather than walked.

And she was still slim, with only the faintest thickening at her belly to tell him what he hadn't known until now, what he'd been afraid to wonder about until he'd finally tracked her down in what had to be, literally, one of the farthest places she could go in the opposite direction of Bel Air. And him.

That she was keeping the baby. *His* baby.

Giancarlo didn't know what that was inside of him then. Relief. Fury. A new surge of determination. All the rest of the dark things he'd always felt for this woman, turned inside out. All mixed together until it felt new. Until he did.

She was keeping their baby.

He would have loved her anyway. He did. But he couldn't help but view her continuing pregnancy as a sign. As hope.

As far more than he deserved.

It seemed like twenty lifetimes before the class ended, and the women in the chairs collected their young. He paid them no attention as they herded their charges past him out into the already-pitch-black night; he simply waited, arms crossed and his brooding gaze on Paige.

And eventually, the last stranger left and slammed the door shut behind her small town curiosity, and it was only the two of them in the glossy, bright room. Paige and him and all their history, and she still didn't look at him.

"You decided to keep it." He didn't know why he said it like that, fierce and low, and he watched her stiffen, but it was too late to call it back.

"If you came here for an apology," she said in a low voice he hardly recognized, and then she turned to face him fully and he blinked because she hardly looked like herself, "you can shove it right up your—"

"I don't want an apology." It was temper, he realized belatedly. Pure fury that transformed her lovely face and turned her eyes nearly gray. As if she would kill him with her own hands if she crossed the wide, battered floor and got too close to him, and there was no reason that should shock him and intrigue him in equal measure. "I spent three months tracking you down, Paige."

Her eyes narrowed and if anything, grew darker.

"Are you sure that's what you want to call me?" she threw at him. "I know that historically you've had some trouble keeping my name straight."

Giancarlo felt a muscle move in his cheek and realized he was clenching his jaw.

"I know your name."

"I can't tell you how that delights me." Her temper was like a fog in the air between them, thick and impenetrable, and he thought she might even have growled at him. "The only thing that would delight me more would be if you'd turn around and go away and pretend we never met. That's what I've been doing and so far? It's been the best three months of my life."

He had that coming. He knew that. He told himself it didn't even sting.

"I understand," he began as carefully as he could, "that—"

"Don't bother," she snapped, cutting him off. He couldn't recall she'd ever done that before. In fact, there was only one person in the world who interrupted him with impunity and she'd given birth to him—and wasn't terribly thrilled with him at the moment, either. "I don't want your explanations. I don't care."

She turned away from him, but the mirrors betrayed her, showing him a hint of the Paige he knew in the way her face twisted before she wrestled it back under control. Another sliver of hope, if he was a desperate man. He was.

Giancarlo walked farther into the studio, still studying her. She was in bare feet and a pair of leggings, with a loose tunic over them that drooped down over one shoulder. She was the most beautiful thing he'd ever seen. He wanted to press his mouth to the bare skin of her shoulder, then explore that brand-new belly of hers. Then, perhaps, that molten heat of hers that he knew had only ever been his. He was primitive enough to relish that.

He'd believed her. It had taken him longer than it should have to admit that to himself. He'd believed her then, and he believed her now—but the fact she'd only ever given herself to him had meanings he'd been afraid to explore. He wasn't afraid anymore.

Giancarlo had lost her once. What was there to fear now? He'd already lived through the worst thing that could happen to him. Twice.

"How did you find this place?" he asked as he walked toward her. He meant, *how did you settle on this small, faraway, practically hidden town it took me three months to find?* "Why did you come here in the first place?"

"I can't imagine why you care." Paige shoved her things into a bag and then straightened. "I doubt that you do." She scowled at him when he kept coming, when he only stopped when he was within touching distance. "What do you want, Giancarlo?"

"I don't know." That wasn't true, but he didn't know how to express the rest of it, and not when she kept throwing him like this. He realized he'd never seen her angry before. Or anything but wild—wildly in love, wildly apologetic, wild beneath his hands. Never cold like this. Never furious. He supposed he deserved that, too. "You're so angry."

Paige actually laughed then, and it wasn't her real laugh. It was a bitter little thing that made his chest hurt.

More than it already did, than it had since that morning in Tuscany.

"You're unbelievable," she whispered. Then she shook her head. "I could be angry about any number of things, Giancarlo, but let's pick one at random, shall we? You told me you never wanted to see me again, and I happen to think that's the best plan you've had yet. So please, go back to wherever you came from. Go back to Italy and ruin someone else's life. Leave me—leave *us*—alone."

He wanted to pull her close to him. He wanted to taste her. He *wanted.* But he settled for shaking his head slightly and watching her face, instead, as if she might disappear again if he took his eyes off her.

"I'm sorry," he said into the tense quiet. "It's not that I'm not listening to you. But I've never seen you angry, ever. I didn't think it was something you knew how to do."

Paige blinked, and pulled the bag higher on her shoulder, gripping the strap with both of her hands.

"It wasn't," she said simply. "Especially around you. But it turns out, that's not a very healthy way to live a life. It ends up putting you at the mercy of terrible people because you never say no. You never tell them to stop. You never stand up for yourself until it's too late."

And when her eyes met his, they slammed into him so hard it was like a punch, and Giancarlo understood she meant him. That *he* had done those things to her. That he was one more terrible person to her. It tasted sour in his mouth, that realization. And he hated it with almost as much force as he understood, at last, that it was true. That he'd treated her horribly. That he was precisely the kind of man he'd been raised to detest. That was why he'd come after her, was it not? To face these things.

But that didn't make hearing it any easier.

"That is not the kind of life my baby is going to live, Giancarlo," Paige told him fiercely. "Not if I have anything to say about it." She tilted her chin up as if she expected him to argue. "This baby will have a *home*. This baby will be *wanted*. Loved. Celebrated. This baby is not a mistake. Or a problem. This baby will *belong* somewhere. *With me*."

As if she really had punched him, and hard, it took Giancarlo a moment to recover from all her fierceness, and more, what it told him. And when he did, it was to see her storming across the room.

Away from him. Again.

"Come have dinner with me," he began.

"No."

"Coffee then." He eyed her, remembering that tiny bump. "Or whatever you can drink."

"And again, no."

"Paige." He didn't have any idea what he was doing and he thought he hated that almost as much as the distance between them, which seemed much, much worse now that they were standing in the same room. "It's my baby, too."

She whirled back around, so fast he thought someone without her grace might have toppled over, and then she jabbed a finger in the air in a manner he imagined was meant to show him how very much she wished it was something sharp she could stick in a far more tender area.

"She is *my* baby!" And her voice grew louder with each word. "Mine. I knew I was pregnant with the baby of a man who *hated me* for *five whole minutes* before you ripped me into shreds and walked away, but believe me, Giancarlo, I heard you. You want nothing to do with me. You want nothing to do with this baby. And that is *fine*—"

"I never said I wanted nothing to do with the baby," he protested. "Quite the opposite."

"We can debate that when there's a baby, then," she hurled at him, hardly stopping to take a breath. "Which by my calculations gives me six months and then some of freedom from having to talk to you."

"But I want to talk to you." And he didn't care that he sounded more demanding than apologetic, then. She might truly want nothing to do with him, ever again, and he understood he deserved that. But he had to be sure. "I want to see how you're doing. I want to understand what happened between us in Italy."

"No, you don't."

And her face twisted again, but her eyes were still that dark gray and they still burned, and he couldn't tell what she wanted. Only that as ever, he was hurting her. The way he always did.

"You don't want to understand *me*," Paige told him. "You want me to understand *you*. And believe me, I already do. I understood you when you were the very wealthy, semifamous director who took an unexpected interest in a backup dancer. I understood you when you were the noble son standing up for his mother against the potential lunatic who had infiltrated her home behind your back. I even understood you when you were the beleaguered, betrayed ex, drawn back into an intense sexual relationship against his better judgment by the deceitful little seductress he couldn't put behind him. I *understood* myself sick."

She pulled in a breath, as if it hurt her, which was when Giancarlo realized he hadn't breathed throughout this. That he couldn't seem to draw a breath at all.

"And then," Paige continued, her voice strong and even, "once I left, I understood that you have never, ever pretended to be there for me in any way. Not ten years ago. Not now. It never crossed your mind to *ask me* why I did something like sell those pictures, just as it never occurred to you to ask me how *I* felt about finding myself pregnant. The only thing you care about is you."

"Paige."

She ignored him. "You never asked me anything at all. You've never treated me liked anything but a storm you had to weather." She shook her head. "You're the damned hurricane, Giancarlo, but you blame me for the rain." She shifted then, her hands moving to shelter that little bump, as if she needed to protect it from him, and he thought that might be the worst cut, the deepest wound. He was surprised to find he still stood. "All I want from you is what you've always given me. Your absence."

The room seemed dizzy with her words when she'd stopped speaking, as if the mirrors could hardly bear the weight of them. Or maybe that was him. Maybe he'd fallen down and he simply couldn't tell the difference.

"You said *she.*"

"What?"

Giancarlo didn't know where that had come from. He hadn't known he meant to speak at all. He was too busy seeing himself through her eyes—and not liking it at all. "Before. You called the baby a *she.*"

"Yes." She seemed worn-out then, in a sudden rush. As if she'd lanced a wound with a surge of adrenaline and the poison had all run out, leaving nothing behind it. "I'm having a little girl in May."

"A daughter." His voice was gentle, yet filled with something it took him a moment to identify. *Wonder.* He heard it move through the room and he saw her shudder as she pulled in a breath, and he knew, somehow, that everything wasn't lost. Not yet. Not quite yet. "We're having a daughter."

"Go away, Giancarlo," she said, but it was a whisper. Just a whisper with none of that fury behind it, and a hint of the kind of sadness he'd become all too familiar with these past few months. And he wanted nothing more than to protect her, even if it was from himself.

Perhaps especially then.

"I can do that," he said gruffly. "Tonight. But I'll keep coming back, Paige. Every day until you talk to me. I can be remarkably persuasive."

"Is that a threat?" She rubbed a hand over the back of her neck, and he thought she looked tired again, but not threatened. "This isn't your land in Italy. I'm not a prisoner here."

"I don't want to keep you prisoner," he said, which was not entirely true. He reminded himself he was a civilized man. Or the son of one anyway, little as he might have lived up to his father's standards lately. "I want to have dinner with you."

She eyed him, and he could see the uncertainty on her pretty face. "That's all?"

"Do you want me to lie to you?" he asked quietly. "It's a start. Just give me a start."

She shook her head, but her eyes seemed less gray now and more that changeable blue-green he recognized, and Giancarlo couldn't help but consider that progress.

"What if I don't want a start?" she asked after a moment. "Any start? We've had two separate starts marked by ten years of agony and now this. It's not fun."

He smiled. "Then it's dinner. Everyone needs to eat dinner. Especially pregnant women, I understand."

"But not with you," Paige said, and there was something different in her voice then. Some kind of resolve. "Not again. It's not worth it."

She turned away again and headed toward the door he could see in the back, and this time, he could tell, she was really going to leave.

And Giancarlo knew he should let her go. He knew he'd done more than enough already. The practical side of him pointed out that six months was a reasonable amount of time to win a person over, to say nothing of the following lifetime of the child they'd made. *Their daughter.* He had all the time in the world.

He'd spent three months trying to find her—what was another night? He knew he should forfeit this battle, the better to win the war. But he couldn't do it.

Giancarlo couldn't watch her walk away again.

CHAPTER NINE

LATER, PAIGE THOUGHT, she would hate herself for how difficult it was to march across the studio floor toward the door, her car beyond, and the brand-new life she was in the middle of crafting.

Later, she would despair of the kind of person she must be, that her heart had somersaulted nearly out of her chest when Giancarlo had stormed in, startling her so profoundly it had taken her a long moment to remember why that instant sense of relief she'd felt was more than a little sick. Later, she would beat herself up about how little she wanted to walk away from him, even now.

But first she had to really do it. Walk away. Mean what she said. Leave him standing—

Her first clue that he'd moved at all was a rush of air over her shoulder and then his hands were on her, gentle and implacable at once. He turned her, lifted her, and in a single smooth shift she was in his arms. Held high against his chest, so she was surrounded. By his scent. By his strength.

A scant breath away from that cruel mouth, that sensual mouth.

Much too close to everything she wanted, so desperately, to forget.

"Put me down."

Her voice was so quiet it was hardly a breath of sound—but she knew, somehow, what that dark gold fury in his gaze was now. It was a warning that this situation could get out of control quickly, with a single kiss, and Paige rather doubted she'd be able to maintain any kind of moral high ground if she let him deep inside her again.

Especially because she wanted him there. Even now.

"First of all," Giancarlo said, in that low and lethal way that still moved over her like a seduction, making her very bones feel weak, "I do not hate you. I have never hated you. I have spent years trying to convince myself that I hated you only to fail miserably at it, again and again."

"Then you only *act* as if you hate me," she grated at him, refusing to put her arm over his shoulders, holding herself tight and unyielding against him as if that might save her. From herself. "That's much better."

He stopped next to the line of old armchairs and love seats that sat against the wall and set her down in the biggest one, then shocked her to the core by kneeling down in front of her. She froze, which was why it took her a moment to notice that he'd caged her in, his hands gripping the back of the chair behind her, putting his face about as close as it could get to hers without actually touching her.

"Why did you sell those photographs?" he asked. Quietly, his dark gaze trained on her face. So there was no chance at all he didn't see the heat that flashed over her, making her cheeks warm.

"What can that possibly matter now?"

"I think you're right about a lot of things," he said, sounding somewhere between grim and determined. And something else she wasn't sure she'd ever heard before. "But especially this. I should have asked. I'm asking now."

And the trouble was, she loved him. She'd always loved him. And she'd waited a decade for him to ask. If he'd asked in Italy, she might have sugarcoated it, but things were different now. *She* was different now.

She owed it to the life inside of her to be the kind of woman she wanted her daughter to become. That strong. That unafraid. That unflinching when necessary.

"My mother was a drunk," Paige said flatly. "Her dreams of riches and fame and escape from our awful little hometown came to a screeching halt when she got pregnant with me in high school, so it worked out well that I could dance. The minute I was done with high school she took me to Los Angeles. She made me use my middle name as a stage name because she thought it was fancy, and everyone knew you had to be fancy to be famous. She decided she made an excellent stage mother, if your definition of a stage mother is that she took all the money and then yelled at me to get out there and make more."

"That is the common Hollywood definition, yes," Giancarlo said drily, but she couldn't stop now. Not even to laugh.

"A drunk Arleen was one thing," Paige told him. "But a little while before I met you, my mother met a meth dealer. His name was Denny, and let me tell you, he was *so* nice to us. A new best friend." Her mouth twisted. "A month later, she was thousands of dollars in the hole and he was a little less friendly. Two months later, she was hundreds of thousands of dollars in debt to him, there was no possible way she could get out of it and he stopped pretending. He laid it out for me." She met Giancarlo's gaze and held it. *Unflinching,* she told herself. No matter that she'd never wanted him to know the kind of dirt that clung to her. Not when his whole life was so clean, so pretty, so bathed in light. "I could work it off on my back, or I could watch him kill her. Or—and this was an afterthought—I could make some money off my rich new boyfriend instead."

"Paige." He breathed her name as if it was one of his Italian curses, or perhaps a prayer, and she didn't know when he'd dropped his hands down to take hers, only that his hands were so warm, so strong, and she was far weaker than she wanted to be if he was what made her feel strong. Wasn't she? "Why didn't you tell me this? Why didn't you let me help you?"

"Because I was ashamed," she said, and her voice cracked, but she didn't look away from him. "Your mother was *Violet Sutherlin.* My mother was a drug addict who sold herself when she ran out of money, and it still wasn't enough. Who wanted to sell *me* because until I met you, I was a virgin."

He paled slightly, and she felt his hands tighten around hers, and she pushed on.

"The first night I spent with you, she realized I'd slept with you," Paige said, aware that she sounded hollow, when still, she couldn't regret it. Not a moment of that long, perfect night. Not even knowing what came after. "And when I got home that next day, she slapped me so hard it actually made my ears ring. But not enough to block her out. I'd already ruined her life by being born, you see. The least I could have done was let her sell the one commodity she had—I mean my virginity—to the highest bidder. She'd had the whole thing planned out with some friends of Denny's."

"How did I miss this?" Giancarlo asked, his voice a hoarse scrape in the empty studio.

"Because I wanted you to miss it." Her voice was fierce. "Because you were my single rebellion. My escape. The only thing I'd ever had that was good. And all mine. And you came without any strings." She dropped her gaze then, to where their hands were clasped tight. "But she was my mother."

He muttered something in Italian.

"I think," Paige said, because she had to finish now, "that if I hadn't met you, even if I'd had a different boyfriend, I would have just slept with whoever Denny told me to sleep with. It would have been easier."

"It would have been prostitution," Giancarlo said, viciously, but she knew that this time, it wasn't directed at her.

"What difference would it have made?" she asked, and she meant that. She shrugged. "I didn't know anything else. A lot of the dancers slept around and let the men help with their rent. They didn't call it prostitution—they called it dating. With benefits. Maybe I wouldn't have minded it, if I'd started there. But I'd met you." She blew out a breath and met his dark gold gaze. "And I was twenty years old. My mother told me a thousand times a day that men like you had a million girls like me. That I'd thrown myself away on you, that you would get sick of me sooner rather than later and we'd have nothing to show for it. And she, by God, wanted something to show for all her suffering."

"How, pray, had *she* suffered?" His tone was icy, and it warmed something inside of her. As if maybe all those foundations she'd thought he'd shattered in Italy had only frozen and were coming back now as they warmed. As she did.

"It wasn't my idea," Paige said quietly, because this was the important part. "Denny insisted that sex sold.

That you were worth an outrageous amount of money. And I thought—I really thought—that I owed her something. That it was just what love looked like. Because I might have ruined her life, but she was my mother. I loved her. I owed her."

"You don't have to tell me any more," Giancarlo said, his voice a deep rumble. "I understand."

"I loved you, too," Paige whispered. "But I'd had twenty years of Arleen and only a couple months of you. I thought she was the real thing and you were just a dream. I thought if it was really a true thing between you and me, you'd try to understand why I did it. But I wasn't surprised when you didn't."

He let out a breath, as if he'd suffered a blow.

"I'm so sorry," he said quietly. So quietly she almost didn't notice the way it sneaked into her, adding fuel to that small fire that still burned for him, for them. That always would. "I wish you'd come to me. I wish I'd seen what was happening beneath my nose. I wish I'd had any idea what you were going through."

"It doesn't matter now." And she found she meant that. She kept going, because she needed to finish. To see it through. "I did it. I got half a million dollars for those pictures and I lost you. I gave the money to my mother. It was enough to pay Denny and then some. I was such an idiot—I thought that meant we'd be fine."

"How long?" he asked, and she knew what he meant.

"Another month or so and the money was gone. Then she was in debt again. And it turned out Denny was even less understanding than he'd been before, because there was no rich boyfriend any longer. There was only me. And he was pretty clear about the one thing I was good at. How could I argue? The entire world had seen me in action. I was a commodity again."

"My God."

"I don't know about God," Paige said. "It was the LAPD who busted Denny on something serious enough to put him away for fifteen years. My mother lost her supplier, which meant she lost her mind. The last time I saw her, she was on the streets and she might be there still. She might not have made it this long. I don't know." She lifted her chin to look him in the eye. "And that's what happened ten years ago."

"You can't possibly feel guilty about that." He sounded incredulous. He frowned at her. "Paige. Please. You did everything you possibly could for that woman. Literally. You can't stop people when they want to destroy themselves—you can only stop them from taking you along with them."

She shrugged again, as if that might shift the constriction in her throat. "She's still my mother. I still love…if not her, then who she was supposed to be."

Giancarlo looked at her for a long time. So long she forgot she'd been too ashamed to tell him this. So long she lost herself again, the way she always did, in that face of his, those dark eyes, that mouth.

"I'm so sorry," he said, his voice so low it seemed to move inside of her, like heat. "I wouldn't blame you if you hated me. I don't think I understand why you don't."

"Because my whole life, Giancarlo," she whispered, unable to hide anything from him, not after all this time and all the ways they'd hurt each other, not any longer, "you're the only person I've ever loved. The only one who loved me back."

He shifted back and then he reached over to brush moisture from beneath her eyes, and Paige reminded herself that she was supposed to be resisting him. Fighting him off. Standing up for herself. She couldn't understand how she could feel as if she was doing that when, clearly, she was doing the opposite.

"Violet adores you," he said then. "And despite her excursions around the Tuscan countryside purely to be recognized and adored, she does not, in fact, like more than a handful of people. She trusts far fewer."

Paige made a face. "She has no idea who I really am."

He smiled then. "Of course she does. She tells me she's known exactly who you are from the moment she met you. Why else would she let you so deep into the family?"

But Paige shook her head at that, confused. And something more than simply confused.

"Why would she do that?" she whispered.

"Because my father was a good man," Giancarlo said, his hands hard and warm and tight on hers again, "and a kind man, but a cold one. And shortly after I told her you'd left she informed me that the only time in my life when I didn't act just like him, inaccessible and aloof and insufferable—her words—" and his mouth crooked then "—was when I was with you. Ten years and three months ago."

"She knew," Paige whispered, trying to take it in. "Is that why she was so kind to me?"

"That," Giancarlo said, a certain urgency in his voice that made her shift against the chair and tell herself it was only nerves, "and the fact that no matter what you might have been taught, it is not that difficult to be kind to you."

"You've found it incredibly difficult," she pointed out, and it was getting harder by the moment to control the things shaking inside her, the things shaking loose. "Impossible, even."

"I am a selfish, arrogant ass," he said, so seriously that she laughed out loud.

"Well," she said when the laughter faded. "That's not the word I would have used. But if the shoe fits…"

"I am my mother's son," he said simply. "I was born wealthy and aristocratic and, apparently, deeply sorry for myself. It took me all of an hour to realize I'd been completely out of line that day in Italy, Paige. It wasn't about you. It was about my own childhood, about the vows I'd made that only you have ever tempted me to break—but I have no excuse." He shook his head, his mouth thinning. "I know you didn't try to trick me. I considered chasing you down at the airfield and dragging you back with me, but I thought you needed space from the madman who'd said those things to you. I took the earliest flight I could the following day, but when I got to Los Angeles, you weren't there. Your things were packed up and shipped out to storage, but you never went there in person."

"That storage facility is in Bakersfield," she said, blinking. "Did you go there?"

"I haunted it," he said, his gaze dark and steady on hers. "For weeks."

There was no denying the heat that swirled in her then, too much like hope, like light, when she knew better than to—

But he was here. He was kneeling down in front of her even after she'd told him the kind of person she'd been at twenty. The kind of life she'd have led, if not for him. The kind of world she'd been raised in. He was *trying,* clearly.

And Paige didn't want to be right. She wanted to be happy. Just once, she wanted to be *happy.*

"I was going to ship it wherever I settled," she told him, letting that revolutionary thought settle into her bones. "There was no point carting it all around with me when I didn't know where I was going."

"What 'all' are you talking about?" he asked, his tone

dry. "It is perhaps three boxes, I am informed, after bribing the unscrupulous owner of that facility a shockingly small amount of money to see for myself." His expression dared her to protest that, but she didn't. If anything, she had to bite back a smile. "My mother requires more baggage for a long afternoon in Santa Monica."

Paige shook her head, realizing she was drinking in his nearness instead of standing up for herself and the little life inside of her. That she owed both of them more than that. That the fact she felt lighter than she had in years was nice, but it didn't change anything. That wasn't happiness, that was chemistry, and she'd already seen where that led, hadn't she? She needed more.

Paige might not be certain what *she* deserved, but her daughter deserved everything. *Everything.* She would use Arleen as her base and do the exact opposite. That meant many things, among them, not settling for a man—even if it was Giancarlo Alessi—simply because he was in front of her. Paige had watched that dynamic in action again and again and again. Her baby would not.

"How did you find me?" she asked, keeping all of her brand-new hopes, all of her wishes and all of her realizations out of her voice. Or she tried. "And more importantly, why?"

"The how is simple. I remembered you said you wanted to see the fall leaves change color in Vermont."

"I did?"

"When we first met. It was autumn in Los Angeles, hot and bright, and you told me you wanted to see real seasons. You also said you wanted to live near the sea and see the snow." He shrugged. "I decided that all those things pointed to New England. After that, I utilized the fact that I am a very wealthy, very motivated, very determined man to hunt you down."

"Giancarlo—"

"And the why is this." He reached into his pocket and pulled out a small box, and smiled slightly when she jerked back.

"No." It was automatic. And loud.

Giancarlo didn't seem at all fazed.

"This was my grandmother's diamond," he said. He cracked open the box and held it out, and she remembered, then, that first night with him in Italy, when he'd stood with his hand out and she'd thought he could stand like that forever, if he had to. His dark gaze met hers, and held. "I had the ring made for you ten years ago."

Paige felt her eyes flood then, and she let them, covering her mouth with her hands, unable to speak. So he did.

"Everything you said about me is true," he told her. "I can't deny any of it. But I want to understand you, Paige. I want to dedicate the next ten years to learning every single thing that makes you *you*. I don't simply want a partner, I want to be one. I want to be yours. I want you to yell at me and put me in my place and I want to help you teach our daughter never to surrender herself to terrible men like her father." His voice was scratchy then. "Not ever."

"Stop," she said, and she didn't mean to reach over to him. She didn't mean to slide her hand along his perfect, lean cheek. "I never gave you anything I didn't want to give. You must know that. It was only that I knew it would end."

"This won't," he whispered. "It hasn't in ten years. It won't in ten more, or ten after that, or ever." He leaned forward, sliding his hand over her belly to cup that small, unmistakable swell, and the smile that moved over that mouth of his broke her heart and made it leap at once. Then he made it far worse, leaning in to press a reverent kiss there. "I love you, Paige. Please. Let me show you."

"I love you, too," she whispered, because what was the point in pretending otherwise? They'd already lost so much time. "But trust is a whole lot more than a pretty ring. I'll always be the woman who sold you out."

"And I'll always be the man who greeted the news of his daughter's impending arrival like a pig," he retorted. "Based on the wild fears of the four-year-old boy I haven't been in decades."

"That sounds like a recipe for disaster."

"I know." He shifted then, pulling the ring from its box and slipping it onto her finger. It fit perfectly, and Paige couldn't seem to breathe. And his eyes were so bright, and she felt three times the size of her skin, and she didn't want to let him go this time. She didn't want to sacrifice him, ever again. "Believe me, I know, but it's not. It only means we've tested each other and we're still here."

He picked up her hand with its sparkling diamond and carried it to his lips. "Wear this and we'll work on it," he murmured, his eyes on her and the words seeming to thud straight into her heart, her flesh, her bones. "Every day. I promise I won't rest until you're happy enough to burst."

"Until we both are," she corrected him.

And then he leaned in close, and he wrapped himself around her and he kissed her. Again and again. Until she was dizzy with longing and love. Until neither one of them could breathe.

And Giancarlo gave her a detailed demonstration of his commitment to the cause, right there on one of the sofas in that bright, big room.

CHAPTER TEN

SHE MADE HIM work for it. And she made him wait.

And Giancarlo had no one to blame but himself for either.

"How do I know that you want to marry me and not simply to claim the baby in some appalling display of machismo?" she had asked him that first night, naked and astride him, when his intentions toward her, personally, could not have been more obvious.

"Set me any test," he'd told her then. "I'll pass it."

She'd considered him for a long moment, her inky hair in that tangle he loved and her eyes that brilliant green. And the way she fit him. *God, the fit.*

"Don't ask me again," she said, her tone very serious, her green gaze alight. "I'll let you know when I'm ready."

"Take your time," he'd told her with all the patience of a desperate man. "I want you to trust me."

"I want to trust you, too," she'd whispered in return.

But the truth was they learned to trust each other.

He flew back and forth from Italy as needed, and didn't argue when sometimes, she refused to go with him. He shared her tiny studio apartment with her in her snowy New England town, a hundred miles or more from anywhere, and he didn't complain. He shoveled snow. He salted paths. He made certain her car was well-maintained and he never pressured her to move.

She told him more about her childhood with that terrible woman. He told her about his childhood with a woman less terrible perhaps, but deeply complicated all the same. And they held each other. They soothed each other.

They came to know each other in all the ways they hadn't had time to get to know each other ten years ago. Layer on top of layer.

Until he came back from another trip to Italy one snowy March weekend and Paige said that maybe, if he had a better place in mind for them to live, she'd consider it.

"I don't know anything about homes," she told him, her attention perhaps *too* focused on the book she held in her lap. "But you seem to have quite a few."

"You make every house I have a home, *il mio amore*," he told her. "Without you, they are but adventures in architecture."

And he had them back in his house in Malibu by the following afternoon, as if they'd never left it ten years ago. The sea in front of him, the mountains behind him and his woman at his side.

Giancarlo had never been happier. Except for one small thing.

"Why haven't you married her yet?" Violet demanded every time she saw him, particularly when Paige was with him. He could only raise his brows at this woman he loved more than he'd imagined it was possible to love anyone, and wait for her to answer.

Which she was happy to do.

"I'm not sure I'll have him, Violet," Paige would reply airily. She would pat her ever-larger belly and smile blandly, and Giancarlo thought that they'd both transitioned from a working relationship to family rather easily. Almost as if Violet had planned it. "I'm considering all my options."

"I don't blame you," Violet would say with a sniff. "He was horrible. I'd tell you he gets that sort of inexcusable behavior from his father but, alas, Count Alessi was the most polite and well-mannered man I ever met. It's all me."

"I don't think anyone thought otherwise," Giancarlo would say then, and everyone would laugh.

But he never asked Paige again. He kept his promise.

"And if a single photograph or unauthorized mention of my daughter appears anywhere, for any reason, in a manner which benefits you without my express, written consent," he told the great screen legend Violet Sutherlin one pretty afternoon, in her office in front of her new assistant so there could be no mistake that he meant business, "you will never see her again. Until she is at least thirty. Do you understand me, Mother? I am no longer that four-year-old. My daughter never will be."

Violet had gazed at him for a long time. She hadn't showed him that smile of hers. She hadn't said anything witty. In the end, she'd only nodded, once. Sharp and jerky.

But he knew she understood that he'd meant it.

Five months and three weeks after the night he'd turned up in Maine, when Paige was big and round and had to walk in a kind of waddle to get down the makeshift aisle, she married him at last in a tiny ceremony on Violet's terrace. Violet presided. The bride and the officiant wept.

Giancarlo smiled with the greatest satisfaction he'd known in his life. And kissed his bride. *His wife.*

"Don't ever torture me like that again," he growled

against her lips when they were in the car and headed home, finally married, the way they should have been more than ten years before.

"Surely you knew I'd marry you," Paige said, laughing. "I've been pretty open about how much I love you."

"I'm not at all certain I deserve you," he said, and was startled when that made great tears well up in her lovely changeable eyes, then roll down her cheeks. "But I've taken that on as a lifelong project."

She smiled at him, the whole world in that smile, the way it had been that long ago day on that set when they'd locked eyes for the first time. And Giancarlo knew without the slightest shred of doubt that this was merely a particularly good day on the long road toward forever. And that they'd walk the whole of it together, just like this.

And then her expression altered, and she grabbed his arm.

"We're going to have a lot of lifelong projects," Paige said, sounding fierce and awed at once. His beautiful wife. "I think my water just broke."

They named their daughter Violetta Grace, after her famous grandmother, who'd insisted, and the less famous one, who'd died before Paige was born and Arleen had gone completely off the rails, and she was perfect.

Extraordinary.

Theirs.

And they spent the rest of their lives teaching her, in a thousand little ways and few great big ones, what it meant to be as happy as they were the moment they met her.

* * * * *

LET'S TALK
Romance

For exclusive extracts, competitions
and special offers, find us online:

f facebook.com/millsandboon

🐦 @MillsandBoon

📷 @MillsandBoonUK

Get in touch on 01413 063232

For all the latest titles coming soon, visit
millsandboon.co.uk/nextmonth

MILLS & BOON

THE HEART OF ROMANCE

A ROMANCE FOR EVERY READER

MODERN

Prepare to be swept off your feet by sophisticated, sexy and seductive heroes, in some of the world's most glamourous and romantic locations, where power and passion collide.

HISTORICAL

Escape with historical heroes from time gone by. Whether your passion is for wicked Regency Rakes, muscled Vikings or rugged Highlanders, await the romance of the past.

MEDICAL

Set your pulse racing with dedicated, delectable doctors in the high-pressure world of medicine, where emotions run high and passion, comfort and love are the best medicine.

True Love

Celebrate true love with tender stories of heartfelt romance, from the rush of falling in love to the joy a new baby can bring, and a focus on the emotional heart of a relationship.

Desire

Indulge in secrets and scandal, intense drama and plenty of sizzling hot action with powerful and passionate heroes who have it all: wealth, status, good looks…everything but the right woman.

HEROES

Experience all the excitement of a gripping thriller, with an intense romance at its heart. Resourceful, true-to-life women and strong, fearless men face danger and desire - a killer combination!

To see which titles are coming soon, please visit

millsandboon.co.uk/nextmonth

JOIN US ON SOCIAL MEDIA!

Stay up to date with our latest releases, author news and gossip, special offers and discounts, and all the behind-the-scenes action from Mills & Boon...

 @millsandboon

 @millsandboonuk

 facebook.com/millsandboon

 @millsandboonuk

It might just be true love...

GET YOUR ROMANCE FIX!

Get the latest romance news,
exclusive author interviews, story
extracts and much more!

blog.millsandboon.co.uk

MILLS & BOON
MODERN
Power and Passion

Prepare to be swept off your feet by sophisticated, sexy and seductive heroes, in some of the world's most glamourous and romantic locations, where power and passion collide.

MILLS & BOON
True Love
Romance from the Heart

Celebrate true love with tender stories of heartfelt romance, from the rush of falling in love to the joy a new baby can bring, and a focus on the emotional heart of a relationship.

MILLS & BOON
MEDICAL
Pulse-Racing Passion

Set your pulse racing with dedicated, delectable doctors in the high-pressure world of medicine, where emotions run high and passion, comfort and love are the best medicine.

MILLS & BOON
Desire

Indulge in secrets and scandal, intense drama and plenty of sizzling hot action with powerful and passionate heroes who have it all: wealth, status, good looks…everything but the right woman.